DAY INTO NIGHT

PORTER CASSEL MYSTERIES
www.davehugelschaffer.com

DAY INTO NIGHT

A PORTER CASSEL MYSTERY

DAVE HUGELSCHAFFER

For Harley,

Hope you enjoy the book!

18-June-2011

Cormorant Books

Second printing, May 2011.

Canada Council for the Arts | Conseil des Arts du Canada

ONTARIO ARTS COUNCIL
CONSEIL DES ARTS DE L'ONTARIO

Canadian Heritage | Patrimoine canadien

Canada

The publisher gratefully acknowledges the support of the Canada Council for the Arts and the Ontario Arts Council for its publishing program. We acknowledge the financial support of the Government of Canada through the Canada Book Fund (CBF) for our publishing activities, and the Government of Ontario through the Ontario Media Development Corporation, an agency of the Ontario Ministry of Culture, and the Ontario Book Publishing Tax Credit Program.

Library and Archives Canada Cataloguing in Publication

Hugelschaffer, Dave, 1967–
Day into night / Dave Hugelschaffer

ISBN 978-1-897151-93-5

I. Title.

PS8615.U315D39 2006 C813.6 C2005-906944-9

Cover art and design: Angel Guerra/Archetype
Interior text design: Tannice Goddard, Soul Oasis Networking
Cover image: D. Hugelschaffer
Printer: Friesens

Printed and bound in Canada.

FSC
www.fsc.org
MIX
Paper from responsible sources
FSC® C016245

This book is printed on 100% post-consumer waste recycled paper.

CORMORANT BOOKS INC.
215 Spadina Avenue, Studio 230, Toronto, Ontario, Canada M5T 2C7
www.cormorantbooks.com

DAY INTO NIGHT

1

BY THE TIME I ARRIVE, the fire has grown to an area the size of a small city. The view from the helicopter is impressive. Ten thousand acres of burning timber in a sea of green trees. A ragged rim of orange flickers at the crescent head of the fire and smoke rises like an erupting volcano in a column twisting miles into the sky, blotting out the sun, turning day into night. Aircraft glide silently around this conflagration like insects around a host. Some watch while others dump pitifully inadequate strings of water and red fire retardant in the path of the monster.

This monster will not be stopped. Not for weeks or months.

The helicopter banks, begins to descend toward a tiny clearing in the forest where men swarm like ants around tiny bulldozers and trucks. Base camp, but I'm not ready to deal with that chaos — my business lies at the heart of the fire. I may already be too late. I look at the pilot, shake my head, speak into the microphone which juts down from my headset.

"Not yet. I want to go for a few laps, take a good look."

The pilot nods, swings back toward the fire. A young guy with red hair and freckled arms, his company is charging the Forest Service a thousand dollars an hour and he doesn't care where he's flying, just wants to keep the machine in the air as long as possible. A fire like this requires long hours and a lot of money. A million dollars a day for aircraft, manpower and supplies. I start to say something but the pilot cuts me off, calling base camp with our change of plans.

"*... base, this is whisky-alpha-kilo, requesting entry into the fire zone.*"

The reply is curt, metallic. We can do a few circuits at 5,000 feet. Too busy farther down. I'd hoped for a closer look but at this stage anyone who isn't moving equipment or dropping something on the fire is considered a tourist. We spend ten minutes floating high above the action. From up here, human effort is invisible and the fire continues on its appointed task of consuming one generation of trees for replacement by another. There's an eerie beauty to it, a serene single-mindedness on a staggering scale.

"You with the overhead team?" says the pilot.

"No. Fire investigation."

There's a pause as the pilot digests this. "They think someone started this?"

"It's a possibility. The LLP didn't pick up anything."

"The what?"

Like any occupation, we have too much jargon, too many acronyms. "The lightning detection system. We've got lightning detectors spread across the province. They haven't picked up anything here this spring. Still too early."

A wry smile from the pilot. "I knew an Indian named Lightning once."

I nod. "It's happened before." When it gets too quiet, the native employment program can kick in. But it's not just the natives that get restless when there's no work. The unofficial Forest Service definition of fire is a chemical reaction that converts biomass into overtime. "I heard of a pilot who used to drop White Owl cigars from his machine."

The pilot's grin widens. "Yeah, I heard that one too."

We watch in silence for a few more minutes, staring down through the bubble windshield. The Ducks have arrived — two bright-yellow planes that can skim water right off the surface of a lake, drop it on a fire and return for more. Nothing better, if you have a lake close by, but this fire is on the slopes of the Cariboo Mountains, a steep plateau rising out of the northern forest. They'll have to skim off the Peace River, 20 miles away.

"So you're going to figure out who started this?" says the pilot.

"That's the idea."

Looking down, he shakes his head. "You've got your work cut out for you."

I agree. As usual, investigation is one of the last thoughts during the initial flurry of actioning the fire, hiring equipment and manpower, setting up camps. No one bothered to flag the area where the fire started when it was smaller and it's grown another thousand acres since I've arrived. The bigger the fire and the more people working on it, the harder it will be for me to do my job — find the point of origin and protect what evidence might have survived.

The pilot is curious. "Where do you think it started?"

"Well ..." I wait until we've done another half circuit, then point. "According to the weather report from the towers, the wind has been continuous from the northeast. The fire probably started over there and, if it was arson, from someplace with access — a cutline or road. With the dry conditions, the firebug would want to clear the area fairly quickly. You can see a group of cutblocks at the tail of the fire, a mile or so off a lease road. That would allow a bit of privacy and plenty of logging slash to get the fire rolling."

"So you think it was arson?"

I chuckle. "Pretty hard to tell from up here. Could have been anything, like an old campfire or the hot exhaust from someone's off-road vehicle. I had one fire started by a broken bottle."

"A bottle?"

"The curve on the bottom acts just like a magnifying glass."

Our conversation is interrupted by a call from base camp. Is Porter Cassel on board?

The pilot looks at me. I nod.

The two other members of the investigation team are at camp. I'm to report back for a briefing. The pilot looks at me and I mouth a question. How much fuel does he have left? The reply — two flashes of the hand — ten minutes. I consider, shake my head. The fire is growing, with men and heavy equipment being deployed at the rear, which will make my job exponentially more difficult. "Can you drop me in that cutblock over there?"

The pilot hesitates. "You got a radio?"

I nod; my gear is stowed on the rear seat. As we descend, the fire seems to grow rapidly in size. The pilot takes a few minutes to pick a safe landing spot and I climb out amid a rotorwash windstorm of ash and flinging bits of charcoal, hunker down with my eyes closed. A minute later the machine augers away toward base camp, leaving me alone in the black.

On the ground, the fire is no longer a serene abstraction. I'm in a wasteland at the rear of the battle, my strategic view replaced by a limited vista of charred stumps and tendrils of rising smoke. The air is hot, acrid and hazy, filled with the pungent scent of burned wood and moss. Visibility is down to several hundred yards. I slip on coveralls and a hardhat, check my radio, shoulder my pack and take a good look at the ground.

A fire is like an animal. It is born, feeds, travels and eventually perishes. And, like an animal, it can be tracked. The beast always travels outward from its point of origin, its behaviour modified by weather, fuels and topography. As it travels, it leaves clues that can be read, like a series of arrows that point to where it has been. One clue taken out of context can be meaningless but the indicators taken together are unmistakable.

The faint whine of approaching heavy equipment floats on the breeze. Cats on a flanking action cutting fire guard. Soon, dozers and men dragging hose will obliterate the finer clues. I must work quickly.

White ash imprints like the chalk outlines of a crime scene are all that remain of the logging slash in the cutblock. The fire here was very hot, indicating the origin is still some distance away. I underestimated the rate of spread and should have had the pilot drop me closer to the rear of the burn. But even here there are clues. The smouldering stumps have bowl-shaped burns, deeper in the direction from which the fire has come.

I walk northeast across the cutblock. I'm wearing new work-boots, trying to break them in; it's working more the other way — my shins and arches are already aching. There comes a not-so-distant thud of metal hitting wood, followed by a deep growl and the crash of falling trees. The Cats are closer and I begin to run, ash rising behind me in a powdery cloud like the wake of a truck travelling down a dusty road. Overhead, water bombers rumble and swoosh. At the edge of the cutblock I pause, check my mental map of the area.

It's easy to become disoriented with a fire this size but from what I remember there are a dozen more cutblocks in this direction, each separated by rectangles of uncut forest. The quickest route is through an uncut patch ahead of me but I'm not crazy about wandering through the stand of immense trees. With their roots burned out beneath them, the trees are balancing like some world record attempt. As if to underscore my concern, a tree topples, taking a dozen more with it as it falls.

I try not to think about it as I enter the stand.

The burn pattern in the treetops and scorch marks on the trunks tell me I'm travelling in the right direction, getting closer to the origin. Once in the open safety of the next cutblock, I breathe easier and examine the ground as my boots stir ash as fine as talcum powder, crunch over blackened debris. The unburned shadow of logs lying on the ground and scorch patterns on exposed rock indicate a fast, wind-driven fire. I cross a dusty logging road and all signs of fire direction are reversed. Here the fire backed into the wind. I've crossed the origin line.

I return to the road, look around.

Smoke drifts along the ground. Along one side of the road are a series of shallow depressions like bomb blasts filled with fine grey ash — the remnants of brushpiles where loggers heaped together treetops and branches. The piles were probably burned this past winter and one of them wasn't properly extinguished. A wind came up and a forest fire was born. I walk along the road, shaking my head at this carelessness. The timber company that allowed this sloppy work has learned the hard way. A good chunk of its forest is gone. For confirmation, I use my hand-held radio to call base camp.

"Where the hell are you?" comes the reply.

"I'm in the blocks —"

"— have been waiting for you for a goddamn hour."

The problem with these radios — you have to wait for the other guy to stop swearing before you can talk. Etiquette is important for ensuring everyone gets a chance to communicate. Patience is a bonus; tempers tend to get short under pressure. "Were these piles burned last winter?"

An annoyed pause; other radios murmur in the background. "What?"

"The piles in these blocks, when were they burned?"

"Uhh ... stand by one."

I wait, walk along the road, inspect craters that used to be piles — the intensity of the fire burned the organic matter out of the soil. A group of firefighters trudge past, Natives carrying rolls of hose, their fresh orange coveralls streaked black. When I supervised these crews, it was easy to see who wasn't working — just look for the guy with clean coveralls. Or black marks that looked suspiciously like handprints. The burn pattern on the ground catches my attention in one area and I spend some time using a stick to rake the ash in several craters.

Nothing. I move on. The ash in the craters is deep. At the fourth site the stick catches something, flipping it out of the ash like a fish rising from the surface of a pond. It's a small square metal pan, like the type used for baking, but this one wasn't used for brownies. In the past two years, I've seen a pan like this several times. Someone is lighting fires when the hazard is at its most extreme — someone we've been unable to identify. The arsonist is careful and the heat of the fire isn't kind to what little evidence remains. Bootprints are wiped out by ground fire and the pan can't be fingerprinted after it's been scorched black by heat. To complicate matters, the other sites were hopelessly contaminated by firefighters. And it doesn't help that I've flipped this pan over, knocking out any residue.

I call base camp again.

"What?" The voice on the other end has forgotten about me.

"The brush piles in the blocks?"

"Oh — right. Stand by one."

A few minutes later, I get a response. The piles were never burned.

The helicopter returns, landing a quarter mile from the fire's origin as directed and raising a maelstrom of ash and grain-sized pieces of charcoal that blast my face, settle under my collar and drift down my back. At the edge of the cutblock, a large spruce snag, like an immense black bottlebrush, sways from the impact of rotorwash and surrenders to gravity. Three men exit the helicopter and run, crouching, toward me. A minute later, the helicopter flies off into the smoke and we blink away ash, tears running down our faces. One of the men — Phil Berton, the fire behaviour specialist on the team — I know. He introduces the others.

"Porter, this is Cam Huspiel, the fire boss —"

Huspiel is tall and so thin his yellow coveralls hang on him like a bedsheet over a cross. His equipment belt, with radio, water bottle and first aid kit, sags lopsided from his waist, despite having been cinched as tight as possible. He offers a sooty hand. "Well, used to be," he says, looking around. "I was initial attack but the overhead team has arrived."

"Aagh," I say, knowing how he feels. First on the fire, you call the shots, make the big decisions, get everything moving, then a team of more senior people arrive, take over and you're relegated to some minor role. Like briefing the fire dicks. "My condolences."

He grins. "It's their screw-up now."

Berton has been waiting politely. He interjects. "This is Darvon Malostic."

I shake another hand, a much cleaner one.

"Darvon is the new investigator on the team."

I smile. Malostic smiles back. He's short, seems too young and disgustingly well-groomed — with a sort of soap opera presence that doesn't quite fit with the setting. Maybe it's because he's the only one out here not wearing grimy coveralls. Maybe it's just because I'm not crazy about the change. "Really," I say. "What happened to Bill?"

"Heart problems," says Berton. "Doctor told him to stay away from stressful situations."

"He's got teenage kids," I say. "He came here to relax."

"Yeah, but the doc said to quit boozing and smoking. So he's avoiding smoke."

I nod, think about Bill Star: overweight, outspoken and a hell of a good guy. I can't see myself having long, philosophical discussions at base camp over a pack of beers with Malostic. But maybe I'm just getting old, set in my ways. Never trust anyone over 30 has been replaced by never trust anyone under 30. I've crossed the grand divide.

"So what's the situation?" asks Malostic.

I look around. "Well, we seem to have a process of rapid oxidation, accompanied by heat and light, compounded in severity by significant air movement."

Malostic blinks, looks confused. I keep a straight face. Sometimes jargon is fun. He looks over at Berton, who tries not to smile. "Porter is saying we have a fire, driven by wind."

It takes Malostic a few more seconds to realize we're poking fun at him, then he looks indignant. "What I meant was, do we have any indication how this started?"

"Follow me."

I had the helicopter land a quarter mile from the origin so the rotorwash wouldn't further disturb the site. We walk along the road to the crater with the pan.

I point. "It started here."

"Right here?" says Malostic.

"That's the point of origin."

Malostic frowns. "You disturbed it."

"A little. I didn't know it was there."

"You're not supposed to move anything until I get here."

Not entirely true. Malostic's job is questioning witnesses, liaising with the police and following up leads while Phil and I locate and document the origin, collect the evidence. But it's standard operating procedure not to disturb anything until the evidence search and documentation is complete. "It was concealed by ash," I say. "I needed to confirm it was the origin."

Malostic sneezes, pulls a Kleenex from his pocket, blows his nose. "You really shouldn't touch anything," he says, shaking his head. "There might have been some residue in the pan we could have analysed. Next time, just wait. Or bring a metal detector."

Berton and I exchange glances. "Good point," says Berton. "We'll add one to our kit."

Malostic nods, looks vindicated. "So, why did he start it here?"

"He used the brush pile to assure ignition," says Berton, staring at the crater and rubbing his chin. Berton is short, balding, trim and tidy. With his glasses, he looks like a high school math teacher. But he's been on more fires than I'll ever see. "He probably used an accelerant like diesel to start the pile. Once the heavy slash in the pile was burning, it threw embers into the block and ignited the logging slash. With a bit of wind, this would produce maximum fire intensity by the time it hit the standing timber, where it crowned out."

"Crowned out?" says Malostic.

I'm not encouraged. "What do you know about wildfire?"

"I've done some research."

"Research?" As usual, it looks like the Forest Service picked the lowest bidder.

Malostic looks injured. "There's some excellent material available."

"I hope so."

"Crowning is when the fire gets into the tops of the trees," Berton explains. "To crown the fire needs wind, ladder fuels and sufficiently dry conditions. When it gets rolling, a crown fire is the most difficult sort of fire to fight."

Malostic is taking notes. "You think the perpetrator knew this?"

"He knew what he was doing."

Malostic sneezes again, reaches for another Kleenex. "Sorry. Allergies."

"You're allergic to smoke?"

He ignores my question. "Why do you think he used diesel to start the fire?"

"Well, the cake pan was used for a reason," says Berton. "Probably to contain a fluid. So the question has to be asked — why use a pan at all when he could have simply sloshed some gas on the pile, tossed a match and run like hell?"

"Time delay?" says Malostic.

"Exactly," says Berton. "But you couldn't use gasoline for any sort of time delay involving an open flame or spark, so he probably used diesel, which isn't as volatile as gasoline and won't ignite until it actually contacts a flame. He probably put a candle in the diesel, which would give him plenty of time to get away from the area before the fire started."

"Makes sense," says Malostic. "Except it wasn't a candle."

Berton and I look at each other. "Why not?"

"The diesel would dissolve the candle," Malostic says. "You see, paraffin is a heavy fraction of crude oil. During the refining process the lighter components are distilled off, leaving behind the heavier components such as paraffin. When recombined, the diesel would act as a solvent."

"A chemist in our midst."

"It was just a minor," Malostic says modestly.

"So it had to be something else," says Berton.

"Sure," says Malostic. "It could still be diesel, but with a different igniter."

Malostic is scribbling in his little notebook. I reach over, use my fingers to smear a bit of soot on his cheek. Now he fits in better. He looks at me, alarmed.

"Mosquito," I say.

He returns to taking notes. I unload my backpack, put on fresh gloves. Berton and I use string and pins to cover the origin area with a grid, then take pictures, make sketches and take notes of our own. We squat and sift through the ash, use magnets to look for metal debris, one section of the grid at a time. We make it to the cake pan without finding more evidence.

More pictures, then I carefully tip over the pan, right side up, examine ash I've inadvertently dumped out. Wood ash from the slash pile, but this time there's something new. Because the pan was tipped over the residue at the bottom is now on top and there's a small smooth black wafer the size of a dollar coin. I photograph and measure this, use tweezers to place the wafer in a plastic container padded inside with cotton. The remainder of the ash from the pan looks unremarkable and I turn my attention to the pan, black and warped, the bottom discolored by heat, hues of purple and blue visible through a coat of char. There's no brand stamped on the pan but it's the same type used in the other fires, which I remark on to Berton.

"You've had this happen before?" asks Malostic.

I pause, look at Berton, who shrugs. "Are you serious?"

Malostic frowns. "You didn't read the files?" I ask, incredulous. "Or talk to Bill?"

Malostic's frown deepens. "I came on short notice."

"Well," I say. "This fire is number five."

Base camp is pandemonium. Helicopters land, refuel and take off. Piles of equipment — groceries, fire hose, chainsaws and pumps — are everywhere. Hastily erected wall tents occupy the forest along the edge of the clearing. A Caterpillar dozer is pushing over trees to make more room. Trucks and vans clog freshly scraped earth and men in orange coveralls and red hardhats scurry back and forth. Two office trailers have been dragged in for the overhead team. One of the trailer doors opens and a tall Ranger in uniform steps out, scans the chaos. He has grey hair, is wearing a green ball cap, and is looking for something. As soon as I recognize him, I swear.

Berton looks up from where we're sitting at a picnic table, reviewing our notes. He looks past Malostic, who's sitting at the other side of the table, then over at me. The man in the ball cap is coming our way, an intent look on his face.

Berton sighs heavily. "Uh-oh."

Malostic looks up. "What?"

"You're about to meet the new fire boss."

By the time Malostic turns to look, the man in the ball cap is standing behind him, glaring at me. Malostic extends a hand.

"What the fuck are you doing here Cassel?"

Arthur Pirelli, 55 years old and chief ranger of the Fort Termination Ranger District, he used to be my boss back when I too was a full-time ranger. We've had what you could euphemistically call a falling out since then. Right now, he's dangerously close to a stroke.

"I'm investigating this little fire you have here, Arthur."

Malostic finally gets the impression that his hand will not be shaken, and withdraws his offer.

Pirelli grinds his teeth. "You've got about two fucking minutes to get off my fire."

I smile, as professionally as possible. "Well, we're not quite done here, Arthur."

"Two minutes," he says. "Before I rip you a new asshole."

Then he's gone, stomping back to the trailer. Malostic looks like a fish pulled suddenly from deep water. "What was that all about?"

I don't want to talk about it. "Arthur and I don't get along."

Malostic means to pry and asks why.

I swallow, look away. "He has this crazy idea I killed his daughter."

2

THE PAST HAS a way of trespassing on the present. You can try to forget it but sometimes it doesn't want to forget you. For me, Arthur Pirelli is the past that won't forget. Not that he doesn't have good reason. At the end of the fire season one year, he threw a party at his acreage to show his appreciation to the staff for a job well done. His daughter Nina was home. She was tall, slim, black-haired and mysterious. While the other guys were busy draining a keg of beer donated by a local helicopter company, I was talking with Nina, drawn by something deeper than pure physical attraction. She had just dropped out of university — business and finance, didn't want to spend her life in an office cubicle, wanted to take journalism instead, work in a field for which she had passion. I told her I knew how she felt; I'd dropped instrumentation in favour of forestry for roughly the same reasons.

Kindred spirits, we began to see each other on a regular basis, but Arthur had plans for his daughter. Hanging around with a member of his staff, ten years her senior, was no way to get ahead. He talked to the university, convinced them to let Nina return, but her reluctance had increased. We had secretly become engaged. Arthur knew little of what was going on and it was exciting, sneaking around, sharing clandestine hours together in my trailer or at a campfire by the river. But it was also frustrating, and one day, dressed in a spare uniform, she came to work with me. We avoided the office, went together on a timber harvest inspection. I was to pass her off as a visiting ranger. A little harmless fun. A way to spend the day together.

Turned out, it wasn't so harmless.

At the logging camp, I parked the truck out of sight next to an idle feller-buncher. The logging foreman knew Arthur, so Nina remained in the truck while I went into the office trailer. Events after that are a little blurry. There was a loud thump from outside and someone came into the trailer, yelling about an explosion. I ran outside, expecting someone had been smoking too close to a fuel tank, but that wasn't it. The feller-buncher next to my truck was on fire, flames shooting from severed fuel lines and hydraulic hoses, engine compartment peeled open. Through smoke and rippling heat, I could see Nina sitting in the truck as if nothing had happened. I assumed she was in shock, stunned by the explosion, as the truck was only yards from the burning machine. I had to get her out but couldn't get close enough. Men were dancing around, spraying with small fire extinguishers from their trucks. Finally, one of the men ran across the yard, started up a big loader and pushed my truck safely past the burning machine.

I was the first one to the truck. The driver-side window was shattered, glass tinkling as I wrenched open the door, and I remember asking Nina if she was okay — her eyes were open but not moving. Then I noticed the back of her head was soaked with blood, matting in her dark hair.

"Just hold still," I told her. "You're going to be fine."

After the autopsy, they told me she was killed by a tiny piece of metal no larger than a pencil eraser. A bomb had destroyed the feller-buncher, planted by an ecoterrorist who called himself the

Lorax. He'd been in the papers for years, bombing logging equipment apparently at random, but had never killed anyone. Not until that day, three years ago.

That was his last bomb. They never caught him.

As for me, I resigned, moved my office to a bar in Edmonton until my savings expired. My sister took me in, cleaned me up, told me to get a job. An old friend in the Forest Service took pity on me and I became a seasonal fire investigator. The dress code was casual — coveralls but no uniform.

Now, the last thing I need is a reminder from Arthur Pirelli.

After the fire, I have to get away from everything connected with the Forest Service. I take my old Land Rover for a drive. From Fort Vermilion, I go south then west toward Dawson Creek. From there, I just keep going.

Music has always been my drug of choice. Turn it up loud enough and you don't have to think. Pink Floyd, Led Zeppelin, Dylan, T-Bone Walker, Hendrix. At Dawson I turn north onto the Alaska Highway, switch tapes, drink a few Jolt colas, have a dozen cups of coffee. No sleep, no thinking, just music, driving and caffeine. By the time I reach Fairbanks 2,000 miles later I'm exhausted, empty and numb. But salved.

Two days of sleep in a motel and I'm ready to head back.

The trip south doesn't require music. I've travelled far enough that distance serves as a proxy for time, separating me from Arthur Pirelli and Malostic's questioning look. I'm content to listen to the hum of my tires, watch the endless green forest slide past.

When I finally reach home, my sister's place in Edmonton, my credit card balance has grown, fed on gas station bills, but I'm back to level. I pull Old Faithful into the driveway behind my sister's minivan and spend a few minutes listening to the engine cool as I try to make out stars through the light pollution of a million streetlights.

No luck. The ancient patterns remain hidden. Closer, a modern pattern emerges as windows light up; Cindy on her way down. She answers the door, dressed in her blue housecoat, her brown hair messed. “Oh, Porter, thank God. Come in.”

Inside is the familiar and comfortingly domestic pattern of scattered toys and clothes. Cindy has three kids, a full time job as a social worker and a deadbeat ex-husband, so housework is low on her list of priorities. I pick up a few strategically hazardous toys near the stairs, drop them in a cardboard box that doubles as toy chest. The clock on the bookshelf says two in the morning.

“Sorry Cin, I shouldn’t have come so late.”

She takes a seat at the tiny kitchen table, smoothes back her hair, waves off my apology.

“It’s okay,” she says. “Someone called for you an hour ago. I was still awake.”

I’m annoyed. No one calls me at that hour unless it’s a fire. “Who was it?”

“A forestry guy.”

“What did he want?”

Cindy frowns. “I’m not sure but he said it was important.”

“It’s always important this time of night.”

She smiles regretfully. “I get those calls and they’re never important. Or sober.”

“Shawn?” I never hear the phone at night when I’m staying here.

She nods, tries to look as though this doesn’t bother her. Shawn, her ex-husband, is not one of my favourite people. “Usually right around closing time,” she says. “He’s drunk and lonely.” She’s playing with an action figure, an overpriced chunk of moulded plastic on steroids, absently sliding it back and forth on the table. Her lip trembles. “He’s struck out with the bimbos at the bar and wants to come home.”

“You want me to talk to him?”

She shakes her head. “Thanks, but this doesn’t have anything to do with you.”

“I could talk to him. He wouldn’t bother you for a while.”

“I’m a big girl now Porter. I can take care of myself.”

I nod, but to me she’s still my little sister. At least with me staying here, Shawn doesn’t come around late at night anymore, restricts his visits to the court-appointed time slots. But I worry about her and the kids when I’m gone. “You sure. I could be convincing.”

“Porter ... no. He used to be my husband.”

She looks at me and I see her pain, her loneliness.

“Okay.” I change the subject. “You got a number for who called?”

Cindy goes to the fridge, rummages on top in a slag heap of old mail, sunglasses and screwdrivers. She comes back with a scrap of paper, hands it to me, watches my face. The name on the paper is familiar, a guy I used to work with. Carl Mackey. His message — it’s happened again. I don’t think it’s a fire and I get a bad feeling.

“What is it?” says Cindy.

“I better make this call.”

3

CARL MACKEY SITS hunched forward, his long arms draped over the steering wheel of his Forest Service truck, not saying anything. We'd talked the night before, small talk to avoid the reason for my early morning arrival. Now, only a few miles from the site, I watch grey tree trunks glide past, shift my gaze to the road, to the Forest Service sticker on the dash admonishing me to drive safe, and it's like I never left. We could be on our way to a fire or logging inspection, but this time Carl is the only one wearing a uniform.

"You sorry I called?" he says.

I shake my head.

"We could turn back."

"No. I need to do this."

We come around a bend and the valley widens. Carl downshifts and I get a panicky, want-to-go-home feeling. Ahead, there's a string of trucks parked in the ditch; extended-cab, four-wheel drives with metal toolboxes and quads in the back. Closer, I can read the decals — Curtain River Forest Products, Puddle Welding, Search and Rescue. Locals and loggers. Two police suburbans are angled to block off a narrow road leading up from the valley. A cluster of about 30 men mill in front of a tiny trailer. We drive past and park.

The sun is still behind the rocks and it's cold this morning, raw and still like you get in the foothills at this time of spring. Carl pulls on winter boots, his heavy Forest Service coat and grabs his tin of sandwiches. He's always eating. When we used to go out together, I'd have to drive, so he could eat. He's like a parking meter — if he goes more than an hour without being fed, he'll expire. I pull on the insulated coveralls he's loaned me and we walk along the road toward the trailer.

The trailer, a boxy little thing with a narrow door and one window, has been hastily set up, the hitch propped on a freshly cut tree trunk. There's a small deck of logs nearby, over-lengths that have been bucked off by log trucks at the intersection of the two roads, and this is where many of the men sit, smoking and sipping coffee out of metal Thermos cups. Carl introduces me to a short, chubby guy upholstered in the latest Gortex outerwear. Casey Fredricks, head of the Curtain River Search and Rescue. He hands me a clipboard and pen.

"Thanks for comin'. You gotta sign in."

I hesitate, wondering if I should use my real name and not sure why I shouldn't. Maybe it's because I don't want to be here. Maybe I want to pretend I'm someone else. I sign my name anyway. Porter Cassel. Next to my name is another column. Organization. I nearly print Forest Service then hesitate again, wondering what to put down. Fredricks notices.

"Just put down Search and Rescue," he says.

I nod and copy from the line above. High security operation they got going here.

Fredricks takes back the clipboard, hands it to Carl. I look around, hoping to see something of the crime scene, but it must be farther up the logging road. We seem to be waiting, so I wander to the log deck and take a seat among the other searchers. Talk is subdued; no one really knows what's going on. Carl chats with members of Search and Rescue, then comes over and stands next to the deck. His Forest Service coat has tiny pinholes burned in the arms, from sitting around campfires.

"So what's the plan?" I ask.

He shakes his head and frowns. "Just wait I guess."

"When did it happen?" Out here, it seems okay to talk about it.

"Shift change," he says. "Between 10:30 and 11 last night."

"He's switched to night operations."

Carl nods, chewing his lower lip.

"What's the damage?"

He shrugs. "Three pieces. Probably worth about a million and a half."

The sun creeps above the jagged, snow-covered horizon of the Front Range, brushing the clouds orange and pink. All heads turn to watch the show and for a moment talk ceases. It's a little like morning prayers but no one's lips are moving. The colour begins to fade as the sun climbs above cloud level. Prayer time is over, for most anyway. I'm saying a little invocation before asking the question that's been on my mind half the night.

"Anybody hurt?"

Carl looks away, toward the trees. "They're not sure."

"Not sure? How can they not be sure?"

My voice is a helium octave higher and a few men glance in my direction. Carl swallows, his prominent Adam's apple bobbing like a gopher peeking out of a hole. He's nervous, doesn't want to freak me out. It's a little late for that. "I was talking with Casey," he says. "A lot of explosives were used. Apparently, there isn't much left of some of the machines." He pauses, the unsaid message hanging heavy. *What if there was someone in one of the machines?* "That's why the cops want help," he says.

"To find the pieces."

Carl nods.

"But they have no reason to believe anyone was hurt," I say hopefully.

"They found someone's truck," Carl says, rubbing a bony finger under his nose. "Near one of the machines. Of course, it could just be a coincidence. You know what these logging operations are like — trucks all over the place. Someone drops his truck off for later, gets a ride back. Or it breaks down. It could be anybody's truck."

He's trying hard to reassure me, but I don't much believe in coincidence anymore — not the type that brings good news anyway. Carl falls silent, gives me a sympathetic look. I've seen him once in the past three years, at a fire, and our previous nights talkativeness has thinned. It's easier to just lean on our familiarity. He makes a big production of sitting down, shifting a loose log on the deck as he gets comfortable, begins to desecrate his lunch box. Fredricks ambles over, the clipboard tucked under his arm, looking important.

Carl pauses, lowers his sandwich. "So what are we waiting for Case?"

The big guy rolls his neck like a wrestler getting ready for a match, gestures toward the trailer. "More cops, some guys from Major Crimes up north. Same guys who're investigating the other bombings. The local boys want to wait until they get here."

The other bombings. A memory fades in like a scene change in a bad horror movie. I'm sitting on the metal steps of a trailer, shivering as much from shock as cold. A stranger leans too close, asking questions. Why did I park there? Did I notice anything unusual? Did the girl work for the Forest Service? Why was she dressed like that? It's taking all of what little control I have left to pretend I'm listening as I stare at the stranger's big nose, grey eyes and the coarse, aging flesh of his cheeks, touched pink from the cold. My attention is riveted on details, unwilling to face the bigger picture. Finally I can no longer stand the look of the stranger's face, the tone of his questions —

"Porter, you okay? You want a sandwich?"

Carl is offering me tuna salad on rye, his generic solution for life's little problems. This one's going to take more than tuna salad. I shake my head and look at Fredricks. "You know any of their names?"

"Who?"

"The investigators from up north."

Fredricks looks down at me and frowns. He gains a few chins.

"Andre Rachet?" I prompt.

"Yeah, maybe. I think I heard that name."

I shake my head and sigh. Fredricks looks at me a little harder, glances at his clipboard as if to assure himself that I should be here. Apparently satisfied, he wanders off. Carl gives me an understanding glance as he lights a smoke. There's a quiet moment, then the door to the trailer opens and three cops get out. The Mounties look us over, go to their car to make a call on the radio, then stand apart from the rest of us and talk. One of them is an older guy with greying hair and his life's savings hanging over his belt. The other two are younger: one dark-haired, the other blonde and thinning. I stand and edge closer, until I can hear what they're saying. They're talking local shop, biding time until the boys from Major Crimes get here. The older guy looks over at me. Not wanting to be conspicuous, I retreat. Good doggie. I sigh and sit beside Carl on the log deck, stare at the trees.

"I shouldn't have called you," he says. "Dredging up all those memories."

He's watching me like the night nurse on a psychiatric ward.

"I'd have heard about it anyway."

"Sure. But it wouldn't have been as bad as actually seeing it."

Interesting theory. I offer him a conciliatory smile to let him know I'm holding up. But I'm not sure I am and wonder again what I'm doing here. Facing my demons? Or maybe I'm just a sucker for punishment. Maybe I need punishment.

Carl looks toward the road and a few seconds later I too hear the approaching vehicle. It's a white car, an RCMP cruiser, and everyone watches it roll slowly to the barricade like a parade float. The engine's so quiet you barely notice when it's shut off. The door opens and three men get out. They're older men, steely grey bristle visible below their dark blue hats — the weary, serious faces of old soldiers. I've seen them before, shared hours in a small room, sweating as they ask me questions I didn't really want to answer. The most pointed questions came from the senior of the three, a tall man with a prominent hooked nose and dark suspicious eyes. Sergeant Andre Rachet. He's grown a moustache since the last time I saw him, giving him the distinguished look of a general. Or maybe it's just the way he carries himself. He scowls, takes a minute to look around. When he sees me, his scowl deepens and I look away. Then his back is turned and he's talking to the other cops. They move toward the trailer and motion us over. I stand at the periphery of the crowd, try not to stare at Rachet as he opens the proceedings.

"Thank you for coming. I'm not sure what you've heard but we've had a bit of nastiness last night." Rachet's manner of speaking is succinct and, with its light French accent, almost formal. "What we know so far is that someone was in here and blew up three pieces of logging equipment — a grader, a feller-buncher and a Cat. A lot of explosives were used and there are pieces everywhere. Our job this morning is to find all the pieces. The scatter pattern will help determine the amount of explosive used and where it was placed —"

Rachet looks us over as he talks. He's all business, laying it out quickly, and I feel a surge of hope. Maybe this time they'll find who did it. But my hope ebbs. In the three years since Nina's death, the cops have had no suspects.

Rachet holds up a jar, filled with loose bits of metal and wire. "Some of the pieces may be from the device itself. It's important to know if you think you've found a piece of the device." He shakes the jar, rattles the contents. "These are examples of what you might find — bits of blasting cap, wire, fragments of casing — so have a good look. If you find anything like this, you will plant a red flag." He holds up a long wire pin with a square of red plastic on the end — the same sort of marker oil and gas companies use to mark their seismic shot holes. "If you find a piece of the machine or anything foreign to the forest environment, you will plant a yellow flag."

The jar is handed to me and I turn it over, look at the bits of metal, the snippets of coloured wire. They could be the remnants of someone's stereo. But I can't help wondering if they're from an actual crime scene, if they killed anyone. If they killed Nina. I pass the jar to Carl.

Rachet continues. "Remember not to move or touch any object you find. Mark everything with a flag, including cigarette butts and pop cans. Do not drop anything at the crime scene. No smoking. No blowing your nose and dropping the tissue. Be careful, watch where you step."

Carl drops his cigarette, grinds it out under his boot.

Rachet turns to the other cops. "Anything more to mention?"

They look at each other, shrug. One of the local Mounties points to a man in the crowd. "Maybe I'll just introduce Al Brotsky.

He's the harvest supervisor for Curtain River Forest Products, and he's the guy who discovered this mess. He's familiar with the layout of the area and he'll be helping to coordinate the search."

Brotsky glances around, nods briefly. He's tall and wiry, looks to be about 45 and in good shape. My immediate impression is he's a serious guy, the type you don't want to piss off at the bar. But then again, he's got every reason to be serious this morning.

"We ready to head up?" asks Brotsky.

"Yes, in a moment." Rachet looks us over. "One more thing. There is a vehicle parked at the crime scene. We've been unable to locate the registered owner." He pauses, lets this sink in. His next words are slow, deliberate, and cause an unpleasant clench in my gut. "If you find anything of a potentially human nature, you will mark the location and immediately notify one of the members."

There's a respectful silence.

"Okay." Rachet nods, purses his lips. "Let's head up to the site."

The cops will only allow two vehicles at the crime scene. We climb into the back of two four-wheel-drive pickups, hunker down on wheel wells and spare tires. The logging road from the valley is narrow and, at this time of spring, rutted and potholed. Squatting in the box of the truck, gripping the rail and hoping the next bump on the road doesn't buck me overboard, I'm filled with a nervous excitement, like I get on the way to a fire. But there's fear too, of stepping into a memory best forgotten. The truck hits a bad uphill stretch and we all brace ourselves. Carl grimaces, his posture tense, his jaw clenched. Behind him, vertigo presses as grey tree trunks and green branches ripple past. Someone yells and points. On the side of the road is the first victim. The frame of the grader is black and still smoking.

The truck ahead of us pulls over but we rattle past.

The Cat is the next casualty, parked downhill on a half-constructed road, its engine shroud blackened and askew. But the dozer is a big chunk of iron and is in better shape than the grader. We thump past, up a long grade, around a corner and into a clearcut on the side of a steep hill. The valley drops away to our left and we have a panoramic view of forest canopy, pocked with clusters of cutblocks like pieces missing from a jigsaw puzzle. In the distance, as though cut out of white paper, is the jagged profile of the Front Range. The truck abruptly slows, throwing us off-balance, comes to a halt in the middle of the clearcut.

Show time. We jump out of the truck box, look around. Centre stage is what remains of the third machine and for a moment there's a graveyard hush. A feller-buncher is a big piece of equipment. It sits on a metal track, like a tank, has a large engine, an enclosed cab for the operator and a long arm on which is mounted a heavy saw and grapple. This machine is capable of consecutively severing up to a dozen trees before its grapple is full and it must lay the bunch of trees on the ground. In the years I've worked with the Forest Service I've seen hundreds of these machines, but it takes me some time to make a positive identification. The cab and a good portion of the engine are missing. What remains of the engine shroud has fist-sized holes through it, the quarter-inch steel plate is curled back like burnt paper. The heavy arm lies twisted on the ground. I look past the smoking metal rubble for what I know I'll find, and when I see it an apprehensive tingle goes up my spine. Spray-painted in fluorescent-orange letters on the branchless lower trunk of a large pine, clearly visible, is the single dreaded word.

LORAX

I'm overcome by a rush of bizarrely conflicting images — a little orange cartoon character popping out of a stump clashes with the frozen, questioning look on Nina's face. My throat cramps painfully and it becomes hard to breathe. Dark splotches invade my vision and I squat on the dusty clay of the road, rock forward and use a hand to steady myself. Rachet is saying something but his voice is hollow, metallic, as though he's shouting from the top of a deep shaft, and I close my eyes for a minute. When I look again, Carl squats in front of me, a worried look etched in his face.

"You okay, Porter?"

I nod, take a few deep breaths, stand slowly, rubbing my palms on my jeans. I'm nervous and it shows. Several members of Search and Rescue are watching, waiting to test their first aid skills. The way I'm feeling, I hope they know CPR.

Rachet is frowning. "Perhaps you should head back."

I shake my head. "I'm fine, just missed breakfast."

He watches a minute longer, as if I might collapse, then turns his attention elsewhere, begins to organize the searchers. I stand with the men as he gives instructions I barely hear. My gaze drifts back to the tree at the edge of the cutblock, to the bright slashes of orange paint. The killer has chosen as his mascot a character from a children's book. The Lorax is a furry little guy who laments the cutting of his Truffula Trees by a faceless character named the Once-ler. Naturally, the Once-ler gets carried away and cuts all the trees, pollutes the environment and has a change of heart only when his empire collapses. The moral of the story is clear, but I don't think Dr. Seuss had this in mind.

Rachet gestures toward the blackened machine, points to a perimeter marked with yellow plastic flagging, like a makeshift volleyball court. The clay within is scorched, covered with a dusting of fine ash. "That yellow line around the machine is the blast zone — we won't be searching there. Forensics will do that. So don't cross it. Constable Lutz will give you your flags and then we'll establish a pattern and begin to search. Remember, take your time, watch where you walk and mark everything foreign to the forest environment."

This morning, we all look pretty foreign to the forest environment.

"Where do you want my men?" says Fredricks.

"We'll start here." Rachet points to the yellow line. "Work our way out."

Fredricks nods, takes charge of his men, his pudgy face intent and serious. "We'll split into two groups — one uphill and one down. Standard search pattern. Complete coverage. Try to stay about six feet apart from your neighbour. Get your flags and let's get started. We've got a lot of work to do."

Rachet gives me a quick glance as he walks past. I want to follow him, ask him a few questions about this bombing, but I might be pushing my luck. No doubt he'll want to talk to me later anyway, ask why I'm here. I go to Constable Lutz and get my flags: a dozen yellow and three red.

The feller-buncher sits at the side of the road, midslope in the clearcut. I pick the more difficult downslope area, where the incline is steepest and there's a thick mat of logging slash. It's more likely something will be missed here. And I don't want anything missed.

I line up between Carl and Brotsky. We begin to search.

Close to the blast zone, there are a lot of big pieces. A section of exhaust pipe. Part of an engine shroud, curled like a cinnamon stick. It seems silly to mark such obvious pieces but I mark them anyway and slowly move down the slope.

One step. Scan. One step. Scan.

Farther from the blast zone, the pieces of metal are smaller and less frequent. Pretty soon I go several yards without seeing anything; I backtrack, just to make sure. The logging slash — broken deadwood, branches and treetops — is a foot deep and it would be easy to miss something small. I want to lift the slash out of the way, pile it to the side, but if we started that it would take a month to clear the area. I lift a branch and peer beneath. There's a small piece of glass down there. I stick a yellow flag in the ground, keep looking. Forty yards farther downhill, the clearcut hits dense timber and I stop. Should I go in? I decide to finish working my sector of the cutblock and start up the hill, six feet to the side of my last pass.

The grade is steep and I stop for a breather, watch the others.

Searchers cautiously pick their way across the green slash-strewn slope, their heads down, a bouquet of flags held at their side. Everyone has developed his own pattern and our tight formation is disintegrating. It's going to be a long day; we'll have to go over this slope a few times to make sure none of it is missed. I begin to work my way up the slope.

My hope is that if I focus on what I'm doing I might be able to stop thinking about the last time I was part of a scene like this. But my thoughts drift back and despite myself I begin to compare. The similarity of both incidents has drawn me here so I look for the differences, hoping they'll somehow make this easier. With Nina, it was winter and the machine was parked close to a logging camp, not on the side of a sunny cutblock in spring. Compared to the blast that killed her, this one was a nuclear explosion. But here at least, no one was killed and this difference is the most reassuring. Then I remember the truck — the missing registered owner — and glance toward the road. The truck is hidden by the swell of the slope.

Carl sees me pause, ambles over. "You're walking kinda funny."

"New boots."

He nods, balancing on a log as he opens his jacket. The early morning cool is gone and we're all overdressed. Clothing has been abandoned all over the cutblock, propped on sticks like deflated scarecrows. A scent of warming pine sap mixes with the smell of burning hydraulic hose. The valley below is a trough of fluorescent green so bright it hurts my eyes and I glance uphill, toward the wreck where Rachet stands and watches. I feel like I'm dreaming.

"You finding much?" says Carl.

"Not for a while. You?"

He shakes his head, gazes toward the edge of the cutblock where the forest has been sheared away, leaving a wall of grey, branchless trunks. I catch flashes of colour as searchers move through the timber. We need another dozen men or we'll be here for days.

"You think it's worth searching down there?"

Carl shrugs. "Maybe. I heard one guy found a piece of the engine in the trees, stuck up in the branches. An exhaust manifold I think."

I look uphill, gauge the distance — a hundred and fifty yards, at least — and wonder how much energy is required to throw a chunk of metal that far. More than is needed to disable a machine. To do that, all you'd have to do is fry a few belts, cut a hose or two. So why use such a powerful bomb? To make a statement? Why after three years of silence?

"You heard anything about what was used?"

Carl hesitates, takes a cigarette from a pack tucked under the shoulder of his short-sleeved uniform shirt like some tough guy from a fifties movie. Carl is a new breed of tough guy: a civil service rebel — The Uncivil Servant. He taps the smoke against his chin. "Not really. Fredricks says they think it might have been some sort of heavy-duty pipe bomb."

"A pipe bomb?" I find it hard to believe a homemade bomb could do this.

Carl puts the cigarette between his lips. "Yeah, or dynamite."

"So they don't know."

He shakes his head. "They got some experts coming from out east."

For a moment, we stand together and watch. It could be just another day from the past: Carl and I on a timber harvest inspection. But those days are gone. We're in a different dimension now and my life has become a bad version of the *X-Files*. "Why would someone do this?"

"The Lorax?" Carl shrugs. "Who knows? Maybe he's frustrated."

"Everyone's frustrated, Carl. That's why they invented beer."

Carl ponders this, takes out his lighter. I motion uphill to where Rachet and another Mountie are talking. Carl pauses, carefully tucks the unlit smoke into his shirt pocket like he's putting it down for a nap. "No nicotine. Now *that's* frustrating." He takes a deep breath, sighs and looks thoughtful. "This country sure has been opened up in the past few years. Everywhere you look you see cutblocks and roads and wellsites. Not much wilderness left anymore." He could be a broadcast journalist working for the CBC — he's got the thoughtful inflection just right. "It's not like up north," he says. "This is the East Slopes and when you change something out here, people notice. There's a population of two million within a three-hour drive and a lot of them come here to recreate. This is their backyard and they don't want to see pipelines and cutblocks. They just want trees."

"You think the Lorax is local?"

"Sure — why not?" Carl pulls the cigarette back out of his pocket, lights it up this time. "You should hear some of the phone calls I get at the office." He takes a deep drag, blows smoke away from me, effects a whiny tone of voice that would be nearly comical if not for the context. "*Why are you letting the timber-hungry bastards cut so many trees? Why are there so many log trucks on the roads? When are you going to put more toilets in the campgrounds?*" His hand shakes as he holds the cigarette. "I tell you Porter, it's like working the complaints counter at a goddamn high school cafeteria."

The CBC was never this lively. "So when *are* you going to put in more toilets?"

For a few seconds, Carl looks at me like I'm a stranger, an annoying tourist. Then he shakes his head, gives me a dry chuckle as he butts his smoke out against a rotten log. "Never," he grumbles. "Build more toilets and they will come. We should stick to a gravel pad and a fire ring. They can shit in the bush. That'll keep most of them away."

I doubt it. The affluent camper today packs his own toilet, along with his TV.

"If the Lorax is local," I say, "why all the action up north?"

Carl shrugs. "Easier targets maybe."

"And why strike here, after three years?"

Carl shakes his head. "I don't know, Porter. How'd your fire up north go?"

With all the commotion I'd forgotten about the fire. But when Carl brings it up the first thing I think about is Arthur Pirelli's offer to modify my anatomy — a detail Carl can do without. "It was a cooker. Hell of a spread rate. Grew a thousand acres while I flew around it."

Carl nods. "I followed it on the Sit-Rep. You peg the cause?"

"Arson."

"Really?" He looks concerned. "You sure?"

"I found the origin. Another cake pan."

"So that makes it — what — six fires?"

"Five. We better catch the bastard soon or we'll run out of trees."

"Any leads on the firebug?"

"No. Betty Crocker maybe, considering all those cake pans."

Carl chuckles. "Good to see you can still joke about it."

"Who's joking."

He slaps me on the back and I'm glad he's here — a friendly face amid the chaos.

"You'll figure this all out someday, Porter."

I nod, unconvinced. Carl moves away, stepping with his long moose legs over the logging slash. Rachet glances in my direction and I resume searching. There's a piece of metal by my boot, a broken piece of some bracket, and I plant a flag and move on. Farther upslope, I catch the intermittent buzz of flies, see something reddish-brown in the mat of green pine needles. Using the tip of my boot, I move aside a branch and find a strip of what looks to be spinal column, about six inches long, ragged bits of rib still attached. I'm hoping it's a piece of carrion from a wolf kill. Or leftovers from a spring bear hunt.

No. It's the registered owner. A dull swell of nausea creeps into my throat.

I try to keep my voice casual. "Hey Carl, come have a look at this."

Carl is downslope and takes a minute to reach me.

"What's up Porter?"

I point. Carl is a hunter. He'll know.

Carl takes one look and swears.

4

WE'RE USING A THIRD colour of flag now. Blue. I've got a lot of company. My sector of the search area has become the busiest corner of the clearcut and I'm bumping elbows with a dozen other searchers and several of Canada's finest. My newfound celebrity is making me nervous; Rachet is watching me as much as I'm watching the ground. He steers me away from the other searchers, far enough they won't hear his questions. We pretend we're searching.

"So what have you been up to?" he asks quietly.

"Funny," I say. "I was just about to ask you the same thing."

"I heard you've become an investigator of sorts."

"The Forest Service calls me in on the occasional wildfire arson."

"And you're here to do a little investigating?"

"This isn't a fire."

Rachet squats and lifts a branch, peers beneath. "But you're here."

"I was in the area."

"How convenient. Doing what?"

I feel my face flush, my ears getting warm. "I was visiting Carl Mackey."

"Mr. Mackey..." Rachet says this like a librarian searching a dusty file cabinet. He's kneeling, peering into the logging slash but

I don't think he sees anything down there. He's avoiding eye contact, trying hard to keep this casual. Or at least trying to make it look that way. "Mr. Mackey helped us with the evidence search the last time this happened," he says. "Interesting, finding you both here again." He glances up at me to underscore his point, his forehead creased and serious. Then he's rummaging in the logging slash like he lost his car keys. "Are you and Mr. Mackey both working here now?"

"I'm not with the Forest Service any longer."

He stands, brushes imaginary dirt off his hands. "You resigned?"

"I had a little issue with wearing the uniform."

"Of course." Rachet shakes his head. "This must be difficult for you."

I ignore the practised sincerity. This is conversation, Rachet style. Half condolence, half cross-examination. I've been through it before. Today, I don't feel like answering questions. I'd rather be on the other side. "Have you made any progress?"

He watches the other searchers. "We've got a few leads."

"Really?" I'd like to believe this. "Like what?"

"I wish I could tell you."

"So there is something?"

"There's always something."

"You really have no idea, do you?"

The look he gives me is not encouraging. "The investigation is ongoing, Mr. Cassel."

I look around — at the cutblock, the other searchers, the black tangle of metal farther up the hill. With Nina, they didn't let me help with the evidence search — I was at the crime scene just long enough for a few basic questions. Then it was a long stretch in a small room with bad coffee and Mounties with sweat stains under their arms. At least here, I feel like I'm doing something.

"What about this?" I say. "What happens next?"

Rachet strokes his moustache. "Since there's a fatality, the Chief Medical Examiner becomes involved. Technicians are on their way from Calgary to collect the human remains. In the lab they'll do a post mortem, determine the cause of death."

That'll be tough — blown to fucking bits. They better bring tweezers.

"As for the rest of this mess —" Rachet gestures with a casual sweep of his arm, "the post blast team will arrive from Ottawa. They'll document the scatter pattern, collect samples, test for residue." He sighs, lowers his voice as though talking to himself. "It's going to take a hell of a long time to analyze this much debris."

"What about the bomb? Any clue as to what was used?"

"Hard to tell at this point."

"You think it was a larger version of the same type of bomb?"

Rachet withdraws a handkerchief, wipes sweat from his forehead, carefully folds the soiled handkerchief and tucks it into a back pocket. "What I think," he says, "is that you've been through a lot of uncertainty these last three years. Now you see the same sort of thing and you're impatient for answers. I don't blame you, but I don't have any answers this morning. We're working on this with all available resources."

I've been dismissed and he moves a few steps ahead, watching the ground, pushing branches carefully aside with the toe of his boot. He's right — I want answers or, if I can't get them, some indication they've accomplished something these past three years. I need a reason to hope. So I divert from my grid and follow him. It doesn't take him long to realize I'm not giving up.

"What do you do in winter?" he asks. "When there are no forest fires."

"My parents moved to Jamaica. I usually spend some time there."

"Jamaica?" He raises an eyebrow. "What part?"

"The Blue Mountains. They bought a coffee plantation."

"Must be nice," he says, glancing upslope. But he won't bite.

"About those remains —"

"Yes," he says. "You've got a sharp eye. Keep up the good work."

Then he's walking uphill, picking his way over logging slash. I move farther downslope where there's little chance of finding human remains, stop at the low end of the cutblock close to the standing timber. From here I have a good view of the scene. Men move slowly across the green slope, their heads bowed like an army of tourists searching for lost contact lenses. Yellow, red and blue flags sprout like timid saplings — the blue flags in a cluster close to the charred hulk of the feller-buncher. My eye follows the brown scar of the road to the treeline, then down the side of the cutblock. Someone else is standing at the bottom of the slope, watching the proceedings.

It's Al Brotsky, the company man who discovered this mess, and I wonder what he saw earlier this morning. I drift in his direction, pretending to search, and stop a tree length away, one boot up on a stump in the classic outdoorsman pose. Out west, you gotta give a guy plenty of room and I wait for Brotsky to take notice. He doesn't.

I clear my throat. "You finding much?"

He turns, looks at me. He looks tired and dejected.

"Hard to see anything," I offer.

"Yeah," he says. "Lots of slash."

He looks at me a moment longer, then turns his attention upslope. He's the only searcher wearing the standard cutblock safety gear — orange hardhat and reflective vest. A few minutes pass and I feel as welcome as a door-to-door bible thumper on a Friday night. But he has something I want and so I gotta get his attention.

"That must have been one hell of a bomb."

No response. I'm about ready to find more lively company, a tree perhaps, when Brotsky turns, gives me a Clint Eastwood look. He clearly doesn't feel like talking but I close the distance, introduce myself and suffer through an unnecessarily painful handshake.

"So this was your logging show?"

"Yeah," he says, looking upslope again. A pale scar extends downward like a fish hook from the corner of his mouth, stretching as he frowns. He takes off his hardhat, rubs a hand over short, greying hair, plops his lid back on and tugs down the brim. "We were just about done for the season," he says, shaking his head. "And then this."

"I know," I tell him. "I've seen this before. Up north."

He looks at me closer. "You with the cops?"

"Not exactly."

"Search and Rescue?"

"Something like that."

He nods, considering, then grins. "Insurance?"

Something I've never been mistaken for but I nod. Seems harmless enough.

"That's quite a knife," he says. "For an insurance salesman."

Back when I had the time and initiative, I used to make knives. I'm wearing one of the better ones: an eight-inch blade with an antler handle, in a beaded sheath. In the city it would probably get me arrested but out here it's a great ice breaker.

"Our bowie knife policy," I tell him.

"Sure." The fish hook scar stretches in the other direction. "Mind if I have a look?"

I pull it out. Brotsky hefts the knife, tests its sharpness by shaving off a few bristly arm hairs.

"Kind of unusual," he says. "Distinctive."

"Made it from an old buggy spring," I tell him. "Good steel."

"Sits in the hand real nice." He doesn't want to let go of it. "What do you charge?"

"I'm not selling," I tell him. "Maybe, someday —"

Reluctantly, he hands back the knife. He's friendlier now, although I doubt he still thinks I'm an insurance rep. I test out our deepened relationship by asking him if he has any idea who was killed. "I'd hate to guess," he says with a pained look. "Until we know for sure."

"Who's truck is that, up there?"

He rubs his chin, hesitant. "A guy by the name of Ronald Hess."

"Was he on your crew?"

"He was the buncher operator. That was his machine."

There's a heavy silence — the implication unavoidable. Brotsky sets a leg against a stump and looks upslope. Rachet and his crew are clustered around something, squatting like a group of tired hikers. They stand and one of the men begins to string yellow ribbon — more human remains. I look at Brotsky in profile. His jaw is clenched.

"Why would Hess have been the only one here?"

Brotsky shrugs, watching the Mounties. "Came in early I guess."

"It happened during shift change, right?"

Brotsky nods.

"What exactly do you guys do at shift change?"

"We shut down, check the machines for loose hoses, stuff like that."

"What about a mechanic? Anybody come in for routine servicing?"

Brotsky gives me a troubled look, like he should be able to recognize me. Without an official capacity beyond a drone with a spare pair of eyes, I'm not sure how far to push this. But he doesn't seem to mind talking about it now. "The last operator didn't notice anything unusual and his machine wasn't due for service for a while."

"How could a person check that?"

"Each machine has a service log in the cab."

I glance upslope. There's a service log that'll never be checked.

There's a lull in the conversation. I'm in no hurry to find more fractions of Ronny Hess. Neither is Brotsky. We linger at the low end of the cutblock, watch the action — a few parked vehicles, a black lump of metal and a scatter of men wandering apparently at random. My eye keeps drifting toward a cluster of little blue flags. From here, they look like a patch of blueberries. It occurs to me that whoever planted the bombs must have been pretty familiar with the operation. To blow up three pieces of equipment several miles apart in the space of a half-hour takes some planning. You'd have to spend a few days watching the operation to establish a pattern to the shift changes. Or you'd have to work here.

"Any of your guys have a grudge against Hess?"

I'm hoping the Lorax slipped up and can somehow be traced. But Brotsky gives me a strange look. "A grudge?" He pulls a tin of chewing tobacco from a back pocket, takes his time working a lump of black goo under his lower lip. "We've got a good bunch here," he says, his lip bulging. "If somebody'd had a problem that serious, I think I would have known about it."

"What about Hess? Was he easy to get along with?"

Brotsky looks thoughtful, working up a eulogy. "He was a new guy. Didn't really know him. Good worker though — could really handle a machine. Real asset to the operation."

"How long did he work here?"

"Couple of months." Brotsky spits a glob of oily sludge, glances uphill toward the epicentre of the blast. "Fuckin' environmentalists," he says bitterly. "Bad enough they harass you and drag you into court, but now when you go to work you gotta worry that some nutcase is going to pop you off." He spits again, uses his boot to rub the mess into the end grain of a tree stump. "It's getting so a guy can barely do his job out here anymore."

I think of Nina. "I know what you mean."

"I don't understand those people," he says. "Bunch of hypocrites —"

He rambles on for a few minutes: the typical hatred for meddling environmentalists.

"You notice anything suspicious when you arrived?"

"Other than my damn equipment was blown up?"

"You pass any unfamiliar vehicles on the way in?"

"It was dark."

"Any headlights?"

He thinks for a minute. "Not that I recall."

He's tiring of my questions and begins to search, kicking branches, walking with a slight limp like he's got a bad hip. We work our way along the timbered edge of the cutblock, past fluorescent blazes on the trees. I keep within a dozen yards of him.

"How many people have access to this area?"

"Everybody," he snorts. "This place is too close to the city."

I'm about to ask if they ever run security out here but he veers off, walking just fast enough that it's clear he has other business. The game is over, score inconclusive. I head upslope, past an area filled with blue flags, newly cordoned off, careful not to look too hard, and meet Fredricks on his way down.

"Head back to the trucks," he says. "We're moving out."

I turn to ask him why we're leaving with so much left to do but he's too far past already, striding across the slash, nearly stumbling in his rush to carry out this vital assignment. Carl comes up beside me. "Miller time," he says.

Men are heading back to the trucks, trudging slowly uphill. Rachet and his crew are nowhere to be seen, probably on the road hidden by the swell of the slope. Looking at a nearby yellow flag, I feel a mild sort of panic. I came here on impulse, drawn by forces I couldn't resist, and now I know why — I want to help catch the bastard. But I have to leave now and there's so much to do, so much they'll never tell me. I squat next to the yellow flag. Nestled among the moss and pine needles is a short, concave piece of black metal about three inches long. Part of the machine — they'll never miss it; they have hundreds, thousands of other pieces.

"Have you got an empty sandwich bag?" I say to Carl, standing behind me.

This late in the day Carl's sandwich bags are always empty. He rummages in a pocket, hands me a lump of plastic which unfolds on its own like a clear flower in my hand. I turn the bag inside-out, use it as a glove to pick up the small chunk of metal.

"Porter, you're not supposed to do that."

Carl's voice is an abrasive whisper. He leans closer, breathing in my ear like an excited dog as I fold plastic over the specimen, seal it in the baggie. To his obvious horror, I slip the baggie and its heavy contents into my jacket pocket, pull the pin with the yellow flag out of the ground and add it to my bundle. No one seems to have noticed. Carl follows me up the slope, whispering fiercely.

"I think you better put it back."

"This one's mine."

"Are you nuts? You could get arrested."

"They've got plenty of other pieces."

He shakes his head. "I still think you should put it back."

We trudge up the slope, past smouldering metal and onto the fresh subsoil of the logging road. More vehicles are parked along the edge of the road now and newcomers are taking cases out of a van, conferring, readying cameras and slipping on rubber gloves. Staff from the Chief Medical Examiner's office, come to collect the remains of Ronny Hess. Rachet is talking to them, briefing them. I wander past, an invisible volunteer.

Hess's truck, a newer Ford four-wheel drive, is pulled off the road at the edge of the cutblock, its driver-side window spider-webbed with cracks, its front windshield blown in. I hadn't paid much attention to it up until now but seeing the damaged truck sends a jolt of fear though me and I'm drawn forward, terrified I'll see a familiar smudge on the window, a stain on the seat.

I step over a thin yellow barrier of flagging.

"Hey — get the hell outa there!"

It takes a moment to realize the shout is directed at me. A uniformed cop is striding toward me, an intent look on his face. "Back away," he says. "Don't touch anything."

I lift my hands as though he might shoot if I make a wrong move, step away from the truck, across the sacred yellow line. He gestures me away. "That's a crime scene buddy."

I mumble an apology, retreat to the truck in which I arrived. Most of the Curtain River Search and Rescue team is already there, squatting in the box, awaiting further instructions. A few stragglers come across the slash, and when all are safely stowed, Rachet saunters over, thanks us for our help. I want to stay, follow what happens next, but it's clearly out of the question. A few minutes later we're thumping down the road into the valley, holding onto the rail of the truck box.

Ten minutes later, I'm in Carl's truck and we're on our way to town.

"How you doing, Porter?"

"Okay," I mumble automatically. The requisite lie.

"You hungry? I think I've got a sandwich left."

I ignore the offering of this minor miracle and stare out the window. As I watch dense timber slide past, I imagine a shadow slipping silently between the trees — a shadow more myth than reality. A phantom who calls himself Lorax.

5

THE CORRAL IS a small building with a red tin roof, on the far side of the Curtain River. At the edge of town, it sits on a barren gravel lot, next to a collection of rusting culverts and unemployed oil field equipment. The only advantage of this location seems to be its proximity to the highway, offering travellers unfamiliar with the town their first chance for a hamburger and cold beer. From what little I've heard about The Corral, it's where the bikers, transients and rig pigs pick fights with local redneck ranchers and loggers. Carl says he likes the place because it has atmosphere. I think he likes it because it's built of logs and fits well with his mental clock, which stopped sometime in the last century.

Carl doesn't like anything new. He doesn't own a television, computer or cell phone. His Forest Service house is furnished in retro pioneer motif, the furniture unpainted solid wood — no pressboard or plastic. His radio is a restored antique Marconi, as large as a dresser; his phone an old hand-crank contraption I'm not sure even works. Elk and moose hides he's tanned himself cover cheap, cigarette-burned carpet. Faded black-and-white pictures of early forest rangers, stations and lookout towers line the walls. I'm staying in Carl's spare bedroom. It's a little like checking into a museum. But that's Carl. Tonight, he's wearing a buckskin jacket with fringes, the same one I remember him wearing in college. Only now it's grungier, more authentic.

Crystals of broken glass glimmer like stars among the gravel as I park my old Land Rover well back from the building. There are only a half-dozen pickups in front of The Corral this early in the evening, but it's Friday night and I don't want to get boxed in. The big knife on my belt stays in the truck, tucked securely out of sight in the coil springs under the seat. We climb worn wooden steps, boards on the veranda creaking under my weight — I should be wearing spurs for the complete auditory effect.

Maybe it's the high ceiling but The Corral seems bigger on the inside, which isn't saying much. There's a dozen crudely finished wooden tables on metal pedestals, a bar without mirrors, whisky bottles lined shoulder-to-shoulder on open shelves. The ceiling and interior walls are rough lumber, unfinished, bark on the edges. Carl was right — the place has atmosphere. Very woodsy. It's a little like being inside a tree. I take a seat along the wall, on a black leather bench which wobbles under my weight, tips forward and tries to slide me off. By leaning on the table, stability is possible. But the table wobbles too. Carl slides in beside me. I work on my balance.

"So you like the place?" Carl runs a hand through his long hair, smoothes it back.

"It's nice," I say. "Sort of like your place."

Carl smiles, pulls out a cigarette, lights it and glances at me, then towards the bar. He seems nervous, keyed up. I'm just tired, burned out. I haven't had much sleep in the past few days. All I want is a burger, a beer and a decade of sleep. A lone waitress comes over. She's wearing an apron with what look like bloodstains on it. Hopefully, that means she's the cook, not the bouncer — jobs she looks equally capable of filling. I glance at the menu:

a hand-printed card in a plastic holder on the table. I can have a clubhouse, buffalo burger or bacon and eggs. I order the buffalo. Carl orders the same and a jug of beer, which I'm hoping he'll drink most of because the last thing I need now is an anaesthetic. The waitress gives Carl a smile and vanishes into what might be the kitchen.

"I think she likes you."

"I'm a regular," he says. "She smiles at all the regulars. We keep her in business."

There's a quiet stretch while we wait for the food. I keep thinking of Hess's truck, dented, the windows shattered. The piece of Hess I found in the cutblock. Already, these events seem distant, as though they happened a week ago and not this afternoon — the same feeling I get at the tail end of a big fire, with the flames long gone and nothing left to do but wander endlessly through the black remains, searching for that last hot spot. At least with a fire, once it's out, it's over. Carl clears his throat, as if he's going to say something, but remains silent, puffing on his smoke.

The door opens and Casey Fredricks comes in, still in Gortex despite the afternoon heat. Maybe he thinks it's a reducing suit — just melts off the pounds. He sees us and grins, comes over, followed by several more Search and Rescue members. "How're you guys doing?" he asks. They stand around our table, making me claustrophobic.

"Fine," Carl sighs. "You guys?"

"Good." Fredricks is sweating; big droplets cling to his cheeks. "Bitch of a day, huh?"

Carl nods, but his gaze wanders. Fredricks takes the hint and his crew search out a table, rescue a few chairs. Our beer and burgers arrive and suddenly I'm famished. Buffalo never smelled so good. By the time I'm finished the big burger, a heap of fries and two glasses of draft I feel bloated but better. I lean back and look around. The place has filled up while I was eating.

A rough crowd mostly, with one exception. A woman sits by herself at a corner table. She has long, curly, light brown hair, pulled back into a sort of a mane; she's wearing a simple but appealing dress that reveals white skin, bare shoulders and subtly muscled arms. In her hand is a glass of dark red wine, which she swirls as she gazes out the window next to her table. Maybe it's the wine, or the contrast between her dress and the heavy metal bars over the window, but she seems out of place. Attractively out of place. I look away, conscious of my slept-in clothes, my tangled hair, and concentrate on the other patrons. I see cowboy hats, jackets coated with sawdust, stern faces and weathered skin, but my gaze drifts back to the woman. She looks at me suddenly and smiles. I'm not used to being smiled at by strange women and look away, stare into my beer and feel 13 years old.

Carl sighs. "Yeah, bitch of a day," he says, as though continuing the conversation Frederick's started a half-hour ago. He's leaned forward, playing with his lighter — an ancient kerosene version that could double as a small stove. He snaps it shut and slumps back against the log wall, stares at the ceiling. I'm still distracted, trying hard to look like I'm not blushing, when Carl says something, so softly I barely catch it.

"You must be pissed at me."

I look at him, wondering why he would think that. "What?"

"Hell of a thing to go through again," he says slowly, shaking his head. "If I would have known that someone got killed, I wouldn't have called you." He looks strained, on the verge of tears. I've only seen him like this once before. "I was just wondering how you're holding out."

"I'm hanging in there."

"Good," he says. "I don't know if I'd get through it a second time."

"Well, we both are."

"Yeah." He smiles ruefully. "You wanna get out of here?"

I glance sideways, toward the woman. She's looking out the window again. There's the trace of a smile on her lips.

"Let's get another jug," I say. "I owe you a round."

Carl slumps into his seat, resigned. "Okay, one more."

I go to the washroom, via a route that takes me past the woman's table. She glances at me as I walk past, smiles again — her smile would melt icicles on a winter morning. I doubt my own smile looks as appealing. But I get an A for effort.

In the washroom, there's a big handwritten sign at eye level as I recycle the beer. The management would appreciate it if I didn't eat the large blue mint in the urinal. I wonder if that's a problem around here. I wash my hands serenaded by the rhythm of someone throwing up in a stall.

Back at the table, the beer comes and I wonder if I'm being overly ambitious — I can barely keep my eyes open. And I usually cut myself off about now. But I fill both glasses and talk with Carl about people we know, where they are, what they're doing. Many of them have moved on to more profitable careers. I sip my beer, only half listening, my gaze wandering toward the corner table. Maybe it's because she has long hair like Nina. Maybe it's just been three long years.

"— always a target," says Carl.

"Right," I say automatically. Somewhere, he switched gears and I make an effort to listen better. The bar is packed now, far beyond the limit on the fire code notice posted by the bathroom door; the jukebox is wailing the only type of music available in places like these, country and western.

"Sorry Carl, what were you saying?"

"The public — they always blame the government guy."

Carl is slumped in his seat, using a pocket knife to carve hedonistic little designs into the edge of the wooden table. The rest of the table has pretty much been spoken for — some day an archaeologist is going to have a field day trying to translate the cryptic gouges and doodles. Carl goes on about the usual Forest Service beefs. Public criticism. Low pay. It's enough to drive you to drink.

"And when you slap a penalty on some company," he says, flicking wood chips off his jeans, "the District Manager kiboshes it. We're supposed to get out of the face of industry. That's the buzz phrase these days. Personally, I think they're just trying to phase us out."

"Can't win," I agree, glancing toward the corner table. A cowboy is hitting on the woman, a big guy who looks to be about 50, maybe older. She's smiling up at him, nodding. She keeps that up, there'll be a line right into the parking lot. I can't believe I'm jealous.

"Nope." Carl raises his glass of draft. "But at least we're not working in the city."

"Amen." We clink glasses.

The pitcher is empty again and I hail the waitress. Yes, another one please. And send a drink over to the lovely lady at the corner table. The waitress nods and smiles. Already, I'm a regular. Carl says something I don't quite catch. Or didn't hear right.

"What?"

"Sometimes I think the Lorax accomplishes more than the Forest Service."

It must be the beer. "I'll pretend I didn't hear that, Carl."

"Think about it. Who's making a bigger impact?"

"The Lorax is a fucking psychopath, Carl."

We're yelling at each other, just to be heard. Carl stares at me for a moment, looks puzzled, as if he can't remember what he'd said to cause me to yell at him like that. Then he grins, leans over and claps me on the back. "Glad you came, Porter." His face is shiny, his eyes glassy. Mine must be too. Better get along, little dogie, or you'll be hurtin' tomorrow. Gotta finish the jug first though. Out here, wasting beer is a hangin' offence.

"— wanted to thank you for the drink."

I turn and there she is, next to the table, the glass of red wine in her hand. She's shorter than I'd anticipated, in a delicate sort of way, and much closer. For a few seconds I'm confused, then I remember buying her the drink, and with stunning bravery, tell her it was nothing and offer her a seat. To my surprise, she accepts and suddenly she's right there, next to me, smelling of flowers and showing more skin than I'm used to unless I'm in the shower. I can't think of much to say, but what I do seems immensely funny.

"What do you do?" she says.

"I'm a forest ranger. Me and my buddy, Carl, here. Twig pigs."

"Really?" She looks intrigued. "That sounds like a fascinating job. Do you sit in lookout towers and watch for fires?"

It's the same idiotic question I've heard a thousand times. Everyone thinks a forest ranger spends his day with a pair of binoculars vigilantly scanning the forest. Or wrestling grizzlies and saving imperilled deer. But it's been a few years and tonight I don't mind. I'm ready to impress. "Yeah, that and there's the tree counting."

"Tree counting?" she says, a look of mild perplexity on her lovely face.

"Yes." I pour another glass of draft for Carl and myself, allow the suspense to build. "We have to take care of the trees right? So, we gotta know how many we've got in inventory."

She nods, following right along.

"So we count them." I point to the other patrons. "One, two, three ..."

"You don't count each individual tree, do you?"

"No." I try to look serious. "We used to, but now we stick bar codes on them, just scan them as we walk past. Makes it easier to tell which ones are missing."

She smiles — she's onto me. "You don't do that."

"Well ... not really. We do something called timber cruising. Use statistics."

Based on reality, the conversation flounders. I sip my beer, try to look jovial. But I'm remembering the last time I tried to show someone what I really did at work — when I really did the work. It's not doing wonders for my mood and I attempt to compensate by drinking faster. Fredricks has been watching the strange and desirable lady seated beside me and drifts over, sticks a chubby hand across the table at her, introduces himself.

"Casey," he says in his most debonair fashion. "Just call me Case."

"Christina Telson," she replies, batting her eyelashes at him.

I'm jealous. I didn't properly introduce myself or ask her name and I frown at Fredricks, who's purposefully oblivious. Under the table, I slide my hand onto her thigh but she gently sets it aside and for the next few minutes I sit still, feeling guilty and rejected. The tiny table is so loaded with drinks the wood is no longer visible and I retaliate by drinking a whisky I think belongs to Fredricks.

Someone leans over the table and shoves me. "Hey! I'm talking to you, shit head."

It's a Neanderthal — short, squat and unshaven. His face is sunburned and dirty. His hair, the colour of oily steel wool, appears to be attempting mutiny and his eyes are filled with a hostile anticipation. I've forgotten the cardinal rule of bar survival — never point — and despite the numbing effects of too much alcohol and too little sleep, I get a nervous clench in my gut. I'm too far gone to defend myself.

"What?" I say innocently. The faces around the table are pensive, waiting.

"You heard me, shit head. You're too goddamn stupid to sit with a woman like that."

I want to point out the hypocrisy of his statement but the Neanderthal is suddenly jerked out of my personal space. I get one quick back glance of Brotsky's face as he tows the intruder to dry dock. "What the hell was that about?" asks Fredricks. I shrug and we watch from across the crowded bar. Brotsky and the stranger stand in a corner by the washroom door. The stranger keeps pointing toward our table, his gestures emphatic. Brotsky meets my gaze and frowns, pulls the Neanderthal into the washroom. I'm half tempted to follow them in, sort this out, but a primitive part of my brain dedicated to self-preservation prevails. Instead, I turn to the woman beside me, determined to redeem myself for neglecting proper introductions. I offer a hand.

"Porter Cassel."

Her hand is warm. "Christina. Nice to meet you."

It all seems so formal. I think furiously about what to say next.

Telson offers me a conciliatory smile. "I'd better get going."

"Why? That was nothing."

She slides off the bench. "Thanks for the drink."

Then she's gone and the bar isn't so much fun anymore. Some guy in the jukebox is wailing about having seven bullets in his six-gun. Where can I get a gun like that? My eyelids grow heavy, my speech slower. There's a fight outside — the caveman has found someone else to play with — and Carl is helping me to my feet, the tassels of his buckskin coat in my face. We stagger home together, both too drunk to drive. I remember mumbling Nina's name as Carl helped me to my room.

Carl's house is quiet late the next morning when I stagger out of bed. I spend a half-hour in the bathroom, in long distance discussion with parties unknown over the big porcelain telephone. I haven't had a night like that in over a year and I conclude my conversation with a familiar farewell. Never again. The operator gushes her condolences, but I know the phone bill is going to be a killer. Serves me right.

As penance, I saddle up my mountain bike.

My first stop is the parking lot of The Corral, where my Land Rover sits alone, dented and forlorn in the noonday sun. No new dents though. I make a loop around the squat little building, looking for what, I don't know, and notice there's fresh blood mixed with the gravel near the rear door. The Neanderthal's handiwork. Have to remember not to point the next time.

I wheel onto the highway, cross the bridge over the Curtain River — the water level is low this early in the year, the channel braided, gravel bars exposed — and head into town. Like most of the towns I've worked in, back when I had steady work, the highway is mainstreet and it's here the majority of the town is strung out: the bars, grocery stores and gas stations. The post office. It's the sort of town where sideburns never went out of style. I veer right at a carwash, spend a few minutes in the backwaters of the town as my legs warm up. Half the population appear to live in trailers but, judging by the additions and the number of old cars in the yards, not many of them are in danger of going anywhere. I get lost in the crescents for a few minutes — an embarrassing feat in a town this small — find my way back to mainstreet.

An old Chevy pulls out from an alley behind me and follows uncomfortably close. I glance back, expecting a pass, but the driver, invisible behind the sun glint of the windshield, is in no hurry. The truck is on old Apache, a classic of sorts. But this one is a Frankenstein truck, the body put together from numerous carcasses. None of the colours match — the doors are red, the hood white, the fenders blue. Rust splotches and peeling paint complete the effect. It's jacked-up, the tires as high as my bike. I'd noticed the truck twice before, behind the carwash and then barrelling through a vacant school zone. The owner must be some kid, burning gas and doing his part to run up the Gross Domestic Product. Not much else to do here. I turn onto the highway, pass the last gas station and head uphill, out of the Curtain River valley.

The truck is still behind me, which is odd given we're both on the highway now and I'm doing about ten miles an hour. If this is a tail, the driver has a lot to learn. I glance back once more — the grille looks like the mouth of a monster with bad teeth. This idiot is way too close and I veer into the ditch, let him pass, crane my neck to see who's driving. But the window is too high and the driver remains anonymous — hammering the gas and leaving me in a blue haze of exhaust fumes. I watch the truck roar up the highway, sounding like a badly tuned Harley, shake my head.

A slug of water from the bottle on my bike and I push on.

Downshift. The throbbing in my head assumes a nasty resonance and it occurs to me this wasn't such a good idea. But I think of Nina and of last night, how the woman's thigh felt under my hand. I deserve some punishment and lean into the hill, sweat running into my eyes. At the crest, I roll into the ditch, gasp, vomit, catch my breath. There's a breeze up here and a view of the mountains, white and jagged against blue sky. I saddle up and keep going.

The highway is narrow, no shoulder, steep ditches. I occupy the last few inches of pavement — any farther and I'll join the broken bottles and chip bags in the ditch. Loaded log trucks blast past in one direction while oversized motorhomes — worth more than the last house I lived in and driven by city dwellers intent on escape — swerve past me at the last second. I'm terrified I'll become a stain on some Luxury Liner's grille, or an unexpected speed bump.

I take the first gravel road heading generally west, thankful to be alive.

I'm in ranching country, rolling and fenced. Driveways are long and winding, framed by gateposts with the ranch's brand burned into the wood. My lungs and legs are lobbying for a cessation of movement, my head seconding the motion, but I want to make it to the edge of the forest: a blanket of green on the slopes ahead, shimmering like a mirage. Amongst the trees, I can rest.

The road begins to rise. Ranches give way to scattered subdivisions filled with immense houses, so new the dirt at their foundations is still fresh. I think of the trailers in town and wonder who owns these mansions, then remember this area next to the mountains is only an hour from the city. Curtain River has been discovered and everyone wants a piece of the rock. Farther up the road, the mock ski lodges end and a sign in the ditch, put up by the Department of Public Lands, informs me I am now entering the Green Area of the Province — a Working Forest where timber is produced, cattle graze and non-renewable carbon deposits are siphoned off.

A 20-minute lounge in the shade and I feel better. Turn back? Shadow angles across the road ahead and I push on. Just another mile or two. The road is fairly level, it's cool in the shade and gravel crunches satisfyingly under my tires. It would be pleasant if I wasn't so hung over. I coast to a stop where the road forks. The main road veers to the left. The right arm of the fork is narrow, rutted and angles up a steep slope, switchbacking toward a hidden summit. I'm exhausted; the road is torture but something I don't want to listen to is egging me on. Think of the top, it whispers. No, I mumble. I'm sick and I'm already 20 miles from town. *You have to do this*, the voice urges, and when I shake my head the voice becomes nasty, calls me a quitter, accuses me of cowardice.

I groan, start up the slope.

Pain and agony. My legs are filled with barbed wire, my chest is too small and my throat pinches so I can't swallow. I downshift again, to the second easiest gear. I've never used the lowest gear — something always holds me back, no matter how difficult the slope. Maybe I want to have something in reserve. Maybe I'm just crazy. I look ahead — a mistake; the top of the road appears impossibly distant. I focus on the next switchback. My mind grows numb against the stress of forcing onward failing tissue and I hope for a sort of nirvana via necrosis. Finally, mercifully, the road flattens to a manageable grade and I'm at the top of a ridge.

There's a small cabin with a rain barrel, generator shed and outhouse in a circular clearing. It's a forestry lookout tower — a tiny red-and-white cupola at the top of a hundred-foot derrick — where there really is a guy with a scope and pair of binoculars who spends his day vigilantly scanning the forest. I drop the bike and stagger weak-kneed across rocky, manicured lawn to a handmade bench close to the edge of the ridge. If it was punishment I needed, then I'm purified. Ten minutes later, I can breathe again and the tune of my pulse has returned from an uneven hip-hop to a good old blues refrain. The door on the bottom of the cupola slaps open and the towerman — resigned to the fact that his visitor won't leave without some prodding — descends the narrow ladder like an insect intent on escaping a spider's web.

“How ya doin’?” he says, coming up behind me. He’s an old guy with a potbelly, long grey beard and sun-burned dome. His vintage tie-dyed shirt is so worn the colours have faded to the point of competing with the sweat stains under his arms. He’s short, wearing sandals, looks like a hobbit from the sixties. Tower people can get a little loopy if they stay in the profession too long, but he seems okay. Of course, it’s still early in the season.

He sticks out a hand. “Gabe Peterson.”

I stand up, introduce myself.

“Out for a little ride?” He’s looking at my abandoned mountain bike. “Get a few hardy souls like that every year. Most just drive up.” His eyes wander back to me. One eye is bright blue; the other, pale grey. It’s a little disconcerting, as though he were put together from spare parts — like the Chevy. “You want something to drink?” he asks. “I made a pitcher of lemonade this morning.”

At the mention of cold fluids, my knees go weak all over again. I follow Peterson into his cabin, which is crowded with stacks of boxes like he’s just moved in. But it’s not natural for a towerperson to have this much gear, even a tower with road access, and I wonder if Carl knows about this. The boxes are stacked to eye level and Peterson vanishes among them, a layer of boxes indented to allow passage for his midsection. One of the boxes is on its side and I can see bundles of little plastic sandwich bags. Curious, I tug a baggie part way out, expecting ganja or something like that. It’s filled with a flattened clod of hair — black mixed with grey — and has a date on it: August 14, 1982. Peterson might be going into the seniors toupee business, but I don’t think so. This is serious fetish material and I shudder to think what else he might have in these boxes.

Suddenly, I’m not so thirsty anymore.

“Yup,” he hollers from somewhere ahead, as though confirming an earlier statement, and I shove the hair back into its filing system.

"Been in this tower for 38 seasons now." He comes around a corner in the labyrinth, sideways, chuckling, two glasses of cloudy liquid jostling in his hands. "I reckon they let me keep coming back so they don't have to move all this stuff."

I nod, take the offered glass, retreat outside.

We return to the bench — it's so roomy out here — spend a few minutes staring across the valley at a puzzleboard of brown cut-blocks on a far slope. Gabe sets aside his drink, which makes me nervous. "You from the city?" he says.

"No. I'm a country boy."

"Good for you. This place is too goddamn close to the city."

There's a pause. I used to take care of a half-dozen towers up north and would visit them once a month, to bring in groceries. Just as important for the towerperson were the few hours of human contact. Most would babble continuously, cram in an entire month's conversation. Others would be sullen and taciturn, couldn't wait for you to leave. "What do you do in the winter?" I ask politely.

"Guns," he says, grinning. "I'm a gunsmith. Out of my garage."

A gunsmith with a hair collection; I'll sleep better knowing that.

"What about you?" he says. "What do you do?"

"I used to be a Ranger."

Gabe nods and something passes across his face. I get the feeling he's recognized me; my picture was in the papers quite a bit a few years ago. If he does, he's polite enough not to say anything. We both gaze at the mountains. The cutblocks across the valley look familiar. The angle is different and I'm farther above them, but they look like the blocks I saw from the bombing site. Which means the site can't be far away. "You notice anything strange in the past few days?"

Gabe scratches under his beard. "Not really."

"Get any visitors?"

"Vistors?" He snorts, rubs a hand over the bald top of his head, like an amputee with a phantom itch, smoothing back imaginary hair. "Too many," he grumbles. "You should see this place on a long weekend. Had one guy come walking up the hill one morning, wearing Hush Puppies and carrying a poodle. Got his motorhome stuck, rolled it halfway over a switchback. Said he wanted to camp up here. Heard the view was nice."

"When was that?"

The old towerman slurps his lemonade. "About a week ago. Guy wanted me to give him a tow." He chuckles, flops a meaty arm over the back of the bench. "Like I got some way of getting him outa there. I called the office and they called CAA. Took a goddamn winch truck." He shakes his head.

"But you didn't have any visitors these past two days?"

"Just you. Heard those explosions though. Three of them. Woke me up."

"Did you notice what time that was?"

"Naw. Middle of the night. Too dark."

"You see any smoke in the morning?"

"A bit. Real black. Damn lucky it didn't start a fire. It's drier than hell out here."

"I've noticed. What's the hazard up to?"

Peterson shakes his head. "Been extreme damn near since the snow left. Not much of a snow pack and a dry fall. What little snow we had went into the air, not into the ground. Sublimated. If we don't get some rain soon, it isn't going to green up."

"Yeah, it's pretty dry."

"Worst I've seen in 30 years."

I point across the valley. "How far do you think those blocks are?"

"Eleven and a half miles to the top of the ridge," he says without hesitation, like he's making a report. Towermen have a good sense of distance. Some of them can read minds too. "A little less to the blocks. And the smoke from those explosions was even closer — about four miles."

"That's close."

"You got that right," he says. "Too damn close for me. With this hazard, a fire that close would be at my door before breakfast. I knew a guy in a tower up north who got burned out. Up in the sand country. Nothing but pine around him, just like here. Said he could see a wall of flame coming across the tops of the trees — like looking into hell. It's not something I want to go through."

"Keane Tower. I heard about that."

A radio crackles over a loudspeaker, calling the tower for a weather report. Gabe swears, runs for the cabin and through the loudspeaker I hear him reading out a familiar prognosis. Moderate build-up to the west; winds light; good visibility. With the hot weather, it makes me feel like I should be working. I should head north, fight some fire, but I'm not quite ready to leave Curtain River.

I wait long enough to thank Gabe for the lemonade, then saddle up.

Part way down the slope, I stop and stash the bike in the bush.

After the bike ride up the hill, it's a long hike. My hangover has reached stage two — sheer exhaustion — but in the trees it's shady and I take plenty of rests. Up north, you couldn't walk through the bush without a compass and map, but here ridges and mountain peaks simplify navigation. I hike downhill for an hour, spend another hour climbing a sidehill to a lesser ridge with a panoramic view where I fix my location. Then it's downhill again, between slender, branchless stems. A half-hour later, I hit the upper edge of the cutblock where the feller-buncher was bombed.

The cutblock is long and undulating, the road below invisible, dug into the sidehill. I catch drifted bits of conversation, the sound of a vehicle engine, but can see little. I follow the edge of the timber toward the valley bottom, using the cover of the forest. This far in, the edge of the block is barely visible, a demarcation of openness indicated by fewer trees. Suddenly, I hear a motor very close, catch a glimpse of blue metal a dozen yards downslope and drop to the ground as a truck whines past on the hidden road. I lay flat for a while, my cheek pressed against pine needles and dry moss, paranoid I've been spotted and will have to explain myself. But no one has seen me and, crouching, I retreat farther into the forest.

I stop and rest, catch my breath, consider my options. It's still an official crime scene and I have no business here. No official business anyway. But the post blast team is probably at work and I want to watch from the anonymity of the forest, just for a few minutes. Unfortunately, the forest is too sparse here, the trees too far apart to offer screening. I don't have binoculars. The smart thing to do would be to get the hell out of here, return to my bike and forget the whole thing. But I can't forget and it seems a shame to have come this far for nothing. If I could find an outcropping, some sort of promontory, I might be able to watch the activity in the cutblock.

I start working my way upslope again, searching ahead for cover.

Near the top of the cutblock, I angle toward the open and see a jut of rock on the other side. From higher on the slope, I could descend through the trees to the outcropping, where I'd be invisible from below. My stomach protests — it's purged the poisons and wants compensation. I'll spend a half-hour watching, no more, then start back, hopefully make it to town by supper.

I make a wide arc through the trees, above the cutblock, and begin my descent. It's much steeper here and the going is slow, the trees providing handholds. I lose sight of the outcropping and when I see it again I freeze.

Someone else has the same idea, and he's considerably more prepared.

He's prone, belly-down on the rock, dressed in forest camouflage, his clothes a pattern of dark brown tree trunks against light grey so he looks like a truncated deck of logs. If he'd been standing still in the forest, I would probably have walked right past him, but he's out of his background — the perpetual problem with camo. He's wearing a cap of the same pattern, the visor crimped like a steeple, his face obscured. He might be a hunter, or a police sharpshooter, but the way he's aiming through the scope of his rifle, I don't think so. It's the Lorax and for a moment I remain frozen in mid-stride, awkwardly clinging to the stem of a slender pine, waiting for the shot.

The shot doesn't come — he's just watching.

Carefully, I take a few steps back and crouch, paranoid he'll hear me breathing, my heart thumping. He doesn't know I'm here and so presumably I have the advantage. But it dawns on me there is little I can do. The Lorax has a gun; I'm unarmed. I could work my way back down the slope, through the trees so he wouldn't see me, and talk to the Mounties in the cutblock. But by the time I explain what *I'm* doing here, and convince them there is someone watching them through a riflescope, he'll be long gone.

I stand up — I can't let him get away.

Everything about me is loud. My breathing, the way I set my feet and even my clothes are sure to alert the man with the rifle lying on the rock a hundred yards away. Any second I'm sure he'll roll over, point the rifle at me. What I'll do then, I have no idea.

A few minutes of creeping forward and I'm close enough to see he's got a knife on his belt and that he's wearing black boots, double laced around the upper. Hard to tell how tall he is though, prone like that. I need something to establish scale —

There's a scrape and dry clatter as a plate of loose rock shifts under my weight, sends a sprinkle of scree rolling a short distance downslope. Instinctively, I freeze. Should have been paying more attention to the ground, but it's too late now — he's turned over and is sweeping the hillside with his scope. That he's using a scope is my only advantage — the magnification at this range makes me difficult to find — and I bolt sidehill and then down, pivoting on tree trunks and jumping over deadfall. I slip, twist my ankle hard enough to know I won't be running much longer, drop behind two crossed logs.

There's a crunch of dry moss from somewhere uphill, then silence.

We're both waiting. I hug closer to a fallen log, cautiously peer over — nothing but trees. I want to go after the bastard but I might not see him and he has a gun. The odds aren't in my favour. Better to make it to the police, let them call in the dogs and helicopters.

I retreat down the slope. The trees are slender pine and offer pathetically little cover. I feel like a cartoon character trying to hide behind a light post as I dodge from trunk to trunk, attempting to keep my chest and head hidden. I'm making too much noise — snapping twigs — to tell if he's following me. Not that he has to. With that rifle, all he needs is a clear line of sight. A long shot would be better for him too, give him more time to get away —

"Don't fucking move."

I raise my arms, turn very slowly. It's a young cop, his face flushed, a pistol in his hand. "I said ... don't ... fucking ... move ..."

He's gulping, trying to catch his breath. How could I have not heard him running up behind me?

"Take it easy. The guy you want is up there."

I point. Once again, a bad idea. He's nervous enough already.

"There's a guy up there with a rifle, dressed in camo —"

"On the ground!" This cop looks like a rookie but when it comes to restraint he's paid attention in class. Or he's played football because the next thing I know I'm belly-down, his knee between my shoulder blades as he cuffs me hands behind back.

"What the —? Why are you arresting me?"

He's breathing in my ear. "We'll figure that out soon enough."

"Are you nuts? Listen —" I'm trying to explain but it's hard to talk with moss and pine needles in your mouth, no air in your lungs. "The guy that did this is getting away —"

He yanks me to my feet, nearly dislocating both shoulders, shoves me forward.

"Jesus Christ." One last try. "Cuff me to a tree. Go after him."

"You are not obliged to say anything unless you wish to do so —"

Given how pissed I am by now, it's a right I waive.

6

THE LOCAL RCMP detachment is in a renovated old house next to the hospital, in the heart of Curtain River's only real residential area. The interrogation room was probably a walk-in closet at one time, or some old ladies' sewing room. Now, it has somewhat less class. There's an institutional brown metal desk, wide enough that it divides the narrow room, trapping me in the end. A few equally appealing chairs complete the ensemble.

Rachet and a younger cop I don't remember having seen before come in. The second Mountie, an older version of the Gerber baby with thin blonde hair, closes the door, which barely misses the edge of the table. Rachet plunks down an old battery-operated cassette recorder, the flat five-button type that was state-of-the art 20 years ago. He unwraps a fresh tape, shoves it into the machine and pockets the crinkling plastic wrap. By way of introduction, he waves toward the other Mountie. "This is Constable Bergren. Local detachment."

I nod to Bergren. He nods back. We all sit down. The two Mounties span the width of the narrow room. I'm exhausted, at the tail end of a hangover and brutal bike ride. My ankle has swollen so that I've had to loosen my boot. They could have offered me some ice. Or taken a few minutes at the crime scene to question me, allow me a chance to explain. But after Rachet assured the rookie I likely didn't pose an immediate threat, they uncuffed me and offered temporary accommodation in the back of a cruiser, my other choice being to limp through the bush to my bike, then try to ride home. Since they wanted to talk to me later, I humoured them and stuck around.

Rachet leans his elbows on the armrests of his chair, crosses his hands. The long day is written on his face and he's ready to go home, prune his rose garden. Bergren too looks tired, eyes squinted and puffed red from the sun. Everyone wants to be somewhere else. "Sorry about Constable Harder," Rachet says. "He's a bit enthusiastic. Watches too many cop shows."

"That's okay. I didn't need those ribs anyway."

Rachet leans forward, stabs a button on the recorder hard enough to make me wonder how the machine survived this long, provides a quick monotone summary of our little meeting. "May 3, 1998. Curtain River Detachment. Interview with Porter Cassel."

"So this is an interview, not an interrogation?"

Rachet shrugs. "Call it what you want."

"Am I under arrest?"

"No. At this point we just want to talk to you. Give you an opportunity to explain a few things. So there are no misunderstandings. Of course, you are not obliged to say anything unless you wish to do so, but whatever you say may be given in evidence."

"So I can leave?"

"Sure, you can leave." But neither of the Mounties move. I'd have to climb over the table, and both of them, to get out. More intimidation, but I'm not really worried. There's little they could charge me with as I'm pretty sure there's no law against walking through the forest, even if it does take you within the vicinity of a crime scene. But I'm more than a little uncomfortable — the last time I was in a room like this with Rachet, Nina's blood was still on my shirt.

"Do you mind telling us what you were you doing out there?"

"I was just going for a walk."

"A walk, eh?" The Mounties exchange a look that clearly indicates they don't believe me. Under the table, I massage my ankle, think about how long it would have taken me to walk back to the tower, bike into town. I'd be arriving just about now. At least I got a free ride out of the deal. Makes the afternoon a wash. But now the meter's running and I want to get back to Carl's museum for a cool sasparilla and a colder ice pack, a fist full of painkillers and a long stretch of shut-eye. "And you just happened to end up at the crime scene?" Rachet says.

"I didn't know it was still a crime scene."

Rachet knits his fingers together, leans back in his chair, settling in. Not a good sign. Bergren is slouched, watching me. When we make eye contact, he looks down. I wonder if they know I took the shard of metal. Did someone see me? The possibility causes an anxious clench in my gut. "So why didn't you just come up the road?" Rachet says. "Or is this an old forest ranger habit, crashing through the bush?"

"Something like that," I say. "Good for the constitution."

The look on Rachet's face tells me he thinks he's being clever, humouring me a bit.

"You know, Mr. Cassel, I don't much believe in coincidence."

That makes two of us.

"So I would like to know what exactly you had in mind this afternoon."

"You catch the guy who was watching you?" I ask. "The guy in camo, with the rifle?"

Bergren pushes himself up on the armrests of his chair and

with an audible series of pops and crackles, straightens himself out. Nice to know I'm not the only one with a back that sounds like breakfast cereal. "What's this?" he says, craning his neck and leaning forward to get that last vertebrae in line. "You were out there with someone?"

I find it hard to believe Bergren doesn't know — another game in their repertoire.

"I thought he might have been one of yours," I say.

"One of ours? Really? How so?"

"He was geared up like a sharpshooter."

The two Mounties look mildly curious.

"Camo, black boots — the whole fashion statement. His rifle looked military."

Rachet purses his lips, traces a damp pattern on the edge of the table. I'm hoping I won't have to repeat the whole story for Bergren's benefit but when Rachet looks over at me he raises an eyebrow as if this were new information. I sigh, rub my ankle — a long day is getting longer.

"We didn't have anybody up there did we?" says Bergren.

Rachet shakes his head.

"So he wasn't one of ours —"

It's warm in here, the buzz of fluorescent lights a soothing white noise, and I begin to fantasize about a Sealy Posturepedic with proper lumbar and neck support, nearly drift off, force myself to concentrate on Bergren. He crosses his arms — a display of white skin and freckles that would encourage anyone to wear sun block. "Let me get this straight," he says. "You were out for a little stroll and you just happened to end up at the crime scene. At the exact spot where there was this mysterious sharpshooter."

I don't want to explain how I thought the rock outcrop would be a good lookout, how I was just going to watch for a few minutes, but I can see they're ready to play this up any way they have to. "Look ..." I raise my hands — I'm starting to talk like Rachet. "I was just out for a bike ride. I went up this road to a forestry tower and when I saw the pattern of the cutblocks I realized the bombing site was only a few miles away. I was curious, so I went for a little walk."

"Curious about what Mr. Cassel?" Rachet says. "You were just there the day before."

"I know, but I didn't think there would be any harm in taking another look."

Rachet gives me a consoling nod. "I see. How did you find the man with the rifle?"

I tell them how I went to the rock for a look, to make sure it was okay before going further down. Not quite the truth, but close enough. Once again, I describe the guy with the rifle, the sort of camo he was wearing. By the end of this, Bergren is cleaning his nails again. Rachet looks bored. "Maybe he was a hunter," Rachet says, looking toward Bergren. "When's the spring bear hunting season over?"

Bergren consults an interior calendar. "Another ten days."

"I had a feeling he was hunting," I admit. "But not bear."

Both cops ponder this. Rachet drums his fingers on the table. "Did you see his face?"

"It was painted with camo. I didn't get a close look."

"How tall was this individual?"

"I'm not sure — he was lying down. Maybe six feet."

"You're positive it was a man?"

I hadn't considered it might be a woman and search my fading impression for a waistline, some clue that might indicate an armed member of the fairer sex. "It would have to be a sturdy woman."

"So you really have no idea what this individual looks like?" Rachet says.

"Like I said, the face was painted."

"Did this individual see you?"

"He must have. I made some noise and he turned on me."

"And you still didn't get a good look at him?"

"He had a rifle. I wasn't sticking around for introductions."

There's a pause, filled by the tape player with a low thumping squeal, like my Land Rover in low gear. Rachet rubs his forehead, massages his temples. He looks ready for an Advil commercial. "An interesting story," he says. "The phantom gunman watches from the shadows."

For some reason, I get the feeling they don't believe me. "Did you go after him?"

Rachet fondles his moustache. "I'm more interested in why you were there."

"Tell me you went after him."

A dismissive wave of the hand. "We sent up a chopper. They didn't see anything."

"He was wearing camouflage," I mumble. They must think I made up the gunman to divert their attention from my being there. Or they're hiding something — they must have looked harder than that. My pulse quickens — maybe they caught him and they're just tying up loose ends. Suddenly, the room seems humid, sticky.

"You caught him, didn't you?"

They look at each other and I realize how wrong I am.

"Did you send any men up the hill? Dogs to track?"

Rachet leans forward, intent. "So, really, why were you there?"

I sigh, lean back, massage my eyes. Maybe when I look again they'll be gone. No such luck. Rachet is still leaning forward, his elbows on the table. I wonder where the file Bergren has open on the table came from — I was pretty sure he was empty-handed when he came in. But then again I was sure they would go after the gunman too.

"You don't think much of our police work do you?" Rachet says. His hands are still and he's watching me carefully. He's picked a bad time to ask that question — I'm furious they didn't look harder for the stranger in camo — but at the moment, honesty may not be the best policy. I shrug. "I haven't paid it much attention."

Rachet's eyebrows go up. "Honestly Mr. Cassel, I find that hard to believe."

This seems a prelude and I get a bad feeling again about the shard of metal I borrowed. I try to remember if anyone could have seen me. I doubt it — Carl is the only one who knows and he wouldn't say anything. I look Rachet in the eye. "I just want the bastard caught."

"As do we. But sneaking around a crime scene won't help."

"I wasn't sneaking —"

"Right — you were going for a walk. But considering your background, that interests me."

"My background?"

Rachet looks at Bergren, gives him a slight nod. Bergren opens the file, flips a few pages, pausing here or there. "A year of instrumentation at college before you dropped out. Then there's a blank in your record while you were bumming around, presumably finding yourself. You enrolled in forestry, became a Ranger. After that bombing killed your fiancée, you quit the Forest Service and spent a year bumming around, losing yourself — there's a couple of drunk and disorderlies on record here." He goes on, reading my personal history as though it were a technical manual, making me feel like a lab specimen, pinned to a slide and under a microscope.

It's disconcerting and I'm pretty sure that's why he's doing it. God knows my resumé has nothing to do with anything. He ends his dissertation on a more personal note — returning to the bombing up north that killed Nina.

"You were cleared," says Rachet. "But no one was ever arrested."

"No kidding."

Rachet looks thoughtful. "That would burn me, piss me right off."

"Is there some point to this?" They're playing a game for which I have no patience.

"Maybe. You tell us." Rachet is staring at me again, waiting for a wrong move, anything suspicious. It makes me *feel* suspicious. Like slowing down on the highway when you see a cop, even though you're not speeding. "Your girlfriend is killed and the bombings stop. Then, all of a sudden, they start again and there's another fatality. Seems odd you've been involved with both."

"You know exactly how I'm involved. I came here to help, for Christ's sake."

They look at me as if they know something I don't. This might work on real criminals who have something to hide but on me it only raises my blood pressure. I want to say more but I'm pretty sure it wouldn't come out well and the recorder is running. Instead I grind my teeth, stare at the table and wait for the pressure to subside. Rachet and Bergren must be able to see I'm close to the edge because they give me a minute. But only a minute. They're like kids with a magnifying glass, torturing an insect, careful not to burn it too much so that it keeps moving.

"Did you know Hess?" Rachet says.

"Did I know him? Only his ribcage, which I met yesterday."

"Hmmm, that's interesting —" Bergren is flipping through his file again like a student looking for a lost research note. "Because both you and Hess worked in the same area when your fiancée — what was her name — was killed."

"Nina," I say coldly. "Her name was Nina."

"Right ... Nina. Here it is." He pulls out a sheet and holds it up. "Ronald Hess worked at KCL Logging out of Fort Termination the same time you were a ranger there."

This is news to me. "A lot of people worked there."

"Did you ever meet Hess?"

"I don't know. What does he look like?"

Bergren thumbs through the file, pulls out a picture of Ronald Hess and his wife, posed against an azure backdrop in some photographer's office. The picture must have been pulled out of a frame because you can see the fade line on the emulsion. Hess's wife is wearing a coffee-coloured long dress. She's blonde, slim, good-looking and seated on a bench beside Hess, who's in a dark suit with an equally serious look — the old school of thought where it's not manly to smile at the camera, even on your wedding day. Especially on your wedding day. He's young — early twenties — has short, dark hair and a tanned complexion.

I shake my head. "Never met him."

"What about Nina?" says Rachet. "She ever meet him?"

I don't like where this is going. "What are you suggesting?"

Rachet shrugs. "Nothing. Just trying to establish a connection."

"There's no connection." If he tries to work some angle that Nina might have been involved with Hess and I was jealous, they might as well arrest me because Rachet is going to eat the tape deck. "I came here to help with the evidence search," I say carefully. "I was told that you were looking for help."

There's a pause. The magnifying glass is pulled back, put away. Rachet punches a button on the tape deck, extracts the tape. "Your assistance with the search is appreciated and I understand you want closure, but you have to understand that this is police business. You cannot involve yourself further." He pauses, his brow furrowed, gives me time to appreciate his sincerity. "You'll have to be patient."

I nod — not in agreement but because I knew he would eventually tell me this.

"Good." Both Mounties stand. "Thank you for your cooperation."

I nod again to keep from saying anything more and we leave the tiny room. At the front counter, sheathed to the roof with bullet-proof glass, Rachet offers me a ride.

"No thanks," I tell him through the glass. "I'll be fine."

All hospital emergency wards are pretty much the same. They all have curtained cubicles filled with moaning victims. It's only a matter of scale. Some have huge waiting rooms where you could die before they get to you. Others have small waiting rooms where you could die before they get to you. The Curtain River Hospital has a row of six chairs just inside the doors. I'm fairly safe because I doubt anyone has died of a sprained ankle. The guy next to me is in a bit more danger though. He's lost several fingers and his hand is wrapped in a bloody towel. He sees me staring.

"Planer mill," he grunts through his pain. Wood shavings cling to his shirt. A name tag above his chest pocket says LEONARD. His hardhat, which he's still wearing and seems not to have contributed to his safety, says Curtain River Forest Products. A nurse appears from the direction of the admitting desk, followed by another mill worker, also still wearing his hardhat.

"And this happened when?" asks the nurse.

"About 20 minutes ago," says Leonard's buddy.

The nurse leans over the injured man, carefully unwraps the bloody towel. He looks away, tries to smile without much success. His face is pale, the skin contrasting with his dark stubble. "Gonna lose our safety bonus this week," he mumbles.

The nurse scowls. "What a terrible place. Third one this month."

"I didn't notice at first," he says. "It didn't hurt until I looked at it."

"Did you save the fingers?"

"I was just going along," Leonard says faintly. "Doing my thing. There was a loose board, come off the infeed. I must have reached too far. Next thing I know, someone is yelling, bringing me my fingers —"

"They're in the truck," says Leonard's buddy. "In my lunch bucket. I'll get them."

"Nine thousand feet per minute," says Leonard. "It makes you dizzy —"

The nurse leads Leonard into a room and the hallway is mine. There's a small table piled with a scatter of magazines — *Vanity Fair, Good Housekeeping* — all obviously selected by the nurses. I'm too distracted to read though, thinking about the lone gunman. I try to remember his face, recall features seen beneath the splotches of black and green grease paint. He turned too fast, was too far away. There was a hat: a baseball cap, the visor crimped in the middle like the gable end of a roof. It could have been a hunter. It could have been anyone. I should have stopped him.

Another nurse, red-haired and younger than the nurse who attended the injured worker, helps me hobble into an examination room, has me take a seat on the bed. She peels off my sock and looks at my ankle, cradles it in her hand and bends it carefully from side to side, asking if it hurts. It does, but there's something reassuring about having a woman tend to your wounds in a room filled with stainless steel. She takes my temperature and blood pressure — a bit elevated for some reason — asks a few generic questions and tells me the doctor will be by in a few minutes. But the medical profession has a different concept of time, because the few minutes stretch into two and a half-hours. By the time the doctor arrives, a pale man in his forties, I'm in danger of having healed. "Stay off it for a few days," he says. "Elevate and ice for the first 72 hours. Take painkillers if necessary."

He offers me crutches — the real reason I'm here — which I accept. I need mobility.

He doesn't ask if I need a ride. If you can make it to Emergency, the assumption is you'll have a ride home after. I do not. An adolescent stubbornness prevented me from accepting Rachet's offer, but a lady in a minivan saw me hobbling along the road. Now I'm on foot, so to speak. Fortunately, nothing is very far apart in Curtain River.

It's been a few years since I've operated a pair of crutches. It takes a block or two to get into the swing of it and when I do, a motorist pulls over and interrupts my cadence. It's a Volkswagen Beetle, a real one, not the newer, yuppy version. The window squeaks down and a familiar face appears, causing me to stumble and nearly fall.

"Well, if it isn't the twig pig," she says. "On sticks."

"Christina Telson," I say, dredging her name out of a mosaic of jumbled images, hoping I have it right. "How are you?"

A wide, lovely smile. "Better than you. Did that guy finally catch up with you?"

"No, an unrelated incident. Do you know him?"

She looks amused. "Need a ride?"

I hesitate, remembering my guilt from this morning. Her hair is loose, falling over her shoulders, and she's wearing a bulky canvas jacket, which makes her look smaller, waifish. I've always been a sucker for a woman in bush gear. "Okay," I say. "If it isn't too much trouble."

It's a bit complicated, fitting a pair of crutches into a tin can that size, but we manage to cram them between the seats. She has a dreamcatcher hanging from her rearview mirror. The seat backs are covered with bead mats, and strings of beads dangle from the top edge of the windshield. The dash is plastered with faded hippie slogans. Blackened bits of incense have collected in the ashtray.

"Where to?"

I think of Carl's place and the long rest that awaits me, then remember my Land Rover. It gets lonely if neglected. With my bum ankle, it would be nice to have wheels handy. "The Corral, if you don't mind." Telson gives me strange look. "To get my truck," I add quickly.

I notice for the first time that her nose is pierced; a tiny silver tear; funny I didn't notice that before. It makes her seem forbidden somehow. Maybe I'm just not hip anymore. "What?" she says as we rattle over the bridge.

"Nothing."

"You had this funny look on your face."

There must be another admirer of vintage Land Rovers in Curtain River because when I turn the key, Old Faithful doesn't stir. It takes a few minutes to track the problem to it's source — the starter is gone; there's a gaping hole in the bell housing through which I can see the ring gear. Overkill if someone doesn't want me driving, or maybe they're just collecting. I swear — it's going to be a bitch trying to find a starter for an old British import out here in the Land of Chevy. Telson watches from her Bug, her expression polite as I fiddle under the hood, crawl beneath the chassis and cover myself with dust, catch crumbling bits of rust with my eyes.

"Sabotaged," I tell her, blinking as I use a side mirror to clean my optics.

"Bummer." She looks appropriately serious, rummages under her seat and offers me what looks like a fluorescent purple banana. "You want to use my cell phone, call the cops?"

"No thanks." The thought of talking to Rachet again so soon doesn't appeal to me.

"Can I give you a ride home?"

I start to nod but my stomach gives a turn, obviously a step ahead. I haven't eaten today and the exhibits in Carl's fridge are for display purposes only. "How about an exchange?"

She raises an eyebrow, looks intrigued.

"A ride for a bite to eat."

She considers. "I can do that."

I use Telson's trendy purple banana to call a tow truck, ask the garage to pull the Land Rover to the Forestry compound. Then we look for a place to eat. There are a surprising number of restaurants in Curtain River, no doubt to service the tourists headed through to the mountains. We wait five minutes for our turn at the only four-way stop on mainstreet, trapped in a long line of motorhomes headed west. In the other lane is an equally long line of loaded log trucks, headed east. It seems a recipe for trouble. We choose the restaurant in the Curtain River Hotel, knowing the menu there will be predictable. We pause at the threshold, look for a seat among the tiny tables. Like a Western movie, the bearded patrons all stop eating, turn to watch us. Forks dangling bacon are suspended in hazy mid-air and there are ten seconds of silence. The only thing missing is the piano player, frozen in mid-tune. The clatter of dishes and hum of conversation resumes and the patrons ignore us. We take a seat by the window, where the smoke is slightly less dense and there's a splendid view of the intersection.

"Did you catch that?" asks Telson.

"What? That doesn't always happen to you?"

She gives me a sarcastic smile. "Maybe they were looking at you."

A sobering thought. Telson hums a few bars from *Deliverance*. She dumps her big coat over the back of a chair. I move my crutches out of the aisle, lean them against the window. Settled in, Telson brushes back hair from her face, gives me a confident and relaxed look.

"So what happened to your leg?"

"Mountain bike accident. Nothing much. Just a flesh wound."

"Where were you biking?"

"Out west." I'm purposefully vague, too tired and hung over to have much to offer in the way of conversation. But I make an effort — it's been a while since I've had this kind of company at dinner. "There's a forestry lookout tower about 20 miles from town. I biked up to that."

She raises an eyebrow. "Ooh, a machocist."

"Only the day after. Had to purge the poisons."

"Did you stay much longer — after I left?"

"A little, but my heart wasn't in it."

Telson looks down, traces a pattern on the placemat. Bold green letters proclaim it's Mental Health Awareness Week and there's a list of the signs and symptoms of schizophrenia. Be on the lookout for social withdrawal, flat emotions, abandonment of personal hygiene. Sounds like a typical redneck. Or a forest ranger. I stop reading, worried I'll recognize too many symptoms.

"So, Miss Telson, do you live around here?"

"Oh sure —"

A waitress comes, bringing with her the usual lull in conversation. By the way she waits by our table, pen and pad ready, I suspect there's not a lot on the menu. She's tall, thin, middle-aged, with the formaldehyde hair and skin of a well-preserved smoker; a workplace hazard — she'd be perfectly cured if she was a stick of salami. We read our menus — a single typed and photocopied page, cheaply laminated. The quality of the fingerprints would drive a crime scene cop wild with envy. My menu lists bacon and eggs, French fries, Monte Christo, buffalo burger and steak — a real cholesterol smorgasbord. But right now my stomach doesn't care, and when the waitress impatiently clears her throat I have to restrain myself from ordering everything and getting so bloated I'd arrive back at Emergency. Telson orders French fries and coffee.

The waitress frowns. "You want somethin' to go with them fries?"

"No thanks, I'm a vegetarian."

"Not too loud, honey," whispers the waitress. "You're in ranching country."

She continues on her rounds, armed with a pot of very black coffee. I look over at Telson, want to make a comment about her dietary restriction — about needing to enjoy the pleasures of the flesh — but control myself. Sometimes my sense of humour goes unappreciated.

"So, how long have you lived here?" I ask.

She tests her coffee, cringes. "Since Monday."

"Really. What happened on Monday?"

"I needed gas. What about you?"

"Friday."

She smiles condescendingly. "Ah, a newcomer."

"So, other than gas, what brings you to this thriving metropolis?"

I'm suddenly worried she's just passing through and I won't get to see her again. Not that I need more to worry about. Telson sips her coffee, looks privately amused. Maybe she can read my mind. "Truth is," she says, "I'm temporarily unemployed."

"Maybe you can find work here. What do you do?"

"I'm not really in a rush to work again."

"Must be nice. You win the lottery?"

"No," she says. "I quit. I had this boring job and I was living with this guy who wouldn't have noticed if I'd dropped dead. So I figured, screw this, you know. Why wait until the New Year to make a resolution? So I bought this used motorhome and got the hell out of there. Life is too short not to be doing what you want."

An impressive personal philosophy. "So you're just passing through?"

"I'm not sure." She takes a long sip of coffee, looks at me over the rim. Maybe it's just a burst of oxytocin but the look she gives me seems subtly loaded with promise. "It's a nice area, so close to the mountains," she says. "I might stay a while."

"Good — I mean, it is a nice area."

She smiles. I feel heat brush my cheeks.

"What about you, Mr. Forest Ranger? Here to count the trees?"

With a twinge of guilt, I remember telling her I'm still a ranger. Was it Mark Twain who said it was always best to tell the truth so you don't have to keep track of your lies? Good advice but I don't want to talk about why I'm really here; don't want to get into the sordid details of the bombing — just doesn't seem good mealtime conversation. "No tree counting, but I am sort of here on business. I'm visiting another ranger, helping out."

"Your friend Carl?"

I nod, remembering she wasn't the only one at the bar last night.

Outside, a white van pulls to the curb, the decal on the side advertising a television channel touting action news, always first on the scene. A guy with a ponytail and a woman with short hair get out of the van and when they step through the door, the *Twilight Zone* pause is even longer than when Telson and I came in. "The vultures have arrived," I mumble once the din has resumed.

"Vultures?" Telson gives me a wry smile.

"I've had a few unpleasant experiences with representatives of the media."

"Really?"

I nod, scare off a fly that's inspecting a blob of something on the corner of my placemat and quell a sudden urge to blubber my life's story to the first attractive woman I've shared a meal with since the bombing up north. "It was a long time ago."

She looks politely concerned. "What happened?"

"I'd rather not spoil my appetite."

The food arrives. Telson picks at her French fries, sucking ketchup off the end of a fry in a way I find very distracting. Not that I couldn't use a bit of distraction right now, but I look away. "They must be here because of that bombing," she says absently. "What a horrible thing."

So much for distraction. I attempt to pilot the conversation to calmer waters.

"What made you want to become a vegetarian?"

"Oh, nothing special." She waves off the omnivorous fly, which has become intensely attracted to her puddle of ketchup. "I just don't care for the taste of meat."

"You're not one of those animal rights people are you?"

"Not really," she says. "But why eat them if we don't have to?"

"Protein. Enzymes."

"You can get that stuff from plants —"

“Sure, but carrot juice is murder too.”

She laughs. “I suppose so. But one has to draw the line somewhere.”

She gazes out the window, toward the white van. “I don’t understand it.”

“Me neither. I could never give up meat.”

“No, the bombings.” She frowns. “This Lorax thing. What is a Lorax anyway?”

“You should get out more,” I tell her. “Read Dr. Seuss.”

“Dr. Seuss?”

“Yeah.” After all the media coverage, I find it hard to believe anyone doesn’t know who the Lorax is, or what he represents, but I briefly explain. Telson is quiet, listening. It’s therapeutic and I have to stop myself from venturing into personal history. She should be a shrink. “Anyways,” I conclude, “that’s what a Lorax is.”

“A protector of the woods,” she says.

“A cartoon character.”

She nods slowly, nibbles on a French fry. “Sort of a noble crusade, in a way.”

“Not really.” I shift uncomfortably in my seat. This attractive lady may be a raging Green — I should have caught on when she said she was a vegetarian — and I can see the conversation deteriorating.

“Sort of Don Quixote-ish,” she says. “Out to save the forest.”

“Deluded,” I say. “They had that in common.”

She tilts her head, gives me an earnest look. “You think so?”

I stare at my burger. I could leave or just refuse to talk about it, but as a former forest ranger, I have ecology in my blood. And ecology is safe enough. Safer than what I really want to say about the Lorax. “Listen —” I lean forward. Telson does the same, the slightest trace of a smile edged lightly in her features, challenging me. “You have to realize,” I say, “that what you see out there isn’t the way the forest has always been, nor will be for long. It’s a dynamic system and all you ever see is a snap shot. The forest has been replaced over and over again, every century or so, for the past 20,000 years.”

I must be boring her to tears, but if I am, she doesn’t show it. She’s watching me, her chin rested in the palm of her hand, her elbow on the table. Suddenly, I want to talk forestry to her all night. Well, maybe not all night.

“There’s always been a replacement event,” I tell her. “Up until now in North America, it’s been fire. In fact, species like pine and black spruce need fire to reproduce. Their cones are serotinous and won’t open without exposure to extreme heat. They’re shade intolerant and can only grow simultaneously in large stands —”

“Oooh, serotinous,” she says seductively. “You *must* be a forest ranger.”

I pause, halfway through a deep breath, on the verge of expounding the virtues of various silviculture treatments, how they approximate nature, when I realize she’s gently poking fun at me. My breath sighs out, my momentum deflated. I feel sheepish, but somehow better.

“Anyway,” I say quietly, “the Lorax is off base. He doesn’t accomplish anything.”

“Well he sure has a lot of people stirred up.”

“Maybe, but he’s a coward.”

“You think so? It takes a lot of resolve to do something like that.”

It almost sounds like Telson is defending the Lorax, admiring him in a bizarre way, and my anger boils close to the surface. There’s darkling shadows on the weather map, and although I’m hoping the forecast is wrong I feel thunderheads building.

"Resolve maybe," I say, "but he's still a coward, hiding behind a fictional character."

Telson rakes a hand through her hair so it cascades like a shampoo commercial. Her expression is calm, inquisitive. To her this is an abstract conversation. For me, it's not so abstract. I've lost my appetite; my burger remains untouched. I feel a distant clap of thunder and hope she'll see the storm brewing before it's too late.

"He's certainly raised the issue of logging to new heights," she says.

"Issue?" I say. "What issue?" Like the fictional Lorax, my dander is up. So is my volume. Telson flinches, glances nervously around. The other patrons have turned to look. "Is that something like the issue of farming?" I say. "How about the issue of fishing? Or carpentry? It's just a way of living, filling a demand, but people don't get *killed* over farming or carpentry."

Telson sits back, startled. It's raining and she's forgotten her umbrella. She raises a hand over the table, like she's going to reach over, pat me reassuringly, but the hand doesn't venture that far. "I'm sorry, I didn't mean —"

My head is throbbing. "Forget it. It's not your fault —"

We're the centre of attention and I feel like an idiot for overreacting. I don't want to explain, just want to get the hell out of here. "I'm sorry," I mumble, make a further spectacle of myself by thumping around while I gather my crutches.

She leans forward. "You don't have to go."

I rummage in my pockets, pull out rumpled bills, toss a few on the table.

"Porter, please —"

A few good swings and I'm out of the restaurant. An old lady coming in holds the door for me, gives me a concerned look. On the sidewalk, the wind lifts the back of my jacket. There's a storm coming out here too, splatters of rain blossoming on the cement. I make it a block and a half before the Bug catches up with me.

"Porter —"

I lurch a bit farther. The Bug whines after me, the driver-side window open.

"Porter, please just stop for a minute."

This is humiliating, so I stop. Telson is looking up at me like a concerned mother. I look away, at the sidewalk. She must think I'm some sort of weirdo.

"I apologize for my behaviour," I say mechanically. "I've had a rough day."

"Let me give you a ride."

"I'm fine. I don't have much farther to go."

"It's raining. You'll get sick."

I lean on my crutches, look at the slate sky. It's just a local storm cell, without much water but with a lot of energy. The wind will only get worse when the storm hits and I glance over at Telson. Her expression is worried. She holds up a white Styrofoam box, opens it a bit so I can see inside. It's the burger I abandoned. "I salvaged your supper."

A man can only take so much. I get into the Bug.

7

THE NEXT DAY I'm on a bus, headed north to Edmonton. Berton called. Representatives from the forest industry are going nuts and the premier has ordered a task force investigation into the arsons. The big boys are taking over and I'm to help Berton and Malostic brief the new team. Because my Land Rover is unserviceable, I get to spend a few quality hours next to a travelling salesman.

"You got kids?" he asks. He's pudgy, has coffee breath. When I admit to being childless, he brings out his wallet, shows me pictures — seven children with three wives: an occupational hazard. He offers me a chew of tobacco — the damn buses won't let him smoke any more — which I decline, tells me the story of his life. The radio tells another story. Nurses to go on strike again. Landslides in Honduras. More unusually hot spring weather. But I'm not really listening to either story. I'm thinking about Telson.

After she picked me up in her Bug, we went to a little park next to the river, listened to the blues — Leadbelly, Muddy Waters — watched the water flow past as I ate my burger. She told me about her old job as a data entry clerk: mind-numbing hours in front of a computer punching in an endless string of numbers. Like working in a salt mine. It offered bad eyesight, left her ergonomically challenged, paid just enough to cover the basics.

"What about you," she said. "What made you become a forest ranger?"

"Wide open space," I told her. "And free polyester shirts."

"Sounds romantic. How long have you been doing that?"

"I'm just sort of part time right now."

"A travelling twig pig?"

"Something like that."

"And when you're not twig-pigging?"

"I take the winters off, visit my folks down south —"

I kept the conversation light, but not without some difficulty. She was so close, so inviting. So damn attractive. But things didn't work out so good the last time and I'm not taking any chances — at least until the Lorax is no longer hanging over me, jinxing everything I touch. When she laid her warm hand over mine, B.B. King was singing "The Thrill is Gone" — one of my personal favourites — and I was starting to feel good enough I might have disagreed with him. But images of Nina intruded and I asked her to drive me to Carl's. The ride was short and quiet, the wind rocking the Volkswagen. Bobby Bland was singing "Stormy Monday" and the blues were bluer than before. She gave me her phone number, on a scrap of paper.

"Call me," she said. "When you need a fix of slide guitar."

The scrap of paper is in my hand this morning, getting soft and frayed like a note you'd pass around in school. I put it in my pocket, sigh and look outside. Double highway surrounded by flat, open farmland. No relief outside, or inside either; nothing to do but listen to the radio — more country music — and to what Travis, the salesman, is saying. I should have brought a book.

I escape as quickly as possible at the bus depot. Berton is waiting and we walk to his car.

I'm sure Berton knows why I was down south — the latest

Lorax attack is all over the news — but he doesn't press, an endearing trait. We get into his car, an old Volvo station wagon littered with Lego, and head down 104th Ave. for the government core.

"So how are the kids?" Berton has two in university, one in playschool.

"Great." He adjusts his glasses, pushes them up on his nose. "Sarah and Colin are getting good grades. Little Casper is starting hockey this winter." He grins. "You should see him go on his little skates. They're so much fun at that age."

We're surrounded by monoliths of concrete and mirrored glass, reflecting each other like unfriendly neighbours. This is where you're promoted to if you're not careful — the pinnacle of a civil service career — to wither away in some cubicle on the eighth floor, the field only a distant memory

We park near the Legislature, hunt in pockets for change to feed the ticket dispenser.

"I'm dry," says Berton. "What about you?"

"We're okay if it'll take lint."

Berton pilfers his ashtray for quarters, peers under the seats.

"So what's the name of this new task force?" I ask.

"Red Flag," he says, reaching blindly under a seat.

A fitting name. A Red Flag Day in the Forest Service is a day when weather and forest moisture conditions have combined to make for unusually extreme fire behaviour. These are the days when you know a fire will give you problems. The days the arsonist seems to prefer. "So are we still in the loop?"

"Oh, I think so." He pulls out a handful of Lego, half-eaten suckers and gum wrappers. And 16 cents. "They still need people with fire experience to do the dirty work," he says, frowning. "That guy over there might have some change."

A few rows over, a guy is fiddling with a car door. I don't usually have much luck when it comes to asking for money in parking lots but he ambles over when I holler at him. He's tall and slim, his jacket worn and loose, and it occurs to me that the car he was fiddling with might not have been his own. If he's planning on mugging us he won't have much more luck than the ticket dispenser. But as he draws nearer, he rummages in his jeans and pulls out a fist full of loonies and quarters like he's knocked off a vending machine.

"I never remember," I say in way of apology.

He shrugs. "This time of day, you don't have to worry. They only check at 8:30."

"Really?" Berton is mentally counting the money he can save.

"Yeah. The tickets aren't time stamped, just sequential."

"Thanks for the tip," says Berton.

We buy one ticket anyway, just to be sure, walk to a black-glass and steel building a block away. This late in the morning, the streets are as peaceful as a manicured graveyard, all the workers inside — peasants under glass — but you don't want to be anywhere near here at rush hour. Or lunch break. The dead can come back to life. A hexagonal sticker on the door is covered with pictograms of people having fun — running, bicycling, rollerblading and skateboarding — over which is superimposed a bright red slash. No cavorting permitted at the Ministry of Indecision. Today it'll be easy to conform to these restrictions. The people in the elevator give me a wide berth as I swing in on my crutches. Upstairs, in the conference room, I'm in for a surprise. Bill Star is seated at a conference table, sipping coffee and eating doughnuts set aside for a later break. He looks up, gives me a beefy smile. "The later they come," he says, "the worse they get."

I grin, shake his hand. "Good to see you Bill."

"You too. What'd you do to yourself?"

"Long story. I thought you were retired."

He chuckles. "If you're tired more than once, you're retired."

"You're back on the case?"

"No." He gives me a good-natured frown. "Just here to fill in the gaps."

The provincial Director of Forest Protection, a squat grey-haired fellow, is standing at the head of the table, waiting for us to come to order. He's the only one wearing a tie and it's too tight, making his face blotchy like he's holding his breath. Or maybe it's just stress; he's the guy with a $30 million budget and $100 million job. Either way, it's a good thing everyone in the room knows first aid. I get a cup of industrial strength coffee — firefighter java — and take a seat between Berton and Star. Malostic is on the far side of the wide conference table, talking earnestly with a cop in uniform. I think Malostic wanted to be a Mountie but couldn't make the height requirement. Star leans over, whispers. "I heard you came up from Curtain River."

I nod.

He looks grim. "Nasty business down south."

"Tell me about it."

"I heard there was a fatality."

"Yeah, guy who worked for the company."

"Any idea how it happened?"

I shake my head. "No, but I helped the cops with the evidence search."

"That must have been a big job. They making any headway?"

"If they are, they're not letting on."

The Director stands up. His expression is dark, his brow furrowed. He reaches into a brown paper bag, pulls out a blackened cake pan, tosses it onto the table where it clatters, alarmingly loud, scattering fine particles of charcoal. He has everyone's attention.

"Good morning," he says. "I'm Gil Patton, and for those of you that don't know me, I'm the provincial Director of Forest Protection. That means I'm responsible for making sure the fires get put out quickly and that as few of them as possible are man-caused." He points a stubby finger at the cake pan. "Right now, it doesn't look like I'm doing a very good job. We've got some firebug out there, lighting fires when the hazard is at its most extreme. Not only is my budget for the entire summer already drained, the forest industry is screaming bloody murder. With every stick of timber allocated, we're allowed only one half of one percent loss due to fire every year. Which isn't a hell of a lot. More than that and mills go hungry. People are laid off. And my blood pressure goes up. And believe me — it's up. Over the past two years, this firebug has wiped out a half-million acres of timber. This can't go on any longer, and that's why you're here. I expect you to stop this bastard."

He pauses, looks at us to see if the message has been received.

"The way it stands today, we're looking at another hell of a fire season. This'll be the third one in a row, and our drought codes haven't recovered. The ground is so dry there was no run-off from the snowmelt this spring. The Athabasca River is low enough the pulp mills are worried about their water supply and the Loon River has gone underground. If this continues, we won't have a green-up this summer and half the province is already under fire ban. My resources are stretched thin and I have no doubt that whoever is lighting these fires will continue to capitalize on the dry conditions."

Having set the tone for the meeting, Patton turns the floor over to a uniform seated beside him. The Mountie introduces himself as Sergeant Don Kirby, then goes around the table for further introductions and history. There are two constables — Eugene Purseman and Derrick Trimble — seconded from rural posts up north, and an undercover native detective who introduces himself simply as Frank. Other than that, it's Berton, Malostic, Star and myself.

"I spent some time as an arson investigator," Kirby says. "That's why I was picked to head up this task force." Kirby is tall, middle-aged, just starting to bulge at the seams. His brown hair is cut to hang across his forehead in what we used to call a bowl cut. "I'll direct the investigation and make sure everyone has what they need to get the job done."

"You'll get whatever you need," says Patton.

Kirby glances at Patton. "Good to hear that." He looks at us. "I'd like to start with a history from the forestry fellows, bring us up to speed, particularly in regards to anything that might not be in the files. Let's start with the previous physical evidence."

"It's all in the files," whispers Star. "At least it was when I left."

Malostic has caught up on his homework and dives right in. "So far, we've had five fires, four last year and one this spring. The perpetrator uses a pan filled with diesel and an igniter which allows ample time to clear the area before the fun begins."

"The cake pan," says Kirby. "What do we know about it?"

"Made by Francis Steel," says Star. "They made a million of them."

"So we can't trace it."

"Well," says Malostic, staring at the pan on the table, "there might be a way. By analysing the variations in the steel recorded by their quality control —"

"Not a chance," says Star. "Even if you could somehow determine where the pan was sold, you'd never find out who bought it. It's not like you need a licence to buy baking utensils."

"What about the rest of the device?" asks Kirby.

"Haven't had much luck," Star says. "All of the other scenes were hopelessly contaminated by the time we arrived; firefighters walking across the origin, dragging hoses across it — that sort of thing. We had one site where a Cat walked right over the pan, turned it into a waffle."

"Not good," Kirby says. "We gotta do a better job of protecting the origin."

Patton glares at me, as if I have some control over the firefighters before I arrive, his face a shade closer to cardiac arrest. I think he just needs to glare at someone who works for him. "I'll get in touch with the Districts," he says. "Every initial attack crew is going to receive training on identifying and protecting the origin. Is there an RCMP course we can get in on?"

Kirby nods. "We'll set something up. What about footprints, tire tracks?"

"Nothing," I say. "Too contaminated and the ground is generally too dry at those hazard indices to hold much of a print."

"Any witnesses?" Kirby says. "Anybody report unusual activity in the area?"

"Not the four I looked at," says Star. "The odd camper, but no one saw a thing."

"Could the campers be suspects?"

"I checked them out and I doubt it."

"Strange," says Kirby. "I've been involved in structure fire investigations and in my experience, firebugs like to stick around and watch. They get off at the sight of flames — fulfills some sort of need for them. A lack of personal power. Anonymity. Repressed sexual urges. They like to watch the monster they've created and we try to video the crowd that inevitably gathers, record licence plates. Too bad we can't do that for a forest fire."

"If he's using a delay mechanism," says Berton, "he's probably long gone."

"Or watching from a distance," I say.

"True," says Berton. "A bush fire is a little different than a structure fire. With a bush fire, you'd have to be a hell of a ways back to watch safely, particularly at the hazard indices at which this guy likes to operate."

"I keep hearing this reference to hazard indices," says Kirby. "What is that?"

"It's our way of measuring the combustibility of the forest," says Berton. "As you no doubt know, a fire needs fuel, oxygen and heat to burn. Take away any one input and the fire goes out. We rate the fuel availability, which is a measure of how damp the various fuel types are — the drier the fuel, the more fuel available for combustion. It's a complicated system — based on weather parameters such as temperature, precipitation and relative humidity — which gives us several numbers to rate how quickly and with how much energy a fire will burn. That's what we mean by hazard indices."

"I see," says Kirby. "Obviously, our guy likes the drier weather." There's a pause as he flips through a file folder. Star looks longingly toward the doughnut box, stranded at another table in the corner of the room. Malostic is consulting his own slimmer sheaf of papers. The Director looks like he's falling asleep. Frank is using a pocket knife to clean under his fingernails. Kirby looks up. "How far back did you go when questioning possible witnesses?"

"Five miles," says Star. "But maybe that should be expanded."

"Good point," says Kirby. "What about the last one?"

Malostic is still shuffling papers.

"Malostic?"

"What?" He looks up, startled.

"How far back from the fire did you question witnesses?" says Kirby.

"Aagh, just at base camp."

"Base camp?" says Star, his disgust apparent. "Why at base camp? You think maybe the firefighters started it? Did you canvass the area around the fire? Take a flight to look for hunters and campers?"

Malostic is frozen. "We were in the middle of nowhere," he says faintly. "I never thought —"

I can't help feeling a little sorry for Malostic. It's tough, your first time in the fire game. My first fire was right after my initial year of college. I'd never been in a helicopter, never seen a wildfire, never used the equipment. We were dropped at the edge of a roaring fire, with nothing more than a shovel, an axe and a piss pack — a water bag with shoulder straps and a hand pump. Someone had to show me how to fill the damn thing, using my hardhat as a bucket. Today, it's Malostic who's being told how to do his job. "It was getting dark and the fire was seven thousand acres by the time we arrived," I say. "I doubt he would have found anything."

Malostic looks at me, then glances away.

Kirby clears his throat. "Let's talk about that fire. What about physical evidence?"

"Started in a brushpile at the side of a logging road," I say. "No bootprints or tire tracks evident. There was the cake pan you see here on the table. And some residue — a small, brittle, black disc — but I inadvertently disturbed the pan and contaminated the fines. A grid search revealed nothing more."

"You searched for metallics?"

"We used a magnet."

"What about ash and soil samples?"

I shake my head. Kirby makes a note. So do I — *take more samples.*

"What did you do with this black disk?"

"Darvon sent it in for analysis."

Malostic examines a sheet of paper, looks relieved to have something positive to add. "The collected residue was polyethylene, impregnated with traces of potassium carbonate and potassium sulphate. Some minor traces of potassium carbonate-sulphate."

"We'll get our boys at the lab to have a look," says Kirby.

"It was probably black powder," says Malostic.

Kirby looks at him.

"I minored in inorganic chemistry."

Kirby looks vaguely impressed. "Well, black powder makes sense," he says. "Diesel is difficult to ignite without direct heat. If the explosion from the gunpowder scattered the diesel as well as igniting it, this would make quite an effective device."

There's a murmur of appreciation around the table.

"What about a fuse?" asks Star. "We've always thought it might be a candle."

Malostic is about to interject his comment about paraffin being a heavy fraction of crude oil but Kirby cuts him off, shaking his head. "Indoors, I'd consider it. Outside, it'd probably blow out. There are lots of commercially available fuses, but they leave a detectable residue."

I think of the Forest Service legend of the pyromaniacal pilot and suggest it could have been a cigar or cigarette. Kirby nods. "There was a guy down in California, back in the early nineties I think it was, who used a cigarette wrapped with matches to burn clothing stores. He'd light the thing, stuff it deep into the fabric of a clothes rack where it would smoulder. Fire wouldn't start until he was long gone. Caused a lot of damage and a few fatalities, as I recall."

"He was a fire investigator, wasn't he?" says Patton.

"Yeah, he was. Difficult case. They caught him though, gave him a few life sentences."

"Would a cigarette leave a detectable residue?" asks Berton.

"I'd have to check with the lab but it would be an organic ash," Kirby says. "I suspect it would be difficult to detect as it would be much like the ash from the brush burned in the fire."

"How quickly does a cigarette burn?" Malostic asks.

"Let's see," says Star, pulling out a pack.

"About seven minutes to an inch," Kirby says.

Star looks disappointed, puts away his cigarettes.

"So we're looking at a possible half-hour delay," says Kirby.

"Or more," says Patton. "If it was a cigar."

"I thought you quit," I whisper to Star.

"I did," he whispers back. "Gets easier every time."

"We'll widen our search area," says Kirby. "Check back on the other fires for credit card receipts at area gas station, things like that. If our guy felt comfortable enough to use a card, we might be able to place him in the vicinity."

"Now we're getting somewhere," says Patton.

"Needles and haystacks," mutters Star.

"What about a profile?" asks Kirby. "We have any idea what makes this guy tick?"

There's a brief silence. "Employment?" says Patton. "It's happened before."

Kirby nods, gestures toward Frank. "Possibly. From what I've been told, your firefighters are primarily natives who depend on firefighting for their summer employment. We've got some intelligence from our sources in the communities, but not much. Frank here is going to circulate through the native communities within the vicinity of the fires, get a read on the mood."

Malostic turns in his seat, looks over at Frank. "What's your background, Frank?"

"Cree," says Frank.

"The guy who's lighting these fires knows what he's doing," I say. "He knows weather and fire behaviour and he knows where to put his ignition source to do the most damage."

"Like a firefighter," says Malostic.

"Could it be luck?" asks Kirby. "Anyone can tell when it's dry out."

Malostic's lab report, which has been passed around the table, reaches me. I scan the details — traces of this or that chemical equation — and it occurs to me that this lab in Vancouver is where I should send the piece of metal I borrowed from the Lorax bombing. Then it occurs to me that they probably have the rest of the pieces and it might look a little odd. "Sure, it could be luck," I say. "But if it was, there's probably a lot of cake pans out there that didn't do what they're supposed to. Lighting a small fire is easy, but lighting one that is guaranteed to get really large requires an understanding of fuels, wind, that sort of thing."

"And where our resources are deployed," says Berton. "That'd help."

Patton looks worried. "Anybody with a computer can access our weather data on the Internet. We've got fire hazard maps of the whole province there. Thank God we're not putting the location of our suppression resources on-line as well."

"Don't have to," says Berton. "They'll be where the hazard is."

"You might want to take that off for the time being," says Kirby.

"Done," says Patton.

"Anything else not in the files?" asks Kirby.

Silence. Heads shake. "Okay then," says Kirby. "Just one more thing. If you get a fire you think is suspect, or have an inkling of the next place that might get hit, we have a surveillance team available. They're called Special O and they can work with Air Services, run our Cessna Caravan with the West Cam. It's got night vision so if there's a chance the arsonist is hiding in the bush near the fire, we'll be able to see him. If they're not on a more serious crime somewhere, they should be available."

"Good to know," says Berton. Malostic scribbles this down.

"Any questions about protocol?" asks Kirby.

The metal fragment from the bombing is in my jacket pocket and I'm wondering if there's another avenue available to get it analyzed. "What about administration?" I ask. "What if I need to spend some money to maybe hire a helicopter or get something analyzed?"

"Our lab will analyze anything you need," says Kirby. "Just send it to me."

I must look nervous because Malostic looks concerned.

"Do you *have* something else to analyze?" he says.

Everyone is looking at me now. Kirby and Patton frown in synchrony.

"Not yet," I say. "But I'm working on it."

Patton has his secretary give me a charge code, which is a little like a Forest Service credit card but considerably more bureaucratic. Now, I can hire a helicopter. I think of isolated trout lakes up north and quell a sudden urge to go fishing. Instead, I have a beer with Berton and Star.

"This place oughta have a steak sandwich," says Star. "Steak is English right?"

"I'm not sure a steak has a nationality," says Berton.

We're in a mock English pub, on the ground floor of an office building. It's gloomy inside, the walls panelled in oak. Snooker finals are playing on TV. The bartender is wearing a little apron and has a handlebar moustache. Not my first choice, but the meeting went through lunch and this place is within hobbling distance. This late in the afternoon the pub is deserted, except for an old guy at the rail nursing a Caesar. He looks like he's been here long enough to need dusting. We take a table beside an American jukebox made in China and I prop my sore ankle on a spare chair. A waiter appears almost instantly.

"What can I get you lads?" he asks a little too jovially. "Coupla dark swipes?"

"What?" asks Berton, peering up through his glasses.

"A fist full of hearty stouts? A jug of ale?" The waiter is young, red-haired and so pale he looks as if they keep him in the dungeon.

"You got any steak sandwiches?" asks Star.

"I'm sorry but lunch is over." By now, the waiter has exhausted all of his colourful English phrases. "The kitchen is closed, but I could get you a beer."

Star sighs deeply. "I sure could use a steak sandwich."

"Let's get out of here," I say. "Go to Raunchy Ronnie's."

The waiter glances nervously around the empty bar. "I'll tell you what," he says, squatting next to the table and whispering as if he's trying to sell us plutonium. "I'll see what I can rustle up in kitchen. There's gotta be something left from lunch. Maybe a ham on rye?"

Star considers. "Yeah, okay."

The waiter rushes off. "Nice kid," says Berton.

"Sure," says Star. "Gonna make somebody a good wife one day." He looks over at me as he digs a pack of smokes out of a coat pocket, lights one up. "So, you helped with the evidence search?"

"Yeah. It was a mess."

"I hear it was a hell of a bomb," he says, snapping shut his lighter.

"It was. Took off the top of the buncher. You hear what was used?"

Bill shakes his head. "They won't let that out. Too early anyway."

"They won't let out anything," I say morosely.

Bill uses his patient tone. "That's the nature of the business, Porter."

"It would be nice to know if they're making *any* progress."

"Well, I can tell you one thing," he says, leaning forward,
causing Berton and me to do the same. "They've spent about two million bucks on the case so far and from what I've heard, they don't have any suspects. After three years, it's a bit of an embarrassment. In fact, they were considering shelving the case until this new bombing came along. That's why they're hitting this one so hard, bringing in lots of help. They're hoping this'll be their break."

"No suspects," I mumble. "I knew it."

"But this could be the lucky one," Berton says.

Not for Ronald Hess, I'm thinking. Now I'm really frustrated that Rachet didn't catch the man in camo. "You know," I say quietly, "I think I might have run into the guy who did it."

Star gives me a sceptical look.

"At the bombing site the next day. I'm going for a walk and I come across this guy out in the bush, on this sort of a ledge. He's dressed like a commando and he's laying there, prone, watching the cops through a rifle scope. Like a sharp shooter."

"What did you do?" says Berton.

"Not much I could do," I say. "He had a gun."

I'm not sure why I'm telling them this. Maybe I just want to tell someone who'll believe me. Maybe Star will have a different perspective. But he looks dubious. "You told the cops?"

“Of course. They didn’t appear particularly concerned.”

Berton gives me a binocular look through his thick glasses, eyes disproportionately large. Star is thinking. I shouldn’t have said anything — he knows there’s more to the story.

“The next day,” he says thoughtfully. “And you were there in what capacity?”

I shift my propped leg, try to get comfortable. Not gonna happen with Star looking at me like that. “It’s kind of a long story,” I say. “I was in the area and wanted to watch the bomb squad, see how they worked — out of professional interest of course — but I didn’t want to disturb them, so I went looking for a spot to watch unobtrusively when I came across this guy. It seems he had the same idea.”

“You were sneaking around.”

“Well, not at first —”

Bill impatiently waves off my explanation. “You said he had a gun?”

“A rifle, with a scope.”

He frowns thoughtfully. “Did you get a good look at him?”

I shake my head. “He was too far away and his face was painted.”

The waiter arrives with a tray. “Well lads, I’m heartened to say —”

“Just put it down,” says Star, cutting him off. The waiter plunks down three frosted mugs filled with creosote-coloured beer, followed by ham and cheese croissants on small plates.

“You guys need anything else?” He’s abandoned the phoney English accent.

“We’re good,” says Star. Then to me, “Isn’t it still hunting season down there?”

I think of Rachet’s interrogation. “Apparently.”

Star grabs a croissant, tears off a bite, talks around his food. "Well, it was probably just a curious hunter." He takes a long draught of beer. "But it is interesting. First bombing in three years. This guy in camo. You, sneaking around like that —"

"I wasn't sneaking —"

"That's where you twisted your ankle, isn't it?" says Star, pointing what's left of his croissant at me and shaking his head. "You gotta let this thing go, Porter. It'll drive you nuts. You gotta let the boys in blue do their thing. Trust in the system."

Star is ex-RCMP. "That still the party line?"

"In your case, definitely."

I don't agree, but don't want to argue, not here anyway. We continue the discussion in Star's Mustang as he drives me to Cindy's. "I can't believe it's been three years," I say. "And the cops still have no idea who's responsible."

"In a case like this Porter, three years isn't really that long." Star drives with his thumb on the bottom of the steering wheel, his other arm flopped over the back of the seat, a bag of potato chips on his lap. "It took 17 years to catch Kazinsky. And that guy who raped the nurse back in the sixties — they're still trying to figure out who really did it. It takes time to build a case."

"Only if they don't shelve the case first."

"I shouldn't have told you that," Star says. "Shelve is probably a bad term. Cases go cold after a certain period of time. Law enforcement is a finite resource you know. It doesn't mean the case is totally abandoned."

"But some of them are never solved."

"That's true," says Bill. "It's not a perfect world."

"Maybe they would be," I say. "If they had a little extra help."

Star looks at me like a father at a deluded child.

"From someone really motivated," I add.

He sighs — a really deep sigh. "Porter, I was a cop for 20 years and I've been a private dick for another ten. They're depressing jobs, both of them, because in the end, it doesn't matter how motivated you are. You only catch the stupid ones, the rush jobs and amateurs. Every once in a while you might get a professional, then he gets a good lawyer and he's out before you're retired and you gotta try to catch him again. This guy, this Lorax, is a professional. He's not a raving nutcase who leaves a lot of clues. He's careful and I'm willing to bet he works alone. Those kind are the hardest to catch."

We drive in silence for a few minutes. Star eats potato chips, the crumbs precipitating onto his belly. I can feel the weight of the metal fragment in my pocket and take it out, look at it through the opaque sandwich bag. Evidence preservation by Zip Lock.

Star looks over, raises an eyebrow. "Don't tell me that's what I think it is."

"I just want to get it analyzed —"

"Jesus Christ, Porter." Star shakes his head, stares at the road, his jaw clenched. For a few minutes he doesn't say anything, which is probably for the best. "That's obstruction," he says finally. "Theft. Tampering with evidence. Criminal Code. Not to mention that you've destroyed the chain of custody in case that hunk of metal has any unique evidentiary value."

"I know, but they won't tell me anything. I want to know what killed Nina."

Star starts to say something then changes his mind.

"I can't send it through the RCMP," I say. "I was hoping you could help."

Star is silent for several blocks. At a stoplight, he slams the transmission into park, turns in his seat and looks at me. "Porter, do you really think this is going to make a difference?"

"It would to me."

"You think you're going to solve this thing?"

"I just want to be involved. Before, with Nina, I couldn't. Then nothing happened so there was nothing for me to do but sit and wait. Well, I'm tired of waiting. Solve this thing — I doubt it, but at least I'll be informed. There's nothing worse than being in the dark."

The light changes and someone honks. Star slaps the car into drive and hits the gas. We surge through the intersection, rock as we take a corner. He's obviously furious with me and, worse yet, he's silent. For the rest of the trip I'm not sure if he'll help me or turn me in. He pulls to the curb in front of Cindy's townhouse, turns to face me, his heavy forearm resting on the steering wheel. For a minute he just stares, then he sighs.

"Give it to me."

"You'll send it in?"

"I'll hang onto it, think about it."

Grateful, I hand him the little package. "Thanks."

I fumble out my crutches. Star watches, shaking his head. "Porter —"

I'm on the sidewalk, balanced on the crutches. "Yeah?"

He points a thick finger at me. "You be careful."

Cindy is paying the babysitter, a 16-year-old brunette who winks at me. The kids are tearing around the house like wind-up toys. Cindy hollers at them to settle down. They actually pause for a moment before resuming their game of tag. She sighs, collapses in a chair at the kitchen table. "I gotta find a man," she says wearily. "A wealthy one."

"Better call the want ads."

"One mom," she says. "Slightly used, but ready to please."

"You'll be reeling them in by the dozens."

She chuckles sadly. "Unfortunately, they all think it's catch and release."

I nod, pat her hand. All day she works with dysfunctional families, violence, incest. When she gets home, she's a domestic engineer with three kids. She's always taking care of somebody, and by evening, she's burned out, has a glazed look in her eye.

"Order a pizza," I tell her. "My treat."

She raises her hands as though offering a benediction. "My saviour."

"Order two." Then she'll have leftovers.

She looks at my crutches, propped against the wall. "What happened to your foot?"

"Twisted my ankle, going for a walk in the woods."

"Bad?"

"Not so bad. Just slap a slow-moving sticker on my back."

"Consider it done. You home for a while?"

I think about the man in camo. "No, I gotta go south again tomorrow."

She nods, begins to clean the kitchen, orders pizza. I head downstairs to my room next to the furnace. The townhouse is tiny but I don't mind living in the basement. I don't need much space; between fires in summer and travelling in winter, I'm not often home. I take a shower in the tin stall next to my room, then flop on my bed and stare at the joists and subfloor that's my ceiling. Overhead, the patter of running children rolls like thunder. I think about the last few days.

At the top of a shelf built of plywood and rough lumber, there's a shoebox filled with my past. I take it down, spread the contents on my bed. Newspaper clippings. An old videotape with the titles of shows Cindy has taped crossed off the label. There's only one show on the tape now, a *Crime Stoppers* segment a minute long. I pop it in my ancient tape player, lay on my bed and watch. There's a brief snippet of some scene from *The Young and Restless*, then the screen flickers and Mike Matchok, the RCMP spokesman for *Crime Stoppers*, takes centre stage. He stands stiffly in the clearing where Nina died, in front of the blackened feller-buncher, and begins to narrate.

"On or about January 12th, 1995, a person or persons unknown ..."

Like a current hit single on the radio, the words are familiar, burned into memory by sheer repetition. The *Crime Stoppers* program provides re-enactments, where perpetrators are played by actors, in hopes of jogging a witness's memory. Constable Matchok provides a brief narrative of what might have happened before Nina and I arrived, while the camera zooms in to show the back of a man, dressed in nondescript parka and wool toque, glancing about furtively and then climbing onto the feller-buncher. He releases a clasp on the machine's engine compartment, plants an indistinct shape that looks in the dim light vaguely like a pipe bomb. The man's face is never shown, but in my mind's eye his face is painted forest camouflage. He retreats and the scene changes. It's morning. A Forest Service truck drives up a narrow logging road bordered on both sides by large trees, laden with snow. Clearly, there are two passengers, and my gut clenches in nervous anticipation. The truck parks next to the feller-buncher and an actor in a Forest Service uniform, playing me, says something to the passenger in the truck, then walks past the camera. There is a synthesized explosion — a bright flash of light — and men are shown running toward the feller-buncher. My real truck, windows shattered, is shown in an RCMP impound lot. Constable Matchok walks in front, wraps up the video segment with the standard plea for information, offers $2,000 for information leading to the arrest and conviction of the person or persons responsible for this heinous act. All calls are kept strictly confidential.

Two thousand dollars. I'd offer more if I had it. I'd offer everything.

I start the tape again, watch Matchok stand in the forest. Cindy comes downstairs, knocks on my door. "The pizza is here," she says. She comes into my room, sees what I'm watching.

"Oh, Porter —"

She sits on the edge of my bed, glances at the newspaper clippings strewn about.

"I heard about it after you left," she says. "I'm so sorry."

I shrug, try to look calmer than I feel. The truck is driving toward the feller-buncher again. Cindy leans across the bed, grabs the remote, shuts off the TV. For a moment, the only sound is the plastic squeal of the worn tape. Then she touches a button on the VCR and that too stops.

"I saw it on the news," she says. "It was bad, wasn't it?"

I nod, mute. She pulls herself farther onto the bed, puts an arm around my shoulder.

"Mom called. They heard it down there too, wanted to see if you're okay."

"Tell them I'm fine."

Cindy studies me. "You're not fine though, are you?"

I don't answer. For a few minutes we sit together in my dim bedroom, staring at the dead TV as though it might have a hidden message. Some people lash out when they're upset; I turn my anger inward, against the advice of my one-time shrink — an East Indian with a Ph.D, on contract to the Forest Service to help the staff with the stress of downsizing. My stress was a little different. We spent a few 50-minute hours together. He tried but I just didn't want to talk about it. I still don't and Cindy knows this. She leans against me, stroking my shoulder. It makes me feel like a child and I flinch away.

She sits up, her concern clear. "What are you going to do?"

I look at the scraps of newsprint scattered over the bed. Partially visible is a picture of Nina, a driver's licence photo like a prison mug shot. In black and white, she looks like ancient history: some file photo from the fifties. I wonder if it'll take me that long to get over what happened. "I don't know," I tell Cindy. "But somehow, I'm going to stop this."

8

IT'S SURPRISING HOW completely you come to rely on your set of wheels; like many things you really don't appreciate them until they're not usable. Then your relationship with your truck gets ugly. You call it names, kick the tires, pound the dash, consider shooting it. But like any grieving process, you move past denial and anger and eventually have to make up. When I was in Edmonton, I stopped at the Land Rover dealer and picked up a new starter. For the price I paid, it should have come with a trip to the UK. But at least I'd be mobile again.

The view beneath Old Faithful is familiar — rusted cross beams and greasy ball joints. Like a Harley driver, I'm intimately familiar with the workings of my vehicle. I can appreciate its underlying form — or the form under which I am lying; Zen and the art of Land Rover repair. I slide farther beneath, shield my eyes from dribbling encrustations. At the periphery of my vision, I see Carl's boots. I've been telling him about my lunch with Telson.

"She saved your food?" Carl is impressed.

"Yeah. Had them put it into one of those Styrofoam trays."

"And this is after you freaked out?" I can see his chin as he peers down through the engine compartment. "I'm starting to like this girl."

"She's probably gone by now," I say. "She's just visiting. Passing through."

Carl chuckles. "Sure. Whatever. Any breakthroughs on the arson fires?"

"No, not really." I search the oily grime around the void where my starter used to be, looking for any clues regarding the disappearance. Occasionally, these things just fall off. But not usually while parked. "It was just an organizational meeting. The cops have been called in and they put together a task force."

"Really?" Carl's voice is disembodied. "A task force?"

"Yeah. They're pretty serious about catching this guy."

"And you're on this task force?"

"They still need someone to do the dirty work." Around the ring gear housing there's a lot of gritty gunk and I'm thinking maybe I should scrape a bit of it away before I mount the new starter. Makes for a better ground. "Can you hand me my knife. It's under the seat, driver's side."

Carl's feet vanish and a door creaks open. There's a moment of silence, then Carl's voice, muffled from inside the cab. "Where did you say it was?"

"In the springs. It's a little hard to see, but it's there."

Scraping sounds. A drop of oil which has been defying gravity plops onto my cheek.

"I don't see it Porter. You sure you didn't take it out?"

At first I'm slightly annoyed with Carl for being so blind and making me drag myself out from under the truck, across an emery board of gravel. Then when I look under the seat, I'm confused. Confusion quickly gives way to anger.

"Shit — someone took it."

Carl scratches his chin, tries to look helpful. "You sure?"

I try to remember taking the knife from under the seat, but the memory doesn't exist. "Last time I saw it was before we went into the bar. I distinctly remember putting it under the seat."

Carl is nodding. "What about later that night? We were pretty hammered."

I hadn't thought of that. "I don't think so. I think someone stole it."

"Your truck was sitting in the parking lot for a while."

"Well, shit —" The passenger-side doorlock on Old Faithful doesn't work and anybody could have taken the knife. I grab a screwdriver and handful of wrenches and crawl under the truck again. More bad news — like some evil psychology test, the bolt holes in the starter housing don't match the holes in the ring gear housing, no matter how hard I try. They gave me the wrong starter.

I worm my way out from under the truck, brush dirt from the orange fire coveralls Carl's lent me. I rest the new starter on the edge of the engine compartment, stare gloomily into Old Faithful's greasy bowels. I'll have to take the bus to Edmonton again, bring the starter as a carry-on. Maybe I'll meet Travis the salesman, sell him the starter. Hell, sell him the truck so he doesn't have to take the bus. Cut my losses.

"Doesn't fit?" asks Carl.

I shake my head, repack the clean but useless component in its box.

"There's a guy out of town collects Land Rovers," says Carl. "He might have a starter."

"Really. Why didn't you tell me before?"

"His stuff is pretty old —"

"So is mine."

On the trip out of town, Carl pulls a box of crackers from under his seat. Some people keep tools down there; others keep knives. Carl stores food — like a squirrel. At least it's fairly secure — I don't think I'd steal anything edible from among the dust and crap that inevitably collects under a truck seat, particularly a Forest Service truck seat. But today I'm hungry and the crackers look fairly well preserved. We munch as we head for Land Rover Heaven. "Just to let you know," says Carl. "This guy is a Jehovah's Witness. You might end up with more than a starter. You might end up saved."

"He can save my Land Rover."

We're both dressed in fire coveralls, like we're working together again.

"I hear they have another big one," Carl says. "Up by Slave Lake."

"Really." Any big fire is a hot topic of discussion. "How big?"

"Grew to three thousand acres overnight."

I think of our buddy Red Flag. No one called me. "Lightning caused?"

Carl nods. When the weather gets hot, there always seems to be a lightning-caused fire somewhere near Slave Lake. There's a lot of muskeg up there, covered with volatile dense black spruce. It's like dropping a match in dry grass. Even if it's not really dry, a lightning strike can smoulder in the moss until the fuel around it is ready to burn.

"What do they have on it?"

"The Electra and the Ducks. Coupla crews."

"What about you guys?" I ask. "You have any action?"

Carl shrugs. "Nothing much. A little camper fire. But our turn is coming."

We ride in companionable silence for a few minutes. Carl glances at my ankle, wrapped in a tensor bandage. "How did you do that?" he asks, no doubt wondering how I made it back to town without my bike the other day. I hesitate, then tell him the story about my walk through the bush, seeing the man in camo. The interrogation. It's the *Reader's Digest* condensed version and Carl is quiet for a few minutes, leaning forward over his steering wheel.

"You think that was him?" he asks. "You think it was the Lorax?"

"Maybe." I'm unexpectedly reluctant to agree. "Could've been a hunter."

Carl nods, chewing his lip. "There's another week of spring bear yet."

We're both watching the trees at the edge of the road. Dense evergreens. The Lorax could be out here and we'd never see him. I shiver, try to shake off a feeling that I'm being watched. I'm suddenly desperate for conversation about anything normal.

"So, Carl, you seeing anyone in town?"

"Why?" he asks. "You available?" His chuckle is a little forced and I get the impression my old friend is very lonely. "The gene pool here is kind of crowded," he says. "What about you? You gonna see this girl from the bar again?"

It sounds so romantic — the girl from the bar.

"I'm not sure. Maybe."

"You should," he says. "Get on with things. You're becoming a monk."

We're both quiet for a while. We never talk about Nina, not directly anyway. When we used to work together in Fort Termination, I think Carl had a bit of a thing for her. She was in the office a fair bit, helping out in the radio room or with the filing.

"Here we are," says Carl. "Get ready for the sales pitch."

Land Rover Heaven is about 20 miles from town, on a large acreage next to the Curtain River. The mailbox, handmade from a section of tree trunk, says Ryerson. The driveway is a narrow lane, pinched together by dense spruce, so the house remains invisible until you're at the front door. The house is old but well maintained. Chickens free range. So do kids. A half-dozen children play on a metal swing set and come running to the Forest Service truck when we stop.

"Are you a forest ranger?" asks a carrot-haired little boy as I get out.

"That would be the other fellow," I tell them, and Carl is mobbed.

"Is your dad home?" Carl has a panicky look in his eye. I think he's childphobic.

A screen door creaks and a tall, balding man in overalls steps out. He looks a little like a character from *Little House on the Prairie*, but around here that's not unusual. We're in redneck cottage country, where nostalgia is the uniform. Wear a suit in the city all day, then come home and assume another identity. The original back-to-the-landers realized that self-sufficiency was too much work and returned to the city. But their middle-aged kids have grown weary of the city and returned to the land. Cosmetically at least. It's a natural process, like the rabbit or grouse cycle.

He extends an immense knuckly hand. "Pete Ryerson."

The hand is calloused and scarred. No wonder he looks so authentic — he's a real hillbilly. I pay more attention, notice a tire swing near the house and a company truck in the driveway. Like everyone else around here, he works for Curtain River Forest Products.

"Can I help you fellers?"

"I heard you might have some old Land Rovers. I'm looking for a starter."

"Yeah —" He scratches his neck. "I got a few of them."

No sales pitch today. He points toward a dilapidated barn. Farther back and barely visible behind a rank growth of weeds I see the familiar blocky lines of several Older Faithfuls. We amble in that direction, followed by giggling children. Ryerson shoos them away, like chickens.

"You kids git on back now."

The kids scatter and we climb over a corral fence. The ground behind the barn slopes toward a beaver pond which has partially submerged three of a dozen old Land Rovers. Some of the trucks are gutted but several are relatively complete. I'll have to remember this place.

"I'm looking for a '63."

"Take your pick," says Ryerson.

I begin to scavenge, wrenches in hand, walking gingerly — I've discarded the crutches, determined to get by on painkillers and willpower. Most of the vehicles have flat tires, which will make crawling beneath them a bit interesting. Ryerson sits on a fender, watches as I peer beneath the old wrecks. "Damn beavers," he says. "A guy can't win against the little buggers. Tear open the dam and they fix it by morning. I'll have to shoot them, then get that guy to blow the dams again."

"What guy?" I'm curious about anyone who travels around blowing up things.

Ryerson thinks for a moment. He's not like any of the JWs I've run into before, preaching about the day of judgment. Maybe he's in the Jehovah's Witness Protection Program. "Can't remember his name," he says. "But he drives an old hopped-up piece of shit Chevy, rusted to hell and as many colours as the rainbow."

I get an apprehensive tingle — it's the truck that followed me on my bike ride.

"You're sure you don't remember his name?"

Ryerson shrugs.

At the edge of the pond, half submerged, is a Land Rover with a starter. I work from the front, pull weeds out of the way and worm beneath the old clunker into a world of dirt and decaying grease that smells like an old garage. Rusty cross beams press above my nose. Bolts give way reluctantly and I skin my knuckles but win in the end and inch myself from beneath the wreck, hair matted with dirt and flakes of rust.

"What do I owe you?"

Ryerson considers. "Fifty bucks."

A born haggler, I'm shocked. "Fifty bucks? That come with a warranty?"

"Take it or leave it. If it don't work, come get another one."

So much for haggling. I drop the starter in the back of Carl's truck, wipe my hands on my coveralls, settle accounts. On the way back to town Carl proposes a detour. He needs to drop off a few pails of drinking water at the lookout tower, check on Gabe and his hair collection. I can retrieve my stashed mountain bike.

At the tower, Carl is in a bad mood. Peterson was supposed to clean out his accumulated junk but there are still boxes everywhere. Offers of warm lemonade do little to sooth Carl. He speaks in short, clipped sentences.

"I told you to get rid of this stuff," he says. "Two weeks ago. This isn't the Smithsonian."

Peterson looks at me as if I might be an ally. I wait outside, gaze across the valley at the cutblocks. The man in camo had to have come from somewhere. Rachet should have checked the roads in the area for parked vehicles. It would have been easy to run a few licence plate numbers, come up with a name, check if the owner had a hunting licence. They caught Al Capone on tax evasion, Charles Ng on shoplifting.

My mountain bike is just where I left it and I hoist it into the battered box of Carl's green Forest Service truck. We ride in silence down the tower road. Carl reaches for the box of crackers, offers me some. As we munch, I think about Ronald Hess. About Rachet trying to establish a connection.

"Carl, did you ever meet Ronald Hess when we were up in Fort Termination?"

Carl looks at me, shakes his head. "No. Why?"

"No reason. Just wondering how he fits in."

Carl gears down as we approach the main road, comes to a halt at the edge of the grade. His long, aquiline face is troubled. "I don't think he does, Porter. He was just in the wrong place."

I nod, swallow a lump in my throat. He knows what I'm thinking.

"Just like Nina," he says softly. "Bad timing."

9

THE STARTER FITS — thank Jehovah — and by dark Old Faithful is capable of once more living up to her name. Sometimes, remaining faithful takes a little work and a fair measure of mechanical skill. We retire to Carl's place and he forages in the fridge, looking for something for supper. He's pretty much a hunter-gatherer, but finding nothing to gather, he loots the freezer, takes out something from his last hunt. "You want steak?" he says, waving a lump wrapped in brown paper. "It's elk, from last season."

The steaks are frozen as stiff as the soles of my new work boots; I could perish before either soften up. But I want to be a good guest, give him a thumbs up. He unwraps the hunk of purple ice, sets it in warm water in the kitchen sink. I wander into the living room, look around, admire the decor. Wood and animal skins. Antlers and crockery. An antique muzzleloader sits on pegs over the window, displayed in contravention of a new law requiring all guns be under lock and key; I can't see Carl complying.

Next to the window are a series of photos; ancient black-and-whites, slightly out of focus. There's a wooden-trestle forestry lookout tower — they stopped building those 50 or 60 years ago; grey cabins; groups of men with pack horses. The men wear suspenders and wide-brimmed hats, pose with their arms crossed.

Captions are inscribed below in neat block printing: *Assistant Ranger Wilfred Marsheldon with Pack Horses, 1944; The Elbow Trail Crew, 1916.* They don't look like the sort of men you want to mess with.

"Aagh, the good old days," Carl says, handing me an open bottle of home brew.

"Maybe," I say. "Maybe not. It was pretty rough back then."

"It built character," he says. "Which we're in short supply of nowadays."

I sip the home brew, which also has plenty of character — and yeast — and look around Carl's living room. His house is like a time machine, slowly regressing. By the time he's retired, he'll be living in a cave.

"Come on," he says. "I'll show you some of my projects."

We descend narrow, complaining stairs into Carl's basement. It's the sort of place both big and little boys love; musty and smelling of sawdust and damp concrete, filled with tools and half-built carpentry projects. A bare bulb throws craggy shadows from a cluttered workbench. There's a vice and reloading press, empty brass cartridges scattered like artillery shells after a minor skirmish. Carl directs my attention to a child's plastic swimming pool in a corner, by a floor drain next to the furnace. Something large, dark and hairy lurks in the pool, like a boneless monster. "Bear hide," he says, poking at it with an axe handle. "I had it salted in the garage since last spring, figured I ought to tan it before the mice chewed it up."

"You go for bear this spring?"

"No." He sips his beer, sets the bottle aside. "This one'll keep me busy."

"It'll make a nice rug."

Carl grins, says it's for the living room. Now, I say, he'll be able to make love on a bearskin rug in front of the fireplace. All he needs is someone to make love to — and a fireplace. He laughs, slaps me on the back, shows me an antique-style dresser he's building. He's quite a craftsman, something I hadn't realized, and for an hour we're lost in the world of carpentry, discussing the merits of various bandsaws and edgers, the mechanics of dovetailing, the subtleties of varnish.

Hungry, we head upstairs. The steak floats in the sink, turning the water pink like the aftermath of a shark attack. Carl prods the meat; it'll be a while yet. I decline another beer, ask if it's okay to go into the office, surf the Internet. I get a strange look — Carl doesn't approve of computers — but he gives me the key.

The service bell on the office door startles me. I climb the few steps to the main floor, look around. It's strange, being alone in a place that is normally filled with people and a hum of activity. But tonight, the flickering fluorescents are the only things humming. Bertie the Beaver — the Forest Service mascot with a toothy smile and plaid jacket — grins at me from faded posters. *Good Little Boys and Girls give Matches to Moms and Dads.* The U.S. Forest Service has a bear; we have a rodent. The radios in the dispatch room buzz and crackle as towerpeople murmur back and forth in a sort of faceless wilderness soap opera. There's not much to miss here, it's just a dumpy old building, but I'm reminded of late nights at the duty desk, of long phone conversations with Nina. It's like walking into a memory to find nothing but emptiness.

In the duty room the sensation is stronger. A large map of the district occupies an entire wall. The map is scattered with magnetic symbols in the form of tiny aircraft and men, colour-coded by crew configuration. It looks like a war room and I sit at the desk, turn down the radios. I'm not in command anymore; I'm here on a different sort of mission. I stare at the district map, pick out the location of the bombing — someone has stuck a little magnetic lightning bolt there. My gaze moves to another wall, to a provincial base map, and I rummage in the desk for a box of push-pins, stand in front of the map and search for the locations where the Lorax has struck, stick a pin at each spot, ending as the Lorax had at Fort Termination. Then one more pin at Curtain River. There are eight pins on the map. The coverage is loose and erratic but relatively thorough. No area has been hit more than once. If there's a pattern, I can't see it.

I pace — all of four steps — contemplate the map.

What about timing?

I review the dates. The attacks occurred apparently at random, spaced out roughly over a three-year period, then nothing for another three years. I had always believed Nina's death was accidental — that the bomber was horrified at what he'd done and there would be no more attacks. Then, at least, Nina's death seemed to have had some purpose.

I can't believe that anymore.

I abandon the map. The computer monitor comes to life with a faint, static hiss and when I've brought up the Internet I hesitate. *Search for?* I type in "Lorax" and in a fraction of a second have a response. Forty thousand matches. Many are about the bombings but some are of a more benign nature — the book by Dr. Seuss is a classic of children's literature. The little orange character with the oversized walrus moustache is everywhere. Other sites are commentary, some merchandising, some just for fun. Then I click on a site that makes my scalp tingle — a website run by an environmental group, greener than most. A primitive animation shows a feller-buncher clipping a tree, laying it down. As it reaches for another tree, a comic book explosion blows the machine apart, the grapple falls to the ground. Below this the word LORAX blazes fluorescent-green and there's a panel of thumbnail photos: bombed machines frozen in mechanical rigor mortis. It's the Lorax fan club. For a few minutes I stare at the screen, watch the feller-buncher explode over and over again. What bothers me most about this absurd little animation is that it shows the machine in use when it explodes. The message is clear — it's okay to blow these things up while people are in them. I wonder if Rachet has seen this, make a mental note to mention it the next time I'm arrested.

I click on the thumbnail photos. Enlarged, they're grainy, not very good quality, scanned from various newspaper articles. Most I've seen, but a few are new and I print them, hoping they hold some clue. I hesitate then print the rest for a full set. I pin them by location to the map, creating a mosaic of destruction.

I return to the computer, try a few more sites. Several are law enforcement, banking on the power of the Internet, hoping for information. There's a reward posted, $100,000, put up by some industry assocation. I doubt it will help — they're dealing with a fanatic. I surf on, each site connected to ten more, following themes of ecoterrorism, environmentalism, ecology. It's like following a fractal image, infinite and ever changing. From the FBI in Maryland to the Greens in Germany, everybody with something to say is on the Net. A billion screaming voices all yearning to be heard. I read a bit here and there — decoupling, shallow ecology, deep ecology. There are sites on how to make your own explosives. Thermite. Amphol. Pipe bombs. If I ever have kids, they'll never get a computer for Christmas. Lego and Play Dough all the way. My vision is starting to blur, my brain going mushy. Tree spikers and nature loving bikers. I'm lost in cyberspace when Carl comes in.

"How you doing, Porter?"

"Surfing," I mumble.

"Steaks are thawed," he says. "If you can pull yourself away."

I close out Netscape like a drunk leaving after last call, knowing he should have stopped long ago. My head hurts and I have surfer's hangover, information overload. Carl is standing in front of the provincial map, frowning. "What's this?"

"I was trying to see if there's some sort of pattern."

"A pattern." He sighs. "Don't do this to yourself."

"I have to Carl. For my sanity."

"It's your sanity I'm worried about," he says, his forehead creased. "You nearly killed yourself after what happened to Nina. Or maybe you don't remember."

"I remember," I say quietly. "That was the problem."

Carl nods toward the map. "Well, this isn't going to help."

"What do you expect? You're the one who called me."

"I know." He's staring at the pictures; instants arrested in eternity. Finally, he looks away, rubs his eyes. He looks tired, eroded. "That was probably a mistake."

"I would have heard about it anyway."

"Yeah, I suppose."

We look at each other for a minute. I used to know what he was thinking.

"Well, if I can't talk you out of it," he says. "I might as well give you a hand."

"Really?"

"Sure. I want this guy caught too."

"I'm not really sure where to start."

"You'll think of something," he says. "Just let me know what you need."

"Count on it."

He stares at the pictures a moment longer, then pulls them down one at a time, shuffles them into a neat stack and hands them to me. "You know, Porter, you could work here for a while. I'm sure there'll be things you'll want to look into."

"I don't know Carl. I've got a fire investigation to run."

"There's a task force now," he says. "They'll call you when they need you."

He has a point and I give it a moment's thought before nodding.

"Great." He grins. "You can sectorboss. We're a little short-handed."

I'm thinking of the advantages of staying local, looking into the man in camo. Maybe I'll make another trip out to the bombing site, once the Mounties are done with it.

Carl is smiling, trying to cheer me up. "It'll be like old times."

Not quite — someone is missing.

"Can you start tomorrow?" he asks.

"In the afternoon. There's something I have to do in the morning."

10

TRUCKS LOADED WITH LOGS rumble past, raising clouds of dust as I pull Old Faithful between two four-wheel-drive pickups in the parking lot of Curtain River Forest Products. I've been thinking about what Rachet said — that Hess worked near Fort Termination when Nina was killed — and I'm here to get a look at Hess's resumé. It could be Hess had some personal connection to this whole business. Maybe it's a place to start. Maybe it's nothing.

I'm wearing a dark blue double-breasted polyester suit and it's 30 degrees in the shade. Ever since I put the damn thing on at the rental place, I've had to resist the temptation to loosen the tie and tear off the jacket. But I have to keep it on because I have a part to play.

I limp across the gravel lot toward the office, a blocky, timber-frame building. Behind is an array of immense structures emitting ominous clanking sounds. Lifts of lumber are neatly stacked in high rows. Huge loaders, their grapples filled with logs, trudge like hungry beetles between the mill and a log deck the size of a small mountain. I go up bare wooden steps to the office door.

Inside, it's not much cooler. Walls, ceiling and front counter are covered with pine boards, oiled to a light sheen like an old-time general store. Carl would approve. A trucker with a thick brown beard is having a polite argument with the receptionist. He keeps lifting his hardhat and wiping sweat from his forehead with the palm of his hand. Somewhere, a radio is playing Dylan, urging us all to get stoned. With heat like this, we'll be hallucinating soon enough. The trucker loses the argument and goes away.

"What can I do for ya?"

The receptionist is an unnatural blonde. Her bare arms are deeply tanned, as is her generously displayed cleavage; the skin just beginning to wrinkle and slide into the abyss. At one time, she was probably quite a catch. A small hand-carved sign on her desk says "Carmen." I smile as professionally as possible for an ex-forest ranger in a suit. "Hello Carmen," I murmur. "I'm with the Insurance Underwriters of America."

Blank stare. She's waiting for more — the sales pitch probably.

"I'm here because of the unfortunate incident."

"Okay." She's nodding, still waiting for more.

"Our company insures the insurance companies that hold the policies for the employees you have insured. I just stopped by as part of a routine audit. I'd like to see Mr. Hess's employment record, so I can cross-index it with the report the member company will submit to us upon claim of insurance."

Carmen continues to nod. Hopefully, she has no idea what I have just said. Which makes two of us.

"Just a copy will be fine," I add.

"Just a moment." She smiles confidently. "I'll go check."

She vanishes through a doorway into what I hope is the file room. A distressingly long period of time goes by, during which I visualize her making a call to the real Insurance Underwriters of America, if they exist. Mill workers in hardhats and reflective vests pass through the lobby. A guy in a white sweat-stained shirt, asks if I've been taken care of. I nod and he vanishes through a doorway above which the word "Sales" is printed in block letters. Finally, as I'm ready to make a run for it, the receptionist reappears, looking relieved.

"Right this way Mr. ..."

"Hassenfloss," I say quickly. "Asper Hassenfloss."

She leads me to the inner sanctum — four offices and a boardroom. Nowhere can I see filing cabinets and I get an uneasy feeling. I'm about to begin making excuses for a hasty retreat when two

men come out of an office behind me, blocking my escape.

"This is Mr. Hasselfruss," says Carmen. "From the insurance company."

The men stick out their hands, which I shake, sweating and smiling and wondering what the hell I've gotten myself into — I'm centre stage now and not particularly enjoying the limelight. Hopefully, the critics aren't paying attention. The shorter of the two men, stocky, balding and a few years older than me, is Craig Whitlaw, president and owner of Curtain River Forest Products. The other guy, Benjamin Faust, is younger, tall, sandy-haired and frowning. He's the company Public Relations Coordinator; even lumber companies have a spin doctor on staff nowadays. I'm ushered into the boardroom and offered a seat at a long table. As I sit down, I notice the table has no legs but is supported by two hefty tree stumps — roots truncated, the bark still on. Flakes of bark are scattered on the carpet under the table, scuffed off by restless boots.

"Sorry to meet you under these circumstances, Mr. Husselfrass," says Whitlaw.

"A terrible thing," says Faust. "For everyone."

"Ronald Hess in particular," I say. "How is the family holding up?"

"As well as can be expected," says Whitlaw, taking a seat across the table from me, his hands clasped together. He seems confident, sincere. "She's a strong woman. And she has a lot of friends here in the community. Thankfully, there were no children."

I nod in condolence, hope I don't look like as much of an impostor as I feel.

"You're working with the police Mr. Husselfrass?"

"No, we run our own sort of investigation."

"You wanted to see Mr. Hess's work record?"

"Yes." I try to look authoritative. "If it's not too much trouble."

"Sure. Is there anything else you need?"

"That will be sufficient for now. I'll just take a copy —"

"Although it seems odd the other insurance fellow didn't give it to you."

Whitlaw is watching me, not suspicious I don't think, but curious. He's got a good stare, subtle but full of authority — he'd make a good chess player. Time for my big scene. "That's not the way we operate. We like to procure our own copies for audit purposes. It's an internal exercise, nothing for you to worry about."

Whitlaw gives me a dry smile. "Good to hear you're keeping everyone honest."

"Who did you say you worked for?" says Faust.

"The Insurance Underwriters of America."

"But we're insured with Gilbert-Fredricks and Associates," Faust says.

"Of course. We're the umbrella under which your local insurance provider operates."

"A sort of industry association then?"

"Sort of. I'll just grab a few copies from the file —"

Whitlaw stands and I do the same, relieved the interrogation is over. But he doesn't go to the door. There's an antique wall clock near a collection of framed pictures — black-and-whites showing teams of horses hitched to wagons piled unbelievably high with logs. He takes a key from a nail on the wall, opens a glass front on the clock and manually rewinds the spring, his back to us. There's something deliberately casual about this ceremony. Faust reads my expression, gives me a patient look, like we're in church, waiting for the pastor. Whitlaw finishes, carefully closes the glass door, hangs the key on its peg.

"Sad thing," he says. "Sad thing that happened to Mr. Hess. We're a small company Mr. Hasselfruss and we take care of our employees. We take care of the community. You can only imagine what an impact a thing like this has. We're not used to outsiders making trouble."

I nod, prepare to say something conciliatory, but Whitlaw isn't finished.

"These environmentalists," he says. "They don't understand that this is a business. People go to work here. We actually *make* something." His jaw clenches. "They just criticize and in a way I can understand that. It's human nature to meddle. But these people that plant explosives —" He shakes his head. "It's just insane. How can we protect our people?"

I think of Nina and don't have an answer. I don't think he's expecting one.

Whitlaw is halfway to the door before he offers me another handshake. "Thank you for coming Mr. Husselfrass. You need anything, you just let us know. Benji here is your man."

"A copy of Mr. Hess's employment record will be fine."

"Carmen at the front desk can get that for you," Faust says. He reaches into his shirt pocket, offers me his business card. It's got little pine trees on it, an elk and a stack of lumber. It occurs to me almost before it's too late that I should ask them a few questions.

"Do you know of any individuals who might want to do this?"

Whitlaw hesitates by the door, looks toward Faust. "We have a few environmental groups in our neck of the woods. They give us a pretty hard time but I wouldn't think they would stoop to this. Benji could probably tell you more."

"Could I have their names?" I pull a small notebook from the vest pocket of my suit. I bought it on my way through town, in case they wouldn't let me take a photocopy of Hess's records. It came with a genuine fake Arrow pen and makes me feel very professional.

"There's really only one significant group," says Faust. "The Mountain Guardians. They're connected to the bigger organizations, so we pay attention to what they're up to. They've dragged us into court a few times, showed up in the cutblocks with reporters, hassled our staff."

I'm scribbling notes. "Where can I contact them?"

"Angela Murtow is their leader. She's quite a character, used to teach philosophy in some university out east. Apparently, she finds activism more stimulating."

"You wouldn't have her number?"

"She's in the book."

Whitlaw is still by the door. "Benji can help you with any more details."

I give him a nod and he vanishes. "What about other groups?"

"There's a few — all small time. They feed off the Guardians."

"Good, thanks." I put away my notebook.

I follow Faust to the front counter. He's bowlegged, which is probably a condition of employment around here. "Carmen, honey, could you get Mr. Hassenhelf a copy of Ronald Hess's work record?"

Carmen gives him a peroxide smile, hustles off.

Benji is restless, has things to do. "You all set here Mr. Hessenhelf?"

I nod. Benji vanishes and I'm alone in the lobby. I take a look around but there's not much to see. A few old saw blades are hung on the wall, painted with winter scenes; old wagons covered with snow. In a corner is a stack of product flyers and some glossy pamphlets expounding the responsible forest practices of Curtain River Forest Products — Benji and the boys in Sales have been busy. I take a flyer advertising treated lumber; maybe I'll build a deck for Cindy.

"Here's your copy, Mr. Hasselhoff."

I take the offered manila envelope. Carmen's smile is dismissive. Just as I reach the door, it swings open. Al Brotsky nearly runs me over. "Sorry," he mumbles at the suit, then sees my face.

"How you doing?" I say as I edge past him.

"Fine," he says, grinning. "You take care now."

I park Old Faithful in front of Curtain River Men's Wear. The rental place is relieved to get the suit back in one piece. I'm relieved to give it back, more relieved to have escaped Curtain River Forest Products without having to explain what I was really doing there. Good news all around. And there's more news in the envelope from Carmen, which I'm not sure is either good or bad. I open the manila envelope and prop Hess's resumé against the steering wheel. By the looks of it, Hess had his resumé done by a professional; his work experience is emphasized in neat little bullets, like you'd find in a magazine or some glossy stockholders report. Overkill, considering the job for which he was applying. I skim over his minimal education, concentrate on his work experience.

The most recent bullet captures my attention.

Hess did work in the area of Fort Termination, as a feller-buncher operator for KCL Logging, and I let out a breath I hadn't been aware of holding. It could just be a coincidence but then why was Rachet so interested? *Were they friends?* Rachet insisted he was just examining the angles, trying to establish a connection. But he'd planted a seed.

The type of seed that sprouts late at night, when you can't sleep.

I shake my head, stuff the offending document into the manila envelope, pop Old Faithful into reverse and back into the street. I'm not ready to consider the possibilities, to incriminate Nina's memory on the basis of such flimsy circumstantial evidence. I drive around town for a few minutes, just to be moving, then turn toward the residential north side where, according to the address on the resumé, Hess lived. His widow might know.

Would she tell me?

Do I have the guts to ask? Do I really want to know?

After a few blocks my resolve begins to fade, afraid of what I might find.

I take evasive manoeuvres, divert to a restaurant, find a cushy booth, order pizza and sit by the window, staring blankly at the road. Logging trucks rattle past, dribbling bark. Motorhomes lumber slowly by, foraging for gas stations and soft ice cream. An orange Volkswagen Beetle pulls into the parking lot and vanishes behind a row of four-wheel-drive trucks with Monster Mudder tires. A moment later Telson comes in, stands by the door, looking around. I'm not sure she's looking for me so I just wait.

She sees me, comes over.

"Hi Porter. I saw your old beater, thought I'd come in and say hello."

She's standing at the end of the table, wearing a tank top and cut-offs, sandals and a green metal bracelet which contrasts nicely with her light brown skin — she's taken in some sun and it gives her a healthy radiance. Her long wavy hair is pulled back, highlighting her strong jaw line, her slender neck. I offer her a seat.

“Thanks.” She smiles, props her elbows on the table. “Where’ve you been?”

“Working. Why, you miss me already?”

She drums her fingers on the table. “Just nice to know *someone* in town.”

We chat about nothing in particular. The hot weather. The mountains. The moose that wandered into town. There’s something about her that makes it seem I’ve known her a long time. But when she asks what work I’ve been doing, I’m purposefully vague. I’ve become protective of my past, hiding it like an animal with a wounded limb. The manila envelope with Hess’s resumé is on the table and when the pizza arrives I use the diversion to slip the envelope onto the bench beside me, out of Telson’s sight. She’s staring at the pizza like a stray dog begging for scraps.

“Go ahead. My pizza is your pizza.”

“Thanks.” She picks the salami off her slice, offers it to me.

“Sure.” I load up. “What about you? What have you been up to?”

“As little as possible.” She yawns with a satisfied cat-like stretch that presses her unrestrained nipples against her tank top. I glance away — eventually. “Just lazing around,” she says between mouthfuls of pizza. “There’s a nice little lake about a half-hour from here. Not much of a beach but an awesome view of the mountains. We should head out there sometime.”

I think bikini, allow that it might be a good idea.

“What about tonight?” she says. “Watch the sunset. Build a campfire?”

How diabolical — she’s offering me the perfect escape. But if I don’t summon the courage now, I may never talk with Hess’s widow and the seed planted by Rachet will grow. Telson senses my hesitation and glances out the window, trying to look casual. "Unless you've got something else planned."

The old Porter would shoot me for this. "Well, unfortunately —"

"That's okay," she says quickly. "You hardly even know me —"

"That's not it —"

"It's okay, Porter. Really. I'm not usually this forward. It must be the mountain air."

She's a little insulted at being turned down — the fragile female ego — and I feel a twist of regret. "I definitely would like to go," I tell her. "Don't get me wrong. I just can't do it tonight. I have some business I have to clear up. Any other night would be fine."

From her look it's clear she thinks it's woman business. She's right, in a way.

"Okay." She smiles — our little secret. We chat between drools of cheese, keep the conversation light. We talk about growing up, the funny little incidents that stay with you, more humorous in retrospect. Like me, Telson grew up on a farm.

"I thought I detected a strain of country girl there."

"Farmer's daughter."

"You milked cows? Killed chickens?"

"No —" She looks shocked. "We had machines for that."

"Aagh, a modern country girl."

"I had my own horse though. What about you?"

"I'm allergic to horses."

"That's terrible." She's grieving. "You can't get near them?"

"Only in the salami form."

She gives me a wry smile. "So much for romantic rides on the beach."

I nod, silently curse my inadequate antihistamines. She's ordered an iced tea and watches me over the rim as she sips. Nina used to do the same thing and I'm stung by a sudden moroseness, deeper and more complex than before. Telson notices.

"What's the matter, Porter? You look kind of pale."

"Nothing. I think I better get going."

We argue over the bill, Telson determined to pay her half. The old-fashioned country boy versus the liberated woman. The liberated woman wins — what a surprise. We split the bill and I walk her to her Beetle where I have a sudden urge to go to the beach with her, watch the sunset, maybe fade into the sunset. Instead, I give her a hug, which she wasn't expecting.

"Take care," I say, and quickly walk to my truck.

It's early evening, the heat of the day just beginning to dissipate as I pull Old Faithful to the curb in front of the Hess residence. The house is larger than I expected, faced in red-brown brick on a lot at the edge of the Curtain River in a newer area of town I missed on my earlier mountain bike ride. The older part of town has small houses on large lots, with room for trees and space for children to play. Here, it's large houses on small lots. Somewhere, our priorities changed — we moved the children from the swing set to the television set. An emerald green minivan sits in the driveway. The walkway is pink cobblestone surrounded by brown lawn. A chlorotic spruce and several leafless birch occupy the front yard, dormant, waiting for rain. I mount concrete steps, press the button under the mailbox. A faint melody clangs from some muffled location deep within the house. A minute passes. I'm about to try again when the inside door opens, sucking air against the seal of the storm door. A woman looks at me through dusty glass.

"Yes?"

It takes me a few seconds to recognize Linda Hess. In the photo shown to me by Rachet, she's blonde, slim, good-looking. Now she looks like a junkie, her face pale and puffy, eyes glazed as if in fever — the face of mourning. Red lipstick only accentuates the effect. Her hair, brown and shorter — reverted I assume to her natural color — contrasts with her white-on-white nurse's uniform; neither does much to enhance her complexion. I'm amazed she's working at a time like this but maybe that's her way of dealing with the denial phase of loss.

"Mrs. Hess, I'm Porter Cassel. Could I speak with you for a moment?"

She frowns. "Well, I'm really just headed to work."

"Just a few minutes. It's fairly important."

She shifts her weight from one foot to the other. "What's this about?"

There's no easy way to do this. "It's about your husband."

"Are you with the police?"

Her hand is on the interior door, ready to slam it shut at the slightest provocation.

"No, not exactly."

She takes a step back. "I really don't have the time." The door begins to close.

"Please Mrs. Hess. I know what you're going through."

The door continues to close — the look on her face: no one knows what she's going through.

"The Lorax killed my fiancée."

At the mention of the Lorax, Linda Hess freezes. She peers from the darkness of her cave, past the half-closed door, like a frightened child, her brow furrowed and her chin tightened into a dimpled knot. I want to reach out, reassure her, but it might send her off the deep end. "I apologize for coming here at a time like this," I say in my most soothing tone. "But like you, I want who ever did this stopped and to do that I need to talk to you. I'll try to be brief."

She's clearly caught between fight or flight. I put on a patient smile.

"Your fiancée," she says, whispering. "What was her name?"

"Nina — Nina Pirelli."

I'm not sure what meaning the name has for her but she opens the door and I step inside.

The house is immaculate. I'm standing on a plastic mat overlaying thick, green shag in her living room. Clearly, the front door is cosmetic, to be used only as a fire escape, or by strangers like me. A stone fireplace set into a cedar feature wall dominates the room. There's a floral print sofa with wooden trim on the arms, matching recliner, magazine rack and coffee table with real fruit.

"Can I get you something to drink?" She's kneading her hands.

I try another reassuring smile. "Water is fine."

She goes for the water and I'm alone in the living room. I slip off my boots, walk across cool, deep carpet, examine framed pictures on the mantle; a graphic history of two converging lives. Ronnie and Linda when they were younger with their parents and siblings, then the obligatory wedding pose which I've already seen. Linda graduating from nursing school. Ronnie fishing. But no kids. I turn, suddenly aware that I'm being watched. A nurse stands by the entry to the kitchen, a glass of water in her hand, and for a second I have the impression she's come to give me my medicine.

I take the water, suggest we sit in the kitchen. Clean living rooms make me nervous.

The kitchen table is polished oak, worth more than my truck. Carefully, I take a seat, set the glass of water on the table. The kitchen isn't quite as clean as the living room; there's an open Styrofoam package of chicken soup. Linda Hess pulls out a chair across from me, providing a wide safety zone, and for a minute or two, we just sit. I sip the water. Oppressively little happens.

"I'm sorry for your loss," I say.

"You too." Her condoling smile is a grimace. "How old was she?"

"What?" I've already forgotten that I told her about Nina. I'm a little nervous.

"Your fiancée?"

"Nineteen," I say quietly. "She was nineteen." I pause, hoping I don't have to talk about Nina's death, but the silence between sentences is ominous. Maybe sharing what happened to Nina will show Linda that she's not alone, help her open up. "She was killed at a logging operation north of Fort Termination."

Linda tucks her legs beneath her. "Yes, I remember that. It was on the news."

More silence. I plunge on. "It happened near a feller-buncher. She was in my truck."

I pause after each statement, hoping she'll say something that I can use to lead into the questions I want to ask. But she's not very responsive, just sits there, her eyes averted, her slender hand wiping imaginary dust off the edge of the table. Like a newspaper article, I continue to give her slightly more elaborate versions of what happened. When I get to the part about how it was my fault that Nina was there, it's my turn to fall silent. Linda looks at me and I see profound loss in the emptiness of her eyes. She shouldn't be alone right now.

"It's so sad, Mr. Cassel. So sad."

I nod, try to swallow a knot in my throat.

"Ronny was a good soul. He wanted kids ..."

She trails off, knotting her fingers together and staring at me with faraway eyes.

"I'm sorry," I say again. "Maybe I should come back later."

"You're here now. But I'm not sure what you want."

That makes two of us. The way I see it, there are only a few possibilities, none of which make much sense. It could just be a coincidence that Hess worked in the same area where Nina was killed. Maybe both Hess and Nina somehow came into contact with the Lorax, although how I can't imagine. Or Hess knew Nina in a way I don't want to think about — the possibility I find most disturbing, for more than the obvious reason. I'm not sure where it leaves me, except the only person with an identifiable motive. Maybe this is what Rachet was hinting, but since I know I didn't kill either Nina or Hess, I'm at a loss. As I look across the burnished sheen of Hess's kitchen table, a final possibility occurs to me, which I like even less. Hess was the Lorax and involved with Nina. After her death, he stopped the bombings, but couldn't forget what he'd done and took his own life. This might explain the large amount of explosives used. If so, had he told his wife?

"Could you tell me what happened that night?"

The widow sighs, glances out the kitchen window. "I've told the police everything."

"I know Linda, but the police don't tell me much."

She looks at me as if I'm crazy, wanting to hear more.

"It's frustrating," I say. "Trying to put it together, so it makes sense."

"It doesn't make sense Mr. Cassel. It'll never make sense. Why go over it again?"

"Just briefly. Please."

She hesitates then takes a deep, steadying breath, tells me what she told the police in a way that makes it clear she's had to repeat this more than once. "Ronny went to work just after midnight, but I'm not sure of the exact time because I was working at the hospital. Our shifts overlap. He wanted to watch some movie on Fox before he went, so I think he did that. The last time I saw him was five o'clock that evening. I got the call at three minutes to three in the morning," she says wistfully. "I remember looking at the clock."

"Was he acting strangely that night? Anything unusual?"

She shakes her head.

"Did he have any enemies? Anyone who might be capable of something like this?"

A deep sigh as she looks at me, insulted that someone would ask that about her husband. But it's been asked before. Asked and answered. "No, Ronny didn't have enemies. He got into the occasional fight at the bar, you know, like all men do. Adolescent stuff mostly and it didn't happen often. He knew I didn't like him doing that." She's on the verge of tears. "He was a gentle soul at heart. He got along with everyone."

I wait, hope the tears don't come.

"Linda, when you were living in Fort Termination, was there anyone that you and Ronny knew who struck you as a little strange? Someone with strong environmental beliefs or someone who might have seemed very quiet when the topic came up. Someone Ronny might have run into because of his work?"

For a minute or two, Linda looks thoughtful. A new expression passes across her face, an uncomfortable mixture of hope and suspicion, a desire for revenge I've seen in the mirror. Then her features go slack, settle once again into the drained, neutral expression.

"No," she mutters. "They were all a little strange."

I take out my wallet, fumble it open, try to extract a photo of Nina but the plastic pouch is taped shut so I slide the wallet over to her, like an open book. She leans forward, looks at Nina's picture without touching the wallet.

"Do you remember seeing her before?"

Linda frowns slightly. "This is her, isn't it? Your fiancée?"

"Yes. Have you seen her?"

"She was very pretty," she says, her eyes still on the tiny picture. "I used to see her on the street and in the stores every once in a while, although I don't think we talked much. A little, you know, like people do when they see each other in the same places. It was a small town. And she came into the hospital once, with a broken ankle. She was in a lot of pain but she never cried."

I remember Nina telling me about this. It happened shortly before I knew her. She'd been riding Arthur's old three-wheel ATV and had put her foot down at the wrong time. The back wheel had climbed up her leg. Her ankle broke. Naked, you could see her one leg was a bit thinner, hadn't quite recovered from the atrophy. It's my turn to get teary.

"What about Ronny? Did he have any reason to know her?"

"No. Why?" Linda's expression is intent but confused, as if part of her mind were processing an unreasonably complex program. I slide the wallet home, tuck it into my shirt pocket where it hangs like an anchor. "It's just that both Ronny and Nina were in Fort Termination and they've both —"

I hesitate, find myself using Rachet's words. "I'm just trying to establish a connection."

She's frowning. "You think there's a connection?"

I massage my forehead. "I don't know —"

The back door creaks open and from the corner of my eye I catch a flash of someone coming in, carrying white plastic grocery bags. "I'm back Linda," a woman's voice calls out. "You okay, honey?"

Linda looks toward the backdoor, then over at me. The look of puzzlement returns and I get the impression I don't have much time. "Did Ronny ever act strange when you were living in Fort Termination?"

"Strange?" she says distantly. "What do you mean?"

I'm not sure I should press harder, but I need to know. I don't get the chance.

"Oh — you have company dear."

Another version of Linda Hess stands at the entrance to the kitchen; 30 years older, more solid, with greying hair and a tired but determined expression. Four bags of groceries hang from each hand; her forearms are as big as my bicep; her calves the size of watermelons. "Hello," she says. "I'm Linda's mother. And you are?"

"Porter Cassel." I stand, unsure of etiquette under the circumstances.

Older Linda looks at her daughter and frowns. "Honey, you really should take that off."

It dawns on me that Linda isn't going to work.

"Mother —" Linda speaks mechanically. "This is Porter Cassel."

"Yes, so I've heard."

"It was his girlfriend that was killed up north."

For a moment, Mother looks uncertain. Then she sets down her grocery bags and comes across the kitchen, gives me a firm, unexpected hug. "I'm Gertrude," she says. She's nearly as tall as me and I get a whiff of shampoo, perfume and cigarettes. "Sad times, Mr. Cassel. Such sad times." She releases me and steps back, a tear in her eye. "Will you stay for supper?"

"No, I really should be going." The last thing I want to do is grill Linda Hess in front of her mother about the possibility that her dead husband was having an affair with my dead fiancée. Come to think of it, I can't believe I'm here. I glance toward the window; it's dark outside. I've been here longer than I realized. "I just stopped by for a minute."

I retreat to the front door, slip on my boots, nearly have to be rude to get out of there. The screen door slaps shut and I hurry down the dim walkway to my truck, fire up Old Faithful and punch the gas, nearly stalling the old girl. When I turn the first corner, I realize my hands are shaking and pull over, force out a deep breath.

Behind me, a set of headlights swing around the corner. Brake lights flash as the vehicle hesitates, then accelerates furiously past me. I catch a glimpse in the beam of my headlights of a dirty, pale blue, old Plymouth with a mudded-over licence plate. The car rocks as it takes a corner and I see an old sideswipe dent on the driver's door. Maybe it's the hesitation when the driver saw I was pulled over, or the way the mud covers only the licence plate and not the bumper, but I get a feeling the car was waiting on the curb, the driver having watched me go into Hess's house. My tail has turned tail and I punch the accelerator, give chase.

We cat-and-mouse for a few blocks, the old car always a corner ahead of me, until it turns onto the highway and I'm blocked by a big truck with an entourage of impatient cars. I nose in as quickly as I can, eliciting angry honks from the lineup, but by the time I have a clear lane on the highway, my one-time pursuer is gone.

11

THE NEXT DAY, I'm playing teacher. The Forest Service requires all firefighters to receive a basic level of training and Gary Hanlon, the chief ranger at Curtain River, took advantage of my temporarily being in his employ to have me give a little spiel on basic fire investigation. The course is being held at the Christmas Creek staging camp out in the bush and I'm standing in a plywood shack, in front of a group of natives, all wearing orange coveralls. They look a little like a chain gang on lunch break, seated at picnic tables in the cook shack, their demeanour subdued, their faces intent and worried. I try to break the ice with a few jokes but the faces looking at me are impassive. I tell them a story about a forest ranger who accidentally started a fire after a long and arduous tree planting project by ceremoniously burning his map. The map scorched his fingers and he dropped it — into the dry grass. Attempts to stomp out the fire failed — I demonstrate with energetic stomping — and the bombers had to be called. My audience likes the story and the room thunders with raucous laughter.

"Man, that must've been embarrassing," says a stocky fellow in the front row.

"I can't *believe* they didn't fire you after that," says another.

"Me?" I say. "That wasn't me."

More laughter. In truth, it was Carl, sitting at the back of the class. He'd been smiling before, watching me play professor. Now his smile is a bit forced. The fire he'd accidentally started wiped out the cutblock he'd just planted.

I move on to the subject at hand, give the class a *Reader's Digest* version of fire investigation. Their role is limited but critical, and I tell them about using burn and scorch patterns to identify the area of origin — stress the importance of marking the origin, cordoning it off with flagging and protecting it. Post a guard if necessary and don't drag hose through this area or spray it down. If it's still smouldering, resist the temptation to put it out and instead extinguish the surrounding area. I don't have a blackboard at my disposal and so scribble diagrams on sheets of paper taped to the plywood walls. As is typical, there aren't many questions about the lecture.

Most of the questions are about the recent arsons.

"You guys figure out who's startin' all them fires?"

"I hear they're using some sort of bomb —"

Like everyone else, they read the papers and they're curious, want the inside track. Even a firefighter isn't impervious to gossip. I decline all questions, except to say the case is ongoing. I'm starting to sound more and more like Rachet.

A question from the back row. "What if we're on a fire and we see the guy?"

Twenty-five brown faces look at me expectantly. Native firefighters are a tough, capable group and if I was the culprit, I wouldn't want to face this crew. Not that our Red Flag suspect would be hanging around anywhere near enough for that to happen. "Just give him a little squirt with the hose," I say. "That'll knock him over."

There's a pause, then more laughter.

Carl's voice cuts through the tail end of the laughter; he's annoyed at my light-hearted suggestion. "You think you've found the guy, you just leave him alone. First of all, how are you going to know it's the right guy? And if it is, he could be armed. You just report it to your crew boss. We'll leave the rest to the cops."

"Right," I say. I should have sidestepped the humour.

My lecture is over and Carl takes his turn, then we troop outside and stand on the bank of Christmas Creek while Carl gives a demonstration on setting up and using a fire pump. He expounds on the virtues of fire foam — water efficiency and the smothering effect — and coats a spruce tree so it looks like the middle of winter. Then it's time for lunch. Carl and I sit on the back steps of the cook shack, in the shade, sandwiches in hand.

"You had to mention the map," he says, shaking his head.

"Too good a story to resist. Besides, they don't know it was you."

"You shouldn't do that Porter."

"Do what?"

"Tell them how their supervisors can screw-up."

Carl sounds unusually serious. I eat my sandwich, don't say anything.

"You know just as well as anyone," he says a moment later, "that a fire is like a military campaign. Safety is achieved through organization and obedience. We can't suggest in any way that the people giving orders don't know what they're doing. Lives are at stake."

I've never heard Carl talk like this, so stern. He's getting a case of green underwear — a sort of overzealousness at being a forest ranger. Or maybe he's right and I was being too flip.

For a few awkward minutes we eat our sandwiches, pretend nothing was said. Carl eats twice as many as me, then lights a cigarette, speaks out of the corner of his mouth. "Sorry for coming across like such a prick. I guess I'm just a little sensitive about that fire. It's still sort of embarrassing. Not that I caused irreversible damage or anything. I mean, fire is a natural process. If we didn't put the fires out, everything would burn eventually anyway. So it wasn't really a big deal. Except for the trees we just planted, I guess."

"Sorry for bringing it up."

"Forget about it," he says, waving his cigarette.

I watch him smoke. He looks older today, skin beginning to wrinkle around his eyes, long hair becoming coarse, streaked with the odd grey hair and receding slightly at the temples.

"So how's your investigation going?" he asks.

I assume he means the Lorax investigation. "When the cops questioned me, they asked about a possible connection between Hess and Nina. That got me wondering, so I went to the mill and got a copy of Hess's resumé. Turns out, he worked for KCL Logging out of Fort Termination, in the south part of the district."

"So you know who he worked for. So what?"

"I'm not sure. I went to see Hess's widow yesterday."

"Really?" He looks surprised. "Why?"

"To see if there was something she could tell me."

"What could she possibly tell you?"

"I don't know. Something that might link Hess with Nina."

"You think they're connected?"

"I can't help wondering if there's some significance, both of them having been in Fort Termination at the same time. Both becoming victims."

"It could just be a coincidence, Porter. She tell you anything?"

"No, she was pretty fried. But I have a feeling there's more to this."

We watch the crew organize a quick game of volleyball over a sagging net strung between two posts. They're competitive and the game is noisy with lots of shouting.

"You find out anything more about that guy in camo?" asks Carl.

He's never been far from my thoughts. "No, not yet."

"What about the cops? They have any leads?"

"If they did, I'd be the last to know."

Carl leans to let a firefighter pass between us on the steps, taps ash off his cigarette. "You know Porter, they could both have been accidents. Both of them could easily have been in the wrong place at the wrong time. From what I've heard, Hess came to work early."

An accident — there's that explanation again, makes it sound so benign.

"Accident or not, it doesn't much matter," I say. "They're both dead."

Carl nods, takes a long drag on his smoke.

"I'm going to need a few days off," I tell him.

"What? You just started."

"I know, but I'm going back to the Fort."

He looks at me, concerned. "What's at the Fort?"

"I'm not sure. But for me, that's where it all started — it's the origin."

Carl shakes his head. "I need you here. The whole province is at an extreme hazard and at the first hint of risk we're going to be manned to the teeth around here. If I let you go, we'll be short-handed again."

"Carl, I'm a fire investigator. I could be gone anytime."

"But you're not," he says. "You're here and there's no fire investigation at the moment."

I'm not sure why he's being so adamant. "I have to do this."

"Porter, for Christ-sake, just wait until it rains. You can play detective then."

Play detective? Carl isn't the only one short-tempered now. "Look Carl, this isn't some sort of game I'm playing here. I'm going tomorrow. You can manage a few days without me."

Carl's frown deepens. He butts out his smoke, interrupts the volleyball game.

We go back to class.

The next day, I'm on the highway, wheels humming against the pavement, valve tappets chattering and front end clacking — all systems normal. It's nine in the morning and already the highway ahead is rippling in the heat. I've got all the windows open but it's no cooler inside, just noisier.

On the drive into town from the camp last night, Carl was silent and sulking. This moodiness was a side of him I'd forgotten; in college he'd sometimes go days without talking to anybody. Not wanting to argue, and having no appetite for the silent treatment, I went out, cruised Old Faithful around town, looking for the orange Volkswagen. No luck. I called her cell phone and a tonelessly polite voice told me the customer I was calling was either away from the phone or out of the service area. I bought take out, ate on a carved-up picnic table down by the river.

Carl was gone when I checked into the Mackey Museum of Nostalgia and I considered driving directly north to Fort Termination, but the thought of remaining alert through eight hours of dark made me feel heavy and sleepy. I wanted to flake out and watch TV for a while, but there was no TV. I was tempted to cruise the Internet but Carl had no computer and the office was locked. So I went to bed. The next morning Carl was in the kitchen, making bannock.

"Morning, Porter. Care for some pan-fry?"

We had breakfast together; Carl cheerful and talkative.

"Sorry for being such a hard-ass there yesterday," he said. "I go to extremes sometimes."

"No problem. If you can't hassle your friends, who can you hassle?"

He wished me luck and we parted with a handshake.

The fields around me this morning are brown; trees leafless and waiting. All we need is a wind and we'll have a big money day — a Red Flag day — and everyone will be working. But I'm optimistic this morning; I'm finally doing something about what happened to Nina and it's good to be travelling. I may not feel so confident when I get to the Fort but it's still eight hours away.

I crank up the music so it can compete with the wind. Creedence Clearwater Revival has me thumping the steering wheel, singing along. A few minutes later I turn it down, pull over; the truck is making a new sound. Once the wind tunnel effect is gone, the chiming becomes recognizable — it's my satellite phone, guaranteed to disturb me anywhere on the face of the earth. I excavate it from beneath a pile of camping gear and dirty coveralls.

"Hello?"

"Porter, is that you?" The voice sounds like it's coming from a box somewhere in China. "Glad I caught you. It's Dirk Ensley at the Drayton Ranger Station. We've got what looks like another one of those arsons."

I know Dirk, worked fires with him, tell him I'll be there in an hour.

"Where are you?"

I tell him and he says they've got a machine closer. They'll pick me up.

A few minutes later hear the throb of an approaching aircraft, like something out of a Vietnam war movie. A yellow helicopter lands in a field next to the highway. It's a Bell 212, a big chunk of metal used by the HAC crews — elite rappel teams who drop by rope into a fire; fondly referred to as the dope-on-a-rope crews. Several cars and a motorhome pull over on the shoulder of the highway as a firefighter in dirty coveralls climbs out of the helicopter, crouches as he comes my way. They're waiting for me at the fire; he'll drive my truck to the ranger station. People get out of their vehicles and gawk. Baseball caps and Stetsons go sailing off to never-never land, caught by rotorwash. Tourists chase hats down the highway. It's amusing to watch as we lift off.

I fumble on a headset, adjust the mike. "How big's the fire?"

We're gaining altitude as we turn and the pilot points to a column of grey smoke about 20 miles away. The colour of smoke from a fire tells me a lot. Thick white smoke is the best, as it indicates the fire is consuming damp fuel, pumping up a lot of moisture. Straw-coloured smoke indicates intense heat and extreme fire behaviour. Black smoke means the fire is burning so aggressively it can't get enough air; grey smoke is sometimes the prelude.

"What've you got on it?" I shout into the headset.

"Just the HAC crew," says the pilot. "And a dozer that was nearby."

The Bell 212 is a helicopter capable of lifting a truck. You need a big, stable base like this to safely drop men down by rope. The cockpit is filled with panels of switches and gauges, like something you'd see in a commercial jet liner. Unlike a jet liner, everything vibrates; my vital organs quiver in synchrony with the rotor blades. Good thing I'm strapped into my seat with a four-point harness, the webbing heavy enough to hold a draft horse. The pilot wears a flight suit and full helmet with sun visor; the effect is distinctly military.

"You do any bucketing?"

"Yeah, about a half-hour," he says. "There's a beaver dam close by."

I study the approaching smoke. No visible flame. Maybe I'll get lucky and the origin will be properly protected. Nearly over the fire, we begin to circle, the pilot banking hard so I have a good view. The fire is small, ten acres, and enclosed by a wide dozer-guard of bare earth.

"You seen enough?"

"Let's go for a few more circuits, a little higher up."

The helicopter quickly climbs another thousand feet. With two turbine engines, power is not an issue. Below, as the fire becomes smaller, I have a feeling there's something different about this one. The other Red Flag fires were much larger, started in areas of continuous, highly flammable conifer forest. This fire was started in a dense black spruce stand. The trees are short, with branches right to the ground — perfect fodder for an instant crown fire — but the black spruce stand is only a pocket in a low boggy area, surrounded by mixed aspen and white spruce. Without significant wind, this fire has only limited potential. The crown fire that developed dropped to the ground where the forest cover changed, creating what looks from this altitude like a ragged hole in the canopy.

Compared to the other arsons, this fire looks less planned, more opportunistic. There's a public road close to the edge of the fire where the arsonist likely parked before walking into the forest. The time of day seems odd; the other fires were started in the mid-to-late afternoon, when the forest was at its driest. This fire was probably started early in the day, when moisture levels are higher, forest fuel less flammable. Or the ignition device was set yesterday and burned very slowly. Either way, it wasn't much of a fire and this could be a bonus; more evidence may have survived.

I use the radio in the helicopter to call the Drayton ranger station, talk to Dirk Ensley, ask if the rest of the Wildfire Investigation Team is on its way. The response is affirmative.

I signal the pilot — time to take a walk in the ash.

The 212 drops like a stone, shuddering, the dash vibrating, then hovers momentarily above the road before settling solidly on gravel. I unbuckle myself, step out and close the door, crouch until I clear the main rotor. A firefighter in charcoal-smeared yellow coveralls is waiting in the trees, his eyes averted from the rotor blast.

The 212 lifts off, thumps away. Brief introductions follow.

"How you doing?" says the firefighter. "Maurice Kochansky."

"Porter Cassel."

Kochansky is the leader of the HAC crew. He's short, slim and young — a university student probably — and like a medic at the scene of an accident he gives me a brief chronology of events thus far. Staged at the Drayton camp; called to the fire at 0846 hours; size at assessment one hectare; fire behaviour moderate; rappelled in and started to bucket; dispatch advised Cat was available six miles away. They had a suspicion the fire might be man-caused and searched for the origin. They found and flagged it. I'm impressed, confirm the origin was not disturbed.

"Well, not much," says Kochansky. "A few footprints."

He leads me into the fire, past black, swizzle stick trees. Already there's a trail here, mashed in by the firefighters. Kochansky walks quickly and I wince as tendrils of pain creep up from my ankle. Three hundred feet from the road we swing off the trail, follow a double set of ashy bootprints. Ahead, I see bright orange ribbon, stark against the black.

"Here it is," says Kochansky.

The origin is surrounded by a denser concentration of slender blackened poles. The HAC boys made sure the site was well marked

— ribbon is hung like parade streamers in a large loop in the remains of the trees. Bootprints lead to a dark square that must be the cake pan.

"These your prints?"

Kochansky confirms. I tell him to wait, follow his prints to the origin, look around a little. The arsonist picked the thickest area to assure a rapid crown fire. And it looks like the same sort of device — it's the same type of pan all right, this time filled with less ash. I'm in no rush to upset anything so I retreat.

"What now?" asks Kochansky.

"Now you stay here, outside the ribbon. Guard this area with your life."

Kochansky nods; he's with the program.

"Have you got a pen and paper?"

He pats a chest pocket in his coveralls.

"Good. I want you to write down everything that happened from the moment you got the call to when you met me. What the smoke looked like en route. Any vehicles you noticed. The names of all your men. The name of the Cat skinner. When you discovered the origin. Who discovered the origin. No detail is too small. In a little while, this place is going to be crawling with cops and they'll want this information, so you'd better get it down while it's fresh and people aren't in your face. Any questions?"

"No sir," says Kochansky. "But I think I'm going to need more paper."

No problem, I tell him, and head back to the road where I take a pad of paper and a clipboard from my pack, swallow a few painkillers. Overhead, the helicopter is bucketing again, trailing droplets of water that splatter around me. The flame is mostly out, but he's running up the meter. I call him, tell him to stay away from the origin, not to dribble on it. His reply is curt, one syllable.

I walk into the fire again, imagine Red Flag pushing his way through dense spruce. Why here? Why stop and light this fire? I give the clipboard to Kochansky. When I arrive at the road again, there's a white minivan pulled over, a Mountie closing the door.

"Hello." I offer a hand, introduce myself.

"Corporal Dipple," he says. "Ident, 'K' Division."

Dipple is a few years older than me, shorter and stockier. His black hair is cut very short; he has a small balding area on top like someone set the mower blades too low. He's a bit pale in contrast to his dark hair and is frowning as he watches the helicopter fly over, its bucket swinging wide on a long line. His gaze travels toward the Cat, a big D-8 sitting on the shoulder of the road, its blade a curved wall of metal.

"So, what've we got here?" he asks.

I briefly explain who I am, name the rest of the team and task force, give him some history on the other Red Flag fires and what I know on this one so far. Dipple flips open a small note pad, writes this all down. He says nothing until I'm finished, then gestures with his pen toward the blackened area of the fire. "Is the origin identified and protected?"

"Yeah, I've got a guy watching it."

"Good. How much contamination?"

"A little," I admit. "But better than the other fires."

Dipple's brow furrows. Contamination is a dirty word. He watches the helicopter pass overhead again. "Does he have to do that right now?"

I reach for my belt radio. "Probably not, but let me call the fire boss."

Kochansky hesitates before answering, nervous about making a call with the police on site, but it's good to keep people in the loop, let them be part of the operation. The pilot cuts in, offers that he needs to stop for fuel soon anyway. Kochansky agrees it would be a good idea to shut down for a while.

Dipple has moved down the road. "Do you know which vehicle made these tracks?"

He's standing near the shoulder of the road next to a distinct pair of tire marks I hadn't noticed. I look around. The minivan is the only vehicle and I shake my head, tell him the firefighters arrived by helicopter; the Cat walked down the road from an operation a few miles away.

He nods, goes to his van.

My crime scene kit is in my backpack. Dipple's fills his van. He pulls out a metal case, takes out a camera and levelling tripod, makes a note of the time and weather conditions, measures the distance to the marks on the road, sets up a digital camera.

"Anything I can do to help?"

"You can search the rest of the road."

I take a quick walk, find nothing else of note, return to find Dipple measuring the distance between the tire tracks, the width of the disturbed area. The tracks are little more than scruff marks on the dry road surface, no tread visible, and I wonder aloud how they might be of use.

"Vehicle types have unique track widths," he says, making a note in his flip pad. He points toward the tire marks. "You can tell he was headed south. By the slight slew in the tracks I'd presume it was a two-wheel drive powered through the rear axle. I'll feed this info into a database, come up with a list of suspect vehicle types."

I make a mental note to look more carefully for tire marks. "What's next?"

"Show me the origin."

We trudge into the fire, Dipple looking around. "There's a lot of tracks here."

"The firefighters were dropped at the road and carried in their gear."

Dipple stops walking, scratches his head. "This isn't good."

"It's hard to protect everything on a fire."

"This is going to waste a lot of time," he says. "There'll be hours of casting."

"These guys didn't know it was an arson when they walked in."

"Given the history, they should have considered it."

It seems a moot point now. I shrug and we walk the rest of the way to the origin. Kochansky stiffens, stands straight when he sees us, looking like a good soldier. I introduce him as the HAC leader. He grins, shakes Dipple's hand.

"You found the origin?" says Dipple.

"Yes sir. I cordoned it off right away."

"What about those two sets of bootprints?" says Dipple. "Those both yours?"

"Only one pair sir." He gestures toward me. "The other one is his."

Dipple looks at me, his forehead creased. "Had to go in for a look?"

"I am a fire investigator."

"My job," says Dipple, his voice even, "is the collection and preservation of evidence at a crime scene. If someone wants my services, I expect only one thing and that is the scene not be contaminated. Contamination wastes my time and can destroy any chance of going to court."

"I realize that but —"

"To do my job properly, I have to account for every activity and alteration in the crime scene. Tromping around in here with your wafflestompers doesn't help."

Kochansky looks at his wafflestompers. I'm determined to remain polite. "Is there something you need me to do?"

"Your job will be to aid in the management of the crime scene, to keep people out of the area. I consider the crime scene to be the origin and the area from the origin to the road. If anyone has to come in, they follow the trail already established, maintain a single line of contamination."

I feel a bit like a kid who's trained for the big game but only gets to warm the bench. I'd hoped to assist Dipple, pick up a few pointers. Dipple asks Kochansky a few questions, is impressed when Kochansky hands him three pages of notes.

"Good work," he tells Kochansky.

Kochansky gives me a wry smile. "Thank you, sir."

Dipple strings yellow police crime scene ribbon around the origin area; it's getting pretty colourful out here. As we walk back along the trail through the fire I hear the crunch of tires on gravel. Berton and Malostic have arrived in a green Forest Service suburban. Introductions ensue, after which Corporal Dipple gives them the speech about contamination and staying out of the crime scene while he works. Malostic takes notes. When Dipple goes to his minivan to make a call, Malostic pulls me aside.

"What was his name again?" he asks, his pencil ready.

"Nipple," I say. "Constable Nipple."

"Oh." Malostic chuckles. "Strange name."

"Yeah. I think he's kind of sensitive about it."

"No wonder."

I smile. It might be fun working with Malostic after all.

"Okay," says Dipple. "The rest of the team will be here in about 40 minutes. I need everyone attending the fire to muster here on the road so I can record footwear."

“I’ll arrange that,” says Malostic.

Malostic doesn’t have a radio and I’m tempted to let him wander through the ash looking for firefighters but call Kochansky instead, pass on the request, tell him to make sure the men walk to the road along the fireguard cut by the Cat. A few minutes later, sooty firefighters begin to trickle in. They cluster on the road, talking and joking. They’re all university students by the looks of it, working hard and having a good time.

“What do you want them to do?” Malostic asks Dipple.

Dipple is readying his camera next to the van. “I’ll need their boots, full pairs, one person at a time. They’ll get them back as soon as I finish photographing the soles.”

“Roger,” says Malostic. He goes to the group of firefighters. “Can I have your attention for a moment. I’m Darvon Malostic. Constable Nipple over there needs your boots for a few minutes, so he can photograph your soles.”

Over by the van, Dipple’s head jerks up and he frowns at Malostic.

“Not my *soul*, man,” says one firefighter; a Jamaican exchange student.

General laughter from the firefighters. Malostic laughs too, but I don’t think he gets it. The firefighters kneel, unlace their boots. Malostic brings them to Dipple, one pair at a time, like a faithful hound dog.

“Thank you,” Dipple says frostily.

“You’re right,” Malostic whispers as he passes me. “He’s a bit sensitive about it.”

It takes Dipple 20 minutes to photograph all the boots, then the firefighters are told to return to work but to stay well back from the origin. The Cat skinner is next, a middle-aged guy with a torn shirt who sits on the tread of his bulldozer as he waits for his boots. Dipple asks him a few questions about when he arrived, what he saw. Nothing unusual. Kochansky and I get our boots immortalized, then Kochansky returns to guard duty and Dipple and I walk along the shoulders of the road, search the ditches.

"So you're a fire investigator," says Dipple.

"Seasonally." I tell him about my years as a ranger, my switch to part-time work.

"Sounds like a good job. Why'd you switch?"

"It's a long story."

Dipple doesn't press. After a quarter mile without finding anything we turn back. "I didn't mean to come across as such a prick," he says. "Most of the scenes I process are more controlled."

"I should have been more careful."

"Live and learn. You want to give me a hand with the casting?"

"Sure."

We're walking down the road, checking the opposite ditch, when the rest of the task force arrive in a police suburban. Kirby rolls down the window, nods toward Dipple. "Where can I park?"

"Anywhere," says Dipple. "The road has been cleared."

Kirby takes charge and we cluster around the front of the suburban for a group hug. For Dipple's benefit, Kirby gives a casual but concise rendition of the other fires. Kochansky is called in from guard duty, presents his report on what transpired before my arrival. I give a short encore. The Mounties slip on blue coveralls and heavy boots, snap on white rubber gloves like a group of surgeons in prep. But it's more autopsy than surgery.

The first order of business is a grid search, from road to origin, looking for what Dipple calls transfer evidence. Before we go in, he downloads his digital camera into a laptop, hooks up a printer, cranks off black-and-whites of our boot soles. He's got more hardware and software in his van than most ranger stations. He goes in first with video and still cameras, records the scene for posterity. We follow, begin to work our way through the ash.

The idea is to examine every bootprint, compare them to the photos, disregard those of the workers on site. It's a tedious exercise, made more so by the way the fire has scorched the duff; there's little structure to the prints; the photos don't help much.

An hour passes. It's like staring at those 3-D puzzles in the Saturday paper, getting nothing but a headache. Then Berton calls to Dipple.

"I got a fresh track here."

Heads turn like there's a pretty girl in the bar.

"You guys keep working your sections," says Kirby. "There may be more."

I complete a pass on my section of grid, which brings me close to Dipple and Berton but not close enough to really see the print. I want a good look but am hesitant to wafflestomp closer. Dipple notices. "Work your way over here," he says. "But be careful."

There's nothing to record in transit but I'm careful anyway.

The print is in a small muddy pocket surrounded by shrivelled aquatic plants. In a normal year, this would be underwater but now it's a patch of fine textured black mud with just enough moisture to hold a print.

"Beautiful," murmurs Dipple.

I get a tingle of anticipation; the print is different enough in its basic pattern that it clearly was made by someone not currently here — our first glimpse of Red Flag. Dipple sends Berton to the minivan to bring back his casting kit, then measures the print, places the ruler next to it and sets up his camera. He fusses with the supports, makes sure the plane of the camera is parallel to the ground, uses a flashlight to shine across the print as he clicks away.

"Why the flashlight?"

"The trick to this," he says, looking through the camera, "is to use an oblique light source to bring out the three-dimensional aspects of the print."

"Interesting." Malostic has come over with Kirby.

Dipple looks up, finds he's at the centre of a crowd, faces peering down like he's a wounded quarterback in midfield. "Okay," he says. "Everyone is just going to have to back away. I'm the only one that needs to be here."

Malostic clears his throat. "I took a course on footwear ident."

"Wonderful," says Dipple. "Now clear out."

We back away.

"Cassel, you can stay if you want to learn how to cast a bootprint."

Malostic scowls in my general direction. Dipple notices, waits until we're alone, asks about Malostic's background. I'm not sure, I tell him. Criminology major probably, with a minor in chemistry, maybe forensics. No experience but educated into a state of helplessness. Dipple nods, opens his casting kit. "We use dental stone," he says. "You should carry some."

He presses a strip of cardboard into the mud to form a low wall around the print, mixes white powder into a slurry, pours it into the mould. The cast will be ready in 20 minutes. He picks up his camera, sends me back to my assigned grid area. No further suspect bootprints are found, nor are any other clues until we reach the cordoned origin. Dipple stresses that he is the only one going in. Malostic and Kirby go for a walk to talk to the firefighters. The two constables — Purseman and Trimble — amble back toward the road, talking amiably. Berton and I linger by the crime scene tape and watch Dipple operate.

Dipple follows the trail in, videotapes the site, takes still photos and maps the area. Constables Purseman and Trimble arrive laden with metal cases, shiny new empty paint cans, a shovel and rake, metal detector and soil sampler. Their foreheads glisten as they set everything by the sacred ribbon. Dipple strings a grid, searches with the metal detector, works his way in toward the pan. The pan is seized the way it is, slipped carefully into a plastic bag, the contents undisturbed. Soil samples are taken, placed in the new paint cans. An exhaustive search is done with the rake and Berton and I get bored, wander back to the road.

"That bootprint is in a strange location," says Berton. "Off to the side."

I'd noticed that too — the print is not in line with the road and origin. "Maybe the fire was started at night," I say. "The guy got disoriented and couldn't find the road so he wandered around in the spruce."

Berton steps around a blackened tree. "Why do you think he started it at night?"

"I don't know why, but I think he did. He's pretty careful. I don't think he would have left a print like that in daylight. He would have seen the mud hole and stepped around it."

"Maybe he's just getting cocky."

"Possibly, but there's something different about this fire."

Berton is sweating. His glasses keep sliding down his nose. "Such as?"

"Look at the fire behaviour."

"Subdued," he says, looking around. "An early morning burn."

"Right." This has been nagging me ever since we arrived. "It's not the usual high intensity event. It's like this was an afterthought, an impulse fire. He was driving past and had the urge."

"Maybe it's not the same firebug."

"Maybe not, but the device looks the same."

At the road, Malostic and Kirby are leaned up against the

hood of the police suburban, deep in conversation about profiling, motives and trigger events. Berton and I drift over. Malostic seems to be holding his own. We listen for a few minutes, learn more about fire as a manifestation of frustrated sexual desires. If that was our profile, most of the male population would be suspects. Kirby turns to us, asks if this fire is different than the others. I tell him my impressions.

"Interesting," he says thoughtfully. "It could be a copycat but there's been no media coverage regarding the nature of the device."

"It could be a break in the pattern specifically to confuse us," says Malostic.

"Well if that's what he's trying to do," I say, "it's working."

The next morning I'm back on the road, headed north. I'd spent the night in Drayton, in a motel room that smelled of pressboard and urine. Breakfast was fried eggs and coffee — not a good idea because now my stomach is churning. But it might not be the caffeine or grease that has my insides turning over — Fort Termination is closer today.

I take a drink from a bottle of water, warm even though it came from a service station cooler 20 minutes ago. Already, the asphalt ahead wavers like something out of an acid trip. I toss the bottle on the passenger seat, amid an assortment of service station junk food designed to appeal to the weary impulse buyer; it looked good when I bought it — I'll end up throwing most of it away. At least it covers my satellite phone, which I feel vaguely guilty for turning off.

The phone rang shortly after hitting the road this morning: Carl irritated that I wasn't returning to Curtain River. The fire should have set some sense into me; dry as a popcorn fart around here; high temperatures and low humidities; afternoon winds with a high probability of dry lightning. Hell of a time to take a few days off.

I work for him less than a week and already he's a slave-driver.

He isn't the only one the dry weather is making jumpy. That little arson fire feels like a prelude — a reminder. Red Flag wants us to know he's still out there. I keep glancing at the satellite phone, half buried under Doritos and Big Chief Beef Jerky, tempted to turn it back on. Another diversion would save me from the conflict that lies ahead.

Then again, that's why I turned it off.

I open the bag of Doritos, nibble on the salty wafers, try not to think too much about what lies ahead. I remember Arthur Pirelli at Nina's funeral. We didn't talk. Some force kept us apart. He stayed on his side of the casket. I stayed on mine.

That fire by Vermilion was our first conversation since the funeral.

"You've got about two fucking minutes to get off my fire —"

The road ahead is straight, the terrain flat open farmland. I hate this part of the drive the most: brown stubble fields and grey earth, a dead landscape. Dust devils waltz across barren ground. Closer, motor oil soaked into the truck's floor mat slowly vapourizes, filling the cab with a refinery smell. The open windows help very little — just more hot air. Sweat beads on my forehead and the steering wheel is slick, my hands leaving a damp print on everything I touch. The sky is light blue, faded like old denim, the sun relentless. For weather like this, you need welding goggles, not sunglasses.

I have lunch at Claire's Diner, little more than a trailer with a stove. Claire is heavily overweight — too much of her own cooking — and has every fan in the place going, blowing grease odours and crazed houseflies in little eddies over the counter. Johnny

Cash is on the radio but can't compete with the rattle of the fans. I try a grilled ham and cheese; it doesn't go down. I buy ice cream instead, eat it fast.

Fields become interspersed with patches of bush. Finally there are no more fields, only mile after mile of trees and a sort of stupor sets in — a good way of making miles without thinking about where they lead. A familiar slough passes on my right, then a sign for the secondary road leading to Fort Termination. The stupor recedes, replaced by an eerie sensation that makes my scalp tingle. I haven't been back here since Nina died.

I pull over at a rest stop, walk into the ditch and sit on a log in the shade of the trees. I've been past here a hundred times but never stopped, always in a rush to leave or make it home. Today, there's no rush — ghosts are patient. I linger, watch semi-trailers swoosh past. I want to turn back; the truth may be out here but I'm not sure I want to find it. I just want relief, want to be free of this nightmare. I return to my truck, hope Old Faithful won't live up to her name.

She starts. No more excuses.

Fort Termination is a hole in the forest occupied by about 700 people. Its name tells its story — at one time, it was the end of the road. For most inhabitants, it still is. Very little here is new. Trailers sport rambling additions. A few cars driven by restless teenagers go very fast; most go slower, sinking into backyard weeds. Despite the poverty, there are riches underground in ancient reefs. Oil and natural gas. Coal bed methane. Millions of dollars flow daily from this region through pipes under the ground, yet there is no real economy on the surface. Oil workers stop on their way through, supporting the grocery stores and bars, but no one stays longer than they have to. The curse of the North.

I stop on a low hill overlooking town, take a moment. A small green sign, streaked with bird shit and riddled with bullet holes, says five kilometres. When I used to jog to keep in shape, it was here I turned back. Then, this sign was a symbol of salvation. Now it seems the opposite.

The five kilometres pass too quickly.

The ranger station is a triple-wide trailer at the edge of town, next to a faded fire hazard sign stuck on Extreme. I pull into the shade of a clump of spruce trees, in a small parking lot in front of the office reserved for the public. I used to park in the back.

In two easy strides I mount the wooden steps, note the handrail is still loose from rot and needs to be replaced. The rug in the entrance hall is the same ugly brown mat. Familiar posters and pamphlets are tacked to the walls. It's like the last three years never happened and I'm coming to work. Except today, I have to stop at the front counter.

I ring the service bell. Never had to do that either.

Darlene McMaster sits at a brown metal office desk and at the sound of the bell looks up from her computer screen. There's a brief pause; a look of disbelief.

"Porter Cassel." She says this as if I were a mischievous kid. But she's pleased.

In the Fort Termination Ranger District, Darlene McMaster is an institution. For the past 27 years she's watched a succession of rangers come and go, seen the Forest Service evolve from horses to helicopters, typewriters to computers. She learned forestry through osmosis, watching and learning, manning the radios, typing letters and reports. She knows more about the business than the rangers.

"Darlene. How're you doing?"

"Oh, you know." She stands slowly, walks to the counter. "Fires, fires, fires."

"Your arthritis acting up?"

No worse than usual, she tells me. She's Metis, hefty and stubborn. And tough — she's worn out three husbands. We make small talk about district business; still the same problems, the same politics. Another bad fire season developing; staff are actually beginning to *complain* about the overtime. She asks about my sister; I tell her about Cindy's divorce. Finally, I have to ask. "Is Arthur in?"

A shadow crosses her face. "He's in the bush with a new ranger."

"He actually made it out to the bush?"

"Yeah. Imagine that."

A moment of silence. Arthur went ballistic after Nina was killed and I never returned to the office, just loaded Old Faithful and headed out. From Edmonton I mailed a letter of resignation to the regional director. As for my trailer, the landlord kept my damage deposit, paid for my overdue rent by selling what little furniture I had. I didn't care. Darlene adopted my office plants, shipped my personal effects south to Cindy. I vanished, like a soldier missing in action.

"Will he be back before closing?"

"I doubt it."

Another pause; there's too much going on under the surface for comfortable small talk. I promise to pop in again before I leave; Darlene looks like she doesn't believe me. After the way I left last time, I don't blame her. But she wishes me luck.

Outside, I have the strangest feeling — I'd expected Arthur would be in. It's like a close call on the highway, a brush with death you're slow to appreciate. Then it hits you that somehow you cheated fate. But I don't read much into it; I'll see Arthur at home, when he gets off work.

Until then, I have a few hours to kill.

I cruise familiar streets and the sensation that I never left settles in. A few people along mainstreet watch me pass, look surprised and wave. I wave back, try to look happy to see them. But I'm apprehensive; I half expect to see Nina coming out of a store. Or strolling along the sidewalk. She'll turn, wave at me, throw me a kiss —

She's an ache in my memory, like a body missing a severed limb.

I turn toward the highway, head into a small industrial area. It's mostly oilfield contractors here at the edge of town. Small offices and big metal-clad shops. Yards filled with oily wellheads, derricks and bundles of pipe. Mixed in are a few logging contractors. KCL Logging is a large cinderblock building in a fenced compound. The gate is open and I pull in, drive past rows of idle skidders, delimbers and feller-bunchers — timber harvesting this far north occurs mostly in winter, when the soggy forest floor turns hard as concrete. I park beside a D 7 Caterpillar, look around. There's no one in the yard. The tinkle of tools on metal drifts from an open shop door in a duet with some music channel I've never heard here before — maybe they've got short-wave. The music ends, giving way to news I can't make out. The radio must have a cracked speaker; the announcer's voice is like something you'd hear at a subway booth.

Better try the office first.

It takes a while to find the right metal door — none of them have windows or signs — and when I do, it's not much of an office: two file cabinets and a metal desk with an old computer, the keyboard covered by a grease-smudged plastic overlay. An old rotary phone is decorated by concentric rings of grime. A parts manual lies open on the seat of a chair.

"Hello?"

No answer. I hesitate, then sweating and nervous, reach over and try the computer, looking for personnel records. The screen is monochrome, probably as old as me; I'm not sure what operating system they're using. Maybe it's a micro-fiche reader with a keyboard. I give up, defeated by obsolescence. The filing cabinet is locked; the metal fire door that leads to the shop isn't.

The shop is cavernous, like an airport hanger, with three bays each large enough to hold a semi. The shop doors are all open, white light from outside mixed with long angular shadows from metal lathes and hydraulic presses. It smells like grease, Varsol and oily concrete. The music is much louder in here, distorted by volume; a cacophony of fiddles. In the farthest bay, a stroke delimber is getting its prostate checked. The checkup doesn't seem to be going well; there are parts scattered all over the concrete floor. A mechanic in grey coveralls and brimless welder's cap stands on the machine's track. His back is to me and he's up to his elbows in engine.

I walk over, watch him work. "Hello."

He jerks, surprised, looks over his shoulder at me. A wrench tinkles through the bowels of the machine, lands on the shop floor. The name tag on his coveralls says Jean and he wears the universal expression of mechanics everywhere when interrupted by someone clean.

JAFOS, they call us: *Just Another Fuckin' Observer.*

"Sorry," I holler over the music. "Didn't mean to startle you."

Jean climbs down from the track, crawls under the machine and retrieves the wrench then walks to a workbench and silences the fiddles from hell.

"Can I help you?"

He's middle-aged with a grey moustache and large hooked nose. I doubt he's worried who I am so I choose the simplest explanation. "I'm investigating the death of Ronald Hess. I understand he used to work here."

"You with the cops?"

"No. I work for an insurance company."

"Insurance, eh." Jean looks wistful. "Yeah, he worked 'ere."

"Do you mind answering a few questions?"

Jean shrugs, unconcerned. "I guess."

"How well did you know him?"

"Not too well. I work mostly in the shop."

"But you saw him around? Talked to him now and then?"

"Sure." Jean uses a rag to wipe grease from his hands, the motion a sort of process that seems to help him think, like he's pondering a puzzling mechanical failure. "I see him around, you know, when he comes into the shop. Sometimes I see him in the bush, when his machine goes down."

"That happen a lot?"

"Sometimes." Jean leans against the workbench, stuffs the rag in a back pocket where it hangs like a grunge fashion statement. His welder's beanie is purple with little yellow flowers. "Some guys are pretty hard on the machines," he says. "All they care about is production. But a machine has its limits you know. Especially in the cold."

"Was Ronny like that?"

"Not really." Jean frowns thoughtfully. "He was a pretty good operator."

I try out Brotsky's phrase: "A real asset to the operation?"

"Yeah, I guess you could say that."

"What was your impression of Ronny? Did he get along with everyone?"

"So far as I know." Jean hesitates, as if deciding whether he should tell me more. "Ronny was a careful guy, real safety minded. The boys here, they get paid by the piece, want to make lots of money, pay for their fancy trucks. They push it too hard sometimes, get careless, but Ronny wasn't like that. Maybe because his wife was a nurse. He'd plod along, sure and steady, didn't like the guys in the skidders pushin' him to work faster."

"Did anything serious ever develop?"

"What do you mean?"

"Did Ronny ever receive threats, get into fights over this?"

Jean looks puzzled. "What's this got to do with the insurance?"

"Maybe nothing."

He's staring at me. "You look kind of familiar."

"It's probably just a coincidence."

"No — I don't think so. Didn't you work around here before?"

"Maybe in another lifetime. Anything else you can tell me about Ronny?"

"No." He shakes his head and I get the feeling he's done talking. He's squinting at me in a way that makes me nervous. More than likely he's seen me in uniform years ago, at a logging operation while he worked on a machine. I thank him for his help. He nods, watches me walk across the yard, get into my truck. When I glance in the rearview mirror, he's still standing in the open bay door of the shop, wiping his hands with a rag.

I dawdle over supper, in one of the two restaurants in town. It's not that the chicken balls are especially good, just that I'm not eager to face Arthur. The way I see it, one of two things could happen — Arthur could shoot me or I could get him first in self-defence. Either way, it won't be pretty. The waitress comes around a third time to offer more tea. The owner, a short middle-aged Chinese fellow, asks how the meal was, if there is anything else I need. I can take a hint and reluctantly pay the cheque.

Using the satellite phone I call Arthur's place. When he answers I hang up without saying anything, sit in Old Faithful a few minutes longer, summoning my courage. I should have faced Arthur years ago — waiting has not made this easier.

I put Old Faithful in gear, drive slowly.

The Pirelli house is a split level, cedar-sided, located in the better part of town. The streets here are paved, the lawns manicured. The heat of day is lessening and slanted evening sunlight makes the lawns and spruce trees a brighter green. I park a few houses away, like I used to when Nina would sneak out to meet me. The memories are as vivid as the sunshine, her absence a painful void in the seat next to me. I sigh, take a deep breath, step out of the truck. Every motion is slow and deliberate. A group of kids play on a front lawn, running through a sprinkler as it arcs away from the sidewalk.

Arthur's green Forest Service truck is in the driveway.

I walk up thc path to the house, ring the bell on the front door.

For a moment nothing happens. Maybe I can still get away unscathed. But I hear the scrape of a chair from within. The inside door rattles and I brace myself. It's Arthur's wife, Madeleine, drying her hands with a small dishtowel. She's short, heavy set, has hair like a poodle and a plump, smooth face — the type of woman you'd see on a commercial for old-fashioned home baking. When she sees me, her eyes widen for a second. Then she opens the storm door. "Porter Cassel," she says quietly. "How are you?"

"I've been worse."

A wry smile. "Haven't we all. What are you doing here?"

"I want to talk to you and Arthur for a few minutes."

She doesn't ask about what but her gaze drifts sideways, toward the stairs leading to the kitchen, where I imagine Arthur is sitting, still in his Forest Service uniform, having a beer.

"Well ... I don't know if that's such a good idea."

"Just a few minutes." As if this helps.

The corner of her mouth twitches. She kneads the dishtowel, works it into a ball and looks at me with a desperate, helpless sort of look. She's pulling double duty — dealing with the loss of her daughter and the rage of her husband. She sighs and her round shoulders slump a bit farther south. "You'd better give me a minute to prepare Arthur."

She mounts the steps, displaying meaty calves, and I wonder how she's going to prepare Arthur: stuffed with a side dish of plum sauce? More likely, she needs time to hide the keys to the gun cabinet, secure any sharp objects. I hear her low murmur. Then Arthur, not so quiet.

"— the *fuck* does he want?"

More murmuring; more unpleasant adjectives spoken through clenched teeth. I wait, stare at a wooden key rack on the wall, gaze longingly outside. It's a good five minutes before Maddie comes back and I wonder if they were hoping I'd given up and gone away. Another minute or two and they might have gotten their wish. Maddie stands at the top of the stairs, motions me up.

Arthur is seated at the far end of a small kitchen table, still in his brown polyester Forest Service uniform, grey hair matted, ball cap and can of Bud in front of him. He's leaning forward, forearms rested on the tabletop, jaw clenched and eyes squinted like he's in the midst of having a boil lanced.

"Thanks for seeing me Arthur. I know this isn't easy —"

"You've got more balls than brains, Cassel."

His eyes are levelled at me like lasers, diamond hard with hatred. With the slightest glance, he could wilt houseplants, cut furniture in two. Maddie pulls out a chair opposite Arthur, motions that I should sit. I ignore the chair for the time being.

"What the fuck do you want?" asks Arthur.

There's no way to make this easier. "I need to talk to you and Maddie about Nina."

He nods, his lips pursed.

"And about what just happened, down in Curtain River."

He's waiting — he doesn't look very patient. Maddie watches, like a referee at a tennis match, her eyes darting back and forth between the opposing teams.

"I went down there and helped the cops look for evidence."

"Well aren't you a Boy Scout."

There's a conspicuous pause; I'm not sure where to start. Arthur is silent, like a Mafia Don contemplating a traitor, deciding on an appropriately gruesome punishment. Maddie stands with her arms clasped close to her body, like she's cold.

"It got me to thinking," I say. "Wondering if there's a connection."

"A connection?" Arthur sneers. "Of course there's a fucking connection."

His fists are clenched and it looks like he's got a wad of chewing tobacco in his cheek — I think he's chewing his tongue. I better give him the executive summary. "I'm talking about a connection between Nina and the fellow who was killed down south."

"You think you're some sort of cop now," Arthur says.

"Turns out, the fellow who was killed down south worked here —"

"Some kinda *private investigator* —"

"Give him a chance," Maddie says sharply. "Take a seat, Porter."

"A chance?" says Arthur. "That's more than our little girl had —"

Maddie shoots him a determined look. "Arthur —"

Arthur takes a sip of beer, chews on it, his chin jutting. He's old and angry; wrinkles and frown lines intersect on his narrow face. I don't much feel like sitting at the table with him but do anyway. This must be how The Chair in San Quentin feels; there's plenty of juice in this room. Maddie sits like a negotiator between me and her husband.

"What kind of connection?" asks Maddie. She's trying not to look hopeful.

"The guy's name was Ronald Hess," I say, looking at Maddie; it's easier to talk to her. "He worked here for 18 months before Nina was killed. The way I see it, there are a couple of possibilities. They both could have known the person who was doing this, maybe had some suspicion —"

"You don't think they were accidents?" Maddie looks frightened.

Arthur sits back, presses his palms against the edge of the table.

"Well, it is possible —"

"Christ!" Arthur pushes back his chair; an abrasive squeak that causes Maddie to wince. He glares at me as he walks past, stands by the kitchen sink, stares out an open window. I turn in my chair, don't want my back exposed. For a minute the only sounds are mosquitoes at the window screen, the tinkle of a wind chime, the muted voices of playing children.

"You think someone purposefully *killed* Nina," Maddie says.

"At this point, I'm not sure of anything."

"Someone killed her all right," Arthur says quietly. "He's sittin' right here —"

Maddie's voice is a husky groan. "Arthur —"

Arthur turns, points at me. "— pretending to be some sort of cop."

I stand. It was a mistake to have come.

"Sit down," says Maddie. She looks at Arthur. "She was my daughter too and if there's something to know, then I want to know about it!"

I remain standing, where I can see Arthur. We're like fighters at a weigh-in. Arthur gives me his best pre-fight glare, then turns it on his wife. Like a good referee, she doesn't flinch. He makes a grumbling noise you'd need a field zoologist to interpret, stares out the window.

"As for you, Porter, finish what you've started."

I swallow, nervous, glance toward Arthur. He's still turned away, staring out the window. "Like I said, both Hess and your daughter might have known the person who was doing this. I doubt they would have realized it at the time but if the killer had any doubts —"

"You make a crappy detective," Arthur says, not looking at me. "The guy who planted the bomb wouldn't have known she'd be there. It was your screw-up that she was."

"I thought of that," I say. "He might have been watching —"

He turns and stares at me. "Unless you did it. That'd explain everything."

"Arthur, I know that fits nicely with your view of the universe, but I didn't do it."

"Guilty, one way or the other," he mutters.

Maddie gives him an icy look. "We know you didn't do it, Porter."

"Thank you."

Arthur mumbles something I don't quite catch.

"Go on," says Maddie.

"Do you recall anyone that Nina knew who seemed suspicious?"

"In what way?" asks Maddie.

"The people she knew — were you uncomfortable with any of them?"

"You, for starters," says Arthur.

Maddie sighs. "I don't think so. It's so hard to say, looking back."

"Waste of time," says Arthur.

Maddie glares at him.

"Well it is."

"We'll think about it," says Maddie. "How can we get hold of you?"

"I've got a satellite phone." I give her the number.

"What are the other possibilities?" asks Arthur. It's killing him to ask.

"What happened to Nina might very well have been an accident," I tell them. "After she died, the bombings stopped until Hess was killed. This could mean the bomber had no intention of killing anybody, that he was horrified when Nina died."

Maddie clearly prefers this explanation.

Arthur stares at the linoleum. "But he started bombing again."

"Maybe it took him a few years to get over what he'd done," I say.

"The bastard," Arthur mumbles.

"Or maybe he couldn't get over it."

I wait, let them make the jump.

"You think Hess was the Lorax," Maddie says faintly.

"I've considered it. Maybe he killed himself."

Arthur is nodding; first good news he's had all day.

"Would he do that if he didn't know her?" asks Maddie.

She leading the conversation to places I've been reluctant to go.

I try to keep my voice even. "Is it possible Nina was seeing Hess?"

"What!" says Arthur. "You mean *sleeping with him*?"

The look on his face — I don't have to answer.

"You're asking us?" he says. "*We* didn't know she was sleeping with *you*."

"It's not like she would tell me," I say, my voice unsteady.

Arthur takes a step toward me. "Listen you little shit —"

I back away, toward the door.

"You be damn careful what you say about my little girl —"

Maddie stands. "Arthur, please —" But any authority she had is gone.

Arthur is fumbling with the cuff buttons of his polyester shirt. He wants to roll back his sleeves, duke it out like in some old-time movie, but he's too angry to make anything that coordinated work. There's no use trying to reason with him and I have no desire to fight Nina's father. When she was alive, I would have fought Arthur to prevent being apart from her but now it just seems pitiful. I retreat to the door, grab my boots, don't bother taking the time to slip them on. The screen door doesn't get a chance to shut behind me — it catches Arthur in the face, further enraging him. I expect him to come after me but he shouts from his front step as I walk away, carrying my boots. The kids stand on the neighbour's lawn, dripping and gawking.

The fighters return to their corners — I climb into Old Faithful, Arthur goes inside.

In my truck, I sit for a few minutes, my head leaning against the steering wheel, in no shape to drive. My throat is so constricted I can hardly breathe and everything is blurry. I'm whispering Nina's name, apologizing over and over. There's a knock on the side window.

Reluctantly, I look up.

It's Maddie. The flesh around her eyes is puffy but she's not crying — she's stronger than both Arthur and me. She motions for me to roll down the window and I wipe my cheeks, attempt some semblance of composure.

"I always knew about you, Porter," she says. "A girl talks to her mother. I didn't mention it to Arthur because it would have made things at work difficult for both of you."

I nod, try to croak a thank you.

"She loved you, Porter. She wasn't seeing anyone else."

"I'm sorry," I whisper. "I shouldn't have come."

She reaches in, pats my shoulder, walks away. She doesn't look back. I feel like an idiot for coming here, stirring things up like this. But I'm relieved.

On the way out of town, I pick up a dozen roses and stop at the cemetery, spend some time with Nina. Tell her what's been going on. Offer an apology for doubting her.

12

I ARRIVE AT Cindy's late that night to find the kids in the kitchen, fighting over who gets to make popcorn. They mob me, cling to my legs like anchors so I can't move. I set my pack by the door, give a round of hugs, then look around the corner into the living room — there's an unpleasantly familiar odour in the house tonight. Cindy and Shawn are sitting on the couch in the living room, watching a movie. Two years ago, this would have been a normal scene. Since then, they've divorced, fought a nasty custody battle which Shawn, quite rightfully, lost.

He gives me the old "hang loose" salute. "Hey buddy, how's it goin'?"

Shawn Marshall is not one of my favourite people. Tall and thin, with receding brown hair and a cocky attitude, he found Cindy when she was fresh out of college. He'd never finished high school, was working as a DJ at a nightclub and not doing that very well. They say you can't pick who you fall in love with, which is a pity because the marriage lasted only long enough to produce the three kids. It ended one night when Shawn's pregnant girlfriend came to the door, looking for Shawn. She found Cindy instead.

"I'm doing fine, Shawn. What about you? The bar close early tonight?"

"Yeah, right." He grins — a nervous grin; he knows how I feel. I shoot Cindy a what-the-hell-are-you-doing look. She's lonely, wants a whole family again; it would be too easy for her to slip into the old role. Shawn wants something a little more immediate. At least they're sitting at opposite ends of the couch. "I heard what happened down south," Shawn says. "Crappy, man."

Cindy must see that I'm ready to unload on Shawn because she gives me a look. *Be patient — he'll be gone soon.* "Shawn had the kids this afternoon," she says. "He took them out for supper and rented movies. You want to watch with us?"

This must be Cindy's way of paying him back for acting like a father for a few hours. I sit on the ottoman — the movie, *Under Seige 2*, isn't very good. Steven Seagal looks bored as he thrashes a couple of villains. Jackie Chan would kick his ass. Regardless, it wouldn't be my first choice for a children's movie. I stay long enough to establish my presence then make myself a sandwich and go down to my room by the furnace. I hear the movie end, followed soon after by the slap and click of a closing door. Cindy comes down, sits on the edge of my bed. I tell her about Fort Termination. She's a good listener.

"Can you stay for a few days?" she asks.

"No, I've got to get back. I had to fight for two days off."

The next morning Cindy makes me a big breakfast — bacon, eggs, toast, hashbrowns, coffee. I play with the kids for a half-hour, build a Lego castle, then fire up Old Faithful and head south through the city on a zigzag course toward Old Strathcona. I've been thinking about how the fires were started and want to find a cigar shop; the Yellow Pages list three in this neighbourhood.

I cross the High Level Bridge, pass girls in Spandex biking up the hill: a different kind of traffic hazard. Old Strathcona is close to the university — an area filled with student housing, little shops and cafes. You can buy just about anything around here — steel guitars, handicrafts, term papers — but at nine in the morning almost nothing is open, including the tobacconists I need to see. I spend an hour in a Java Hut, read the paper. There's plenty about the Lorax but nothing new.

Ten o'clock finally arrives. I've had too much coffee and walk light-headed and jittery to the smoke shop. The store is small and narrow and mostly empty. Cigars are displayed in wooden trays inside a glass case, neatly arranged like miniature brown artillery shells. The smell is pungent but vaguely pleasant, like the memory of a father sitting in his living room, puffing on his Sunday cigar. An older fellow in a T-shirt stands behind a cluttered counter, flipping through a magazine. He's got plenty of hair under his chin but none on his head; the classic inverted hairline.

He watches me inspect his cigar display. "Can I help you?"

"What's the longest cigar you carry?"

"The longest cigar ..." He strums his fingers on the counter and peers over the top of his bifocals — the scholarly tobacconist. "We've got a couple of brands that come in an eight inch," he says. "They're pretty long."

"Could you show them to me?"

He joins me at the glass cabinet and we peer together into the tobacco aquarium. To a rookie like me, cigars all look pretty much the same. I was hoping for a brand or two which might be distinctive enough to be traceable to a purchaser.

"What I really need is the longest-burning cigar."

He looks at me through his glasses, head tilted slightly back, eyes magnified to comic proportions. "Longest burning," he mutters. "Well, that would be a function of length and diameter, or what we call ring size. It also depends on how tightly it was rolled."

I nod in respectful ignorance. "So which one of these would fit that bill?"

"Well ..." He tugs on his beard. "Hard to say really. They're not rated like that."

"Could you hazard a guess?"

"You could just buy a few," he says. "Try them out."

"I could. But I don't smoke."

He strokes his beard and frowns, no doubt wondering what a non-smoker is doing in a cigar shop. A heathen in the vicarage. He looks nervously toward the counter where a group of university students are impatient to ruin their health, waiting to pay for their cigars.

"I'm an arson investigator," I add quickly. "I think a cigar was used as a fuse."

The old man adjusts his bifocals, suddenly intrigued. "An arson investigator? Really?"

"Any advice you could give me could prove invaluable."

"Well —" He turns back to the display case. "Let me think."

"I'm looking for a cigar that would take quite some time to burn down."

"Fascinating," he says. "Pity you don't smoke."

"Yes, but I was hoping —"

"Cigars that is. Because then you'd know that they're damp." He looks at me like an opponent in a chess game, waiting to see if I can overcome his latest strategy. It takes me a second to see the significance.

"Damp?"

"Yes, quite damp. In fact, they're stored in a humidor to keep them suitably moist."

"But they do burn or people couldn't smoke them."

He allows himself a faint smile. "Yes, of course."

"So why wouldn't they work as a fuse?"

"Try smoking one, young man."

"No thanks."

"They're rather fussy. They tend to go out unless you draw on them."

My theory is rapidly going up in damp smoke.

"Now, if it was *me*," he says, placing a hand on his chest, "I'd take a pin and poke holes through the outside leaf, then dry it on a windowsill or in an oven. That should dehydrate it sufficiently and allow it to draw in enough air as it burns."

I'm impressed. "Have you given this advice to anyone else?"

He looks taken aback. "Oh no, not at all."

"So, if it *was* you, what sort of cigar would you pick?"

He peers into his cabinet, deep in thought. Suddenly, he brightens. "I've got *just* the thing," he says, going to his counter. Ignoring the students, he rummages below the cash register, mumbling to himself. When he stands, he has a long narrow brown wooden box in his hand, a father-of-the-bride look on his face. "This," he says dramatically, "is an Emperador cigar. They don't come any longer, unless you get them custom made. Fourteen inches. It would make Lewinsky blush."

The university students are impressed, peer curiously over my shoulder as he hands me the box; mahogany by the looks of it. Beside the brand, pressed into the wood, is a smeared announcement, boasting that it's the largest marketed cigar in the world. A Guinness World Record, it's the H-bomb of cigars — let's hope we never have to use it. The back of the box says Mexico. A tiny warning label on the end advises, courtesy of Health and Welfare Canada, that danger to health increases with amount smoked and to avoid inhaling. It seems a little like telling an alcoholic to avoid swallowing.

"You sell many of these?"

"Not many," he says regretfully. "Mostly around Christmas. They're special order."

"What about this one? Who ordered it?"

"Some guy, a lawyer I think. His wife was going to have a baby, so he ordered a dozen of them. When his wife lost the baby, I felt sorry for him, gave him a refund."

Probably the first time anyone felt sorry for a lawyer.

"Do you keep a record of who orders these?"

He shakes his head. "I just order them."

"So there's no way of knowing who bought them."

"Not unless they paid with a credit card."

I doubt the arsonist used a credit card but it's worth mentioning to the task force — they'd have the authority to obtain the sales records. "Who else sells these?"

"Any good smoke shop. Or you can order them over the Internet."

Wonderful. I thank the tobacconist, buy the cigar; $18.95 plus tax.

The students clean out the rest of his Emperador inventory.

Carl is on the duty desk when I arrive in Curtain River later that afternoon. He's busy answering radios, making notes, ordering supplies. There's been a fire and he doesn't have time to talk. I sit outside the duty room for a few minutes, try to chat with the receptionist — a large lady with a passion for one-way conversation — but even she's too busy. The only other person in the building is Gary Hanlon, who's bent over his desk, a frown on his face.

I wait for a lull in the radio talk, stick my head into the duty room.

"How's it going, Carl?"

He gives me one of those I-told-you-so looks. I take a seat opposite his desk.

"I've been meaning to get rid of that chair," he grumbles.

"How big is your fire?"

He's rubbing his eyes. "Forty acres, close to a campground."

"Man-caused?"

He sighs, slumps in his chair, swivels absently back and forth, making me wait. He's got that glazed, stressed-out look which usually takes days to acquire. "Yes, it was man-caused. Would have been nice to have a fire investigator around, but since we didn't we sent out one of our field people." He gives me a disapproving look to make sure I know how this inconvenienced him. "No cake pan on this one though. Some damn random camper. What about you? How'd your little fire go?"

"Cake pan, same guy."

He nods, thinking about this. "You any closer to catching him?"

"Maybe. We found a bootprint."

"A bootprint?"

"Yeah, the guy stepped in a muddy area, left a fairly decent impression."

"So, I guess that's progress."

"Only if we can find the boot."

"What about the Fort?" he asks. "You find out anything about Hess?"

I think back to the mechanic in his purple-flowered beanie. "Not much. It seems he was a pretty average guy. A little better than average actually. Which leaves me nowhere."

Carl runs a hand through his hair. "Well, what did you think you'd find, Porter?"

"I don't know — something."

"You talked to Arthur?"

I nod.

"How'd that go?"

"Pretty good. He managed to control himself for nearly five minutes."

Carl's got a wistful half-smile, picturing it. "He went ballistic?"

"Intercontinental. I left in a hurry."

"How's Maddie doing?"

"Better than Arthur."

For a minute or two we both stare at the floor, grieve for the past. The radio demands attention and Carl sighs, deep and weary. There's a fire status change. An equipment order. A firefighter who needs to go home for urgent family business which, it turns out after some back-and-forth questioning, is actually a court case. Carl is not impressed; the firefighter knew about this and shouldn't have gone out. When Carl's done he looks over at me. "You're back to work?"

"Until the next crisis."

"Good, you're going on man-up. The sector boss went to the fire so you're it."

Carl returns to his radios, directs operations. I've got a half-hour to spare and return to Old Faithful, operate on my backpack, give it a quick checkup. It's in need of major replacement surgery; I ransacked it at the last fire, so I run downtown, buy replacements. I also pick up a small bottle of pop, which will come in handy later when I conduct a little experiment, play with my big cigar. When I get back to the ranger station, the helicopter is late so I make a call from a phone in the empty coffee room.

It's answered on the fifth ring. "Hello?"

"Hello." I switch personalities. "This is Brent Hancock. Is this Angela Murtow?"

"No, this is Kim, her assistant." The voice is curt, but polite.

"Oh ... Is Angela around?"

"No, she's gone to a rally. Can I take a message?"

"Well ... umm ... maybe you can help me. I just moved to Curtain River and I've heard lots of good things about your group, the Mountain Guardians. Like you guys, I'm appalled by the horrendous clearcut destruction of the pristine west country and I'd like to attend your next meeting."

Kim is excited; the path to an environmentalist's heart is paved with adjectives. The more, the better. She tells me the next meeting — a special gathering to discuss recent events — is at the Chowder Creek community hall this Wednesday night at eight o'clock. I tell her I'll be there and she says she's looking forward to meeting me, asks why I moved to Curtain River. I tell her I want to open a health food store, sell organics and hemp T-shirts, maybe some handicrafts and local art. By the time we disconnect, we're practically soulmates.

Now all I have to do is convince Carl to let me come in Wednesday night.

The helicopter arrives, flown by a pilot I know. We chat during the flight. From the air, the staging camp doesn't look like much — a cluster of tent frames close to a helipad where we'll remain to wait for a fire call. But after recent events, it'll be a holiday. We land and I haul out my pack and bedroll. Men in bright yellow coveralls and red hardhats stand among the trees; fluorescent natives watching the pilgrims alight.

"Well if it isn't Mr. Porter Cassel."

The crew leader is a tall, wide native with an ugly scar on his cheek and a smile that lends him the air of a pirate. I've worked with him before; his crew is top-notch.

I shake his beefy hand. "How come you're not on the fire, Alphonse?"

Alphonse lives for flame and he makes a disgusted sound, like a bear finding an empty picnic basket. "Damn dispatch," he grumbles. To a firefighter, Dispatch is a mysterious god, capable of moving men and equipment anywhere at a whim. "They sent the south crew even though we're closer. Said we needed to stay put because of the hazard."

I'm kind of glad they didn't send him. "Who was your sector boss?"

"Frank Whiteknife," he says, shaking his head. "He got to go too."

"Everybody but you."

"Yeah, that's a humbug."

I slap him on the shoulder. "Don't worry, your time is coming."

Before you arrive on man-up, everything is a rush. Pack your bags. Get a briefing. Catch the helicopter. When you arrive at camp, time begins to slow, like an Eatmore commercial. Man-up is sitting at a strategic location in the forest, waiting for a fire. So long as radios are manned and equipment is ready, there's no hurry to do much of anything. I check the gear, Alphonse following, watching to see if I find anything amiss. I want to give him a hard time about something but the pulaskis are sharp, the pumps and saws clean and ready; everything is squared away. I concede, tell him they've done a good job. His smile grows wider, like he's found a galleon loaded with gold.

"Now what, boss?" he asks. "Pump practice?"

"Too late in the day. We could get a call."

Alphonse looks disappointed — he's a man of action.

"Let's try the creek," I suggest. "Go fishing."

He brightens, wanders off to collect his fishing gear. I dump my pack and bedroll in a vacant tent frame, take out my world record cigar, peel the plastic wrap off the box. It's one hell of a stogie and I hold it to my lips, like something out of a corny gangster movie.

"I didn't know you smoked." Alphonse, at the door of the tent

frame.

I lower the cigar, feel a bit sheepish. "I don't. This is for an experiment."

"An experiment?" He laughs. "Like Bill Clinton?"

"Not that type of experiment. I want to see how fast it burns."

"Oh." He looks puzzled. "Want me to smoke it for you?"

"No, I need to know the smoulder rate. Besides, I wouldn't do that to you."

He sits on a bed frame across from me. "What sorta experiment?"

"One that involves explosives."

Alphonse rubs his hands. "Count me in, boss."

I read the fine print on the green band of the cigar, a guarantee by the manufacturer, slip the band off and put it in my pocket. I'll check with them later. I rummage in my pack, find a compass, use the ruler on the side to measure the length of the cigar. Thirteen-and-a-half inches. I use a pocket knife — still haven't found my hunting knife — to trim off the end of the cigar so it dries faster, leaving thirteen inches; measure the diameter, write all this down in my handy-dandy notebook. Alphonse leans forward to see what I'm writing. From a first aid kit, I take out a safety pin and begin to poke holes along the shaft of the cigar, through the tobacco-leaf wrapping.

"What a shame," he mutters. "A perfectly good cigar."

I set the perforated cigar on the top of the tent frame wall near the door, where it'll receive plenty of heat and airflow. "Okay Alphonse, let's go fishing."

At the creek, we test our radios, make sure we have contact in case of a fire call. Firefighters in coveralls and hardhats lounge on the shaded bank like construction workers in the Garden of Eden. I unfold my portable fishing rod, attach a small fly. Alphonse has nothing but a tangle of fishing line.

"Where's your rod?"

"Rod?" He grins. "I'm an Indian. I don't need no stinkin' rod."

His fishing kit is a dozen feet of line and several lures he's obviously made here, out of materials at hand. He selects the cut-off bottom of a small fork — the tines bent into hooks, scraps of plastic flagging for colour — ties the line to a long willow branch. I laugh at him but he catches a trout while I get skunked.

"Take that, white man."

"Yeah, yeah ..."

By ten o'clock the next morning, the cigar is as dry as it's going to get, the outer wrapping beginning to crack and separate. And it's brittle. The arsonist would have to transport a cigar this dry in a box or it would break. I organize the crew, explain that we're going to do a little test, have them collect deadwood from the forest, make a pile in a bare area behind the camp. As a precaution, we set up a pump, string some fire hose; I don't want this turning into another Forest Service legend. From my pack, I take out the rest of the materials I brought from Edmonton.

A cake pan, about eight-inches square and two-inches deep.

A small can of "F" black powder.

My polyethylene pop bottle.

To be prudent, I assemble the device in my tent. Alphonse

stands guard but since he's facing the wrong way, spying through a flap in the tent, I don't think he'll be all that effective. I cut off the bottom quarter of the pop bottle, pour in an inch and a half of gunpowder and stick in the cigar — which is far too long and topples over. Some sort of additional ballast is needed. I consider adding a base of sand but doubt this is what the arsonist used; we would have found traces mixed with the residue. Then it occurs to me that a cigar this long will produce a lot of ash and a hot ember on the gunpowder would result in a premature ignition. An ash skirt is needed, perhaps a cardboard disc with a hole in the centre; this would also stabilize the cigar. I cut a disc from the flap of a cardboard box, make a hole in the centre for the cigar, find the disc snaps tightly into a groove in the top of my pop bottle cup. The cigar is held firmly in place; the device tight, stable and fully self-contained. I may be onto something.

The next step must be done in the open.

I carry the ignition device to the brushpile, position the cake pan under the edge of the pile and set the device in the centre of the pan. From a jug of diesel meant for the generator, I pour in three fingers of the thick, greenish liquid. Unlike gasoline, which explodes within feet of a spark, diesel has a low flash point and won't ignite unless in direct contact with a flame. Regardless, the firefighters hang back in the shade of the trees. Alphonse crouches behind me like SWAT team backup as I pour the diesel.

He takes a step back when I pull out a lighter. "Careful there, white man."

The cigar is difficult to light, standing up like that. I pull it out, hold the lighter to the end, take a few test drags to get it going. Bad idea for a non-smoker; it tastes like a barn fire. I gasp and sputter. Now I know why Health and Welfare Canada advises against inhaling.

Alphonse laughs. "Good stuff, eh?"

My tongue feels like it was dipped in acid. "Here, you try."

"With pleasure." He puffs casually on the cigar, holding it as though he were an oil baron out inspecting his holdings, puts on an exaggerated English accent. The noble savage meets Monty Python. "I say there — old boy, smashing nice weather we're having."

"Give me that."

The tip of the cigar is grey and hot, pungent smoke wafting around us. Carefully, I insert the other end through the hole in the cardboard disc, seat it firmly in the gunpowder, set the smoking device in the pan of diesel.

"Now what?" asks Alphonse.

I make a note of the time. "Now we wait, old boy."

I lit the cigar at 9:46 this morning. At 4:32 in the afternoon there's a cannon-like blast from behind the tent frames. Naturally, I'm in the latrine and miss the initial ignition, but I get out in time to see a white cloud mushroom into the air. When I arrive the brush pile is engulfed in flame — the blast from the gunpowder has splattered the diesel.

From down by the creek, I hear the rumble of a fire pump. Firefighters appear from the shade of the trees, headed for a nozzle at the end of a nearby hose. Good response time, but I don't want the fire put out and gesture with a hand across my throat; kill the pump. The firefighters hesitate, ready for action. The hose fills with water like a snake coming to life. There's a cough and sputter from the nozzle and a thin jet of water rockets through the air. I shake my head and the firefighters look disappointed, idly spray the ground around the fire. I make a call on my radio and the pump falls silent. The nozzleman looks at me like a kid with an empty water pistol.

"What's up boss?" Alphonse, arriving from the creek.

"I'm going to let it burn. I want to see what's left in the pan."

He gestures to his men. They retreat to the shade of the trees.

He's sweating, big droplets running down his cheeks. "Gunpowder worked good, huh?"

"What gunpowder?" He wasn't supposed to be watching when I put it together.

"I sorta peeked."

"Yeah, I figured." I don't want anyone getting ideas. "Just don't pass it along."

He grins. "My lips are sealed. Omerta, man."

I sit in the shade of the trees, do some math as I watch the pile sizzle and settle. Total elapsed time from ignition to initiation was 6 hours and 46 minutes. Considering I seated the cigar an inch and a half into the gunpowder, that leaves a fuse length of eleven and a half inches. Simple division gives me a burn rate of about 35 minutes per inch. If the arsonist travelled away from the device at a rate of 60 miles an hour, how far away would he be at the time the fire started? The problem echoes like a word question from sixth grade math class. My answer: 406 miles. Mathematically, this is correct. Practically, this means we'd have to search half the province.

"What do you figure, boss?" Alphonse, lying on his side on the moss, the natural angle of repose. "You think this is how he's doing it?" He watches the news like everyone else.

"Maybe." I ponder the flickering pile. "He sure knows what he's doing."

"How many fires has this guy started?"

"Too many, Alphonse. You think any local boys are looking for work?"

For a minute Alphonse is silent. Natives can be touchy about the suggestion they've started fires in the past despite this being a traditional method of native grassland management. Now it's a traditional method to manage unemployment. "No," he says, "I don't think so. It's been pretty busy the last two summers. Even without them fires, everyone would be working."

a half-hour later, the fire is pretty much out. All that remains is a circle of ash and smouldering branch ends the fire couldn't reach. Toward one edge is the cake pan, no longer shiny and new.
We stand around the circle like worshippers at a henge.

"That was a pretty hot fire," says one of the firefighters.

"What exploded like that?" asks another.

"I saw him put in some gas —"

"It was diesel —"

"Diesel don't explode like that."

Alphonse gives them a look and conversation ceases. I squat, inspect the contents of the pan. Grey wood ash, fine and powdery. I blow lightly, which lifts some of the ash out of the way. There's a loose, cylindrical lump of coarse ash — the remains of the cigar — and a thin black scab about two inches in diameter, probably the pop bottle. The evidence is fragile, easily disturbed. I'm going to have to be more careful, like the boys from Ident.

"You figure out what you needed to know?" asks Alphonse.

I nod, pick up the pan. "You can spray this area down now."

Three hours into Saturday afternoon we get a call and my holiday in the woods is over. I spend a few days in smoke and ash, favouring my good ankle, working in heat like the blast out of a jet engine. The fire isn't large, but because the ground is so dry the fire has burned deep into the forest floor. I call the fire extinguished on

Wednesday morning and by Wednesday afternoon I'm in the duty room, still wearing my hardhat and charcoal-smeared coveralls, weighed down with a radio belt and water bottles, ready to be debriefed.

"Take a load off," Carl says, waving away an imaginary cloud. "And shower."

I unclasp the belt, drop it with a clunk on his desk.

"Not here," he snaps. His desk is cluttered with grocery orders and smoke messages. His face is cluttered with stress lines and he hasn't shaved in a few days. The big wall map is busy with magnets — when I was in the ash there were three other fires going, all started by careless weekend campers. *Good little boys and girls give matches to moms and dads.* One of the fires is still out of control, trying to climb out of a gully and overtop a ridge. The bombers have gone to higher priority fires up north, leaving us without major airstrike capability. Carl's patience is thin.

He rubs his fists against his eyes. "How'd the fire go?"

"A lot of work for a few acres."

"Any clue who started it?"

"No. It was abandoned. Random camping area."

"I know the place," says Carl. The radio squawks; the debrief is over.

I wait until he's finished on the radio, consider telling him about my cigar experiment but now probably isn't the best time. Later, when we can both relax. "You need me tonight?"

"Why?" he says. "You got a date?"

"There's a Mountain Guardian meeting I want to go to."

Carl gives me a disgusted look. "Waste of your time, Porter."

The radio demands attention again, asking when the drinking water is coming out to the fire. An anxious voice claims the men are getting pretty thirsty. Carl frowns, shifts through a sedimentary scatter of paper. "Shit," he mumbles, looking at me. "I forgot to send some. Can you run some water out there?"

I look at the map; it'll be a quick trip. "Sure."

Carl keys the mike. "CR-3, this is dispatch. Your water is on its way."

I pick up my radio belt. "You sure you don't want to come?"

"To that meeting?"

"Yeah, see what it's about?"

Carl shakes his head. "A bunch of self-appointed do-gooders sitting around and talking. They don't understand ecology and the only thing they ever accomplish is pissing off a few loggers."

"So you've been to a meeting?"

"Porter, they think the Forest Service is secretly splicing the genes of Arctic char into pine trees, so they'll be frost resistant. Like we've got some secret laboratory in a cave somewhere. Trust me, the Mountain Guardians are a waste of your time."

"So, that would be no?"

"Regrettably, I'll be stuck here. But feel free to pass on my regards."

I borrow Carl's forestry truck, drive to the cache behind the office. The cache is the name given to the building behind every ranger station where basic supplies are stored and minor maintenance is carried out on chainsaws and hand tools. During fire season the cache gets pretty cluttered, and today I have to pick my way over piles of dirty hose. I search for empty water pails — a scarce commodity because no one ever seems to return them — fill several from a garden hose and load them in the back of Carl's truck.

The fire is 30 miles out of town and I drive through pastureland, simmering under rippling waves of heat, and into the forest, dormant, waiting for rain that is weeks overdue. From a rise in the road I see an anvil of grey smoke and call a nearby helicopter to ferry in the pails of water. When the bird lands, I'm tempted to jump in, lend a hand at the fire, but instead load the machine and watch it auger away. The fire will be here tomorrow. Or there'll be a new one.

On the way back to town I get a flat tire, make it to Carl's place just before eight o'clock. I'm faint from heat, work and lack of food, but there's no time for rest or chow. I take a two-minute shower and take 20 minutes to find the Chowder Creek community hall.

13

THE CHOWDER CREEK community hall sits across the road from a tiny church and graveyard. The hall is an old, white-painted clapboard building scarcely larger than a house, no doubt built at a time when people travelled by horse and buggy. Back then, people worried about surviving in the shadow of the mountains. Today, a different generation is meeting here to help the mountains survive.

Or so they believe. Opinions differ.

A handmade cardboard sign tacked to a fencepost by the driveway announces the meeting and a dozen vehicles fill the parking lot in front of the hall, but there's no one in sight. I'm late and park along the shoulder of the road. An orange Volkswagen Beetle with a dented fender crouches among the minivans and I feel a twist of anticipation.

The hall door is propped open and I go in.

"Your name please?"

A young woman, short and plump, dark hair and pale face, stands just inside the door. She holds a clipboard. "Brent Hancock," I say. She smiles, offers me a warm hand to shake. It's Kim, Murtow's assistant, and she's glad to see me. I tell her I'm glad to be here.

“The meeting is just about to start Mr. Hancock. Please take a seat.”

The hall is long and narrow, the floor made of pine boards darkened with age and use. Plastic stacking chairs, stencilled on the back with the name of the hall, are arranged in uneven rows. Most of the people are in the middle rows. I search for Telson. She’s off to one side and I squeeze along the wall. She has a pad of paper in her lap and moves her knee politely out of the way, then glances over to see who is taking a seat next to her.

“Porter.” She’s surprised to see me.

“Mizz Telson. How are you?”

She brushes hair back from her face. “Good. I’m good. How about you?”

“I’m doing all right. Are you a member of the Mountain Guardians?”

She laughs lightly. “No. I was driving past and saw the sign.”

“Really.” I glance at her pad of paper. It’s blank. “You here to take notes?”

“This?” She looks at the pad. “I was going to write a letter.”

I nod but say nothing. I’m not sure I believe she was just driving past, but don’t want to press her. It’s none of my business if she has a bit of a green side. When it comes right down to it, I think we all do, forest rangers probably more than most. They say if you scratch a logger, you find an environmentalist and vice versa. Lately though, the battle lines have pretty much been drawn. Which is why I’m here. My cruise on the Internet mentioned something called decoupling — a strategy used by some environmental groups to separate their legitimate from their illegal activities. An example of this might be a group which secretly engages in ecotage — sabotage to further environmental objectives — then uses its popular name to receive supposedly anonymous communications from the saboteurs. The sabotage is denounced, giving the group the illusion of respectability while gaining media coverage for both the saboteurs and the group. The Lorax may be a decoupling strategy and I look around for anyone of the same build and size as the man in camouflage I stumbled across near the bombing scene. Hard to tell with everyone sitting.

"What about you?" she asks. "Why are you here?"

"I was just driving past, thought there was a party."

"I doubt this will be much of a party."

"Then I won't bring in my veggie tray."

She smiles as though privately amused, doodles on her paper.

"I was looking for you the other day," I say casually.

"Really?" She raises a critical eye.

"I was hoping to take you to the beach."

"Maybe I don't want to go anymore. It's not wise to keep a lady waiting."

I'm not sure if she's serious, but the meeting is getting underway. A tall, thin woman walks to a plywood podium. Her hair is long and slate grey, pulled back from a stern, bony face. In her youth, she must have been a striking woman. Now she could be the aging headmistress of an English boarding school. Or the nanny from hell. This must be Angela Murtow, former philosophy teacher, now head Mountain Guardian. She pulls half-glasses from a pocket and coldly stares down the barbarians.

The general murmur of conversation peters out.

"Good evening." Her voice is strong. "It's good to see so many of you here. As you know, I called this meeting to discuss recent events. In particular, I'm talking about the resurgence of activity of this so-called Lorax." She pauses, looks over the top of her half-glasses to check if her class is paying attention. "Until now, we've avoided this topic — in my experience, extremism rarely garners sympathy. But this time the Lorax has struck in our backyard and people will look to us for a comment. We have a duty to respond. How we respond will further define how we are perceived. I'm opening the floor for discussion."

There's a long silence. Murtow stands and waits, the patient hall monitor. There's about 20 people here, more women than men, everyone dressed in jeans and Western shirts. I'm tempted to give her my opinion of the Lorax, but doubt it will be well-received. I want to remain inconspicuous. Finally, an older lady in the front row speaks up, her voice thin and tremulous. "I think we have to abhor the violence," she says. She's knitting, needles poised, yarn wrapped around one finger. If nothing else, she'll get a pair of socks out of the meeting. I'm tempted to tell her I take a size eleven.

"Yes," Murtow says. "Violence is rarely sympathetic."

There's a murmur of agreement, interrupted by a guy in the second row.

"Well, I don't know about that," he says loudly. He's about 50, overweight, with a bulbous varicose nose set in a grouchy face. "Maybe them loggers brought it on themselves. They must be doing something wrong or the Lorax wouldn't have gone after them."

There's a mummer of assent I find troubling. Clearly, the group believe the Lorax is in the right.

"They're probably part of that gene experiment," someone says.

"Yes," comes another comment. "And they're cutting *way* too many trees."

"That's why they're doing the experiments — they need to grow the trees faster ..."

The meeting continues on a predictable trajectory. The usual myths and misconceptions are aired and the consensus seems to be that logging should be outlawed. You'd think none of them live in wooden houses or use toilet paper. Emotions run high and voices rise in excitement. It's like watching a talk show without a moderator and finally, I can't take it anymore.

"If the forest wasn't logged," I say, "it would burn."

Heads turn and there's a shocked silence. I've blasphemed.

"It's a dynamic system. It isn't always going to look like you see it today."

A long moment of silence; they may burn me at the cross. Murtow peers at me over her glasses, her expression demanding an explanation for this insolence. I suppose I could just stop, go to the principal's office and take my 50 lashes. But of course I don't. "The forest around here is pine and pine regenerates through fire. So unless you want it to burn off, or allow it to become infested with pests and disease, it'll have to be cut." Another silence and for a moment I think I'm getting through, then Murtow looks away, shuffles a few papers and the meeting resumes. I've been disregarded and understand why Carl didn't want to come.

"I see you came to make friends," whispers Telson.

"Good thing I'm close to the door."

A discussion ensues on how it might be possible to publicly abhor violence while still drawing attention to the underlying problem of clear-cutting. Sounds a lot like decoupling. From somewhere behind me, a deep voice cuts through the conversation.

"You've got it all wrong. Why denounce violence?"

It's a man in the back row, sitting alone. He's young, wearing a jean jacket, ball cap and work boots. He looks to be the same size as the man in camo, but the ball cap isn't crimped in the middle and the boots are brown, not black. But these are superficial differences, easily changed.

"Those bastards should be scared when they head out to the bush," he says. He's leaned back, an arm flopped over another chair, relaxed. "They should know someone is watching, that there's going to be consequences when they screw up."

I wonder how he thinks Nina Pirelli and Ronald Hess screwed up and stare at him, wanting to make eye contact, to see if there's a flash of recognition, something that might give me a clue, but Murtow has his attention. "We all know your opinions Reggie, but someone died here. We can't endorse that kind of violence on either moral or ideological grounds. That's not what we're about and the merest suggestion would destroy any community support we might have."

"What community support!" says Reggie. "Everyone works at the sawmill."

"All the more reason to be careful how we present ourselves."

Reggie grumbles a bit, but is quiet. I make a mental note to look him up.

The meeting drags on. Telson doodles unicorns and rainbows. We play tic-tac-toe. Finally, it's decided the Mountain Guardians will release a comment denouncing the bombing as an unacceptable reaction to a genuine concern. One way or the other, they're determined to get some mileage out of this tragedy. I'd like to infiltrate the group, but I'm pretty sure I've blown my chance. I need help from someone they wouldn't know, look over at Telson — the gypsy vegetarian doodling smiling flowers on her pad of paper — and dismiss the thought. Perfect as she would be for the job, I have no intention of placing any more women in harm's way.

The discussion swings toward more mundane concerns — housekeeping and fundraising. Bake sales and raffles to save the world. Telson leaves with me and we stand in the parking lot near her Bug. It's dusk, cooler but pleasant. Soon the first few stars will come out.

"You have any supper plans?" I ask.

She considers, gives me a sly smile. "Why? Are you asking me out?"

Once again, she makes me feel like a teenager. "Maybe. Yes."

"Well ... I sort of have plans."

I must look comically crestfallen because she laughs. "I'm kidding, Porter."

We agree to meet at a restaurant, where she parks her Bug. I suggest we get take-out, find a spot with a view and watch the stars come out over the mountains. She's agreeable and with two warm, brown paper bags in hand we climb into Old Faithful, head out of town.

"Don't you find it strange to have the steering wheel on the wrong side?" she says.

Old Faithful is an English machine. "You get used to it."

There's a ridge facing west, overlooking the town, which I spotted on my helicopter trip in from the fire. It takes a while in the dark to find where the trail leaves the main road, Telson stomping an imaginary brake pedal as we round corners, but we clear a line of trees to find a panoramic view of dark mountains, sparkling sky and the Christmas tree sprawl of town lights.

"Wow." Telson sits up. "This is really something."

We get out, sit on the dry grass; it smells of sage and juniper. We dig into our paper bags. The food is in little Styrofoam trays and is still hot. Neither of us says much as we eat and I steal a glance at her now and then. There's a sliver of waning moon and she's a mysterious figure in the moonlight, long, wavy hair and slender hands. The tiny metal stud in her nose gleams like molten metal. She's so different from Nina, but in a way that's comforting.

"You see that really bright light over there," I say. "That's Jupiter."

"Really?"

"And that one to the left and down, that's Saturn."

She sets aside her Styrofoam tray. "I always thought those were stars."

"No, they're planets. With a good pair of binoculars, you can see their moons."

She sighs, leans forward and hugs her knees. "People don't look at the sky enough."

For a long time neither of us say anything. I want to move closer, put my arm around her, but somehow feel it's the wrong thing to do right now. Or it's the right thing and I'm an idiot. Neither possibility is very comforting.

"Porter, are you married?" She says this without looking at me.

"No, I'm not married. Why?"

A long pause. "No reason," she says.

There's always a reason for a question like that. Next, she's going to ask if I'm gay. I make a pre-emptive strike by moving over, sitting closer. She looks at me and smiles.

"You seem married."

"To a ghost. It's an awkward arrangement."

She brushes hair away from her face. "Just my luck."

"I've had a little experience with luck too. The bad type anyway."

Her hand finds mine. "You want to talk about it?"

"No," I say. "But this helps. Let's leave it at that for now."

14

CARL IS FINALLY OFF the duty desk. He's frazzled from the stress and long hours, is talking in short sentences, like he's still on the radio. It's Saturday, but like everyone else in the fire business, he needs the overtime and so he's still working. We head out together to demobilize a fire camp. It's a nice, mindless sort of job.

"It's a split shift Porter. You're supposed to gear up slowly."

"I am gearing up slowly."

I'm driving an International three-ton stakebox so old that if it breaks down we're going to have to go to the museum for parts. Carl is slumped in the passenger side, wearing sunglasses and knawing on a hunk of homemade deer jerky.

"Pull that button up when you shift," he says.

"You want to drive?"

Carl says nothing, inscrutable behind his sunglasses. If it was up to him, we'd be doing this with a team of horses and a buckboard, which would probably be just as fast. I skip a gear or two and the truck lurches, the old stake sides creaking and flopping. Carl slides a few degrees farther down the seat.

"You meet the crazies?" he asks.

"The Mountain Guardians?"

"Yeah. What'd you think?"

I picture Angela Murtow at the podium, lips pursed — the picture of piety. The lady who was knitting. Reggie, frothing at the mouth. "They're a different bunch. I made the mistake of trying to explain pine ecology."

"Which I'm sure they appreciated."

"Not exactly."

Carl chuckles. "Porter Cassel — leaper of small buildings and dispeller of myths."

"It wasn't a total loss. Christina Telson was there."

"The girl? She a Guardian?"

"No, I think she was just curious."

"Uh-huh." He gnaws on his jerky. Ahead, the mountains are cloaked, the air filled with a fine solution of wood smoke and road dust. The fire we're headed to is extinguished, but others are still burning farther north and to the west. The air smells like burning bark and grass.

"How'd they react to the bombing?"

"The Guardians? They're milking it."

Carl nods as if he expected this, gazes out the window. I'm thinking about Murtow's little group — locals concerned about their backyard; maybe a few from the city. Watchers and whistle-blowers, they struck me as mostly harmless. Except for one.

"Carl, what do you know about a guy named Reggie?"

"Reggie Barnes?"

"I didn't catch his last name. Young guy, long brown hair, sorta chunky."

"Yeah — that'd be Reggie Barnes. He worked for us a few years ago, as a warehouseman. Not our best warehouseman; he had a little problem with inventory. We're flying a patrol one day and pass what looks like a small man-up camp — Forest Service tents. When we stop, these guys come out, drinking beer, just pissed.

They've got Forest Service lanterns, chainsaws, campstoves. They're Reggie's buddies. Said he lent the stuff to them."

"Really?"

"Yeah. Reggie had a different concept of lending. We had to let him go."

We grind uphill on a gravel road. Empty, the truck is lugging, everything vibrating. Dust rises in sheets from the floor, the door panels, behind the seat. I open the window to let this airborne portion of the road return home but it doesn't much help, just sucks in wood smoke. The abrasive mix doesn't seem to bother Carl, who lights a cigarette.

"How can you do that?"

He blows a smoke ring. "Do what?"

"Smoke when you're engulfed in smoke."

"This smoke is better," he says. "It has nicotine."

I downshift, turn onto a narrow logging road. The gear from the fire camp we're demobilizing will be flown to the road by helicopter. I park, call the fire boss, confirm that we're ready. As usual, they're behind schedule and we'll have to wait.

Carl pulls out a paperback — one of those wilderness adventure, turn-of-the-fur trade books. The character on the cover looks a little like Carl with his buckskin jacket — all he needs is an Indian princess to rescue. I look around, wishing I too had brought something to read, end up reading the Forest Service stickers on the dash. Safety First seems to be the main character; they don't have much of a plot. "Carl, do you think Reggie could have done it?"

Carl looks up. "Done what?" He's still stuck in the story, riding into the hills.

"The bombings. You think he's capable of doing something like that?"

"Reggie?" Carl shakes his head. "He's too lazy."

I think about this for a minute. "What do you mean?"

"God forbid they actually decide to do something, get their hands dirty."

"You're talking about the Guardians?"

"They're such a bunch of hypocrites," he says, closing his book and sitting up. "We're supposed to be the ones protecting the environment — us, the Forest Service — and they hate us. They think we're only here to help the sawmills rape the land. At one time we were respected. It was a badge of honour to be a ranger. Now, we're just bureaucrats, civil servants. We've lost our credibility. That's why these sorts of groups are springing up."

"And you think they should be doing something? Getting they're hands dirty?"

"That's not what I meant," Carl says. "They'll just never be effective."

"Like the Forest Service?"

"Like the Forest Service should be."

Carl sounds like one of those old time rangers, complaining about how soft the Service has become. In their day, they rode horses, slept under the stars. His green underwear is too tight. But he does have a point — we used to get out a lot more when I first was a ranger.

"We have to get back to our roots," he says. "Our core business —"

"You run next fall, I'll vote for you."

Finally, I hear a deep throb and the dark shape of a helicopter materializes in the smoke, a net full of gear hanging from a long line. Carl's campaigning is over for the time being. The net is dropped by the truck and the helicopter augers back to the camp. We hump tents and melons of dirty hose into the truck, fold the net to exchange for the next full one. I'm thankful for the work; there's something soothing about manual labour, so thoughtless and fully absorbing. By the time the camp is out and the truck is loaded we're both content to rattle back to town, thinking only of air conditioning and ice cream. Carl finds a station on the old AM truck radio and we listen to Willie Nelson as the road ahead ripples in the heat and warm air flows in the open windows.

At the edge of town, pickup trucks with horse trailers line the side of the highway like a redneck protest, clog service roads.
There's horseshit all over the pavement and mainstreet is barricaded by a police car. Looks like the James Gang is in town, robbing the local Treasury Branch, and they're getting a posse together. Carl gears down, the old stake sides creaking against three tons of shifting fire gear.

"Rodeo week," Carl says. "They're getting ready for the kickoff parade."

"We're pretty much done right?"

"Yeah," he says. "I guess so."

I haven't seen a parade since I was a kid. "Let's go watch."

We park the truck in the Forest Service compound, slip off our coveralls, walk the few blocks to the parade route. Mainstreet is barricaded, motorhomes and big trucks being rerouted at the four-way stop, drivers gawking as they crawl through the intersection. The street is lined with spectators, forming a gauntlet of lawn chairs; blue porta-potties interspersed like guard booths. Pickup trucks are backed to the sidewalk; families crowd on tailgates. Teenagers lob water balloons and kids squat, intent and restless, ready to dash for candy. There are more people here than the proclaimed population of the town.

I look around, hoping to see Telson.

"Who are you looking for?" asks Carl.

"Nobody. Just looking."

It occurs to me that at least half the people are wearing the same type of blue jacket. I read the logo on the jacket of a man standing next to me. Curtain River Forest Products. The guy's got a company watch and ball cap too. No doubt about this being a company town.

We sit, wait for the action. The sidewalk is uncomfortably hot, but I'm too tired to stand.

I hear the parade before I see it.

First come the town fire truck and ambulance, weaving from curb to curb, horns blaring loud enough to blow off a loose toupee. Children cover their ears and scream. Next march the Legion veterans, no doubt selected for this position because they can't hear the fire truck, followed by the rodeo queen in a gleaming red four-wheel-drive. Candy is thrown and kids scamper into the street. Water-balloon-throwing teenagers are blasted by the firemen and retreat. The local Member of Parliament sweats in a new suburban, the window down. It's going be a long parade — every business or charitable organization within a hundred miles seems to have a float.

Curtain River Forest Products has three entries. One is fairly elaborate — a papier maché version of Paul Bunyan and his blue ox, framed between lifts of lumber. Little kids with oversized hard-hats dispense candy from a large barrel. A banner proclaims Logging Helps Communities Grow and Prosper. The other two entries are semis pulling highboys loaded with lumber that look like they're trying to sneak through instead of using the detour.

A last minute entry eases into the parade from a side street. A team of Clydesdales pulling a heavy wagon stops to let it in. As it draws nearer, I get the feeling this isn't a registered entry and I nudge Carl.

"Take a look at that."

It's not an elaborate float but gets the message across efficiently enough. Pulled by a shiny sport-utility vehicle is a small trailer, pine saplings wired along the front and back, scruffy stuffed black bear posed in the middle. There are a few obligatory balloons and a Mountain Guardian banner is hung on the side of the trailer, urging us to protect our natural heritage. Seated in handmade willow chairs are two men in flannel shirts and overalls, whittling sticks. As the float draws near I notice two alarming details simultaneously. Reggie is one of the men and one of the balloons, tacked to a short chuck of tree trunk, is orange, with a hand-drawn face — crude, but with the bushy walrus moustache, obviously the face of the Lorax.

I stand up. "Oh shit."

"What?" asks Carl, joining me.

"Look at that balloon."

Carl looks at it without much interest, suddenly frowns, then laughs.

"You think that's funny?"

He cuts short his laughter. "I just can't believe they're doing this."

Me neither. I look around at the crowd, at all the blue jackets. As the Mountain Guardian float passes in front of me, Reggie is grinning. He won't be grinning for long if anyone else recognizes that balloon.

The pace of the parade seems to slow. I'm expecting a lynch mob but the crowd seems oblivious. As I pan across the crowd, looking for signs of trouble, I notice for the first time the white van from Action News and can't help wondering if they have some inside information. Riots always look good on page one. But maybe they're just hanging around for the parade, for a few colourful pictures. Then I hear a child, pointing to the float.

“Look Mommy, it’s the Lorax. Like from my book.”

I’m close enough that I hear the first curse from a man who’s tall, large and not amused. He cranes his neck toward the passing float, smacks the arm of another man standing close to him and points. I hear the word Lorax used in a new and interesting way. Others begin to notice and the crowd becomes restless. Reggie must sense something is amiss. He stops whittling.

“Fuckin’ murderer!”

An aluminium lawn chair sails across the street and hits the corner of the Mountain Guardian float, knocking pine saplings loose so they lean and sway. The Clydesdales pulling the wagon behind the float balk and whinny. There’s a ripple of outrage from the crowd, like a low moan from a distressed animal. Reggie and the other man stand and glare into the crowd. For a minute it seems this will be the extent of the violence, then the man who threw the lawn chair strides onto the street and heads for the float. He’s slim, bowlegged — not a big man but he’s got the wrath of the crowd behind him. He walks alongside the float, shouting at Reggie.

“The *fuck* are you doin’? You pansy-assed *motherfuckers*.”

Reggie points at him, whittling knife still in hand. “Back off asshole.”

The man in the street lunges at Reggie, snatches away his pocket knife. Reggie trips against his handcrafted willow chair, nearly falls off the float but is rescued by his companion. He regains his feet just as the protestor uses his knife to pop the offending balloon.

Reggie screams, “You tree-killing pig!”

Bad choice of verbiage. From my perspective on the sidewalk, I have a ringside seat. A horde of blue-jacketed men charge the float from both sides — women and children scurrying for cover like a gunfight in a Western movie. Reggie lifts his arms in a defensive kung-fu sort of motion then freezes when he realizes the immensity of his problem. He's surrounded by screaming mill workers and no longer seems so sure of himself. They rip pine saplings from the float, tear off the limbs. Reggie and his partner narrowly escape a similar fate by jumping from the trailer to the hitch and scrambling onto the roof of the SUV. It's a little like watching the evacuation of the American embassy at the end of the Vietnam war. Only there's no helicopter coming and Reggie's vehicle is stopped, marooned in a churning sea of blue. The rest of the parade continues ahead, leaving the Mountain Guardian float stranded like a decoupled rail car. Reggie screams at the driver, stomping on the roof, which buckles suddenly, throwing him off balance. He nearly falls to the lions, but regains his footing. The crowd begins to rock the vehicle.

"Cool," says a teenager close by. He's got blue hair and a lip ring.

A reporter strides past, followed by her camera crew, fumbling to get their gear up and running. They shoot several minutes of Reggie doing the SUV jive, then look around for someone to interview. There's no one close except Carl, me and a group of teenagers. A microphone is thrust in my face. "Do you know what prompted this sudden attack?"

I shake my head, point to Blue Hair. "You'll have to speak with my agent."

The microphone automatically swings away. I grab Carl, who seems stunned, and we make a run for it, mix with spectators down the street. With any luck the reporter didn't recognize me. A look back confirms Lip Ring is enjoying his 30 seconds of fame.

In the street, Reggie and sidekick are rapidly losing ground.

Carl looks worried. "Maybe we should do something."

"Sure. Let's watch."

Sirens approach; news of the commotion has reached the front. Spectators part like the Red Sea as fire trucks lumber to the rescue. I'm caught in a retreating tide of rubberneckers, swept into a gas station parking lot where I watch from an eddy as firefighters blast the mob with water — they break like sand washed from a driveway. Reggie and sidekick are pulled to the safety of the fire truck. Police suburbans emerge from a side street, lights strobing, sirens warbling. Soggy cowboys and mill workers retreat. They're still angry but the mob energy has dissipated. Reggie is assisted into a cruiser and whisked away. Elvis has left the building. The show is over.

"Unbelievable," mutters Carl.

"Was that the Reggie who worked for you?"

"That was him," he says, shaking his head.

The reporter is looking around like an anxious mother at a shopping mall — Reggie is gone and she wants a follow-up. Nose Ring isn't credible enough for the six o'clock news. I grab Carl by the elbow, lead him in the opposite direction. I've had enough of reporters and Loraxes for the day. Ahead in the parking lot of a video store I see a familiar figure standing in the back of a pickup truck. She's got a camera with a zoom lens pointed at what's left of Reggie's float.

"Doing a little work for *National Geographic*?"

Telson is looking through the public eye and is startled, nearly falls out of the truck.

"Christ, Porter, didn't your mother tell you not to sneak up on people like that?"

"Let's leave my mother out of this."

She's wearing army pants cut very short and a baggy red T-shirt with an interesting graphic involving a chicken, a rabbit and an

Easter egg. Very becoming in an adolescent grunge sort of way. With the camera it makes her look like she's on assignment for *Mad Magazine*. Carl is looking at her like she's a piece of home-made deer jerky.

"This is Carl," I say. "My partner in crime."

Telson smiles sweetly. "We've met."

"Aagh yes," Carl says. "The girl from the bar."

Telson's smile turns sarcastic. Carl has a way with women.

"Nice parade," she says. "They always this festive?"

Carl shakes his head. "Not usually."

"What started it?"

I help Telson down from the truck, hold her camera. "You didn't notice?"

"No." She takes back the camera, fits it into a Pelican case. Now she looks like a drug courier. "I saw the chair, then this guy came running onto the street and started fighting."

"It's parades," I say. "Too many horses. Makes the cowboys antsy."

She gives me a dry smile. "Right. What really happened?"

"Who knows." I don't want to talk about the Lorax.

"Okay," she says. "So what now, boys?"

The Mountain Guardian float has been pulled to the side and the parade is starting again, fitfully like an old windup toy. It's mid-afternoon but I don't feel like working any more. Neither, apparently, does Carl.

"Let's grab something to eat," he says.

We end up going for pizza which, next to buffalo burgers, is the food of the West. Sentimental fool that I am, I pick the same booth Telson and I shared a few days ago, wishing we had it to ourselves. I glance over at Carl, notice his hair is light grey with ash, his hands and face dirty, and realize I probably look the same. I excuse myself and go to the washroom, clean up as best I can. When I get back, Carl and Telson are deep in conversation and I feel an embarrassing twinge of jealousy. Maybe it's because I know Carl is lonely and Telson is the best-looking girl in town. Maybe it's because three years is a long time. Carl looks up at me as I sit down, notices I'm cleaner than he is and excuses himself.

"Funny guy," says Telson.

"Carl?"

"He's been telling me all about you. All those embarrassing college stories."

"The traitor."

She grins, savouring her newfound leverage. "Like the time you poured pepper into the heat ducts of that security guard's car —"

"There were mitigating circumstances — "

"Or the time you hired a girl to do a strip-o-gram during the statistics class —"

"Enough." I hold up my hands. "That's sensitive information."

Telson flutters her eyelashes. "Your secrets are safe with me."

"Okay," I sigh. "What's this going to cost me?"

She places an outspread hand on her chest, looks shocked. "Cost? Oh no, you've got me all wrong. I would never use such embarrassing information for personal gain. Never. As a matter of fact, I don't even want to talk about it anymore. Let's talk about something else. Did you know there's a midway in town, with rides and games and cotton candy?"

Oh, she's smooth. "Okay, okay, I'll take you."

Carl returns from the bathroom, looking like he took a bath: hair wet and combed back, face and hands scrubbed nearly pink. A strand of paper towel hangs like a fashion statement from behind one ear.

"Nice earring," I say.

He gives me a puzzled look. Telson casually signals there might be something by his ear and Carl pulls off the strip of paper towel. I've never seen him blush before.

"What?" He scowls, trying to regain his composure.

"Nothing."

We read menus, order an extra-large — hold the salami, hold the ham. Basically, we're ordering cheese and bread. We talk about the weather of all things — a bad subject to get into with forest rangers; self-proclaimed experts who feel they must explain the nuances of weather and fire hazard. Telson listens politely as Carl gets into drought codes, relative humidities. I'm sitting next to her and under the table her hand slides onto my leg. My relative humidity rises.

"It seems very dry out lately," says Telson.

"Oh, it is," says Carl. "The BUI is over 100 and we're talking about drought codes well over 400. Which is amazing for this early in the season." He's practically babbling. "When it gets this dry, the forest just wants to burn and it's hard to stop it. Did Porter tell you he's on the provincial fire investigation team?"

She shakes her head.

"He's working on those arson fires. You've probably heard about them."

"Yes, I've read about them. They've caused a lot of damage, haven't they?"

"A half million acres burned so far," Carl says, divvying out pizza like this was a pit stop at a race track. "Not that they won't grow back. But that's a lot of trees up in smoke."

"And you're investigating those fires?" she says, looking at me.

"Well, there's a team of us ..."

Her hand begins to slide slowly back and forth across the top of my leg. The hazard rises to extreme and it's hard to concentrate.

Carl gives me an odd look and I reach under the table, stop the hand from moving but keep it where it is. The ground can react violently to rain after a long drought. Carl talks about Curtain River; its past as a logging and ranching town. He's a virtual cornucopia of historical information. By the time the pizza is gone he's taken us from the last Indian battle to the present. I had no idea he had such a gift for casual conversation.

"You should write a book about it," says Telson.

"I just might." Carl, the buckskin scholar. "Now what should we do?"

Telson looks at me, gives me a pleading look.

"Okay, okay."

I haven't been to a midway since I was eight, don't remember so many horse trailers, so many little surprises scattered like mines over the grass. The wobbly Ferris wheel looks like a death trap; the midway looks expensive; the cotton candy inedible. I must be getting old.

"Just like I remember," says Telson, grabbing my hand.

"That Ferris wheel looks like it's going to fall over," says Carl.

"Where do you want to start?" I ask Telson.

She grins. "Everywhere."

We start with the Ferris wheel, which lists to one side as we sit down. The view from the top is splendid but I'm distracted by memories of unrenewed life insurance. I've been skydiving and it seemed safer — this is too close to the ground and I don't have a parachute. Telson shrieks with delight. In the Gravitron I find out how a blood sample feels in a centrifuge; my T-cells have pretty much separated by the time we're done. I pass on the Zipper, feign back pain to avoid being unzipped. Carl sees his big chance, goes for a flip with Telson, spends a few minutes after the ride bumping into things. Telson is just getting warmed up. They've got a bulk discount on tickets. She buys a whole roll.

In the dark, with lights on all the rides, I get infected with carnival fever. Carl produces a mickey of rum from a pocket inside his buckskin coat. I lose 50 bucks trying to win a two-dollar toy for Telson. Carl wastes another 50 and finally wins. Telson gives hugs all around. We ride the Gravitron until we're all a few inches taller and can't walk straight. Around midnight, the lights start to go out. Grouchy carnies begin to shut things down.

"I think they're trying to tell us something," says Carl.

"Now what?" Telson's got cotton candy stuck to her nose.

I take a few bowlegged steps. "When in the West, do like a cowboy."

"Let's go steer wrasslin'," says Telson. "Yee-ha. Let me at 'em."

"Steer?" says Carl. "I don't think I'm in any shape to drive."

Nobody wants the night to end, so we follow the rodeo crowd to The Corral. It's standing room only — you could roll a ball bearing from one side of the room to the other on the brims of the cowboy hats. We lounge by the wall, beers in hand. Telson wants to dance but there's no vacant floor space and I'm not sure my ankle is up to the job. Undaunted, she dances in-situ, elbowing cowboys out of her way. Carl points to the bar, challenges me to a shoot-out. After a year of altered states following Nina's death, I've been relatively careful with the drinking but tonight I'm tired of being careful, accept Carl's challenge. The shooters go down so quickly I barely notice. Someone in the crowd shoulders me. I think it's a drunk cowboy in a rush to find the privy but the shove comes again. It's the Neanderthal, pug-nosed, unshaven, glassy-eyed and chewing a cud of tobacco.

"Watch it asshole." Like the shooters, my response is too fast.

He shoves me again and grins. Another challenge.

"Listen buddy, I'm trying to have a good time here."

Another shove; he's not big on talk tonight; I'm thinking it's overrated anyway. Time to teach this throwback some manners. Telson tugs at my arm, tries to lead me away. The Neanderthal spits a glob of black phlegm onto my shirt. But tonight, I'm invincible.

I swing first.

15

I'M ON PAINKILLERS and wearing sunglasses as I drive Old Faithful north to Edmonton. Even so, it's too bright out and certainly too early to be moving — the Monday morning from hell. Sunday was pretty much a blur, on account of Saturday night at The Corral. I doubt the Neanderthal learned any manners; the last I thing remember is a bright flash of light. I came to on Carl's couch, feeling like I'd been run over by a cultivator and pressed in a waffle iron, my shirt a curious mixture of fluids. There was a lot of dried blood, most of it mine by the look of my nose. And Telson? Well, she was long gone.

"She wasn't impressed with your little show," Carl told me.

"I should have known better. She's not that kind of girl."

Carl's laugh was a little too smug. "Your Jackie Chan impersonation didn't help."

Sometimes when I drink I think I'm an Asian crime fighter. "Did I win?"

"You were entertaining. Until you hit the floor."

"I take it that's a no."

"Your face looks like bad plastic surgery."

The mirror confirmed it. I'm going to need more than sunglasses to cover these bruises — the full Groucho mask with the plastic nose and fake moustache might work. As for the rest of me — I'm like the Tin Man in *The Wizard of Oz* before Dorothy showed up with the oil can. No oil for me though; Dorothy has gone back to Kansas. Carl offered something stronger: codeine washed down with warm beer. It helped a bit and we sat on his back deck in the shade, like patients at a convalescent home. Watching the ravens fight over the dumpster in the alley. Sleeping away the afternoon.

The ravens woke me in the dark, pecking my chest, fighting over my shirt.

The second formal meeting of the Red Flag Wildfire Arson Task Force takes place at the palatial new RCMP "K" Division headquarters in Edmonton. The old building, a familiar landmark blue cube, has been replaced with a red brick and glass structure developed by an architect with visions of grandeur. The effect is wasted on me this morning as I pull Old Faithful into a visitors' parking spot, check in at the front desk — an enclosure of bullet proof glass.

"I'm here for the Red Flag meeting."

The commissionaire frowns at my bruised face. "Are you a member?"

He has a tattoo of an anchor on his forearms, looks like an aged version of Captain High Liner. Behind him is a bank of television screens showing surveillance views of the parking lot and doors; I didn't notice any cameras. He's conducting his own surveillance, waiting for my answer.

"No. I was hoping for a complimentary first visit."

"They usually are," he says. "Who do you need to see?"

"Try Don Kirby."

The commissionaire hands me a clip-on visitor tag and log book to sign in. He calls Kirby, tells me to take a seat. I watch uniformed members pass back and forth, their handguns at eye level. Kirby appears, passes me through a security door, leads me down silent, tiled hallways. At the boardroom, I'm the last to arrive. Malostic and Berton are here, but Star is absent. So is the florid Director of Forest Protection. Dipple is seated beside Frank, who's dressed in a beaded buckskin jacket. The two constables from up north — Purseman and Trimble — sit together like starched bookends. It looks like a meeting of The Village People. Except for me; I'm *Night of The Living Dead*. I take a seat next to Berton, who does a double take when I remove my sunglasses, display my shiner.

"You look terrible," he whispers.

"You should see the other guy's knuckles."

There's a counter with a coffee urn and an unopened box of doughnuts I'm guessing won't last long in this place. Other than the chairs and table, there's not much for furniture — this is a war room. On a wall is tacked the game board — a large provincial map with the Red Flag fires indicated by bright stick-on dots. Kirby clears his throat, wastes no time on preliminaries. "I'm sure all of you have met the corporal from Ident. As his services are very much in demand, I'll have him go first."

At the head of the table, Dipple sets up a small easel with two enlarged black-and-white photos. He looks very trim and capable this morning, his movements and speech efficient and practised — the manner of someone familiar with courtroom presentation.

"Good morning." He rubs his hands together as if warming them over a fire. "I've met all of you except the gentleman in the buckskin coat. First, a few comments on the general scene. Contamination was a problem due to the level of activity in and near the point of origin. I understand some of this was necessary, but this should be better controlled in the future."

Kirby glances at me, one eyebrow raised like a judicious father.

"The point of origin," continues Dipple, "was located 147 metres directly west of the road. Physical evidence seized at the origin included a metal pan ten-inches square and two-inches deep. Within the pan were found several specific identifiable compounds. There was a quantity of wood ash as well as an ash plug approximately an inch and a half in length. Microscopic analysis of this plug revealed a leafy, dendritic structure, pointing to a substance of plant origin. This was further substantiated by the presence of calcium oxalate."

"So what are we talking about here?" asks Kirby. "Some kind of cigar?"

"Possibly," says Dipple. "Although my observations are consistent with many materials of plant origin and do not apply exclusively to tobacco. The size and shape of the plug does suggest a cigar but vehicle vibration as a result of transport deteriorated the plug's morphology."

Kirby is making an impatient cranking motion with his hand.

"If I had to guess," says Dipple, "I'd say it was a cigar."

"Thank you."

"Wouldn't a cigar be too damp?" asks Berton.

"Apparently not," says Kirby.

"I did a little experiment," I volunteer. "I built a device using a cigar which had been perforated and dried out. The cigar was inserted into a cut-off pop bottle filled with black powder and then set in a pan full of diesel."

"Really?" Kirby looks impressed. "And you set this thing off?"

"In a brush pile. It worked like a damn."

Malostic is staring at me, probably wishing he'd thought of this first.

"That what happened to your face?" asks Purseman.

"No, that was a different kind of explosion."

"This cigar," Kirby says. "Did you record the time it took to burn down?"

"Seven and a half-hours, give or take a few minutes."

"*Seven hours?*" Kirby can't believe it. "What kind of cigar did you use?"

"That's the interesting part." I take the Emperador box from an inside jacket pocket where it's been concealed like a sawed-off shotgun, set it on the table. "I figured if the arsonist is using a fuse, he'd use the longest one he could find. So I looked around a little. According to what it says on the box, this is the longest marketed cigar in the world."

The empty box is passed around. Frank sniffs the wood like a good smoke.

"I doubt this is what was used," says Malostic. "Too traceable."

"We're going to have to widen the search area," says Purseman.

"Yeah," mumbles Frank. "To half the province."

Kirby studies the imprint. "Who sells these?"

"I got this one here in town, at a little shop in Old Strathcona. It's special order, from some wholesaler in Ontario, but you can get them over the Internet."

Kirby sights down the box like he's checking a pool cue. "You can get anything over the Internet, but it's a place to start. I'll have someone trace the distribution of these things. You say you used gunpowder?"

"Black powder. Single F in a cut-off pop bottle —"

Dipple clears his throat. "I've got a burglary to do this morning."

"Right," says Kirby. "What else did you find?"

"In addition to the organic ash there was a small mass of polyethylene impregnated with traces of potassium carbonate and potassium sulphate —"

"There's the gunpowder," Malostic says happily. "Just like I predicted."

Dipple glowers at Malostic. "May I finish?"

"My apologies Mr. Nipple. Please proceed."

"It's *Dipple*," he says frostily. "*Not* Nipple."

Malostic colours, gives me an injured look.

"As I was saying," Dipple continues, "potassium carbonate and sulphate compounds. There were also traces of a hydrocarbon,

most likely diesel." He pauses, refers to notes then gestures toward the photo enlargements on the easel. "As for transfer evidence, we found a single bootprint in the area between the road and origin. Relatively good as far as bootprints go." Using a pencil as a pointer, Dipple indicates a lug on the heel of the boot. "As you can see, there are numerous accidental characteristics, such as this prominent gouge, that will aid identification."

"Like a fingerprint," says Berton.

"Yes. Boot types are fairly diluted but wear patterns and damage tend to be unique."

"What if we just find the boots?" asks Malostic.

"If the boots have been worn for more than a few weeks — and I'd hazard to guess these have — it's possible to compare interior wear patterns to a person's foot."

"And if they wore someone else's boots?"

"Then we'd be out of luck."

"What about the tire marks?" asks Kirby. "You come up with anything?"

Dipple's pencil swings toward the other photo. "The surface of the road was too dry and coarse to leave a tread impression, but the track and surface width indicate a light half-ton, two-wheel-drive pickup, likely a Chevrolet."

"A Chevy," mumbles Frank. "That narrows it down."

Kirby is eyeing the virgin doughnuts. "Anything else?"

"I took soil and flora samples in case you need a comparison."

"Good point," says Kirby, looking around at us. "Anyone think they may have a suspect, let us know right away. If there are bits of organic matter on their clothes, pine needles or moss or stuff like that, we may be able to do a DNA match and tie the sucker to the site."

Malostic is taking notes. "How reliable is that?"

"Just another piece of the puzzle," says Dipple. "Any more questions?"

There are no further questions for Dipple and he gathers his photos, heads to his burglary. Berton and Frank use the lull to go for a quick coffee. Kirby moves in on the doughnuts, spears two with his index finger. He licks frosting off his fingertips, continues the meeting from beside the coffee urn. "We're going to have to widen the search radius, look for traffic tickets, credit card gas receipts," he says, waving a doughnut at us. "Anything that might place a person within the vicinity of these fires. We'll develop a suspect list, reference this against registered vehicle types. It's a wide net, but it's a place to start. Frank, you find anything in the native communities?"

Frank sits on the edge of the conference table, stirs his coffee. "Nothing."

"Nothing?" Kirby frowns. "People must be talking."

"Yeah, but it's just talk. There's been plenty of work to go around."

"What about a pattern? Can we predict where the next hit will be?"

I look at the provincial map. Somehow, the distribution looks familiar.

"Anywhere it's hot and dry," says Berton. "Which is everywhere."

"Can we narrow that down a bit?"

"Maybe," says Berton. "We could use drought codes ..."

Suddenly, I make a connection. The map reminds me of a similar map I developed in the duty room of the Curtain River Ranger Station. The fire map has fewer sites but the distribution isn't that much different. It could be a coincidence — there's only so much forested area in the province and any two maps with dots on it could be seen to have similarities — but it strikes me that what the

Lorax has been trying to do is remarkably similar to what the arsons are actually accomplishing — disruption of the timber harvest. The Lorax temporarily interrupts work but the fires remove the timber supply. It's a leap I can't help making.

"Maybe it's the Lorax," I say. "Maybe he's the arsonist."

Berton stops talking. Kirby lowers his doughnut. "What?"

"The Lorax might be the one lighting these fires."

Kirby looks sceptical. "The bomber?"

"Think about it. Some guy blows up the odd piece of logging equipment and what happens? He generates a few headlines but the equipment is replaced the next day. So what has he accomplished, other than raising insurance rates?"

Kirby shrugs. "Brings attention to his cause."

"Sure, but if his aim is to shut down logging, he's fighting a losing battle. And I think he knows that. There's a better way, one far less risky and guaranteed to have a significant impact. Light a fire that'll get big and you'll really throw a monkey wrench into things."

Malostic shakes his head. "The Lorax is supposed to *protect* the trees."

"That depends on what you mean by protect," I say. "In the story, the Lorax tries to stop the loggers from cutting down the trees. He's trying to protect the trees so it seems ridiculous to think of him starting fires. But if you consider fire in its natural context, it makes perfect sense. In this climate, fire is part of the ecosystem. I don't know about Truffula Trees but our forests are fire-dependant communities — they need fire to reproduce. People don't see that for the same reason they think clear-cutting is terrible. In reality, they're both just different versions of the same thing; they're both replacement events but only one is natural."

Kirby is still frowning. I don't blame him. The idea seems ludicrous if you don't have an appreciation of ecological cycles. Which leads me to believe the Lorax must be educated or well read. A self-made biologist maybe. Kirby is rubbing his forehead, having difficulty with this.

"You're saying the arsonist has an ecological motive?"

"I think he's trying to re-establish the natural cycle."

Malostic looks puzzled. "But they can salvage trees after a fire can't they?"

I nod. "Some of them yes, but a mill can't run like that — everything at once and then nothing for the next century. They need a steady, reliable supply of timber. And if the fires are too large the mills won't have the capacity to handle the enormous amount of salvage. After a few years, the burned wood is useless."

There's a thoughtful silence. Kirby goes to the map, contemplates the dots. We drift over like kids drawn to a TV on Saturday morning. The fire locations are represented by red dots; I use my pen, add crosses where the Lorax has struck. It looks like we're playing a random version of tic-tac-toe. So far, the other team is winning.

"Seems unlikely," Kirby says. "Changing his MO like that."

"If fire is more effective," says Malostic, "why is he still blowing things up?"

Kirby looks at me. "How does that fit in with your theory?"

"I don't know. But I've got a feeling there's some connection. What about the device?"

"Those bombs are a lot more potent than some cigar," says Frank.

"They both could have used gunpowder. Is there some way of checking?"

"We can check with the other task force," says Kirby. "Compare notes."

I picture Rachet's face when he hears it was my idea. "Anyway more convenient?"

Kirby gives me an odd look. "I think we have to examine the possibility right away," I add quickly. "The fire hazard in most of the province is extreme. If we can establish a link, we might be able to predict where he'll hit next, move resources to that vicinity."

Berton looks sceptical, then reads my expression. "Yes, that would be a good idea."

Kirby scratches his chin. "Well, we could check with the CBDC — the Canadian Bomb Data Centre. It's a national police service out of Ottawa that coordinates information on bombings, theft of explosives, that sort of thing. They could tell us what was used in the bombings. Of course, it would be just as easy to check with the other task force."

"Why bother them until we have some supporting information?"

That look again, of concern over my impatience. "Well ... Why don't you guys grab another coffee while I run to my office, look up the CBDC on my computer."

There's a movement toward the counter; the doughnuts are getting scarce. I intercept Kirby, ask if he minds company. He shrugs, leads me through more tiled hallways. Despite the quiet, my pulse is racing. In his office, I take a chair opposite his desk.

He pecks at his keyboard. "You seem pretty eager."

"I don't want any more big fires."

A few minutes of silence as Kirby navigates cyberspace. His office is small, cramped by desk, chairs and filing cabinets. Pictures of his kids hang on the wall next to wanted posters. I'm sitting across from him and can't see the face of the monitor.

"What have we got here?" he says, frowning. "Nope, the Lorax used dynamite, not a pipe bomb. Of course, that doesn't mean there isn't a connection." He taps a few more keys. "Let's see what we've got on PIRS, the old Police Information Retrieval System. They've got everything there."

Kirby hums an ambiguous tune deep in his throat. I stare at the back of the monitor as though the information might somehow seep out. The humming stops and he shifts in his chair. "Hmm, that's interesting." He leans forward, a concerned look on his face.

"What? What is it?"

"You," he says. "They've got you on observation."

"What does that mean?"

"It means that any member who comes in contact with you is supposed to file the particulars here. What you were doing. Who you were with. Where you were going. It's the sort of thing they usually tag a suspect with." He peers past his computer. "Anything you want to tell me?"

I think of Rachet's interrogation, get a sick feeling in my gut. "It's a long story."

"I'll clear my schedule."

I explain; he's not satisfied with the *Reader's Digest* version. He sits back, hands knitted together over his belly, his face neutral. My face feels a little warm. After I'm done, he chews his lip for a minute or two. "I thought you looked familiar."

"So now what?"

"For you, nothing. I've got to talk to the other task force before we discuss this Lorax theory any further. Until then, it's business as usual. You keep doing your job, protect that point of origin."

"So that's it?"

"That's it."

I swear under my breath. Foiled again, thanks to Rachet.

16

I STEW FOR A WHILE on the way south. The initial rush brought on by my revelation the Lorax might be lighting the fires has worn off and now I'm not so sure. Maybe I want to catch the Lorax so bad I'm seeing him everywhere and I poke at the theory, worry it like a dog with a toy, see if it holds together. I have a thinking problem — I'm overly analytical and will analyze an interesting thought to death, suck out all the juice until it's lost its flavour. This latest theory is no different and after an hour of rolling possibilities in my mind like clothes in a dryer, I decide to give it a rest. I use the satellite phone to call Telson's cell phone. She picks up on the fourth ring.

"Hello," I say, changing my voice. "It's your secret admirer."

A pause. "Who is this?"

"General Chong. Calling from Taiwan."

"General Chong, huh? You sound more like a skinny guy with a black eye."

"Close enough." I drop the cheesy accent. "You want to go out tonight?"

"To Taiwan?"

"Sure," I say. "Weather's here, wish you were beautiful."

A really long pause. I've pushed it too far, trying to be funny.

“You were a real jackass Saturday night, Porter.”

The Neanderthal had more coming than I could offer, but I try to sound remorseful.

“I’m sorry. It wasn’t the real me. Give me another chance.”

“Well ...”

“We’ll go to this spot I know by the river, roast spareribs over the open fire, watch the stars come out, have a deep meaningful conversation.”

“I’m a vegetarian.”

“So we’ll roast tofu.”

Another pause, like a taped delay at a ball game. “I don’t know —”

“Garlic toast? Asparagus? Brussels sprouts?”

“Well ... I am a sucker for good garlic toast.”

She’s in. I agree to pick her up around seven at an RV park at the edge of town. I’m curious to see this mobile abode of hers, learn more about her. She’s a bit of an enigma: this girl travelling around by herself, taking an interest in me. I pull into Curtain River in a better mood than when I left. It’s 6:30 — just enough time to run to the grocery store for garlic toast, take a quick shower. Carl is flopped on his couch, reading an old hunting magazine.

“How’d your meeting go?”

“No time,” I say. “Tofu now. Talk later.”

I hum a tune in the shower, drag a razor over my stubble, slap on a bit of whatever cologne I can find, try with limited success to wash it off because it smells so terrible, then dress and run for the door.

Carl sits on the couch, puzzled. “Did you say tofu?”

I’m fumbling with the cuff buttons on my shirt. “Telson’s a veggie girl.”

"Oh, I see." He grins. "Give her my best."

"No — I'll give her *my* best. See you later."

Old Faithful lives up to her name and I wheel into the IGA parking lot with five minutes to spare. An old man with a walker takes his time crossing in front of me and I impatiently strum my fingers on the steering wheel. I'm not normally this anal about being on time but after Saturday night at The Corral I don't want to push my luck with Telson. I plan to be in and out of the IGA quickly, pick her up, drive into the sunset ...

One of the vehicles in the parking lot catches my attention — an old multi-colored Chevy Apache parked in front of the laundromat. It's the Frankenstein truck, the one which followed me on my bike ride, the truck driven by the guy who used to blow beaver dams for Pete Ryerson. I look for the driver but the vehicle is uninhabited.

I'll wait, just a few minutes.

Five minutes pass, then ten. I sit in Old Faithful and fidget, glance at my watch like a kid in math class. I'm going to be late. Finally, I get out of my truck and stroll past the laundromat. Inside, two old ladies are playing crib. I veer toward the Chevy, make a wide circle, jot the licence plate number in my little notebook. Glance at my watch again and look around, trying to decide what to do. The driver might not be back for hours.

I casually saunter over to the Chevy.

It looks like a garage workbench in there, greasy parts scattered over the seat, bearings stacked like stale doughnuts on the rod of the gearshift. An oil pressure gauge is propped on an open ashtray, dripping onto the floorboards. The dash is cluttered with chainsaw files and wrenches, empty cigarette packs. A cluster of faded air freshners dangle from the rearview mirror; big-breasted ladies in coy positions. The passenger door isn't locked but is hard to open, gives an alarming metallic squeal — a backcountry burglar alarm.

The interior smells of dirty oil and rat shit, like an abandoned blacksmith shop.

Still no one in the parking lot. I move quickly now. The glove compartment holds more old bearings and burned-out fuses but no registration or insurance. At the bottom is what could be a used condom and I back out quickly, close the door and return to

my truck, ponder what to do. I'm already late but if I go into the store, I might miss the driver. I agonize for another few minutes and am ready to throw in the towel on my impromptu surveillance when the driver of the Chevy appears.

It's the Neanderthal — the same curly, steel wool hair, heavy stubble and dark, brooding face from the bar. Like me, he moves like he's a bit stiff today. Unlike me, he doesn't appear to be wearing Crayola mascara. He sets bags of groceries in the back of the truck, shoves his shopping cart roughly out of the way, climbs into the cab and fires up his beast. The truck coughs, gives a staccato roar, pistons misfiring, tappets out of alignment — nothing a good stomp on the accelerator won't fix. He backs out of his parking spot, chugs across the lot and roars into traffic.

I ease Old Faithful onto the highway and follow.

We head west and I hang back a good distance. Traffic is light and, like the Neanderthal, I'm driving a fairly conspicuous vehicle. Ten minutes into the drive he turns onto a gravel road and I'm hidden in his dust cloud. I emerge suddenly to find the road ahead empty; he's turned and I take a hard left, sliding part way in the ditch, crawl out in four-wheel-drive.

This road is narrower, less frequently maintained, forested on both sides. Ahead, I see his dust trail drift into the trees. The road dips, passes through an area of dense lowland spruce, rises and turns sharply to the left. I slow to make the steep turn and see a rusted mailbox at a road approach, a driveway partially hidden by trees. Beyond this the road turns again but with dust lingering it's difficult to determine if the Chevy turned into the driveway or kept going. I gear down, creep slowly toward the driveway to take a look as I roll past. Too late I realize the old Chevy is parked in shadow on the driveway, the driver looking back. I swear, gun the engine and spray gravel as I pass. But as I race away, I'm pretty sure he knows I followed him.

By the time I return to town daylight is failing. I rush to the IGA; they're just closing but let me in when I dance in front of the door like I have to go to the washroom. The girl at the till is coldly polite; she too has things to do tonight. I should have asked her where the RV park is because it takes some time to find it, longer to locate Telson's motorhome amid crescents winding through spruce trees. Her box on wheels is an older model, more suited to parking than driving. The orange Bug is there but Telson isn't impressed with my punctuality.

"You really give a girl a sense of worth, Porter."

She stands in the narrow doorway of her motorhome, doesn't look like she's going to come out. I don't want to explain why I'm late, tell her I had vehicle trouble. I've got grease smudged on my forearm; I must have touched something in the Neanderthal's truck. Telson seems to accept the explanation. But she remains in the doorway, looking down at me.

I give her my best sad puppy look. "Can I make it up to you?"

She leans on the doorframe. Her look isn't encouraging.

"I brought garlic toast. Pre-baked potatoes. Chinese food."

A long reluctant sigh. She steps down, inspects the damage to my face as though admiring a powerful but disturbing piece of art, tilts my head like a doctor taking a good look. I flinch when she touches the edge of the bruised area.

"Hold still. Don't be such a baby."

"If you look carefully, that cheek has a print of his boot size."

She raises a critical eyebrow. "Don't expect a lot of sympathy."

I wait outside while she gets a flashlight and bottle of wine; hold open the door of Old Faithful for her. She straps herself in; she's seen me drive before. By now it's dark enough that I have to turn on the headlights.

She crinkles her nose. "What's that odour?"

Carl's cologne. I think he left a bottle of Hoppes No. 9 in the bathroom.

"Motor oil," I tell her. "I spilled some on the exhaust manifold."

The drive takes about 20 minutes. She's quiet, making me self-conscious, unsure. I turn off the highway, bump and thump down a dark rutted trail. Old Faithful whines and grumbles. In the headlights, trees cast eerie shadows.

"You okay?" I ask. "You mind coming way out here?"

"This is fine."

Her tone is flat; I can't read her. "I'm sorry I was late."

"Don't worry about it."

The trail ends. I park, shut off the truck and suddenly it's dark and very quiet. Too quiet and I suggest we get out, look at the stars. The squeal of Faithful's door hinges is arthritic; bone grinding against bone. In the dark Telson is a vague shape standing by the truck. Invisible below us, the river is a soft roar. Wind sighs gently through treetops. I wish she'd say something.

"Do you want to go back?"

"No," she says quietly. "Let's stay a while."

"Great. I'll make a fire."

I blunder about looking for firewood, navigating by starlight, bump into trees. The area has pretty much been picked clean but I break off dry branches, hit the jackpot at an abandoned campsite where someone filled their days of leisure by cutting wood. I return with an armful of split firewood, ready to impress Telson but she's gone. I hope she's just visiting the ladies room; there are steep banks along the river. I start a fire, provide her a beacon. When it's popping merrily, I lay out a tin-foiled feast of garlic toast, potatoes, Styrofoam deli trays of Chinese stir-fry. Telson still isn't back so I amuse myself by dragging immense chunks of wood close to the fire so we have something to sit on, then sit on them and worry that she fell into the river. I'm just about to look for her when she appears out of the darkness.

"Thank God," I say. "I thought maybe you fell in."

"You were worried? How sweet. Would you have rescued me?"

"Absolutely. I'll need your help to push the truck out. I think it's stuck."

"You're a hopeless romantic."

"Or just hopeless."

"Now you're getting closer."

She seems in a better mood, sits on a log close to the fire, tells me she was watching the whole time. Cheap entertainment, watching me drag those logs around; she thinks I must be nesting. I watch her as she talks, thinking she's too good to be real. Her hair is touched gold in the firelight, her face glowing with the warmth of the flames. The small circle of light is intimate and I find her intensely attractive.

"You okay, Porter?"

"Couldn't be better. Why?"

"You've got this primitive gaping look on your face."

My face gets warmer. "So what have you been doing to keep yourself busy?"

She shrugs. "Going for walks. Relaxing. It's so peaceful out here."

Peaceful isn't how I'd describe my time in Curtain River.

"What about you?" she says. "You said you were here to help Carl."

"Yeah — that's right. I fight the odd fire."

"And you're an investigator too. How's that going?"

"You win some, you lose some. But let's not talk shop."

"Okay." She stands, warms her butt over the fire, sits next to me. We eat Chinese; she's amused by my attempts to use chopsticks. "They're supposed to be in the same hand, Porter," she says, laughing. She goes to the truck, comes back with the bottle of wine. We don't have a corkscrew, use my pocket knife and butcher the cork. We don't have cups either and pass the bottle back and forth like teenagers at a bush party.

"My dad used to take me camping," Telson says, poking the fire with a stick. "Just the two of us. He worked in an office and by the end of the week he couldn't wait to get outside. He used to say this was the real world and the rest was just make believe."

"I thought you grew up on a farm."

"What?"

"You said you were a farm girl."

"Oh, I was. But we went bust and the bank took the land — just like one of those country songs. We urbanized and my dad took a job in the city. But he missed being outside."

"Don't we all."

Telson smiles. I hope I don't remind her of her father. "Is he still working?"

"No," she says quietly. "He's gone now. Lung cancer."

"I'm sorry."

"Yeah — me too." She gives me a wistful smile, raises the bottle. "To memories."

She passes the bottle and I take a swig. "To the real world."

We sit for a while and watch the dance of the fire, don't say anything. It's been a long time since I sat with a girl by a fire like this. Telson looks at me, moves a little closer, slides her slender hand onto my thigh and I tense.

"What's the matter?"

"Nothing. Just that ghost again."

Her look doesn't waver. Neither does her hand. She waits.

"It's been a while."

She looks pleased. "Relax, Porter, this won't hurt."

The vegetarian reintroduces me to the pleasures of the flesh.

17

THE NEXT DAY is Cindy's birthday and I beg off work, tell Carl I have official business in Edmonton. As usual, he grumbles about being left short-handed. I think he just wants me to stick around because I'm more likely to cook supper than he is. Tonight, he'll have to order pizza. Or thaw another slab of elk meat from his freezer. Cindy has a babysitter scheduled. I'm taking her for a well deserved night out — and introducing her to someone.

"How can you eat this stuff?"

"I'm sorry but they didn't have any tofu bars."

Telson has her boots propped on Old Faithful's dash as we cruise between rolling fields along the big double highway heading north. She's rummaging in the bag of goodies I picked up at the last gas station, pulling out plasticized strips of beef jerky, Rice Krispies squares that look like fire-starting cubes, reading the ingredients. "Monosodium glutamate, sodium nitrate, disodium inosinate —"

"The three basic food groups."

She shakes her head. "I'd hate to see what your colon looks like."

"Me too."

Last night, after the event, we'd lounged by the campfire until well past midnight, not saying much, just being together. Finally, reluctantly, I'd taken her home then found that despite being dead tired I couldn't sleep. I had too much to think about. Lorax. Red Flag. Nina. Telson. But finally, after hours of tossing and turning, I lapsed into a sort of trance-like coma.

"You okay Porter? You look a little dazed."

"Fine," I say after a yawn. "Just a little tired. Alien abduction will do that to you."

"You're calling me an alien?"

"Well, you did conduct a few experiments."

She laughs. There's a new intimacy between us this morning.

"You sure your sister won't mind my tagging along on her birthday?"

"Are you kidding? She'd love some adult conversation."

Telson unwraps a Rice Krispies square, sniffs it and begins to nibble. She's wearing reflective sunglasses, a man's canvas work shirt with epaulets, green pleated shorts and black workboots. Like she's on her way to a militia training camp. She leans against the door, slides the sunglasses down her nose and gives me her best Freud look. With the accent, it's a bit of a contrast. "So, young man, dell me about you childhood."

We play this game for a while. I actually end up telling her a lot about my childhood. She really should be a shrink; they could use a few that aren't as crazy as their patients. The drive passes pleasantly enough and by the time we reach Edmonton, my throat is sore. I'm not used to talking so much. I slow Old Faithful to a speed that doesn't rattle the windows. Even mid-morning on a Tuesday, Gateway Boulevard is bumper-to-bumper.

"Look at that big lightbulb," says Telson.

"What? Where?"

“On the roof of that building.”

It’s not a lightbulb — it’s a promotional hot air balloon. Soar With the Eagles, says the caption. A station wagon swerves in front of me, cutting me off and I hit the brakes, scattering junk food like a kid emptying a Halloween bag. Soaring with the eagles beats driving with the turkeys and I pull in. The guy at the counter asks if I’m interested in booking a flight for me and my wife. Telson gives me a crazy grin. Comes with a certificate that proves I’ve flown in a balloon, and an embossed champagne glass. I’m thinking this would be an interesting birthday gift for Cindy and ask how much. Three hundred bucks. What about economy fare, without the wine glass? Three hundred bucks. No point arguing with a guy whose business is hot air so I make a reservation for later that afternoon. The guy takes my Visa, tells me if it gets too windy, I’ll have to reschedule. I get a coupon that looks like Monopoly money, which the guy assures me is good for a year. If not, Cindy can use it to buy Pacific Avenue.

“Does your sister like to fly?” Telson says, back in the truck.

“Sure. Don’t you?”

Telson glances heavenward. “You don’t expect *me* to go up there?”

“There’s room for three, in their Hindenburg model.”

She looks horrified.

“You’re not afraid of heights are you?”

“You know they can’t steer those things,” she says.

I can’t help laughing.

“It’s not funny, Porter. I can’t climb a chair to get a can of soup.”

“You need a parachute. Build your confidence.”

“I don’t think so.”

“I saw one in the paper the other day. Used once. Never opened. Small stain.”

"You're horrible —"

We cross the river, head north through downtown. It's lunchtime and all the secretaries are out on the street, catching a few rays, smoking, showing off their legs. Telson catches me ogling, tells me to stop drooling. Already, she's territorial. I'll have to invest in a darker pair of sunglasses.

"I'm drooling at you, dear."

Beneath her reflective shades, her smile is unamused. "Nice try."

The red brick building of "K" Division looms ahead. Except for all the cop cars, you'd think it was some fancy corporate office. Telson sits up as I wheel into the parking lot and I tell her I need a half-hour, offer to drop her at the mall a block away. She says she'll be fine here, follows me inside, but has to wait in the lobby as Captain High Liner gives me a visitor's tag, calls Constable Eugene Purseman.

"Nice shiner," Purseman says as he passes me through security.

Purseman is young, tall, smooth-skinned, beefy and looks to be the most junior member of the Red Flag Task Force, which is why I asked for him. We wander to the coffee room where he pours two cups of coffee, hands me one. "So, what can I do for you?"

"What's involved in running a licence plate?"

He drops in sugar cubes, stirs his coffee. "Why? You find something?"

"Someone has been following me."

"Really?"

"Yeah. An old beat-up Chevy."

"And you're sure he's following you?"

"He's got my attention."

Purseman leads me to a narrow office that smells of cleaner, has shelf brackets on the wall. There's nothing but a desk, computer and a single chair. It looks like solitary confinement. "A hundred thousand square feet of space," he grumbles, "and they give me a closet."

"Nice. Very Zen."

"You'll have to stand," he says. "I haven't had the decorator in yet." He takes a seat, types in his user name and password, looks at me over his shoulder. "All we got to do is patch into Motor Vehicles. What's the plate?"

I read the Neanderthal's plate number from my little notebook, watch the screen. A form pops up along with a drivers' licence photo; he's unshaven but this simplifies identification. The name — Zeke Petrovich — is vaguely familiar but I'm not sure why. The address is a box in Curtain River.

"He's registered a 1963 Chevrolet Apache," says Purseman. "And a 1974 Lada."

"He's not driving the Lada."

"Twelve demerits," says Purseman. "Bad boy."

His abstract reads like the Duke boys. Speeding. Stunting. Left of centre.

"What else can we find out about this guy?"

"You shopping for anything in particular?"

"Can we check if he's got a criminal record?"

"Sure." Purseman leans back, sips coffee, cruises cyberspace like it's the strip on Friday night. I'm keyed up, worried that Kirby will wander in, give me shit for not clearing this through him. But Purseman is a willing conduit. He uses PIRS to search Petrovich. A list of entries pops up.

"Ho, ho," says Purseman. "What've we got here?"

What we've got is fairly obvious. Two arrests for assault in the last three years; held for questioning, no charge. Victims unco-operative. One victim, a white male, was in a coma for six weeks.

Trauma to the head and neck — Petrovich likes to use his boots. Looks like I got off lucky.

"This the guy who redecorated your face?" asks Purseman.

I nod. "Can you print that?"

"Sure." He pecks at the keyboard; a one-finger typist like me. "You know, we could charge this asshole," he says. "With his record of assault, he'd go down. All we need is a victim with the balls to stand up in court."

"Maybe later. For now, I just want to know who he is."

Purseman looks disappointed. "What else do you need to know?"

"Does he have a job? What does he do?"

A few more keystrokes reveal another layer of Zeke Petrovich's life. He's a mechanic, which explains the loose parts in his truck, but it's where he works that's really interesting — Curtain River Forest Products. I wonder if he followed Hess around like he followed me. Not that he had too; he'd have access to Hess's machine. And if he's the same guy that used to blow beaver dams, he'd know explosives. "Can we tell if he bought dynamite recently, say in the past five years?"

"Dynamite?" Purseman frowns. "What's that got to do with anything?"

"I'm not sure. I heard he used to blow beaver dams."

"A lot of guys do."

"But they're not following me."

Purseman shrugs. "Okay. Let's have a look."

Ten minutes of cruising police databases produces nothing. "I don't think it's covered here," says Purseman. "I thought the Canadian Bomb Data Centre would track that sort of thing but apparently purchase records aren't recorded. You'd have to go to the retailer."

"You think they'd give me that information?"

"Probably not."

I can't think of anything more I can get Purseman to look up for me. He retrieves my copy of Petrovich's record from some distant printer, escorts me to the lobby. I thank him for his time. He aims a finger at me. "This guy keeps following you, you let me know."

"Count on it."

Telson looks up from her newspaper. "The secret agent returns."

"That's me, double-o nothing."

"You gotta start somewhere. Find anything interesting?"

"No. Let's get going."

I drop Telson downtown, tell her I'll pick her up in an hour. She's not thrilled at being abandoned again, but I don't want her asking a lot of questions about my investigation — I'd prefer to keep that part of my life separate. She recovers well though, says she needs to do a little window shopping anyway. We part with a brief kiss and I head west. There are only a few places to buy dynamite and two of them are in Edmonton, so I take a drive into the industrial area of the city. It's a homey neighbourhood — oily streets, chain link fences topped by barbed wire, yards filled with strange machinery. The company I'm looking for, X-Pert Explosives, is hard to find. I keep ending up at the wrong compound, but finally there it is, sandwiched between a fire extinguisher company and a place that makes shock absorbers. You have to wonder if there's some sort of logic at work here.

The building is brown, metal-clad, with three unmarked doors. I select door number one, next to a small, sealed window. There's a counter, computer, file cabinets and long hall. A sign over the counter tells me I'm in the Customer Induction Area. But it's eerily silent and there's no one around, no bell to ring for service. Maybe I'm in the Customer Abduction Area.

"Hello?"

Nothing. I wait, drum my fingers on the counter.

The building is new, the walls clean and very white. The floor is grey tile; the same colour as the filing cabinets and countertop. There are no promotional displays or unfinished filing lying around, in fact no paper visible anywhere, which indicates care in record security — not a good sign as far as my prospects of obtaining information. On the wall near the door is a photo of the X-Pert Explosives softball team — proof that at one time people worked here. I clear my throat as noisily as possible.

A man in blue coveralls appears at the end of the hall, saunters toward the counter. He's young, has black shaggy hair and a grease smear on his cheek, doesn't look like a person who might rummage through files for me, dredge up old records. But you never know. As he comes closer, I read a name tag sewn on his coveralls. Colin.

"Can I help you?" He stands a few yards back from the counter.

"I hope so. I was looking for some information."

"Information?" Colin frowns. They handle explosives here, not information.

I hesitate. On the drive here I toyed with several explanations. I'm a private investigator. I'm a journalist. I'm a customer who needs a copy of a bill of sale. I'm a student doing research. Finally, I'd decided on telling the truth. Now, I'm not so sure.

"My father bought some dynamite for blowing beaver dams on the farm. Of course, he lost the receipt. Now he's doing his tax and he needs it. You wouldn't have a copy would you?"

Colin frowns. "What's his name?"

"Petrovich," I say. "Zeke Petrovich."

"When was that?"

I try to look thoughtful. "A coupla years ago."

"He needs it now?"

"The old man doesn't do his taxes very often. It's not like he gets much back so he's never in a hurry. And when he gets around to it, he's lost most of his receipts."

Colin allows a half smile. "Just hang on. You better talk to Rufus."

He vanishes into an office down the hall and I hear a mumbled undercurrent of talk, then Rufus comes to the counter. He's older, short hair, dark complexion, shirtsleeves rolled back to display solid forearms. He's a serious-looking guy; I can picture him slinging crates of dynamite. He stands squarely behind the counter, his arms crossed. His frown isn't encouraging. "What's this about a receipt?" he asks. His voice is deep, with a coarse edge.

I repeat my story, which sounds flimsier this time.

"I'll need ID," he says.

I make a show of looking for my wallet. "I must have left it at home."

"No ID, no receipt."

"Well ..." I sigh, look dismayed, which is easy enough. "I'm just in town for the day. I guess he doesn't really need a receipt unless he gets audited. Maybe you could just tell me the date and the amount."

Rufus scratches his head, rummages under the counter, produces a pad of graph paper with the company logo — a cartoonish explosion — and asks me to repeat the name for which I want the receipt. Zeke Petrovich, I tell him and he prints the name in neat block letters. Now we're getting somewhere.

"And your name again?"

"Barry Petrovich."

"Well Barry, I'll tell you what I'll do. I'll look up Zeke and if we sold him anything, then I'll call him and tell him the amount so he can do his taxes."

"Oh, great." I try to look positive. "But he doesn't have a phone."

A look of annoyance. "No phone?"

"No, he's kind of strange that way."

"I could mail him a copy. Registered."

"That would be fine," I say, trying not to look disappointed. Maybe there's some other information Rufus can give me, so the drive out here isn't a total waste. "He said he might need another case for blowing stumps. Could I pick one up now?" I'm pretty sure the answer is no, but I want to find out what procedure Petrovich had to follow.

Rufus snorts, shakes his head. "Not a chance. You can't buy explosives for someone else. Your dad would have to come in himself. There's forms he's got to fill out and there's a waiting period. I'll need a criminal record search and might have to clear the purchase through the RCMP."

"But he could get more if he needed it?"

"Like I said, there's a procedure. From what I hear, they're talking about prohibiting that sort of sale altogether, which would be for the best. Dynamite isn't something you want to mess around with. Your dad should hire a licensed blaster. Most counties have one."

"How could I find out if a guy's licensed?"

"Ask to see his license. Or hire one through the county."

With Petrovich's record it seems unlikely he could purchase dynamite or get a blaster's licence. But up until a few years ago, he didn't have a record. "How long does the stuff last?"

"Dynamite has a one- to two-year shelf life, after which it begins to deteriorate." Rufus leans against the counter, seems to relax. We're talking his language now. "Nitro doesn't biodegrade, but the other components would. The product would get unstable after that."

"So he should only buy as much as he needs."

"Absolutely. You don't want unstable dynamite lying around. By law, a farmer only has 90 days to use or dispose of it anyway."

"What sort of product would you sell to a farmer?"

"Depends what he wants to use it for. From what you've told me, probably a nitro-based gel in a 50 mm x 800 mm configuration. That's a pretty skookum charge. It would displace about one cubic metre of material, take care of his stumps in no time."

I think of the feller-buncher at Curtain River. That was a pretty skookum charge.

There don't seem to be any more questions I can ask without a detailed explanation, which I doubt would further my cause with Rufus. I thank him, leave the Customer Induction Area. As I back out of my parking space I see a face in the window by the door. Rufus is frowning, probably writing down my licence plate number.

I head back into the city, silent and agitated. The wind has picked up, rocking Old Faithful and blowing hamburger wrappings across the road like tumbleweeds. It doesn't look good for a balloon ride today. Just by chance, I glance in the rearview mirror, see a light blue Plymouth a few vehicles back drift toward the shoulder of the road, then pull back into the lane. The car has a familiar ugly wrinkle on the driver's door, just like the car that was waiting for me after I left Ronald Hess's widow in Curtain River. But it was dark then and I can't be sure. I slow down and the intervening cars begin to pass, but the blue car also slows and is passed, making it impossible to get a clear view of the driver or car. I pull over abruptly, enter a service road leading to a string of gas stations and restaurants.

The old blue Plymouth coasts past, the driver looking in my direction. His face is shielded by a ball cap pulled low and he's hard to see against the glare coming off the side window, but I think his baseball cap has a crimped visor — like the man I found watching the cutblock. I try to follow but by the time I get back into the heavy flow of freeway traffic, he's gone.

We go to Bourbon Street at West Edmonton Mall. It's like the real Bourbon Street in that you can get something hard to drink at both places, but that's about as far as my imagination can stretch it. This version is inside, for one thing. They've dimmed the lights, put in a few statues and wrought-iron benches, but it's still just a hallway in a big shopping mall. Make that a gargantuan shopping mall; I need a compass and hip chain just to figure out where I am. It's a nightmare but Cindy likes the place — it's got lots of stores crammed close together, makes spending money highly efficient.

"Damn. I should have made a reservation."

"Don't worry about it, Porter," says Cindy. "We'll get in somewhere."

She's wearing a short dress — a simple print outfit — and a relaxed smile. The place is crowded but she doesn't seem to mind; tonight none of them are her responsibility. She'd probably be content to just wander around, holding my arm. By the looks of this crowd, that's all we might be able to do. There are long lines at restaurant entrances.

"What about that place?" asks Telson, pointing to a small eatery with a smaller fenced-in patio. A dozen people sit at plastic tables, gloat at the crowd milling on the other side of the fence. But there's no lineup at the door. I'm not sure that's a good sign.

"They have black beans." Telson is reading a menu by the patio. "And dark beer."

"Beans and beer. A dangerous combination."

"You'll be fine," she says. "Just stay away from the grill." She's on my other arm, wearing a leather mini-skirt and halter top that's turning a lot of heads. The gawkers aren't the only ones with their tongues hanging out — a street juggler walks past, at the edge of heat prostration as he flips bowling pins. The humidity in here is the other thing this version shares with the original. A group of Japanese tourists cluster like platelets, point toward the bean

place. I sense an impending lineup and steer the two women toward the restaurant door, trying to cut the tourists off at the pass. We all attempt to look like we're not running. The Japanese aren't happy about losing the race.

We're shown to a table in the non-smoking section. By the looks of it, our table is the non-smoking section. But the haziness adds to the ambience — a New Orleans motif. I can imagine a riverboat captain stopping by for a mess of pan-fried shrimp, a table of gamblers in a corner. But then again, I have an active imagination. I cough, rub my eyes.

"The smoke bothering you?" Telson asks.

"Only when I breathe."

"The big firefighter."

"That's a different kind of smoke. More organic."

At least it's cooler here — air conditioning works better in a small space like this — and dim. I order the Bayou Burger, which I suspect is pretty much like any other burger, and a mug of dark draft. Cindy isn't usually a big eater but since she doesn't have to cook tonight she orders potato skins, two salads, New York steak and a bottle of wine. Telson orders the beans.

"How long have you and Porter known each other?"

"About a week," says Telson.

"So it's a long-term relationship."

"Longest one in three years," I say. There's an awkward pause.

Cindy sips her wine. "So what do you do, Christina?"

Telson smiles faintly, toys with her beans. "I'm sort of between jobs right now."

"What did you do?"

"I worked as a receptionist at a software company."

"What happened there?"

"They got bought out, replaced all the staff."

"Even the receptionist?"

Telson nods, sips from her mug of stout.

"I thought you worked as a data entry clerk," says Cindy. "At least that's what Porter told me."

Telson gives me a vaguely annoyed glance. "I did that too. Talk about a dead end job. All day, you hunch over your keyboard, type in numbers. It's like copying the phonebook. I felt like some fourteenth-century scribe with carpal tunnel syndrome."

"So you've had a lot of jobs?" Cindy is merciless.

"You'll have to excuse my little sister," I say. "She's professionally inquisitive."

"Really?" Telson leans forward. "What do you do, Cindy?"

The food arrives and conversation is temporarily interrupted. Waiters must feel a bit like prison guards, the way people clam up when they come close. "I'm a social worker," says Cindy, between forkfuls of salad.

"That must be a demanding job."

"Helps to be a bit crazy. Sort of a prerequisite."

"You must hear some sad stories."

"I try not to dwell on them too much."

"No doubt. Speaking of stories, what was Porter like when he was younger?"

Suddenly I'm invisible as the two women talk; Cindy telling

embarrassing stories about my childhood. How in junior high school I tried to dismantle the building until someone discovered a pail of screws and bolts in my locker. My clandestine experiments with pyrotechnics in the science lab. Stuff like that. I glare at Cindy, hoping she'll take the hint, but she's purposefully oblivious and I give up, bide my time, gaze through a single-paned window at the lineup in front of Tony Roma's. A few expectant patrons have planned ahead and are reading books. Someone moving through the crowd catches my attention. He's not waiting, he's looking. He's wearing a baseball cap with a sharply crimped visor. I can't help thinking it's the driver of the old blue Plymouth — circled back from the freeway and followed me here.

I excuse myself, join the herd outside.

The crowd is dense, the lights dimmed, and it takes a minute to spot him. When I do, he's too far across the hall to get a good look at, too many intervening tourists. I can't see anything more than his head; an impression of short hair; a glimpse of a man's face in profile. Nothing clear enough to recognize. He's headed away, toward the main part of the mall, keeps looking from side to side; the ridge on the visor of his ball cap plainly visible. The crowd eddies in behind him and it's hard to move quickly; no one is in a hurry. He vanishes now and then, like a boat in rough water bobbing among the waves. He remains 40 of 50 yards ahead and I'm like a man overboard, watching the boat drift beyond reach. If only he'd turn back, take a good look my way. Or stand close to one of the fake streetlights.

By the time I reach the end of Bourbon Street, he's nowhere in sight.

Cindy and Telson think I've been in the washroom, which suits me fine. It was the burger, I tell them. Or the Crocodile Fries. I give

Cindy her birthday present — the Monopoly money coupon, tell her it was supposed to be a hot air balloon ride. She's pleased, but right now anything would please her; the bottle of wine is empty and she's started on a second. Telson is all for squeezing into one of the bars but I can see Cindy is on the thermocline between a warm glow and a cold front and suggest a movie instead. We end up watching *Firestorm*, a nice relaxing film that takes my mind off work.

18

I MANAGE TO GET the same dark blue, double-breasted polyester suit. The clerk at Curtain River Men's Wear thinks I'm spending too much on rentals and tries to talk me into a nice cotton getup. Four rentals and it's paid for. He'll even throw in shoes at ten percent off. I'm not interested, rent the suit and cruise around town for a few minutes. Everyone waves. I feel like the mayor. Maybe I should run, but when impersonating an insurance investigator it's best to stay low key. I drive out of town, follow the scent of drying timber. At Curtain River Forest Products they must be having a staff meeting because the parking lot is full. I create a parking space out back, leave Old Faithful to fend for herself, cut across a thumbnail of lawn. Inside, the air conditioner still hasn't been fixed and Carmen, the same Marilyn Monroe wannabe, is behind the reception desk. I'd hoped for someone different.

She purses her lips, raises an eyebrow. "Mr. Haffenflaff. What can I do for you?"

"Hassenfloss." I try to sound professionally offended. "Asper Hassenfloss."

"Right ..." She clasps her hands together, gives me an imitation sweet smile.

"I have just one small detail left to clear up."

She's chewing gum. "What might that be?"

"I just need to check your personnel records one more time."

"Sure. Just a minute sweetie." Carmen vanishes down a hallway. She's wearing a short skirt and I get a good look at tanned cellulite. When she returns, she takes a seat and turns to her computer screen. "Files are in the back," she says without looking at me. "Down the hall, fourth door."

"Thanks. I'll just be a minute."

The file room is long and narrow, with banks of grey four-drawer lateral filing cabinets lining the walls like safe deposit boxes in a bank vault. Some of the cabinets have labels, some don't. It takes me a while to find current personnel. There are hundreds of files, jammed in tight, but they're alphabetical and I find Petrovich, Zeke, employee number 0004532. I lay the file open across the others, flip back through Petrovich's employment history. Pay records. Vacation notifications. An employee commencement form indicates he's a mechanic. His starting wage is higher than any wage I ever made as a ranger. Behind this is what I've come for. As I scan his resumé, I get an eerie feeling, like some archaeologist who just found the missing link. Petrovich worked for every company that was hit by the Lorax at about what seems the right time. I pull out the resumé, walk to the reception desk. Carmen is on the phone.

She looks up at me. "I'm on hold. What do you need?"

"Can I use your photocopier?"

"You can try, but it's on vacation."

I return to the file room. I'm tempted to take the resumé but it would be better for Rachet to find it in situ. I jot down a few notes in my handy-dandy detective notebook — when and where

Petrovich worked — slip the resumé into the file and close the drawer. When I turn to leave, twin versions of Paul Bunyan block the door.

I try to slip past them. "Excuse me fellas."

They move in, eclipsing the hallway light. "You just stay put."

They're mill workers wearing hardhats, work boots and reflective vests. They stand with their arms crossed; judging by their size, these guys could be the backup in case the forklift breaks down. Someone must have thought to check if there really is an Insurance Underwriters of America. "If you'll just let me slip past, I've got another meeting."

The forklifts don't move. There's no other way out.

"Okay guys, I'm losing my patience."

Maybe I can get past them. If I hit low —

Carmen's voice, from down the hall. "He's in here."

The mill workers step back and two Mounties in uniform fill the gap. It's Harder — the rookie who escorted me from the bombing scene, and Bergren.

"Well, what have we got here?" says Bergren.

"You again," says Harder.

"I can explain. There's something here you've got to see."

"Let's go for a little drive," says Bergren.

"It's right here." I move toward the file cabinet.

"Turn around," says Bergren. "Slowly."

I turn. Slowly. Their guns aren't out but Harder is a little too eager for my taste, his hand resting on his holster. They don't cuff me but lead me out by the arm like bodyguards. Carmen and the other girls from the office muster to watch the action. The Mounties let me drive my truck to town.

Bergren is my silent passenger.

I spend some time alone in the interrogation closet of the local detachment, contemplating the walls. They should put up some pictures, pin up a few anti-drug slogans, maybe a wanted poster or two. Liven the place up a bit. Or they could do one of those IKEA commercials were they redecorate a public bathroom, make it look like a palace. I'm mulling over the possibilities when Bergren comes in, closes the door, uses a damp sleeve to wipe sweat off his forehead. "Christ it's hot out there. I used to want to work in the tropics. So much for that."

"I used to want to be a cop," I say. "Until I saw the suicide rate."

"Touché," Bergren says. He seems to be in a good mood, chuckling as he sits down. "Insurance investigator. Not terribly original. And not terribly bright, doing it twice in a row."

"I was a little worried about that."

The door opens again, bumping Bergren's chair. Rachet comes in. He's out of uniform, in shorts and a polo shirt, looks like a tourist. Sweat beads on his face like condensation on a cool glass. In the confines of the small room his odour adds a new sense of urgency — I want to wrap this up quickly. "I actually had a day off Cassel. I was on the seventh hole, my first game all year. Twelve hundred bucks for a membership and I get to use it once."

"Maybe you should pay as you go."

"Maybe." He pulls up a chair, leans back and crosses his meaty legs, displays enough black hair and white skin to frighten a tarantula. "So what have we got today? A little Mickey Spillane? A little more Mike Hammer action?"

"More like Cluseau," Bergren says.

"At least Cluseau was funny. I had to drive an hour and a half because you wanted to play detective." Rachet frowns at me. "I don't see a lot of humour in that. Let's just dispense with the niceties and you tell me exactly what you thought you were doing. So I can salvage something of my day off."

"I think I found something."

"Really," he says. "Surprise me."

"A clue?" says Bergren. "I'll try to contain myself."

Up to now, they've regarded me as a nuisance but I'm pretty sure they'll be interested in what I have to tell them. "Do you know who Zeke Petrovich is?"

"Petrovich?" Rachet looks thoughtful.

"The mechanic," Bergren prompts.

"Right, the mechanic. Works for the mill here. What about him?"

"Do you know where else he's worked?"

"What's that got to do with anything?"

"Turns out, he worked for every company that's been bombed."

Rachet swats at a fly, doesn't look concerned.

"At about the right time," I add. I can't believe they don't see where this is going.

"The right time for what?"

"For him to be the Lorax."

The Mounties exchange a look I've seen before. It's not encouraging. "You don't find that even vaguely suspicious? That he had the opportunity and means to plant the bombs?"

"Opportunity and means," Rachet says. "You've been reading Agatha Christie."

"Look —"

"The only company Mr. Petrovich has worked for that's been bombed is this one."

"What?"

Rachet gives me an impatient look. "Zeke Petrovich has worked here for the past eight years. Before that, he worked for a garage in Nova Scotia."

"No —" I dig out my notebook. "He's worked for every one of them."

Rachet leans forward, holds out a hand. "May I see that?"

I hand him my notebook. "I pulled this info from his resumé —"

"Interesting. You've been busy."

"I'd rather you didn't —"

"What's this entry here? Debris sample to be analyzed?"

"That's nothing. Another case."

"So you're branching out?"

"Something like that. I'd like my notes back."

"In a minute." Rachet lingers — the discriminating reader — hands my notebook to Bergren, who vanishes, leaving Rachet and me alone together in the tiny room.

"Don't you need a warrant or something to confiscate my notes?"

"That's the least of your problems."

"Look, I *saw* his resumé. I had it in my hands —"

Rachet sighs. "We looked into Petrovich. He was the last person to do any work on Hess's machine. But he checked out, so far anyway. I don't know what you thought you saw but we've done the work. Petrovich was nowhere near the other bombing sites."

Something isn't right. "He's used dynamite before —"

"That why you went to X-Pert Explosives?"

"What?" That wasn't in my notebook.

"The guy called," Rachet says. "He was suspicious, took your licence plate."

"I thought it would be worth looking into."

"Did you, Mr. Barry Petrovich? Or should I call you Mr. Hassenfloss?"

I massage my eyes, take a moment. "You're missing the point."

"No, you're missing the point." Rachet stabs a finger at me. He doesn't look so casual anymore. "You're dangerously close to interfering with a police investigation. This is no game you're playing here."

"You don't have to tell me —"

"Apparently I do. If I'm to have any chance of catching the bastard that's doing this, I can't have you blundering around. Impersonating people. Questioning people. Creating expectations and doubts. The only thing you'll succeed in doing is destroying opportunities for professional investigation. And if that notation in your notes about analysing debris has *anything* to do with this case then you're farther across the line than you realize. Make no mistake, I'll lock you up to protect the integrity of this investigation."

There's an uncomfortable silence, broken by Bergren's return. He hands the notebook to Rachet, who hands it to me. I pocket it, protectively. "Maybe you've seen the wrong resumé."

Rachet shakes his head.

"Did you look at the one at the mill?"

"If it'll make you feel better, I'll send someone over for it."

"That would make me feel better."

Rachet nods to Bergren, who leaves again.

"There are other things," I say. "Petrovich has been following me around. My first day in town, I was taking a bike ride, he nearly ran me over. Twice he's picked fights with me."

"That what happened to your face?"

"That was Petrovich. He seems to have it in for me, which makes sense if he's the Lorax. And then there's the dynamite. A local guy told me that Petrovich used to blow beaver dams."

"Why do you think the Lorax is using dynamite?" Rachet's expression is deadpan. He lets me twist for a moment. "I know about the Red Flag Task Force," he says. "You shouldn't be using your access for anything outside the authority of that investigation."

"Is that why you put me under observation?"

"I put you under observation because I thought you might do exactly what you're doing."

"Did you stop to think that it might be embarrassing for my arson investigation?"

Rachet looks unconcerned. "It's an acceptable inconvenience."

I want to object, but have been overruled. Once again, I've been found out-of-order and dangerously close to contempt. I try to redirect. "The Lorax is using dynamite though. We can agree on that?"

Rachet gives me a noncommittal shrug.

"So there could be a connection to Petrovich."

"You're fishing," Rachet says. "But I will tell you that if the Lorax used dynamite he wouldn't have used the type your buddy Petrovich would have bought for blasting beaver dams."

"What type would he have used?"

Rachet hesitates, clearly wondering how much to tell me. "Seismic gel," he says finally. "It has traces of barium sulphate, a densifying agent not found in the composition of what your friend would have used for blasting beaver dams."

"You found this at all the sites?"

Rachet gives me a half-smile. "How is your arson investigation going?"

I debate telling Rachet my theory that there may be a connection between both cases. Maybe when I have some evidence, something more than a hunch. "Slowly," I tell him.

"No suspects?"

I shake my head.

"Frustrating, isn't it."

Bergren returns, empty-handed, and Rachet gives him a questioning look. "Same resumé we have on file," says Bergren. "He's worked in Curtain River for the past eight years."

"That's impossible. I saw it —"

Rachet shakes his head, gives me a sad but understanding look. "I think, Mr. Cassel, that you want to find this Lorax so bad, you're seeing him everywhere." He lifts his hands in an expression of helplessness. "But your judgement is clouded."

"My judgement is not clouded. I saw the damn resumé —"

"Which is why I feel I should not arrest you for interference. This time."

I have more to say but don't. Rachet's message is clear.

"Go home, Mr. Cassel. Stay out of our way and let us do our job."

19

AFTER THE DEBACLE at the mill and the resulting interrogation, I'm ready for some distraction and jump at Carl's suggestion of a poker game. Beer, music and a group of socially maladjusted forest rangers and firefighters. Perfect. Carl pulls his heavy, wooden kitchen table away from the wall and by eight o'clock there are a half dozen of us dealing, drinking and telling the usual stories about fires, deranged tower people and helicopter crashes.

"You hear about the guy who tried to steal the 206?"

Jason Kermicki is telling this one. The local initial attack crew leader, he's a big guy and the youngest at the table. He came highly recommended, meaning he brought beer. But an hour into the card game, he's won more than his share and siphoned off most of the beer he came with. His decibel level has been increasing steadily, drowning out Jim Morrison on a portable CD player someone brought

"Yeah, I guess this firefighter was pissed right up one night and figures he's seen the pilot take off and land enough times, figures he can do just as good."

"I heard this one," says Carl. "It's bullshit."

"No, it really happened —" Kermicki talks with an earnestness you only see in salesmen and the severely intoxicated, his face showing a nice, rose-coloured glow. "So he got the helicopter fired up and a few feet off the ground before he hit the old deadman's arc and flipped her over."

"I remember that," says Gary Hanlon. "He never got it off the ground."

Hanlon has been quiet and everyone is waiting for him to loosen up so they don't look too much drunker than the boss. Everyone except Kermicki, who cracks his last beer. "Told you it happened."

"You were like five years old then," says Carl.

"I've heard the story."

"Drink slower and play faster," says Carl. "You've got to work tomorrow."

The game continues. I drink more than I win, but I'm content. When I was a ranger, I went to a lot of games like this — it takes me back to a better time. I sip my beer, watch the faces, listen to stories I've mostly heard. Kermicki begins to lose his concentration and winnings. Carl pulls ahead.

"Hey, we're outa beer," says Malcolm, the warehouseman.

"Should be another case downstairs," says Carl.

I fold. "I'll get it."

Carl studies his cards. "It's on the shelf."

Downstairs, I go to a shelf at the far side of the basement. The shelf is built of heavy planking, chainsaw carpentry, and extends from the hot water tank to the end of Carl's workbench. Boxes and paint cans fill the shelf. I can't see any beer so I begin to shift the boxes around. Nails, scraps of leather, junk. I think I see what might be a beer case on the top shelf, have to climb onto a lower shelf to see. I move a bag of steel wool out of the way. No beer, just the case, filled with more junk. I'm about to jump down when something catches my attention. At first it looks like the end of a piece of wood but then looks familiar. I pull it out. It's an Emperador cigar box; The Largest Marketed Cigar in the World.

I step down from the shelf, ponder the box, slide it open. It's empty.

Has to be a coincidence. When I look around the basement my eye falls on Carl's reloading press, and a shelf on the wall above, lined with cans of gunpowder. Smokeless powder. Black powder. Just another coincidence? I turn back to the shelf, slap the cigar box idly against the palm of my hand. Hendrix drifts through the floorboards, singing about castles in the sand. Carl has a muzzle-loader which takes black powder and I shake my head, remember what Rachet told me. Maybe I am getting paranoid. I should put the box back. Behind me, the stairs creak.

"That was a hell of a cigar," says Carl. "Took me a week to smoke it."

I look at the box, feel like a thief.

"You find the beer?" he asks.

"No."

Carl looks around. "I thought it was on the shelf. Or maybe I put it in the root cellar." He opens a narrow door, pulls a string hanging from a bulb. Carl is the only guy I know who has a root cellar. We had one on the farm when I was growing up. But we also had a wringer washer and you could buy half a dozen bags of potato chips for a dollar. The beer is next to a hundred pound sack of potatoes. "Here we are."

I'm still holding the cigar box. "Carl, where'd you get this?"

"Christmas present," he says. "Guy I met in Mexico sent it up."

A reasonable explanation. Carl hands me the beer. "What's the matter, Porter?"

I shake my head, set the box on the workbench. "Nothing. Let's play cards."

Upstairs, we receive a round of applause. Out west, a hero is the guy who finds the last case of beer. Runner-up is the guy who passes out first. I'm feeling just good enough that if I don't watch myself I'm in danger of capturing both titles. Ross McPherson, an old cowboy with a sweat-stained hat and kerchief around his neck, deals us back in. It's only nickel and dime stuff but an hour later I've lost 20 bucks which to me is still a lot of money. The phone rings for a long time before someone answers — they probably figure the antique wall phone is just a gag. It's for me, which is just as well because the boys are tired of playing for pocket change and the paper is coming out. I grab the phone, lean against a big old grandfather clock; Carl's only stationary timepiece.

"Hello?"

"Hey Porter, it's Bill. You sound kinda faint —"

I look at the antique wall phone. "I'm in a different time zone."

"What's that noise. Are you staying in a bar?"

"We're playing poker. You should come on down."

A short chuckle. "Sure, I'll crank up the plane. Be right there."

I'm overcome by a sudden nostalgia and want Bill to join us. We had some good poker games over the last two years. But it's a three-hour drive and by then the beer will be gone, someone will have won all the money and will have to run for his life. It'll be funny, watching someone run with 20 pounds of change.

"You still there Porter?"

"What?" My mind is wandering. Look out for a little grey squishy thing.

"I got the results back on that metal. Had to send it to a place in the States."

"Oh yeah? Who won a medal?"

A sigh. "The metal, Porter. You remember, the piece you gave me?"

It takes a moment to realize what Bill is talking about. "Oh right. Let me guess, it was seismic dynamite with traces of barium phosphate or sulphate or something like that."

There's a pause. Bill must be wondering how I know.

"No, Porter. It was C4."

"What?"

"C4, Porter. They found traces of RDX and microcratering."

"Use English, Bill."

"Microcraters are tiny little craters in the metal formed by extreme heat and force. You only get that with high explosives, not with dynamite. RDX stands for Research Development Explosive. It's a military term. You can't get this stuff at the corner store. You either steal it from the military, or you buy it on the black market."

There's a burst of laughter from the card table. I watch McPherson slap Kermicki on the back, pull a pile of bills home to papa. I'm sobering fast, trying to make sense of what Bill is saying — two different types of explosive, one more powerful than the other.

Bill's voice cuts in like a loud speaker. "You still there buddy?"

"I'm here."

"They said the sample had to come from pretty close to the centre of the blast."

There's more noise from the card table as Kermicki argues with McPherson, trying to get his money back. Kermicki's having a hard time getting the words out; he sounds like an old record at half speed. McPherson is grinning.

"So what are we talking about here Bill? What sort of expertise do you need to use this stuff?"

"Any halfwit can wire up a bomb. The ones that are no good at it don't last long — there's a fairly quick process of natural selection at work here — but who ever did this had access to C4. So why use this kind of shit when there are a hundred other more accessible explosives? You could just toss in a few sticks of dynamite. Or even easier, mix up something in your garage; a little nitrogen fertilizer and diesel."

"You think this was a professional job?"

"Think about it for a minute —" Bill has music on in the background; Holly Cole singing about a one-trick pony. That pony is having more luck than me lately. "Those machines were down for what? A half-hour? The guy got in during a pretty small window and managed to hit multiple targets. That takes timing Porter, and surveillance. This wasn't spur of the moment and it wasn't some kid with a pipe bomb. I'd say you're dealing with a career-minded individual here."

Six feet away, the alcoholic ante has just gone up — Malcolm has a bottle of vodka, Silent Sam — it's about the only thing silent around here. Hanlon rummages in the fridge for mix, trapping me in the corner with the fridge door. He sounds like a hungry bear going through a camper's icebox. My experience with Carl's fridge leads me to believe he will emerge disappointed. "You have any sort of database of people that might be able to do this Bill? Anything you could look up?"

There's a reluctant sigh on the other end of the line. I can picture Bill running his hand through his hair. "I can run a profile through CPIC but it would be pretty general, so I don't think that would help much. And it's not like I have an open conduit there either. I'm not an active member anymore."

Hanlon has resorted to squeezing the juice out of an orange. It's not a pretty sight.

"What about military records?"

"That's a whole other universe, Porter. They're not exactly

thrilled to lay open their database to outsiders, even law enforcement. I know a guy that might be able to help if I ask real nice. But I don't want to bother him unless we know what we're looking for."

I close the fridge door before anything gets out. "Any suggestions?"

"None that you'd like. What was it you said earlier about seismic dynamite?"

"That's what the Lorax has been using. Up until now."

There's a pause. Holly Cole has moved onto "Romantically Helpless" — my personal theme song. Carl is motioning me over to rejoin the festivities. He's got two shot glasses in his hands with a red liquid that looks suspiciously like vodka and food colouring. I hold up my hand — give me five minutes. "You know, Porter," Bill says, "that's a little unusual, changing his MO like that. Which could mean several things. We could be talking copycat. Or he's upgraded, accessed some new product. Or maybe it's just some nut from down south, practising. The operations in the U.S. have been hit enough they're becoming cautious. Hunting here might be a little easier."

"You'd think people here would be cautious enough after the other Lorax attacks."

"Yeah, you'd think." Bill sounds tired now. "But who knows. All those attacks, then nothing for years. They probably thought he'd gone away."

"We should be so lucky."

There's a pause filled with static.

"Would it do any good to tell you to back away from this?" Bill asks.

"I doubt it."

"So what are you going to do?"

"I don't know. But thanks. I owe you one."

"More than one, Porter. So be careful. I intend to collect."

I stop drinking after I hang up the phone, turn down Carl's experimental shooters, wait for my head to clear. The game continues on its predictable trajectory. Kermicki charges straight into the vodka, gets louder and drunker. Ross McPherson, the only real gambler, wins all the money. By general consent, we stop playing at about midnight. Carl stands, begins to collect the dead soldiers, tosses them at a recycle box. Good thing they're cans, not bottles.

"Good time," says Hanlon. "Let's do it again next week."

"Count me in," says McPherson, pocketing our money.

"Aw shit," says Kermicki. "I don't feel so good."

"Go outside before you puke," says Carl.

There are a few grunted goodbyes and then it's just Carl and me, straightening up. We clean off the table, push it back against the wall. There's a beer spill on the floor where Kermicki sat, like a bloodstain at a murder scene. Carl goes for a mop, moving in slow motion, using the walls for support. He changes his mind, sits on a chair in the middle of the kitchen. His eyes are puffy — he's exhausted but like most drunks refuses to give in. "We should go to the bar," he mumbles, staring at the floor. "The night is young."

Younger than us. I'm not 18 anymore. "We have to work tomorrow."

"Screw that," says Carl. "— just a waste of time."

I find the mop, clean up the spill. Carl lifts his feet out of the way like we're playing Simon Says but has a hard time keeping them up. He kicks at the mop. "Come on Porter. What are you doing, cleaning at this time of night? Let's go party, like the old days. You remember the way we used to party."

"I remember," I say. "That was too much work."

Carl snuffles at some memory. "Who was on the phone?" he asks sleepily.

"Bill Star," I tell him. "You remember Bill —"

But Carl is snoring, slumped forward on the chair, his legs splayed out. I leave him like that, put away the mop. Outside, Kermicki is puking in a hedge, his wide back lit by the porch light, making sounds like a sump pump in reverse. Thank God I'm not 18 anymore.

There's no moon tonight; streetlights are the only sign of life. I need to go for a walk, think and clear my head. But I'm tired. I'll just go a few blocks, let the tension and noise of the evening disperse. Before I know it, I'm across town, staring down the highway. The last streetlight looks like the end of the world; I go past there I'm liable to fall off. I linger, not ready to return to Carl's little house and the hard, empty bed in his spare room. It's comfortably cool out here and I feel a bit better, decide to keep walking, pretend I don't know where I'm going.

A narrow side street along the river leads to the RV park. Away from the streetlights it's so dark I sense rather than see the road, use a gap in the trees to navigate. Gravel crunches underfoot and I smell damp rock and vegetation along the river. Motorhomes are faint white rectangles like relics from some lost civilization. I walk faster, looking forward to seeing her more than I want to admit. But when I find her stall the Bug is gone, her motorhome locked up tight. Disappointed, I sit in a plastic lawn chair, listen to night sounds, let the last of the drink clear my head.

I wonder where she is, hoping she'll come back.

I wonder if she misses me.

I walk back into town, watch stars bob past pointed tree tops. Research Development Explosive. Seismic gel. Two different types of explosive, one more powerful than the other. Why start bombing again after a three-year break? Is the C4 an escalation of the Lorax's technique? Or, as Bill suggested, was it a copycat who killed Ronald Hess? A professional?

Who would have the most to gain? Is gain even a consideration?

I'm in a dim alley behind a Chinese restaurant. Streetlights cast long craggy shadows. Maybe the bomber is a follower of the Lorax who's frustrated the bombings stopped. Maybe it's more than that and Hess's death wasn't accidental — the Lorax nothing more than a convenient scapegoat. It would be easy to dump a body in an idle machine, toss in some high explosive, spraypaint a calling card on a nearby tree. Easy, but when the police begin to look more closely, the killer gets nervous, decides he needs a Lorax, picks Petrovich, a single guy with a criminal record, known to have used dynamite. That would explain the second, incriminating resumé. But it wouldn't hold up to scrutiny — Rachet already knows it's not Petrovich. So why go through the effort, only to yank the resumé?

Maybe the killer had second thoughts, knew it wouldn't work.

I'm behind some building, a furniture store judging by the size of the empty boxes stacked by the door. Modern folk art waltzes across the back wall. Maybe I'm getting old but the scribbles don't make sense. We used to write useful credos like "Clapton is God" and "Cream Rules." This stuff is just cryptic. But then again, so is my theory. Why bother with such a weak frame when up until now they haven't been able to catch the real Lorax?

From a distance come the sounds of an argument, voices rising and dropping. I'm staring at the scribbles on the wall, wondering why someone bothered painting graffiti no one can read, when it comes to me.

It's not the message that's important, it's the fact that it's there.

For a long time, there's no answer at Linda Hess's door. But her minivan is in the driveway and so I keep pressing the doorbell. I can hear the muffled buzz from deep within the house — if there's anyone home they've probably called the cops by now. I'm about to give up when the door rattles. Getrude Hess glares at me through the glass of the storm door.

"I'm sorry to wake you like this but I need to speak with Linda."

Gertrude is bleary-eyed, stands holding herself in a floral print nightgown. A wedge of light from deeper within the house lights her hair from behind, projecting a frizzy halo. This is Linda Hess in 20 years; she should enjoy her youth.

"It's two o'clock in the bloody morning."

"I know — I'm sorry — but I need to talk to your daughter."

"Linda is sleeping." Her voice has a coarse, halting rasp, the timbre of a serious career smoker. It doesn't make her any more friendly. "She took a pill and she's sleeping. I think you should go home." Her hand is on the edge of the door, already closing. I've got about two seconds to present my argument. It may be all I need.

"Ronny's death might not have been an accident."

The door doesn't stay closed for long. Gertrude looks at me like a grizzly trying to decide if I'm edible — it's enough to make you want to play dead. We stare at each other for a moment through the imaginary safety of the storm door. "You want to run that by me again?"

I pick my words carefully. "There's a possibility it may have been more than accident."

"A possibility? What the hell's that supposed to mean?"

I don't want to elaborate too much, standing on her doorstep. I want to talk to Linda. But security around here is tougher than at an English airport. "I've been looking into a few things. Some of them just don't make sense. If I could just —"

She takes a step forward, pointing at me. "You gotta hell of a

nerve, mister."

I raise my hands — a defensive manoeuvre recommended against attacking bears and cougars; better they get your arms than your throat. "Maybe I should come back in the morning."

"Now you want to come back in the morning. Isn't that lovely."

Maybe I won't come back at all. "Once again, I apologize —"

I'm turning away, heading down the steps, when she calls after me.

"It's hard enough already," she says. "Linda doesn't need this."

I agree but hesitate, caught in mid-flight. Her anger is fading, replaced by a desperate sort of curiosity. Like me, she has to know. She stands on the concrete top step, the door half open, like a woman talking to a salesman. I wait. She bites her lower lip, glances inside, looks at me again. "Just a minute," she says quietly. "I'll see if she'll talk to you."

A minute later she's back. She holds open the door. "Come in."

As I pass her, I smell the fabric softener in her gown, the nicotine in her sweat.

"Stay right here."

Gertrude heads down a hall, nightgown rustling behind her. I stand on the little plastic mat just inside the door. In the filtered light coming from the kitchen the room looks different, and it takes me a minute to see why. The furniture has been rearranged, the couch moved to the opposite wall, the recliner closer to the fireplace. Grief management through redecoration — maybe I should have tried that instead of the bottle. It helps to have the furniture to rearrange. A few long minutes are filled with the tick of an invisible clock. A door opens. Someone coughs. Linda shuffles into the kitchen and a chair drags on the floor.

Linda's mother calls to me. "Take off your boots Mr. Cassel."

I leave my boots, still coated with ash, on the floor mat, walk across the carpet. Moisture soaks through my socks; they've been steam-cleaning recently. Linda is seated at the big oak table. She's wearing a blue terry housecoat. Beneath the table I see pale legs and a pair of slippers shaped like big bear's paws. Her hair is a mess and she looks zonked out, staring at nothing. Her eyes track across the kitchen and come slowly to rest on me. I feel a twinge of guilt at rousting her from her bed. But it's too late now.

"I'm sorry to wake you Mrs. Hess —"

"Just ask her what you need to know."

Linda's mother stands behind her like a presidential bodyguard. The kitchen smells of pine-scented cleaner and the chrome faucets gleam like jewels. Linda pivots her head and looks at me. I pause, rub my hands, pull out a chair and sit down so I'm not so threatening. Linda watches, expressionless.

"Linda, I need to know if Ronald had any enemies at work."

She blinks. Her expression doesn't change.

"Was there anyone he didn't get along with? Anyone he disagreed with?"

Linda glances up at her mother, who puts a hand on her shoulder, gives her a grim but encouraging nod. Still, it takes her a minute to answer: a delay like a conversation from deep space.

"No," she says, almost whispering. "I don't think so, not that I knew of anyway. He didn't like to talk about his work. I told them that. The police — I told them everything."

I shift uncomfortably in my chair, wonder what I'm doing here at this time of night. She's so tired and doped up it's a miracle she can talk. I tell myself that if I can solve this, it'll help her like it'll help me — a leap of faith for us both. I try to make eye contact but her gaze drifts away and she stares at the table like a reluctant little girl in trouble. "Linda, I know you've been through all of this before, but I believe someone Ronny worked with might be involved."

Linda frowns, still staring at the table: a sleeping frown, a bad dream frown. Her mother stares at me, concerned. Under her concern is a harder look, a vindictive desire for revenge that twists down the corners of her mouth. "Why do you say that?" she asks quickly. "Is there something new?"

I'm not sure how much to tell them because I'm not sure how much of it means something. I don't want to create expectations. "I don't know anything for sure," I say carefully, "but someone at the mill feels uncomfortable enough to be tampering with their records."

"Tampering?" Gertrude's eyes narrow. "What do you mean?"

"It may be nothing, but there were some inconsistencies."

"At two in the morning Mr. Cassel, it had better be something."

"A mechanic," I say. "His employment record was manipulated."

Gertrude takes a seat next to her daughter, holds Linda's hand but it's me she's watching. "So what does this mean Mr. Cassel? Why would someone manipulate these records?"

"I'm not sure. That's why I wanted to talk to your daughter."

Gertrude turns her attention to Linda, strokes her daughter's arm. "Think about it honey." Her tone is soothing, like she's talking to a four-year old. "Did Ronny ever have a disagreement with a mechanic? Is there anything that he said? Anything you've forgotten until now?"

Linda looks at her mother, then reluctantly at me. She clutches with a pale hand at the front of her gown as if it might open. She's fighting depression, exhaustion and sleeping pills. For a long moment the three of us sit together in silence, then she sighs, shakes her head. "No, I don't think so. He never talked about any mechanics. We've only been here a few months. We didn't really know anybody ..."

Her head begins to bob. She's drifting again.

"Linda, how were things going for Ronny on the new job?"

It takes her a moment to lift her head and when she does, her eyelids flutter against the light and her hand slips away from the front of her gown, rests on the table like a pale, wilted flower. I'm running out of time. "Things were going okay," she says faintly. "He was taking correspondence. He wanted to become an engineer. He liked to build things."

"So he wasn't going to make a career out of this?"

"He had trouble with the math," she says, like a parent reporting after teacher interviews. "Polynomials confused him. But he was trying. We talked about a tutor —"

"Polynomials confuse everyone. What about his job? How did he like that?"

"He got frustrated, sometimes."

"What frustrated him?" Her eyes are closing again. "Linda — what frustrated him?"

"So many people got hurt ..." Her head sinks as though in prayer.

"Who got hurt Linda?"

Her mother puts an arm around her. "Just a few more minutes, honey. Then I'll put you to bed. Just try to think about it. What did Ronny say about people getting hurt?"

Linda looks at me, dreamy, as if in a trance. "Just people," she says, raising a limp hand. "A finger here, a thumb there. I saw them at the hospital, in the Emergency. So many injuries ..."

"Did Ronny ever talk to anyone about this?"

She frowns. "He just called them barbarians."

"He didn't try to bring this to anyone's attention?"

"I wanted him to give it up but he said we needed the money. But we didn't need the money. We could have made out ..." Linda's face begins to crumple and she wails. "I tried to tell him and now he's gone —"

"That's okay baby —" Her mother leans over, holds her tight, rocking her like a child. She glances over at me, her expression worried but capable.

"I'm terribly sorry." I can't think of anything better to say. "If there's anything —"

"Good night Mr. Cassel."

I pull on cold boots, close the door. I hear her sobbing long after I leave.

20

I don't sleep much the rest of the night. My circadian rhythm demands I go to bed early to get a good night's sleep or I toss and turn, can't stop thinking and have weird dreams. Last night was worse than usual. I finally fall into a trance-like half-sleep around five o'clock. At seven the alarm does its best at dragging me back to the real, no less confusing world. I hit snooze by yanking the clock radio out by the cord and tossing it under the bed. A half-hour later its owner subs in, shaking me and rummaging around the room.

"Time to get up Porter."

"Uh-huh."

"Have you seen the alarm clock?"

I pull the blankets over my head. "What alarm clock?"

But Carl can't be set to snooze and ten minutes later I'm in the kitchen, feeling like a Picasso — nothing in quite the right place. I think my body is rejecting itself. "You look like shit," he says. He's in uniform, seated at the table and eating a grapefruit. "You go to the bar with Kermicki?"

Kermicki must have a death wish. "I went for a walk."

"Maybe you should have gone to the bar."

I look in the fridge for the source of the grapefruits. Carl is a binge shopper — there have to be 40 or 50 grapefruits in there, piled like cannon balls. Or some school is having a fundraising drive and an enterprising student caught Carl at the office. I grab a grapefruit, cut it in half, take a seat across from Carl. "How much did McPherson take off you last night?" he asks.

"About 40 bucks. Which is most of my retirement savings."

Carl chuckles. "Yeah, he's a shark. So where'd you go? You see Christina?"

"No, she wasn't home."

"She lives here in town?"

"She's just visiting. Carl, what do you know about Curtain River Forest Products?"

"Not much to know." He squeezes grapefruit juice into a bowl. "They've been around for about eight years. Whitlaw came up from Texas and bought the old mill along the river, spent a few years running that. Then he put a proposal in to the government for a bigger timber area and when he got it, they built the new mill."

I gouge out a piece of grapefruit. It sprays juice all over my shirt, into my eye. You need goggles to eat these things. I squint, look through blurred eyes for the emergency eyewash station. There isn't one — Carl's kitchen isn't up to Workers' Compensation standards. I may have to file a claim. "When was that?" I ask, dabbing with my shirt cuff.

"The new mill?" Carl looks thoughtful. "About fours years ago."

"They have any problems?"

"What kind of problems?"

"Well, this is kind of a sensitive area to cut timber isn't it?"

"You mean environmentally? Yeah, it's sensitive. Since day one, the environmental groups have been all over the company about the expansion. They lobbied the government against giving

Whitlaw the larger area, staged protests, even took him to court. But he got his way, just like every other big project."

"What about safety problems? People getting hurt?"

"It happens. It's a dangerous business, Porter. Lots of machines. Steep slopes. Inexperienced operators. They used to have one of those signs by the mill, the type that lists how many days they've been accident free. But they took it down."

"They took it down?"

Carl slurps juice from his bowl. "Yeah. Probably got tired of starting at zero."

I ponder this while Carl makes himself half a dozen sandwiches for lunch. "I need you to do a tower service up north," he says over his shoulder. "A fly-in job. The grocery order has to be picked up. There's no rain in the forecast so you'll have to bring plenty of drinking water."

The phone rings while I'm in the bathroom. Carl hollers that it's for me.

"Yeah?" I hold the spindle of the earpiece with a damp hand.

"Is this Porter Cassel?"

"Sometimes. The mirror doesn't always agree."

"This is Porter Cassel, right?" A deep, coarse voice — annoyed and more than a little anxious. But I still recognize it. I picture his face just as he tells me his name. "This is Zeke Petrovich. The mechanic. I need to talk to you."

I hesitate, wonder why he would call me. I doubt he wants to discuss his resumé or the finer points of dynamite usage. Maybe he's just run out of people to pulverize and I've come up in the rotation again. "Is this the Zeke Petrovich who drives that piece of shit old truck?"

"Uh, yeah, that's me —"

"And whose boot print is still tattooed on my cheek?"

"Oh, right." A forced chuckle. "Sorry about that."

I'm silent for a minute. Why would he mention that he's a mechanic?

"You still there?"

"What do you want, Petrovich?"

"Like I said, I need to talk to you."

"See that thing in your hand?"

"What —"

"That's a phone Petrovich. So start talking."

"Very funny. Look — I can't talk on the phone."

"Why not?"

"It's kinda complicated."

I can't imagine him doing anything complicated. That he's a mechanic is frightening enough. "So you want to meet me somewhere?"

"Yeah." He sounds relieved. "That'd be good."

"Okay." This might be an opportunity to clear up a few things. "When and where?"

"Now, at my place." There's a pause, a half-beat long. "You know where it is."

"I'm a little busy this morning —"

"I got to talk to you now."

I look over at Carl, who's still making sandwiches. "This can't wait until tonight?"

"No. This can't wait."

I consider for a moment. "I'll be there in a half-hour."

"Come by yourself," he says. It's almost a whisper. "I don't trust nobody."

The line goes dead. I replace the mouthpiece, wondering why he trusts me after what's happened. Maybe it's easier to trust someone you can beat to a pulp. Maybe he thinks we've bonded.

Either way, I'm taking no chances. "Carl, can I borrow your shotgun?"

"What?" He's puzzled. "You don't need one for tower service."

"It's not for tower service."

He sets aside his sandwiches, gives me a worried look. "What's up?"

"Nothing, I hope. I need an hour or two off this morning. Can the service wait?"

"What's going on, Porter?"

I'm not sure I want to involve him further. "It's probably nothing."

"A 12-gauge nothing?" He isn't going to let this go.

"You remember Zeke Petrovich?"

"Sure — guy that redecorated your face."

"That was him on the phone."

"What did he want?"

"He didn't say, but I think he may be the Lorax. Or I did. Now I'm not so sure."

Carl frowns. "What makes you think he could be the Lorax?"

I tell him about my second visit to Curtain River Forest Products, finding the resumé — how Petrovich worked at all the bombing locations. Or at least that's the way it was supposed to look. Carl's frown deepens when I tell him what the Mounties had on file for Petrovich.

"This is a set-up," he says. "Why didn't you tell me about this earlier?"

"I'm not sure about any of this, Carl. I didn't want to bother you."

He points a finger at me. "You didn't want to bother me? Porter, you're here because I wanted to help you — I got you this job because I knew you couldn't leave this thing alone. I wanted to be here for you. But what do you do? You get yourself into trouble, then ask to borrow my shotgun, telling me it's probably nothing."

I don't know why he's so worked up about this. "I appreciate what you've done for me —"

"Yeah — right." He waves it off.

"And your concern, Carl. But let's not blow this out of proportion —"

He turns away in disgust, paces into the living room where I can't see him. I stay in the kitchen, give him a minute to calm down. This is a little odd — Carl is usually so laid back. I've never seen him this agitated. Maybe he still feels responsible for getting me involved because he called me after the bombing. I hear him breathing heavy in the other room. The grandfather clock says 7:40. I've got to get going.

"Look, Carl. I didn't know this meant so much to you."

A few more minutes pass before Carl comes back into the kitchen. When he does, he's rubbing his forehead and frowning. "I'm just trying to be a friend here, Porter. Trying to give you a little bit of support. If the situation were reversed, I'd hope you'd do the same."

"Of course —"

"But quite frankly, Porter, it seems like you don't want my help."

He chews his lip, staring at the floor. I try to sound conciliatory. "That's not it. I appreciate everything you've done for me. I know it was tough to call me after the bombing but I appreciate that you did. I need to get this out of my system — to see this end — but I'm not sure it's such a good idea for you to become too deeply involved. The cops are already giving me a hard time and you have to live in this community. You've got a job here. I don't want you to jeopardize that."

"That's it?" he asks, looking me in the eye. "That's the only reason?"

"Yeah, that's it. I'm trying to be a good friend too."

He seems to relax a bit. "So you're going to meet this guy?"

I nod.

"You still think he might be the Lorax?"

"I don't know." I can't help a frustrated sigh. "He's involved, somehow."

"Then I should come to back you up."

"I really don't think that's a good idea."

For a minute we look at each other. "You're sure?" he says. "I wouldn't mind —"

"I'll be back by ten for the tower service."

There's a pause. I'm sure he's going to insist but he nods, not looking at me. "Okay. I'll have someone pick up the groceries and fill the water pails. If you can make it back by ten, that would be fine. The shotgun is in the closet by the back door. Shells are on the top shelf."

I find the gun — a short, police model with a long magazine in the pump. It takes seven shells. Carl stands at the top of a short flight of stairs, watches me load. His narrow face is creased and unhappy but he doesn't say anything. I fill my coat pockets with extra shells.

We part silently.

Old Faithful's gas gauge doesn't work well below one-third but the station at the edge of town is busy, crowded with motorhomes lined up like sheep at a dipping station. I'm in a hurry and Petrovich's place isn't that far so I bypass. I've got travel insurance — a can in the back with some chainsaw gas. I spend the few minutes it takes to get there wondering why Petrovich called me, what exactly he could want to talk about. How he might ambush me. Shortly before eight I pull off the road a quarter mile from Petrovich's driveway, four-wheel across the ditch. There's an old seismic line, a narrow overgrown trail into the bush that swallows my truck like a child vanishing into a cornfield. I continue on foot.

A low draw choked with alder slows me, but at ten minutes past eight I'm crouched under a border of ragged spruce trees, watching Petrovich's place. The view from behind isn't impressive. At one time there was a homestead here, people working hard to tame the land. Now the land is taking it all back. A grey log house without windows or doors leans like a tired fighter. The roofline of a barn sags. A fleet of scrap cars and trucks lie in weeds, most of them on their sides or upside down, like buffalo after a slaughter. I use the rusted carcases to work my way closer to Petrovich's small trailer.

Gotta watch where I'm walking — I stumble on something in the grass, an anvil that could have fallen from the sky like a gag in a Saturday morning cartoon. Junk is strewn behind the trailer like a coral breakwater. A flock of abandoned shop tools — rusting drill presses and band saws — stand like awkward birds. There's enough lead in a pile of old batteries to ballast a sailboat. I tread lightly, work my way along the back of the trailer, peer around the corner, the horse my only witness — more entertainment than she's seen in years.

The monster truck is parked in front of the trailer; it doesn't look much better than the vehicles in the grass behind me. I try to peek into the trailer from a side window but the drapes are drawn. Like a kid with a seashell I place my ear against the side of the trailer — maybe I'll hear the roar of the assembly line. If Petrovich is home he's not moving around. The only sound comes from another quarter — the horse, snorting, swatting flies with its tail.

Despite my best efforts, the trailer stairs creak under my weight.

I open the door.

The trailer is dim; heavy brown drapes conceal the windows. I'm an easy target framed in the light of the doorway and step inside, close the door. My brief sunlit glimpse of the interior revealed a complete lack of housekeeping skills but no housekeeper. But then again I only saw part of the trailer and I stand silently, gun ready, waiting for my eyes adjust. Waiting for a noise.

"You there, Petrovich —"

My voice vanishes like a call in the night and the ensuing silence becomes more profound. A dripping sound, slow — a leaking faucet. Enough light seeps in below the heavy curtains that it doesn't take long before I see dirty newspapers scattered on the floor, a kitchen table cluttered with dismantled carburetors and cylinder heads. This guy needs his own shop in a bad way. A fridge next to the door screens my view. Where other fridges have clipped cartoons and kids' drawings, Petrovich's has Playboy centrefolds — a different kind of art. Past the fridge I find the source of the dripping.

"Oh Christ —"

Petrovich is in a chair that's pushed back from the table, his dirty hands folded neatly in his lap, his head tilted back against the panelboard wall. He could be taking a nap except for the raw gash in his neck — a drip not even the best plumber could fix. Blood is soaked into the newspapers littering the floor, wicking like a blossoming rose.

Blood that is still pooling.

I spin, raise the shotgun, pump a shell into the chamber. There's no one — no sound except the buzzing of a few flies, the squishy thump of my heart. The splat of thickening blood dropping onto newspaper. I'm breathing like a weightlifter doing aerobics. My eyes track across the table, the countertop, to a partially closed door at the end of a short hall — a perfect ambush. Gun at the ready, I approach, newspapers rustling under my boots. The door comes off its hinges when I kick, rattling wood, rattling me. The bed is unmade, clothes and a fortune in empty pop bottles strewn everywhere. The latest Snap-On Tools calendar hangs crookedly on the wall; big-breasted girls hold torque wrenches, pose next to a toolbox the size of a small car. On a dresser next to Petrovich's bed are kitchen knives with blackened ends, the cardboard tube from a roll of toilet paper, a small propane torch. Burnt crumbles of hash are littered like fly shit.

I use the muzzle of the shotgun to pull aside the corner of a drape.

Nobody outside either.

The bathroom.

I edge out of the bedroom, use my boot to nudge open the narrow bathroom door, yank aside a shower curtain. Mildew and a dank odour of rotting pressboard are the only hazards here. The sink is filled with mould or stubble, I can't tell which. The open toilet has been shellacked yellow. I return to the kitchen, take another look at Petrovich. One cut from ear to ear. No sign of a struggle, although it would be hard to tell in this dump. Still, he's a tough character — the killer must have taken him by surprise.

What could he have known that made him worth killing?

I stare at oily engine parts on the kitchen table, a half-eaten cinnamon bun, a moulding cup of coffee. I should check the cupboards, the drawers — this is the only chance I'll get to look over the crime scene. I set the shotgun on the table, search the kitchen. The usual bachelor staples — cans of soup and beans, instant coffee —

but nothing to suggest a motive. In the corner, Petrovich watches me with blank eyes, and I turn away, shuddering involuntarily.

Nothing suspicious in the bedroom. The bathroom is on its own.

I return to the body, careful not to step in blood. That his hands are neatly tucked in his lap is somehow more ominous than if they'd been frozen in some awkward death spasm. The killer waited until the struggle was over, probably held Petrovich down, then took the time to tidy up. Made him presentable. I can't help thinking it's a statement of some kind, although what it's supposed to say I don't know. I step on something hard, hidden under newsprint. Probably more engine parts, some bracket or shaft, but I squat, peel back layers of yesterday's news.

It's a knife with a bloody blade.

It's my knife.

A tension spider crawls up my back, nests on my scalp. I've stepped into this trap with both feet. The perfect suspect — I can hear Rachet telling everyone how I thought Petrovich was the Lorax and killed him out of revenge. Doesn't help that I didn't report my knife stolen.

But I found it again — that was fortunate.

My watch says I've already been here ten minutes. I need more time to look the place over but I can almost hear the sirens, sub-audible. Whoever set this up certainly would have called the police. I should have brought my camera but it's in the truck, crammed somewhere in a backpack. I'll have to read about it in the papers like everyone else.

Time to exit stage left.

There are plastic freezer bags in the cupboard. I pick the knife up between two fingers, bag it like leftover Thanksgiving turkey. It looks a little less appealing and I wonder if this is the proper way to store biological evidence. Will it degrade in there — rot or something? I'll worry about it after I get the hell away from here.

Fingerprints — what else did I touch?

I quickly wipe cupboard handles, the door — anything else I'm pretty sure I touched. I'm not really sure how much to wipe — there may be prints here from the killer. It's not the sort of situation they prepare you for in ranger school. In my rush, I nearly forget Carl's shotgun, have to dash back into the trailer. Then I'm running through the trees. Running for my life.

I place the knife in a clean Tupperware container from my humble crime scene kit then dig a small hole in the forest floor like a grieving boy about to intern his pet. I'm not sure I didn't leave any fingerprints in Petrovich's trailer and if Rachet finds the knife I'll be the one in a hole in some federal penitentiary. Better it stays here, hidden until I can figure out what to do. I mark the spot like a pirate burying treasure.

A dark, terrible treasure.

21

ON THE TRIP BACK to town, Old Faithful begins to lurch and spasm then stops altogether. I'm out of gas and my travel insurance has expired — sometime in the last year I've been cutting firewood. I sit on the fender for a few minutes but no one comes along. Finally, I use the satellite phone to call Carl.

"Carl, it's Porter. I'm out of gas."

"What am I?" he says. "The damn CAA?"

There's a silence. Carl is still mad at me. The road ripples in the heat. Grasshoppers buzz and crackle in the ditches. A heavy sigh over the ether. "Okay," he says finally. "Where are you?"

"A few miles north of that turn off with the big sign about acreages for sale."

"Just stay put," he says, as if I have a choice. "I'll send someone."

There's a click and the phone goes dead. I sit on the shoulder of the road, my back rested against a tire where I'm invisible to traffic. Now that help is on the way, I'm not eager to talk with any Good Samaritans. The scene in Petrovich's trailer is stamped on my memory like the afterimage of a camera flash. It's all I can do to quell a rising panic and I focus on my surroundings in an effort to remain grounded. Cows graze in a brown pasture shimmering with heat. Nine o'clock in the morning and it's already 30 degrees. I pass the time by tossing bits of gravel at a fence post, a sport I was markedly better at as a boy. Several vehicles roar past, immersing me in clouds of dust. A few minutes later, brakes squeal and gravel crunches — too soon for it to be the help sent by Carl.

I heave myself up. "Thanks for stopping but —"

It's an RCMP suburban. Constable Bergren has his elbow out the window, turns his reflective sunglasses in my direction. He's sweating heavily; the freckles on his cheeks look like specks of damp rust. I take a deep, steadying breath, force a calm I do not feel over my features.

"What are you doing out here, Cassel?"

He's interested in more than offering assistance — I'm still officially under observation.

"See those cows?"

Bergren turns to look.

"Well, I'm conducting a survey on bovine flatulence. Oh — there goes another one."

Bergren stares at me and I watch myself in his mirrored shades. I couldn't really look that haggard — it must be distortion. The distortion extends beyond the sunglasses to Bergren's face. He's not amused. By now they must have found Petrovich.

"I haven't got time for your bullshit, Cassel. Where did you come from?"

I turn, take a look at my truck, point toward the rear bumper. "I'm not sure, but I think maybe I came from that direction. Of course, I'm not a real detective like you guys so you might want to check this out for yourself."

Bergren's freckles begin to blend in with his face. "You stick around," he says. He slams his suburban into gear and races off, leaving behind a complimentary dust storm. I'm getting a pretty good tan; too bad it'll wash off in the shower.

Carl shows up a few minutes later, hefts a plastic gas can out of the back of his Forest Service truck and goes straight for Old Faithful's gas cap like a pit crew at a racetrack. He doesn't say anything, doesn't look at me until the gas is in the tank and Old Faithful is running, then leans on the door, looks through the open window. "What's going on, Porter?"

"You don't want to know."

"There's cops everywhere."

"What've you heard?"

"Not much. Talk to me."

"I'd rather not saddle you with this."

"Uh-huh." He looks past me, looking for something. "You use my gun?"

I shake my head, pull the gun from under the seat. "Here, take it back."

Carl takes the gun, sniffs the muzzle.

"Jesus Christ Carl — I didn't use it. What've you heard?"

"I heard there was a murder," he says quietly, still looking at the gun. He checks the chamber, makes sure it's unloaded. I hand him the shells, wondering how he could have heard about Petrovich so quickly. "Who told you?"

"Turn on your radio."

The killer must have called the reporters as well as the cops; he wanted me caught at the scene and he wanted it public. But he didn't count on my getting away. Or finding the knife.

"Did you know there's blood on your hand?"

I look at my hand, turn it over — there's a dried streak of blood on the ham and I stare at it as though it were an unexpected wound. Petrovich's blood, it must have come from the knife when I picked it up, or the newspaper. Did Bergren see that?

I put my hand down on the seat, out of sight.

"That his blood?" asks Carl.

"I don't think we should talk about this."

Carl places a bony hand on the edge of the window and stares at me. A cow bellows in the pasture, a lonely desperate sort of sound, and we both flinch. "I'm your friend, Porter. You can tell me anything. If you're in trouble, I'll help you. Any way I can."

I hesitate, stare at the dash, listen to the thrum of Old Faithful's tappets.

"It's Petrovich's blood," I say finally.

Carl nods as if he expected this. "You kill him?"

"No. Someone cut his throat. With my knife."

"Your knife? You mean the one you lost?"

I nod and Carl swears softly, hangs his head.

"You were right, Carl. It was a set-up. The phone call. The whole thing."

I'm expecting an I-told-you-so but Carl is silent, standing next to the truck, toeing rocks on the road and frowning. I don't blame him for being angry. I should have told him more. But it's too late now. "So what did you do when you found him?" he asks.

"I took the knife."

"You took the knife?"

"What else could I do?"

"Nothing, I guess. What did you do with it?"

"It's gone."

"Probably best," he says, a grim look on his face. An approaching car slows, then suddenly accelerates. I get a brief glimpse of two old ladies, probably alarmed at seeing Carl standing by the roadside with a shotgun. After the blast of dust settles, Carl says, "Any idea why someone would want to set you up?"

"Not really." My voice is a little shaky. "But they did a hell of a job."

"How bad could it be?"

"Bad, Carl. The cops think I believe Petrovich is the Lorax."

"But you said they had pretty much ruled him out —"

"That's not the point." I grip the steering wheel. "They know I think Petrovich could be the Lorax. I told them as much — Christ, I tried to convince them. He's used explosives before. He has access. I saw his resumé and it seemed so obvious. But when the cops went looking for the resumé, it was gone, which makes me look even more deluded. Even without the knife, they're going to be wondering. Revenge is a hell of a motive."

Carl wipes sweat off his forehead. "Christ, Porter. Who do you think did it?"

"I don't know. Maybe the Lorax killed Petrovich."

"The Lorax?" Carl is puzzled. "How do you figure that?"

"Think about it. The Lorax almost certainly knows who I am, probably knows I'm looking into this. Maybe he thinks I'm getting too close so he sets up Petrovich as the bomber. He isn't worried about convincing the police — only me. My big mouth does the rest. Then he steals my knife and uses it to kill Petrovich and I'm out of the way."

Carl shakes his head. "Doesn't make sense. You're no closer than the cops."

"No — that's where you're wrong, Carl. I am closer than the cops. Back at the bombing scene, I think I saw him — the guy in camo with the rifle. If I could recognize him, he'd want me out of the way. In fact, I'm pretty sure he's been following me around."

"Following you?" Carl looks concerned. "What do you mean?"

"Keeping an eye on me. Monitoring my investigation."

Carl tucks the shotgun under his arm. "So that's the guy we need to find."

"Right, but I'm not sure where to start. I doubt he'll be following me anymore."

"True, but at least you know he's local."

It takes me a second to realize how Carl knows this. "Of course — the resumé."

Carl is nodding. "We need to figure out who put it there."

"It had to be someone with access," I say, excited now. "Someone who knew when I was there and when I left. They'd have to know I'd looked at the resumé, then they'd have to take it out of the file and replace it with the real one. Quickly, before the Mounties returned to check."

"Why didn't you just make a copy?"

"The photocopier wasn't working," I say. Then it clicks.

"Carl, what do you know about the girl at the front desk?"

"Which one?" he asks. "There's three that work there."

"Carmen — blonde. Big hair. Lots of cellulite."

Carl gives me a half smile. "I took her out once, right after I moved here."

"Spare me the details. But do you know where she lives?"

On the way into town I call Curtain River Forest Products, make sure Carmen is working, then follow Carl's directions to her house. It's a pink stucco place near the river. I cruise past, note there's no vehicle in the driveway, but a garage in back. I park a few blocks away near a playground, walk into the treed river valley, work my way to the back of Carmen's house. The fence around her yard is open to the valley, just runs to the break. I peer into the garage. No second vehicle and I move on to the house. The back patio is edged with ceramic gnomes. The door is unlocked. You gotta love small towns.

I ease the door shut, stand in the entry for a few minutes, listening. Nothing but the tick of a clock, the hum of a refrigerator. I take off my dirty boots, stow them out of sight in a coat closet, pad around in my socks. The kitchen is clean, the counters bare, the fridge covered with magnetic knick-knacks, but no crayon pictures or report cards. There's beer in the fridge, leftover take-out. The living room is fairly clean. The curtains are pink frill. Fashion magazines cover the coffee table: the latest light summer looks — earth tones are in. So are nipples — anyone could have told her that. Three bedrooms in the back: one a sewing room, one a guest room, the third her bedroom.

A large painting over the headboard distracts me for a moment: two lovers locked together in an interesting upright position. Risqué but hardly incriminating. In fact, nothing I've seen so far is going to help me. I look around, wonder where to go next. Nothing but last year's fashions in the walk-in closet. As for her dresser, I'm not going through her drawers — a guy's got to draw the line somewhere. On a night table is a lamp and several framed pictures. Two kids, probably relatives. Her and some guy on a beach, ocean in the background. The guy looks sort of familiar, despite too much tan and not enough clothes. I pick up the picture, look closer. It's Al Brotsky, the harvest supervisor.

Something about her and Brotsky bothers me. I'm not sure exactly what.

I put the picture back, go into the ensuite bathroom, wash Petrovich's blood off my hand. The lavender air freshner is so strong I get dizzy. I make a pass through the basement, just to be thorough. Boxes and more boxes. A dartboard and old couch. I can picture Brotsky down here, tossing darts, a beer in his hand while Carmen lounges on the couch, doing her best Cleopatra imitation. There's a workbench in the utility room. Plenty of cobwebs and lint but no tools except a pipewrench and utility knife. I realize what bothers me about Brotsky and Carmen. Back at the bombing scene, Brotsky looked at my knife. *Sits in the hand real nice.* Then I saw him at the bar with Petrovich, right after I stowed my knife. The next time I see my knife, it's covered with Petrovich's blood. And with Carmen's access to the files at Curtain River Forest Products, it would be easy to switch out Petrovich's resumé when I arrived, tidy up when I left.

Maybe the Lorax is a team.

I open a few boxes, find books and old clothes. It's not like she would store dynamite or c4 in her basement anyway. Maybe in the garage. But the garage is locked and deadbolted and I'm not willing to leave evidence that I've been here. I doubt Carmen has anything incriminating here anyway — Brotsky would take care of that. And from what I've seen in the house I'm willing to bet that Brotsky doesn't live here. He's just a Friday night guest.

22

I WANT TO LOOK into Brotsky, but a camper's fire walks away and Carl sends me to the bush. Forty acres of pine are burning, winds are unpredictable and it would be good for me to act like it's business as usual for now. For the next few days I battle flames, trudge fireline, lead the crews. Life seems almost normal and I only think about the bloody knife at night, when I'm in my tent, trying to sleep. Like the telltale heart, it's buried, hidden but waiting, goading me to do something about it. Find the killer, it whispers. Nina's ghost whispers in the other ear with the same message. I'm exhausted, but don't sleep much.

Four days later the fire's not out, but it's under control. Carl pulls me off, sends me home for a shower. Or least that's the reason he gives over the radio. When I climb out of the helicopter, he pulls me aside, his long face pensive and weary. There's a different kind of fire burning here.

"The cops want to talk to you as soon as you get in."

I take a shower, put on clean clothes. I'll find Telson, treat her to a veggie pizza. Maybe we'll spend the night in her box on wheels. The Mounties can wait. But as I drive downtown, a cruiser flashes its red and blues, pulls me over. Bergren's wearing his serious cop face when he comes to my door. He raps a knuckle on my window when I don't roll it down fast enough.

"Good evening officer. Nice night out, isn't it."

"Didn't you hear that we wanted to talk to you as soon as you got in?"

"Last I looked, I wasn't working for you guys."

Bergren points a thick finger. "Follow me to the detachment."

"Am I under arrest again?"

"One thing at a time."

"Then I'm going for supper."

"You can drive yours or sit in the back of mine."

Bergren's eyes are bloodshot and baggy. He looks tired and pissed off, his hand resting on his holster. Since it's probably not a good idea to antagonize someone who can legally shoot you, I decide to follow. Bergren returns to his cruiser, waits for me. I pull out, do an illegal U-turn across mainstreet. Bergren's face is stony in my rearview mirror.

There are a lot of new uniforms at the detachment. Some are wearing flak jackets. All are wearing guns and have handcuffs on their belts. The new faces stop what they're doing and turn to watch when Bergren leads me in. I get the uncomfortable feeling this may be a one-way trip.

Rachet is at a desk piled high with papers. He gets up, leads us to The Room.

I'm shown my usual spot on the far side of the table. I'm becoming such a regular, I have the urge to decorate, hang a few familiar pictures, get a houseplant. There's no tape recorder this time, no file. It's just the three of us.

"What were you doing the day your truck broke down?"

No small talk either.

“I was out for a drive. And it didn’t break down. It ran out of gas.”

“Were you alone?”

“Did you see anyone else when you stopped to provide assistance?”

Bergren shakes his head. “Sadly, it looked like you were alone. Which is kind of the shits for you. It’s a bitch to be stuck in a jam like this with no alibi. You should have thought that one through a bit better.”

“Bad planning,” says Rachet.

“Yes,” says Bergren. “Sometimes they don’t think when they do things like that.”

“True enough,” Rachet says. “Crimes of passion.”

“Rage,” Bergren says, raising a fist. “Revenge.”

“What are you guys talking about?”

“Games and more games.” Rachet makes a deprecating gesture with his hands, as if to express his lack of interest in my question. “That’s okay, Mr. Cassel, we’ve got plenty of time to play. We’ve gone through this sort of thing before. Many times. In fact, you could sort of say we’re experts at this game.”

“Do you guys practise together at home?”

Rachet leans forward, places his elbows on the table, looks at me like a concerned newscaster. Mansbridge with a moustache and uniform. “The way it works is we ask you some questions and you lie to us for a while, then you get tired of lying and tell us the truth. Why not save us all a lot of time — just tell us the truth right away. Call it a professional courtesy between investigators.”

My first thought is they found the knife. It’s sitting in an evidence locker or on its way to forensics. But I doubt it. If they had anything, they would have arrested me.

“So let’s try again,” Rachet says, leaning back, settling in for a long haul.

“Where were you coming from the day your truck ran out of gas?” asks Bergren.

“Look, I was just out for a drive. I’d had a bad night and wanted to clear my head.”

“Why the bad night?” Rachet askss, looking concerned.

“Trouble sleeping,” I say. “Ever since some nutcase killed my fiancée.”

“Who was the last person to see you?” asks Bergren.

“No one. I just got out of bed, went for a drive.”

“No breakfast?” asks Bergren. “You gotta have breakfast. Most important meal of the day.”

“You didn’t talk to anyone that morning?” asks Rachet.

Carl wouldn’t have told them anything. But they might have traced Petrovich’s call.

“No. I was alone.”

Bergren sighs, looks dismayed. “That’s rough. Bad morning to be alone.”

Rachet raises an eyebrow. “Do you know Zeke Petrovich?”

“Of course. You asked me —”

He waves a hand, cuts me off. “Right, right — sorry. I forgot we talked about him the last time we were together. You told me you thought he was the Lorax. You’d been investigating him and making considerable progress from what I recall.”

“I would hardly call it progress. Did you ever question anyone about that resumé?”

“The resumé.” Bergren chuckles. “Right.”

“Someone put it there. Someone also took it away.”

“Maybe it was invisible ink,” says Bergren. “Maybe it self-destructed.”

"Perhaps you misread it," Rachet says generously.

"Perhaps you guys should do a little more investigating," I say, beginning to lose what little patience I had. "First you don't bother going after the guy with the rifle who was scoping you in that cutblock — I'm willing to bet you didn't even bother to check the area for parked vehicles — then you ignore blatant evidence tampering and misdirection. I'm not convinced you even want to catch this guy."

"Evidence tampering," Rachet says. "Funny you should mention that."

Sucker punch — I didn't see it coming. "What?"

"Never mind," Rachet says casually. "Just another one of our imaginary investigations."

They've knocked me off balance and go for a quick combination.

"You still think Mr. Petrovich is the Lorax?"

"When did you last speak with Petrovich?"

I may be on the ropes but I'm not going down.

"Who knows," I say, reeling. "Maybe you're the Lorax."

I missed the bell but it seems the opening round is over. There's a momentary lull as Bergren rubs his eyes, Rachet smoothes his moustache. I shift in my chair, sit up a bit straighter. I'm tired and hungry, sweating a little more than usual. I get the feeling I'm in the wrong weight class. Time for round two.

"So you were out for a little drive," says Bergren. "How pleasant."

"You make any stops?" asks Rachet.

"Like where?"

"Like Mr. Petrovich's residence."

"We're not really on speaking terms."

"Right." Rachet touches his cheek. "He assaulted you. That make you angry?"

“A lot of people try to hit me. Why is he special?”

“Because he’s dead,” Bergren says, pulling a hand across his throat, lolling his tongue. Karloff would be impressed. “Someone cut him all the way through to his spine. Just a couple of days ago. Right about when you were out joy riding.”

“I’m sorry to hear that. He was an asshole, but it’s a crappy way to go.”

“We just want to know if you were in the area,” says Rachet. “If you saw anything.”

“I wasn’t in the area. I didn’t see anything.”

“Do you know where Petrovich lives?”

“Lived,” says Bergren.

“I’ve never had the urge to visit.”

“So you don’t know where he lives?”

“What are you getting at?”

“Someone saw a Land Rover in the vicinity, right about the time Petrovich got whacked.”

“It was speeding,” says Rachet. “So they reported it.”

Bergren tugs at his shirt collar. “Not many Land Rovers in these parts.”

“There’s a guy by the river,” I say. “Got about 20 of them.”

“Yeah, but they don’t run. Yours does.”

They’re just dancing around, trying to tire me out.

“I see you’re not wearing your knife,” Rachet says.

I give them a blank stare.

“That big toad-stabber you were wearing at the crime scene. The one in that nice custom-made sheath. You wouldn’t be able to tell us where that is would you?”

I’m thinking this is going to take more than a blank stare. This is going to take lawyers: Johnny Cochrane maybe. “You guys are unbelievable. You haven’t arrested me. You haven’t cautioned me.

But you're questioning me. Seems to me that might be a bit unethical. And it's just plain bad manners —"

"You can talk to us now," says Bergren. "Or you can talk to us later."

Rachet's hands are up like a cop in an intersection. "Just calm down, Mr. Cassel."

My chair scrapes the floor as I stand. "The next time you want to talk with me, either caution me or do it like civilized people. Don't pull me away from my supper. Buy me a pizza and do it somewhere amicable. If I'm a suspect, tell me straight out. If you want to know what I know, then ask me. And don't dismiss my suggestions. That resumé was there and now it's gone."

Rachet lowers his hands. "You *are* a suspect Mr. Cassel."

"I didn't kill Zeke Petrovich."

"Then you've got nothing to worry about."

"I feel so much better. Now if you'll excuse me —"

"We'll be in touch," Rachet says as I squeeze past them toward the door.

"Definitely," says Bergren. "But don't hold your breath for pizza."

After that little circus, I don't feel much like pizza, or eating alone. I drive to the RV park along the river. Telson is sitting in the shade, feeding granola to the squirrels. They scatter as I pull up, head for the safety of the trees. "You're scaring the poor things," she says.

"They'll be back. You're living in their yard."

"Maybe you should shut off your truck."

Old Faithful is still coughing and sputtering — her carbon is building up and sometimes she doesn't know when to stop. I have the same problem. I hold up my hand — give it a minute. The old girl's coughs deteriorate to intermittent gasps, then a long death rattle.

Telson looks concerned. “Is it supposed to do that?”

“Another one of her tricks,” I say. “It took years of training.”

She offers me an open handful of granola. I pick out a few nuggets.

“So where’ve you been?” she asks. “A girl could get lonely out here by herself.”

“Working. Fires.”

“Another one of those arsons?”

“No — just a naughty camper who didn’t douse and mix properly.”

“Smokey the Bear,” she says, grinning. She’s wearing a red-checkered flannel shirt, cut-off jeans and sandals. She looks very outdoorsy, very beer commercial. It’s working — I want both her and a beer.

“Beaver,” I say. “You’re thinking American.”

“One thing at a time,” she says. “You naughty boy.”

“No — Smokey the Bear is American. We have a rodent here. Bertie the Beaver.”

She looks a bit disappointed. “Oh. You want a beer or something?”

She’s gone a minute, comes out of the trailer with a six-pack of Big Rock in hand. “Have you heard all the commotion?” she asks, handing me a beer. I shake my head — I came here to get away from it. “There’s been a murder. That guy you had a fight with at the bar. It’s all over the radio. They found him in his trailer, although they didn’t say how it happened. They’re being very close-mouthed about it.”

“That’s the police,” I say. “Very close-mouthed.”

“And the killer’s still at large. Kind of gives you the creeps.”

I must have a strange look on my face. “Are you okay, Porter?”

"Fine," I say quietly. "Just missed breakfast. Most important meal of the day."

There's a silence — I can't look at her. If I do, I'll blubber the whole miserable story to her and I don't want her mixed up with this. She could get caught in the crossfire. But she's a good listener and knowing that makes it more difficult. I shouldn't be here right now but can't bear the thought of leaving. I stare at brown spruce needles scattered on the ground. Telson comes over, squats in front of me.

"Hey, what's the matter? You don't look so good."

"Just tired." I try to avoid her gaze but she uses a finger to move my chin so I'm looking at her. "It's nothing you should have to worry about," I say, trying to sound annoyed, hoping she'll just drop it, but she gives me an encouraging smile. "Come on, what's the matter, Porter?"

"I have to go. I just stopped by for a minute or two. Thanks for the beer."

But when I try to stand she holds my arm. It doesn't take much to keep me here. Her expression is concerned but determined, and I won't get away without creating some bad feelings. I glance at Old Faithful, torn between my need and my dread of putting another girl in harm's way. "It's a long story you really don't want to hear."

"Believe me," she says. "I want to hear it."

She won't let me look away. Shamefully, my need wins. "Sit down," she says, pulling another chair close. She sits so she faces me, leans her elbows on her knees, gives me an earnest look. The doctor is in, but I don't know where to start. She must be able to see this.

"The beginning, Porter. Just start at the beginning."

I look around. We're in plastic lawn chairs amid the spruce trees: a suitable location for a shrink's office when in therapy with an ex-twig pig. And I guess that's what she's doing — offering therapy — although I doubt she'll be able to give me much practical advice. But maybe that's not the value of a therapist; maybe just listening is the secret to the trade.

"You said you were married to a ghost," she says. "Tell me about the ghost."

I take a deep breath, and it all pours out — the visit to the logging operation, Nina in uniform, the bombing. The story bears an eerie resemblance to the *Crime Stoppers* video. But I'm not quite as smooth as Mike Matchok; my voice is a little shaky. I stop short of telling her about more recent events — that'll be a different video. When I'm done, Telson sits back in her chair, lets out a long breath. "I remember that," she says. "I didn't realize she was your girlfriend."

"Yeah, that was Nina."

She shakes her head. "That must have been so hard. Then coming here ..."

"Yes, it was hard." I pause and something shifts inside, like a record that's been skipping and finally finds the right track, and I continue the story — a chapter that was edited out long ago but remains in long-term storage. "I never told anyone this, but Nina had a headache. She didn't want to go with me out to the bush that day. I talked her into it, told her she'd feel better with a bit of fresh air. Imagine that, I thought she'd feel better —"

Suddenly, I can't talk. It feels like I've been kicked in the gut.

Telson kneels in front of me again. "Porter, you can't blame yourself."

"Like hell I can't."

She takes my hand. "You can't drag this around —"

But she's wrong. I can drag this around forever. I stand up. "I've got to get going."

"Porter, it's not your fault."

"Don't tell me it's not my fault. It was my fault."

I make it to Old Faithful but Telson gets in front of me and blocks the door.

"Don't run away."

"I'm not running, damn it! Get out of my way."

But I am running and I know it. I just want to get into Old Faithful and drive. Crank the music up until my nose bleeds, until it fills my whole world. Becomes my whole world. But she won't move and my bravado crumbles. I turn away — I hate to let a woman see me crying — and she finds my hand. She's insistent. She leads me away from the truck and up the steps. Inside her trailer, she takes off my boots, lays me on her bed. I feel like a little kid. She climbs under the blankets with me.

"It's my fault," I whisper. "God —"

"Sssh ..."

We lie together for what seems a long time.

"Give me your hand."

Her breast is warm and soft, fits perfectly in my cupped palm. I hesitate and she pulls me closer and suddenly, urgently, I'm in the most secret of places, then we're lying together, damp and breathing hard. We don't say anything for a while, just lie naked together.

"How are you doing?" she asks finally.

"Okay." I may never leave, just hide with her in this little aluminum cocoon.

She lifts her head, props her chin on her arm. "You hungry?"

"Hungry enough to eat tofu."

She gives me a lopsided smile. "Satisfy one basic need only to reveal another."

She gets out of bed, slips on her clothes. I feel a pang of regret, watching her cover herself. "I don't have much here," she says. "If you're willing to wait a few minutes, I'll run to the store, get some of that nasty man-food."

She tells me to stay in bed, she'll be right back. I'm in no hurry to leave. A minute later, the Bug rattles to life, roars away with a sound like a kid who's found a sheet of bubblewrap. I lie on my side and gaze around her trailer. It's small but cozy, filled with her things. Black lace underwear. Glow-in-the-dark stars. Pictures of planets. I've discovered a whole new universe.

I wonder if she has another beer in her little fridge — the six-pack is outside and I'm not particularly inclined to leave the trailer until she gets back. The fridge is small enough that I have to stoop to peer inside. Agh, yes, there we are. I rummage to pull out the can. Strange — is that bacon? I pull a greasy package out from the back of the fridge. Telson must have had a carnivorous visitor. I consider frying the bacon but decide not to do that naked — I'm not quite that brave. I'll wait, see what she brings back. But I get hungry, smelling the bacon, and go looking for my underwear. They're hanging from the corner of a small cabinet near the bed. I chuckle, shake my head. The fabric catches on the corner of the cupboard door, accidentally pulling it open and dumping the contents in a scatter onto the floor. A laptop rides a landslide of loose paper.

As I squat to pick up the laptop, I notice what's on the paper.

Newspaper clippings — familiar; I have a shoebox full of them. Lorax attacks — the headlines just as disturbing as the day they were printed. Inset in the articles are pictures of mangled machinery; pictures of Nina; pictures of me.

I'm confused until I dig a little deeper. Then it gets real clear.

The sheets below are covered with typing, lines neatly double-spaced, scribbles here and there indicating corrections or new ideas. ... *look into P. Cassel's past ... how did P. Cassel and N. Pirelli meet ... start new chapter here ...* She's writing a book about the Lorax, about everything I don't want her mixed up with. I'm her research project.

And tonight? Just a little more investigative journalism?

I have to get dressed. I have to get out of here.

I'm pulling on my shirt when I hear the Volkswagen, meet Telson just as I open the trailer door. She stands on the step, a bag of groceries in one hand, a fresh six-pack in the other, smiling. "I got all the manly necessities —"

"Get out of my way."

Her expression falters. "What is it, Porter?"

"When were you going to tell me?"

"Tell you what?"

"Were you going to wait until the book was out?"

She looks pained. "Porter, it wasn't supposed —"

I push past her. "Save it."

"Just let me explain. You have to understand —"

"I understand just fine." I'm opening the truck door. "I'm just your source."

"That might have been how it started, but things have changed —"

I'm not sticking around for the detailed confession. I slam the door, fire up Old Faithful, jam her into gear. Telson is trying to block me from leaving, yelling to be heard over the sound of the racing engine. I pull past her and in the rearview mirror see her standing on the road, gripping her hair. I wonder if she was this good in her high school drama class. I tell myself I don't care.

Then I'm on the road, cranking up the music. I need to drive.

23

I GO WEST, as far west as a fool in a truck can go. Hard rock this time — Scorpions, AC/DC, Ice House. The primal power of the music resonates with my mood. By the time I reach the coast twelve hours later I'm drained of anger and sick of heavy metal. I spend the night in a motel at Horseshoe Bay, walk the streets, get rained on. Then I head back to Curtain River to finish what has been started.

I make it back Saturday afternoon. No rain here, just sun and the smell of drying lumber. The locals are inside or on benches in the shade. Only the tourists are moving, buying gas and booze, crowding mainstreet with campers and motorhomes. I buy an ice cream at a drive-through burger place. The kid in the pickup window wishes me a nice day. The ice cream tastes like powdered milk.

I eat it as I drive out of town.

Brotsky has a little acreage set amid scattered spruce trees in the old Curtain River flood plain. The house is a cheap Spanish-style knock-off with arched doorways, crumbling stucco. The yard is gravel and chickweed. But it's neat; the chickweed is mowed.

Brotsky is next to the garage, splitting wood. He stops when he sees the truck, rests the head of the axe on the chopping block. The way he just stands and stares makes me think he isn't real happy to see me. I don't know why; if he is the Lorax I've been looking forward to meeting him for years.

I park in front of the house, walk closer.

"Porter Cassel," he says without moving. "How've you been?"

I'm tempted to tell him. "Getting by. How about you?"

"Still breathing. That's enough."

He's been working hard: his grey hair is damp with sweat, his work shirt soaked and clinging to his lean frame. There's a pile of split firewood taller than either of us. Strange thing to do in this kind of heat. The sleeves of his work shirt are rolled up and there's a tattoo on his forearm, buried deep in hair and faded like old newsprint, but the motto is unmistakable — *Airborne.*

"You were in the service?"

He grins — someone out there has a nasty scar on their knuckles. "Born to serve."

"I spent a few months in the reserve."

"A few months, huh?" He's not exactly dazzled by my lengthy military career.

"It was one of those youth employment programs."

"I've heard of them," he says. "Bunch of college kids burning off a summer."

"That was pretty much it."

"What branch were you in?"

"Navy. Not that we ever saw a ship. Did a lot of marching though. What about you?"

"Special forces." That grin again, like something off a heavy metal album.

"Really. Why'd you give it up?"

Brotsky's smile vanishes, lips closing over broken teeth like a man sinking in quicksand. "I got injured," he says, rubbing his leg. "Fucked my joints up on a jump. Hit the ground too hard."

Not hard enough, I'm thinking. "That's rough."

"Yeah, life's a bitch. What can I do for you, Cassel?"

"I need to ask you a few questions."

He leans on the axe, squints at me. "What sort of questions?"

"I need to know about Zeke Petrovich."

"Petrovich, huh?" He sniffs, takes a step back, kicks pieces of firewood to the side. There's a disjointedness to the way he moves, like his undercarriage is loose. Maybe he needs new tie roads, fresh ball joints. The axe remains in his hand, a counterbalance, tilting like a metronome. "What do you care about Petrovich?"

"A lot of people care about Petrovich lately."

"Yeah, I hear he got murdered."

"I heard that too."

Brotsky draws an imaginary knife across his neck. "Got his throat slit."

"You knew him, didn't you."

"Sure. He worked for me."

"You don't seem too shook up."

"In the service you see things," he says. "You get used to it."

"So you saw a lot of action?"

"You could say that." He props a boot on the chopping block, leans an arm on his thigh like a weary sergeant ready to rally his troops. "Covert assignments. Black ops. Sort of shit you see on TV. But if I told you, I'd have to kill you."

Coming from him, it doesn't sound so corny.

"You ever use explosives, do any demolition work?"

"Sure." He chews his lower lip. "Why you asking?"

"No reason."

He stares at me, chews his lip a moment longer. I can imagine him crawling through the mud under barbed wire and loving it. He'd make a hell of a recruitment poster — be all you can be — but he'd scare away the minorities.

"You working with the cops?" he asks.

"Sort of. We have an arrangement."

"An arrangement." Brotsky chuckles. "Really."

"I try to find the killer. They make my life difficult."

He's amused. "So you're going to find the killer?"

"I'm going to try. You said Petrovich worked for you —"

"Tell me something, Cassel." He pulls a tin of chew from his back pocket. The look he gives me I've seen before — Eastwood in *Heartbreak Ridge*. He takes his time working a glob of chewing tobacco under his lip. "Why do you want to find the killer?"

"I've got my reasons."

"I'll bet you do," he says, with a grin that leads me to believe he knows exactly why I'm here. "You were a forest ranger at one time weren't you?"

"A long time ago."

He pockets his can of chew. "So why'd you give it up?"

He's smiling a little as he says this and I don't much care for his tone. I'd intended to push him a bit, piss him off to see where it went — maybe enough that he'd let something slip. Maybe enough that self-defence could be seen as justifiable homicide. But it's a thin line with the courts these days. And he's better at it, quicker on his feet. "I had issues with the uniform."

He sets a fresh chunk of wood on the chopping block. "We all got issues."

"Some more than others. What did Petrovich do when he worked for you?"

Brotsky swings the axe. Clunk. Two halves fly off the block. "Mechanic."

"How long has he been with the company?"

He kicks the halves aside. "About eight years."

Eight years is consistent with Petrovich's real work record.

"What about you? How long've you worked here?"

Brotsky reaches for another chunk of wood. "None of your goddamn business."

His response is casual. He knows he's holding all the cards.

"What about enemies? Petrovich piss anyone off?"

"Petrovich pissed everyone off. That much you oughta know."

I touch my bruised cheek, a reflex action. Brotsky halves another chunk of firewood, burying the axe deep in the chopping block. He leaves it there, wipes sweat from his brow. A few light clouds hover overhead, trying hard not to evaporate. Brotsky is waiting for me to leave, trying hard to be patient. I can see it in his squint, his frown, the way he keeps flicking his index finger.

"You were his boss. You must have done a performance appraisal or two —"

"Sure. He was a good mechanic. A real asset to the operation."

The kiss of death — Hess too was an asset to the operation.

"Did Petrovich get along with Hess?"

"So far as I know."

"How about you? You get along with Hess?"

The clouds don't make it; I feel sun on the back of my neck like a kid with a magnifying glass. Brotsky's patience has also evaporated. He yanks the axe out of the chopping block with one violent thrust. "I get along with everybody," he says, raising the axe and splitting the chopping block with a single swing — massive halves reeling off to either side. He's got the axe at chest level, like he might be lining up another chunk of firewood. But there's no firewood in front of him.

"You got any more questions?" he says, breathing hard.

"Maybe later," I say, taking a step back.

As I leave, I'm thinking I'll be seeing him sooner than later. When the sun broke through those clouds Brotsky pulled a folded ball cap from the back pocket of his jeans. Thing about carrying your cap like that — you have to fold the visor down the middle, crimp it like the gable end of a house.

24

IT'S BACK TO THE BLUES as I cruise north to Edmonton — Muddy Waters, John Lee Hooker, "Lonesome Mood." Soothing music. Ripples of heat on the road seem to match the beat. The big double highway is nearly empty; ribbons of grey concrete waver like an acid trip hallucination. I'm on a different sort of trip, no less confusing.

"That girl keeps calling," Carl told me this morning. "You should call her back."

I'd slept in Old Faithful, down by the river. Carl was worried.

"You two were a cute couple," he says. "What happened?"

"She wasn't who I thought she was."

"When it comes right down to it, Porter, you never really know people."

"You got that right."

I went for a mountain bike ride around town but it took me a half-hour to lose the unmarked Caprice Classic that floated behind me. An excursion into the trees finally did the trick but they knew I'd come out sooner or later. If they didn't find me, there was always Brotsky, who's been following me since I arrived in Curtain River. Or Telson — I'd seen her dented orange Beetle several times, looking for me. Like they say in the Westerns, it seemed a good idea to leave town.

This morning the sun beating through the windshield makes the steering wheel slick, leaves a black smudge on my palms, like a kid playing with briquettes. I'm in a mobile greenhouse and have all the windows open. It doesn't much help; I'm withering anyway. We've got to stop this problem with the ozone layer. At a gas station I soak my canvas hat in water, put it on sopping wet, get strange looks from the tourists in their air-conditioned minivans.

The kids wave — *look at the funny man.*

I drive slow, let what little traffic there is pass me, keep an eye on the rearview mirror. It remains mostly empty but I'm getting cautious in my old age. Just because you're paranoid doesn't mean they're not out to get you. It takes me longer than usual to reach Edmonton.

I stop at Cindy's, but the house is locked. She's at work, the kids at daycare.

Downtown, everyone is driving slow. Intersections are blocked by vehicles with vapour locks. The owners stand like mourners beside their immobile vehicles, gazing under the hood, perplexed. *It just stopped — just like that.* Traffic flows past the clots. You can count the cars without air conditioning — the ones with all the windows open, drivers' tongues hanging out.

On the north side, I turn into Castle Downs, a residential area tangled with crescents and cul-de-sacs designed to frustrate the unfamiliar driver. You could lose years here — every street I'm looking for is one street over, with no visible way to get there. I four-wheel-drive over a few backyards. Even so, it takes a long time to find Bill's house.

A bald teenager answers the door.

"Yeah?" His T-shirt proclaims, "Everything Sucks."

"You must be Mark. Is your dad home?"

Mark is suspicious. I'm over 30 and know his name. "Just a minute."

I wait in a wedge of shade in front of the house — a vinyl-sided unit exactly like all the other vinyl-sided units. Developers don't just build houses anymore; they build whole neighbourhoods: a production line, like plugging chips into a circuit board. Even the landscaping is the same — one mountain ash and two spruce trees. There isn't a gum wrapper anywhere and the lawns have no dandelions. At night, they roll up the sidewalks.

"Porter Cassel —"

Bill stands on his concrete front step, thumb hitched in a belt loop. He's not nearly as immaculate as the neighbourhood; his thinning hair is unkempt, his shirt rumpled.

"I was in the neighbourhood —"

"Come in. Come in."

I hesitate, suddenly reluctant to involve Bill any further. Retired and recuperating from a heart attack, he really doesn't need this. But I need his counsel. I leave my boots on the front step. As I pass, Bill gives me a guarded look that makes me nervous. In the kitchen, Mark stands in front of an open fridge, waiting for his nostril hairs to frost over, complaining there's nothing to eat. Bill gives him a twenty, sends him to the Winks around the corner. "Kid eats all day," he says, rubbing his stomach, something he must do a lot — there's a bald spot on the belly of his velour shirt. "I wish I had his metabolism."

He makes coffee. I fidget, wonder how to start. "How's retirement treating you?"

"Retirement," he says scornfully. "What a crock. Sit around all day watching soap operas, weed the garden. And cleaning — I never thought I'd be cleaning just for something to do."

"The place looks great — you could film a Windex commercial."

He pulls out a chair, sits down heavily. "You see what I'm reduced to?"

"Bill ... I wanted to thank you for analyzing that debris."

"Don't. It was a stupid thing for me to do."

"Well I appreciate it —"

"Maybe, but that's not why you're here."

I pull up a chair, start to say something but falter. Retired or not, Bill is still plugged in. And that could be a problem — he might still be enough of a cop that he'll turn me in.

"A situation has developed," I say. "To a friend of mine."

"What sort of situation?"

"One where he can't go to the authorities."

"Why not?"

"It's sort of complicated."

He looks amused. "Tell me about this problem your friend is having."

I have a vision of telling him I stole evidence from a crime scene — again — and of Bill clutching his chest and toppling off his chair. Another casualty of the Porter Cassel school of investigation. "Your health isn't so good. I wouldn't want to get you all worked up."

"What?" He looks offended. "All of a sudden I'm an old lady?"

"Okay — but you gotta promise to stay calm."

"If I was any more calm, I'd be dead."

"That's what I'm worried about."

"It couldn't be that bad."

"If you've got any pills you need to take, you better take them now."

He waves off the suggestion. "Just start talking, Cassel."

"Someone he was close to was killed and he starts poking around, asking questions."

"Why not leave it the cops?"

"The cops aren't making any progress —"

"So your friend thinks he's going to swoop in and save the day?"

"He can't help himself. He needs to find out who did this —"

"I know a guy with a problem like that," says Bill. He's leaned back, beefy arm flopped over a nearby chair. He looks relaxed but he's watching me closely. "How far did this friend of yours get before he got into trouble?"

"He developed a suspect."

"Really?" Bill looks skeptical.

"But there was a problem. Turned out to be the wrong guy."

"That's why they're just suspects, Porter."

"I know, but it gets complicated. His suspect was murdered."

"Did your friend kill the suspect?" Bill asks slowly.

"No, but it looks that way."

"Why would it look that way?"

"A number of things," I say carefully. I'm into confessional territory now and he's wearing his serious cop face. I tell him about my investigation into Petrovich — how he publicly assaulted me; the suggestion that he was proficient with explosives. The resumé and my attempts to convince the Mounties that Petrovich was the Lorax. Petrovich's call and my finding him with his throat cut. Bill listens, slouched in his chair. He looks like he'd rather be mopping the floor.

"So what do you think, Bill? How bad is this?"

"Well, it's not good," he says, rubbing his forehead. There are lines there that can't be smoothed out. "No alibi and plenty of motive. They can trace the call and probably put you in the general area. But it's all circumstantial. If you're innocent, you've gotta go in, explain what happened."

"I'm not ready to do that."

"This is an unexplained death — a fucking murder, Porter. It could haunt you for the rest of your life. Something could come up years from now. Think about how it'll affect your family — your sister — your own kids when you have them. Being a murder suspect is not how you want to spend the rest of your life. And all because of some circumstantial evidence."

"It's a little more than circumstantial."

Bill's eyes narrow. "What do you mean?"

"The killer used my knife."

"And you know this how?"

"I found it at the murder scene."

Bill chews his lip. "What exactly did you do?"

"The only thing I could under the circumstances. I took it."

"Jesus Christ, Porter." Bill slaps a hand on the table, rattling our coffee cups. "You stole the fucking murder weapon —"

"It wasn't really theft. It was my knife."

Bill shoves back his chair and stalks out of the kitchen. A screen door sighs shut and I'm alone in his house, listening to the icemaker in his fridge. I wait a few minutes to let him cool off, find him on the patio, sitting at a plastic picnic table, his back toward me.

"I had to take it, Bill —"

There's a moment of silence, as quiet as it gets in the suburbs. Lawnmowers hum like a distant horde of locusts. Bill turns to look at me. His face is flushed and he's smoking. He waves the cigarette at me. "You know, Porter, if this shit doesn't kill me, you will."

"I'm sorry to bring this to you Bill —"

“No — Goddamnit, Porter, I’m serious. This isn’t some game you’re playing here —”

“You don’t have to tell me that.”

“Don’t I?”

“Nina’s death was no game. Neither is this.”

Bill puffs furiously on his cigarette for a moment. I pull out a chair, sit across the plastic table from him. The table has an umbrella coming out through the centre: a vinyl cloth covered with paisley flowers that doesn’t quite match Bill’s balding velour. My coming here matches his retirement even less.

“I shouldn’t have brought this up.”

Bill sighs, rubs a wrinkled hand over his face. “You still have the knife?”

I nod.

“Is it here? Do you have it with you?”

“No, but it’s safe.”

“What do you mean — safe?”

“I buried it.”

“You buried it.” Bill shakes his head.

“In a suitable container,” I tell him. “Give me some credit.”

“You didn’t put it away wet did you?”

“I let it dry.”

“Good — that’s one thing you didn’t fuck up.”

Bill smokes in silence for a few minutes then butts the cigarette out among marigolds and petunias. “I suppose you left fresh prints all over the knife when you picked it up,” he says, crouched by the flowerbed. “And all over the crime scene.”

“I don’t think so. I tried not to.”

“Are your prints on file?”

I shake my head.

“If they charge you, they’ll take your prints.”

“I’m hoping it won’t come to that.”

“It’ll take more than hope,” Bill says. “It’ll take a fucking miracle.” He stands up, leans on the back of a plastic lawn chair. “So what are you going to do with the knife?”

“I don’t know. I was hoping you’d have some suggestions.”

“Oh — I have some suggestions. Like maybe you should turn it in before they find it.”

“How could they find it?”

“Grow up Porter — this isn’t the Forest Service you’re dealing with here. These are professional criminal investigators. They can use dogs and run along the edges of the road — you had to get out of your truck somewhere. When they pick up your scent, the dogs’ll lead them right to the knife. It would look better if you turned it over.”

“Do you have any other suggestions?”

Bill thinks about this for a moment.

“Why should I turn it over?” I ask.

“There could be some trace left on the knife,” he says. “The DNA sequencing technology they got nowadays is amazing. If there’s anything caught in the grip of the handle — skin cells, mucous — they might be able to build a profile. All they need are a few cells.”

“That’s not all they can identify,” I say. “They can identify Petrovich’s blood.”

Bill doesn’t want to answer but he doesn’t have to — the look on his face is enough of a match. The handle on my knife is smooth and I can’t see Brotsky not wearing gloves. But there’s plenty of Petrovich’s blood on my knife, which links me to the murder. Combine this with motive and other circumstantial evidence and it’s not a pretty picture. I’m starting to agree with Mark’s T-shirt.

"What about a suspect?" Bill asks. "You got any idea who capped this Petrovich?"

"I think so. An ex-military guy. He may also be the real Lorax."

"Ex-military?" Bill nods. "That works in with the c4. But why set you up?"

"I can identify him —"

A door rattles, Mark back from the Winks around the corner. He comes onto the patio, eating potato chips, a bottle of Pepsi in his other hand. "You call that food?" Bill says. "Tell me you bought something wholesome."

"I bought beef jerky," says Mark.

"That's not food."

"It's meat. Can I have a smoke?"

Bill hesitates.

"Come on Dad. You can't fool me."

Bill sighs, pulls out a rumpled pack. "I'm quitting again."

"Sure." Mark takes the smokes, goes inside.

"Not in the house!" Bill yells after him.

I lower my voice in case any windows are open. "Bill, do you think you could dig something up on this ex-military guy? What he did when he was in? Why he left? There's got to be something."

Bill sighs, clearly torn. I'm still thinking he may turn me in.

"I don't know," he says finally. "Maybe. I worked a case with a guy from the military police a few years back. He might be persuaded. What's this guy's name?"

"Alvin J. Brotsky."

"I'll see what I can do. But if this doesn't pan out, you gotta come in."

"I'll think about it."

"You think hard. And take care of that knife."

Cindy is surprised to see me. So are the kids, who tackle me, hang onto me like a koala to a tree. Uncle Porter only comes home when it rains. There's a storm brewing all right, but it's one they can't see. I'm in town for a meeting, I tell them. It's close enough to the truth.

"What a day," says Cindy. Am I staying for supper? I nod and she opens an extra can of Irish stew. It's the same sort of stuff I eat on the fireline, but she's too overwhelmed tonight to do more than open and warm. The cops busted a child prostitution ring and she spent all day talking to eleven- and twelve-year-olds that have been having more sex than a housewife sees in a lifetime. Runaways, all of them, she tells me as she tosses dirty laundry down the stairs. Most of them don't have much of a home to return to, which is why they ran away to begin with.

"We can only hold them for 72 hours," she says, finally sitting down.

Her grey office jacket is damp with sweat, her brown hair plastered to her forehead. This sort of work hits her hard; Bethlehem, her oldest daughter, is seven. She lies on the floor, playing with a Barbi that, much like Cindy's clients, has seen better days.

"So what happens to the kids now?" I ask.

"We try to send them home."

"And if that doesn't work?"

"Their pimp beats them for three days of lost production —"

While the stew is warming I follow Cindy to the basement, where she gathers a week's worth of laundry from the bottom of the stairs. I wait until she's stuffed the machine full and it's swishing merrily away before asking her for the favour I need.

"Can you get hold of a cell phone?"

"I've got a cell phone, Porter. You know that."

She checks the dryer. It's crammed full. More work.

"A cell phone that can't be traced back to you."

She leans against the dryer. She's too tired to worry much more.

"Something bad happened," I tell her. "And someone set it up to look like I did it."

"You're being framed?" She looks puzzled. "For what?"

"Someone's been killed. Someone I'm investigating."

She frowns. "They're blaming you?"

"They're trying to."

She gives this some thought. "There's a girl at work who's on holidays — I could borrow her cell phone. But you'll have to wait until tomorrow before I can get it to you."

"The cell phone is for you. I just need the number."

"Okay," she says slowly. She knows there's more, but I hesitate, not wanting to tell her how ugly this might get. When I do, her expression scarcely changes — I keep forgetting how really tough she is. "So what do you want me to do?"

"Keep an eye on the news. If the cops are looking for me, I'll need your help."

"Is it really that bad?"

"Bad enough. I'm not going to prison while Nina's killer goes free."

"Don't do anything crazy," she says. "Anything you can't take back."

"Make sure your passport is up-to-date because if the cops come after me, I'll need you to take a vacation. Leave as quickly as you can, before they start to watch you. Pack a bikini and drive south. Bring the cell phone —"

"Porter, I can't just —"

"Tell the office it's a family emergency. Don't tell anybody where you're going."

"But the kids —"

"Take the kids. Keep the cell phone on. I'll need you to make a few calls."

Cindy has a helpless look on her face. "Are you sure there isn't something better?"

"You remember what it was like after Nina was killed?"

She nods, looks unhappy.

"If you stay, there'll be cops and reporters all over you and the kids."

I don't tell her my fear that Brotsky may come after them to keep me quiet.

"It'll be better this way," I assure her. "I'll have this sorted out by the time you return. You can tell me all about your vacation and I'll tell you about mine. We'll swap photos."

Cindy nods reluctantly and we go upstairs, don't talk about it anymore. The kids are hungry, foraging in the cupboards. We eat Irish stew out of plastic bowls, sitting on the couch, watching a Disney movie. Cindy sits close to Beth. I sit with the younger two. It doesn't get any better than this.

Sunday afternoon traffic heading west — I'm stuck behind slow-moving ranchers towing horse trailers, pickups loaded with hay. By contrast, the other lane is like the wrong end of a shooting gallery — motorhomes roar east toward the city. My destination is just as urgent; I want to get back to Curtain River and retrieve my knife. Despite Star's insistence that I take care of the knife, I can only see it linking me to Petrovich's murder. No choice but to toss it into some deep pool in the river. But a dented Ford with a lopsided box won't let me squeeze past and it's hard to see what's coming. Anxious, I start to play chicken with oncoming Luxury Liners. Old Faithful whines and complains from the depths of her transfer case. Despite my rush, the trip drags on: hours in the blistering heat. Fields along the highway are mostly barren rangeland, the grass still too short to pasture cattle. Not much to look at. Not much to do but think. Despite everything that's going on — Brotsky and the knife; the Lorax and the arsons — my thoughts keep finding their way back to the little trailer in the woods; the campfire we shared by the river. I know I should just forget her but I'm not good at forgetting.

Half an hour out of Curtain River, I top a rise on the highway, see smoke. A thin column, rising steadily. A fledgling forest fire. Has Red Flag made his way this far south, or is it just another negligent camper? Either way, I'm more concerned with the location — the fire looks to be in the vicinity of where I buried the knife and I have visions of a firefighter finding it during line construction. Chances are low, but I drive faster, sweating, breathing hard. Finally, the sign for Curtain River is in sight and I gear down. In three minutes I'm past The Corral, the bridge and the four-way stop and at the other side of town. No sign of Telson, Brotsky or the Mounties.

I head through ranching country, into the woods. So lovely, dark and deep.

Evidence I cannot keep —

A helicopter is circling the fire a few miles away, droning like a bored insect. Smoke drifts across the road in places like patches of early morning fog. The odour is earthy and rancid — ground fire that has been burning for a while, waiting for a drop in humidity, a bit of wind. Judging by the amount of smoke, the fire has grown to a size beyond the capabilities of the aerial attack crew. Soon this area will be crawling with firefighters and equipment. I've got to dispose of the knife before someone spots me. Heart pounding, I slow Old Faithful, watching the side of the road for the strip of orange flagging I left as a marker. The forest is loaded with ribbon from timber cruising and seismic programs — no one will pay attention to another ribbon — but as I spot the marker it seems as conspicuous as a highway off-ramp. A chill dread works its way up my sides as I approach the dead snag next to the cache.

Someone knows.

When I pull back the carefully placed flap of moss and dig, the package is there. I fill the hole carefully, conceal any sign of disturbance, tear the ribbon from the tree by the road and stow the shovel in the back of the truck. The knife I tuck under the seat — not the most secure place historically speaking but it won't be there long. I'll take back trails down to the river, then go for a hike, toss the knife into the current along the cut face of a cliff at some bend where the water is nice and deep. In a few days it will be covered with sand — part of just another layer in the riverbed; a primitive artifact. Ten thousand years from now, some archeologist will be thrilled.

But it's not that simple.

As I turn a sharp corner, RCMP suburbans and cruisers block the road like something out of a prohibition era movie. The road is narrow, timbered on both sides — no chance for a quick turn. Not that I could outrun their police interceptors. Or their radio waves. Men with flak jackets and automatic weapons are poised strategically by the vehicles. I have little doubt this picnic is for me and am impressed I'm drawing this much firepower — they must expect I'll come out blazing like a gangster. The rum-runners might have had a chance in a situation like this but I'm pretty much screwed. Rachet stands in the centre of the road, fashionably attired in body armor. I have a fleeting image of revving up Old Faithful, crashing through the barricade.

Rachet strolls up to the truck, stands in front of the open side window.

"Porter Cassel. How are you doing, my friend?"

"You guys look a little undermanned. You need some assistance?"

The assault team surround the vehicle, ready to pounce. Rachet holds up a hand.

"You could step out of your vehicle. That would be of assistance."

Nervous, I shift just slightly — not a good idea with that many pea-shooters aimed at your head. I keep my hands squarely on the steering wheel, in the ten and two o'clock position they teach you in driving school. "What's this about?"

"Exit the vehicle now," Rachet says, getting formal. "Hands where I can see them."

An officer in full riot gear graciously opens the door, his automatic aimed squarely at my chest. Rachet waves him back — this is his bust — leads me to the front of the truck, has me lay my hands on the hood, spread my legs, pats me down. Other Mounties surround us. Bergren leads a group which begin to search my truck, toss tools around, go through the burnt-out fuses and broken sunglasses in my glove compartment.

"Look at this," says one Mountie, examining the shovel. "Fresh dirt."

Rachet is behind me, his hand pressed in the middle of my back, ready to shove me forward and slap on the cuffs, which I'm surprised he hasn't done already. Maybe they need the knife. Maybe he's just savouring the moment. "You been doing a little earth work, Mr. Cassel?"

"Gotta bury the bodies somewhere."

"That's great," Rachet says. "In my line of work, I love comedy."

"Maybe if you told me what you're looking for, I could help you out."

"We're looking for whatever you dug up."

"I was digging soil pits," I say. "Checking structure. Measuring coarse fragments."

"That so?" The hand leans against my back. "You ever heard of Special 'O'?"

"There's a new breakfast cereal?"

"Surveillance," says Rachet. "We've got planes, infrared cameras, shit you've never dreamed of, Cassel. We've been all over you. You went to the store, we knew about it. Your girlfriend's trailer was rocking pretty good the other night. Your trip to the coast had us a little worried but in police work, you gotta have patience and faith. I'm not that patient but I had faith that you'd screw up. Later, I'll show you an interesting little video of you in the forest, digging a hole."

"I couldn't find the outhouse."

The Mounties have exhausted the obvious hiding places and are starting to get creative, probing Old Faithful's more intimate crevices. It won't be long now before they find the knife. When they do, they'll match Petrovich's blood, and the chances of someone believing me will be about as good as finding free parking in downtown Calgary. Forget making bail — I'm looking forward to spending the rest of my life worrying about more than if my room mate snores. I have an unpleasant decision to make. I make it fast.

"Don't worry, Cassel, where you're going, it'll be easy to —"

I slump toward the hood, twist and roll my shoulder. Rachet wasn't expecting this and he stumbles, his leaning post gone, grabs after me like a weekend fisherman trying to land a laker. My two days of self-defence training are starting to pay. I sprint for the patrol cars — the least defended spot — roll like a good injury faker over a hood, crouch and dash into the trees. I'm expecting bullets but none come — they must be pretty sure they can catch me. I have maybe a half-minute lead before the woods are full of Canada's finest. Then there'll be dogs and helicopters and who knows what else — the fucking military.

But for now, all I can do is run.

The road cuts sideslope and I go downhill, where I can make better time. There's also the possibility of dense cover at the bottom. These pine forests are like running through a city park — no undergrowth — and at first the chase is nothing more than a game of tag where everyone but me is it. My only advantage is I'm not wearing body armour and 30 pounds of gear. I hear shouts from behind as trees flash past like pickets at a raceway.

"— he's going right —"

"— cut him off —"

I zigzag, jump over deadfall, cringe as my ankle sends up warning flares. Any second it'll twist again, fold under me like a poor poker player. Then I'll be out of the game; the ante has become a little rich for my blood. The ground becomes steeper and I slip, grasp trees, pivot around them like a gymnast. Ahead and below I see dense young spruce in a drainage at the bottom of the slope and I run like a hunted deer for cover. A shout grunted from behind. "Get him before he reaches that draw —"

A shot rings out, wild, way above my head — a warning shot to stop me from running but I keep going anyway, crash into a wall of dense, young spruce and fir. I go low, charging between slender trunks. Branches slap my face, scratch my hands. I'm suddenly through — in a narrow natural meadow, a cleft in the slopes filled with dry grass and shrub. I cross the meadow, worm my way into the dense spruce on the far side, vanish into the foliage. If I can stay out of sight, I have a chance. Voices behind curse, mix with the sound of thrashing from the other side of the clearing. The ground drops away in front of me, slope tangled in alder and black spruce. I'm headed downslope, following the edge of a ravine that deepens into a gorge. I stop and listen. A moment later so do my pursuers, unable to track me without a noise trail. I creep forward, as quickly and quietly as I can. I seem to be gaining ground, for the time being anyway. Soon, there'll be dogs out here; infrared scanners — but for now I keep running, unsure of where I'm going. I just need a little distance. Time to think this through. The gorge, tangled with deadfall, widens, the trickle of water turning into a small stream. There's more water ahead, thrashing over boulders — the Curtain River.

I stand on the bank, watch the water roll past, serene and icy.

The river is too fast and deep to cross. But I have to do something — my pursuers will fan out, trap me against the impassable river. It's smoky down here in the valley, reducing visibility, a point in my favour. I'll follow the river as quickly as I can, stay out of sight. Somewhere closer to town there are cottages. Maybe I can steal a boat, float out under cover of dark.

After that? One catastrophe at a time.

I'm barely back under tree cover before a helicopter descends into the valley, dips its dangling bucket in the river. I'm closer to the fire than I thought. When it's gone, another appears, this one without a bucket but with blue uniforms inside. I crouch behind deadfall. They make a slow pass over the river, searching, faces in the bubble window intent and solemn. The helicopter rises, banks away.

I keep moving, scrambling over rock between the trees.

Bombers arrive, a group of B-26s. The bird dog plane screams overhead, its warble warning of an impending drop. Much higher, I catch sight of another plane, doing a wide circuit. Special "O" — looking for me. The wind shifts, filling the river valley with thick grey smoke. A lucky break: visibility is down to about 30 feet; the smoke is too dense to fly. But it means the fire is turning, heading in my direction.

I pick up the pace, head downstream.

Another lucky break — a blue canoe stashed in the trees above the high waterline. I can make a break for it on the river as long as the smoke holds, have the canoe manhandled nearly to the water before I have second thoughts. The rapids on this river have killed people and the wind may shift again, leaving me exposed. I use a sharp rock to punch a small hole in the bow of the canoe — it'll be a good half hour before it goes under if it doesn't get ground to pieces in the rapids. If I'm lucky they'll find the debris, assume I've drowned. I toss my denim jacket into the canoe and shove off, watch the canoe sweep sideways down the river until it vanishes into the smoke.

The sun through the smoke is an eerie shade of red and it's becoming difficult to see where I'm going. Despite the very real danger of being overrun by the flame front, this fire may be my ticket out of here. I head upwind, toward the fire, my eyes teary and raw. I'm not setting any speed records — my ankle is throbbing and I don't want to risk twisting it again. The wind shifts subtly, clearing the valley, forcing me farther into the trees. Helicopters come in every few minutes to dip their buckets, rising like busy insects against a twisting convection column of smoke. Bombers circle like seagulls waiting for scraps. I'm not sure what I'm going to do when I reach the fire, but it's the last thing they would expect.

Ahead are low flames — the fire eating a path along the side-slope of the river valley. There's no one here, no fireguard except patchy swathes of red retardant from the bombers, indicating the fire has become fairly large for the resources deployed. This is in my favour, as the first day on any fire is chaotic; right now I need as much chaos as possible. I'll find the staging area, steal coveralls and a hardhat, get dirty and blend in. Hopefully I can sneak into town in the back of some truck.

What I'll do there I don't know — I just can't stay here.

Near the crest of the valley I hear the tread clank of heavy equipment, the crash of falling trees. They're cutting fireline and they're close. I hide behind deadfall — they won't run heavy equipment down the steep valley slope. But I'm wrong — a dozer operator with too much ambition or no brains teeters a big D-8 on the valley break like a child's toy, then slides down the incline. Trees topple before him like rotten fence boards. Even from here, I can see the grin on his face. He's having fun playing with gravity and 40 tons of iron.

Thankfully, he's too busy to notice me.

He grinds down toward the river; I go up. Dozers usually work in pairs, the second dozer cleaning up after the first, but this guy seems to be on his own. No aircraft within earshot so I sprint down the fireline — a ragged scar through the bush. Ahead, in a small clearing edged by splayed trees, is a cache of equipment dropped by helicopter. Two drums of diesel for the dozer, a few thousand feet of hose in cardboard boxes, a portable water tank and a black garbage bag. Someone sent a crew kit instead of a fire pump for the porta-tank; a screw-up but a bonus for me. I open the bag, take out a bright clean pair of orange coveralls and red hardhat. A pulaski completes the ensemble — I'm fashionably rigged for a day of fun in the bush. A smearing of ash and charcoal completes the effect.

I don't walk far before someone yells at me.

"Hey you — come here."

It's a big guy in clean orange coveralls and a blue hardhat, standing on the dozerline. The blue skidlid means he's a crew leader. I pull my hardhat lower and trudge over. He has a two-way radio strapped to his equipment belt. And a knife as big as a machete.

"Where's the rest of your crew?" he asks.

"Back there." I avoid eye contact, point vaguely down the fireline.

"What're you doin' here?"

"Squad boss told me to look for the rest of our equipment."

"Figures." He shakes his head. "Our pump is missing."

I wait, look at the ground respectfully like a good grunt. His radio crackles and pops with non-stop chatter: crews calling one another, aircraft calling dispatch. He must have it on scan.

"You find an extra pump, you have your squad boss give me a call. Harvey Kleg."

I nod.

"And keep your eye out for some guy wearing a blue jacket."

"Okay."

Kleg continues down the fireline. I watch until he's out of sight — he doesn't call on his radio. Sooner or later someone is going to realize I don't fit in. Before that happens I have to contact Carl — I heard him on Kleg's radio, answering as fire boss. He's in a helicopter, directing operations from above. All of the resources on the fire are at his command and I have an idea, if I can just catch his attention.

I walk slowly uphill along the fireline, stopping occasionally to knock a few burning clods of moss apart so it looks like I'm patrolling. Near the road a clearing has been pushed into the trees where vehicles are parked, equipment is piled. Workers unload fuel drums from the old Forest Service stake truck. Carl's helicopter will land here to refuel — my chance to talk to him. But there's a problem — the Mounties have set up their command post at the far edge of the clearing. Rachet stands in front of a police suburban, in deep discussion with fellow officers. I hang back along the fireline, whack away at a burning snag. Two firefighters wander over, give me a hand. One of them has a chainsaw and cuts down the snag.

"That'll take care of her," he says.

"Thanks." Now I'll have to find another way to look busy.

They wander farther down the fireline. I keep whacking at the downed snag. One of the cops looks over, watches for a minute, then goes back to listening to Rachet. I try to estimate how long it's been since the Forest Service helicopter arrived, how long until it refuels. Finally, ten minutes later, a helicopter thumps into view, raising a dust storm as it lands. Carl is in the front seat and I roll over a barrel of turbo fuel — just another helpful firefighter. Carl and the pilot climb out. To my horror, Rachet comes over, meets Carl a dozen yards from the helicopter. I turn my back, help the pilot flip up the heavy drum. I need a believable reason to talk to Carl so I pick a box of fire hose from a pile of equipment, set it beside the helicopter. Carl finishes with Rachet and walks back.

He taps me on the shoulder, shouts over the scream of the turbo engine.

"Where's this hose going?"

I turn so he can see my face. "Somewhere safe."

Carl's eyes widen for a second. He glances toward the cluster of Mounties at the edge of the clearing, their backs toward the helicopter to avoid the rotorwash, motions that I should put the box of hose in the tail cargo hold, then shields me from view as I climb into the back seat of the helicopter. We lift off, veer out over the fire.

"Okay Johnson," Carl says into his headset. Neither he nor the pilot can see me from the front seat. "This is how it's going to work. We're going to the northwest helipad where I want you to jump out and drop that box of hose. Then I'm going to whip you into town to help at the warehouse, if that's okay with you."

I key my mike. "Fine with me boss."

We descend into a small helipad and I drop the box of hose, climb back into the rear of the helicopter. The machine rises high over the smoking chaos. A few minutes later we land behind the Ranger Station. I crouch as the machine takes off, Carl peering down like an astronaut through the nose bubble. I give him the thumbs up; I'm not sure how I'll ever repay him for taking such a risk.

No one gives me a second glance when I exit the back gate of the compound.

In Carl's house I change out of the fire gear, collect a bag of food, fresh clothes and bedding. I consider taking Carl's shotgun but leave it — it's too bulky. I wish I had my satellite phone but it too is bulky and they could probably use it to locate me. Instead, I ransack Carl's poker jar, fill my pockets with change; I'll use the pay phone.

In the basement, I find a place to hide and wait for dark.

25

SUPPER IS A LATE NIGHT gourmet affair involving a can of tuna and several grapefruits. I have a table in the non-smoking section of a condemned old house, walls decorated with neolithic graffiti and skylight compliments of an indoor campfire. The neighbourhood is equally appealing: a defunct gas station with boarded windows and a storage yard filled with dented culverts. Reminds me of *Cannery Row* by Steinbeck; I picture the culverts occupied by sleeping vagrants filling the night with amplified snores.

I'm the vagrant tonight and won't be sleeping.

The nearest pay phone is next to a gas station at the edge of town. It takes several discreet, well timed throws from the shadows before I manage to knock-out the streetlight above the booth, the light popping like an old vacuum tube, glass tinkling onto the pavement. No one seems to notice but I wait a half-hour anyway, then pump in a fistful of quarters.

Four rings before I get an answer. "Yeah?"

I change my voice. "Is this Christina Telson?"

"Depends. Who's this?"

Her cell phone isn't local and my budget is somewhat restricted, so like a Japanese poem, economy of words is to be strived for. But content is equally important; the Mounties are monitoring the airwaves. I glance toward the gas station. A sign in the window advertises smokes, beer and video rentals. "It's Andre at the Express Gas. Your movie rental is overdue and I was hoping you could bring it down. There's a customer in who's pretty anxious to rent it."

"What movie?"

"*The Fugitive.* You rented it a few days ago."

There's a pause. "Give me a minute. I'll be right there."

I retreat into shadow, watch teenagers stop to buy $5 of gas and $20 of beer. They lounge in the parking lot, joking and laughing. Telson's Bug passes on the road, then again going the other direction. She doesn't turn in — something must be wrong. I could work my way across town to the RV park but the Mounties might be watching her trailer.

So I wait, crouched beside a fragrant dumpster.

Twenty minutes pass. I'm getting nauseous from rotting fast-food scraps and consider a move to a more olfactory-friendly location when a cop car cruises slowly past. The teenagers in the parking lot hide their beers, looking suspiciously casual. A few minutes later they're gone, leaving behind a half dozen empties on the concrete curbstops. I'm ready to fade back when Telson's VW pulls past the gas pumps. I give her a quick, shielded burst from my flashlight. She walks into the dark alley.

"Over here. Behind the dumpster."

She takes a quick sidestep, her arms held together in front of her. There's something dark in her hands and I realize why she's so brave. She's either a cop or has come to bring me in — the climax to her book. "I've got a gun and I can see you. Don't move."

I could shine the flashlight in her eyes and run like hell —

"Sorry Porter —" The gun descends. "I wasn't sure it was you."

I stand up, keep an eye on the gun. "Careful with that thing."

“Don’t worry.” She tucks the big semi-auto under her jacket. “I’ve been shooting since I was 12. Took the provincial championship at 16. I can draw faster than most of the pros.”

“A skill every girl needs,” I say. “For those Saturday night shootouts.”

She looks toward the parking lot. “We’ve got to find a better place to talk.”

She leads me around the back of the Express Gas, along much the same route I took, then veers into the bush. There’s no trail here, no moon and very little light coming from the stars. She’s a dim shape ahead of me, bending aside branches, feeling her way through the dark. I follow too close, get a branch slapped in my face, stumble and nearly fall.

“Slow down —”

“Some forest ranger.”

The slope increases then levels off and I hear water. We’re in the river valley near one of the rapids in the Curtain River: Rapids of the Drowned — a wonderful tourist attraction. But we’re here for another reason. The noise will cover the sound of our voices; you’d have to be mighty close to hear what’s being said.

“So what exactly is your line of work, Mizz Telson? If that’s really your name.”

Her face is a pale oblong framed by dark hair. “Journalism.”

“Most journalists don’t carry a Colt .45.”

“This isn’t your usual journalism.”

“I gathered that,” I say, my reply a touch caustic.

“Look, I’m sorry about what happened Porter —”

“I don’t want to talk about it.”

“Well I do.” It’s too dark to read much of her body language but her tone is clear enough. “I started out not wanting to care about you, Porter. I didn’t expect to find you here — I’d already done plenty of research on you. I was here because of the bombing. Then I went to the bar and there you were."

"Ready for the fleecing."

"I was just going to talk to you a little."

"Yeah? Well, we did more than talk."

There's a strained silence and we stand awkwardly, like kids who've sneaked out together to smoke our first cigarette. This could be as much of a mistake. "Can we be friends here?" she says finally. The perpetual female myth.

"Sure," I say. "Why not."

"I'm trying, Porter. Maybe you could do the same."

She's trying to sound matter-of-fact but I detect an undercurrent of emotion. She's not the only one; I remember the hour spent in her bed, the night by the river. I want to rewind everything, but if I could I might run out of tape. Better to let it play, see what song comes up next. "I don't want to talk about it," I tell her. "Let's stick to business. Let's talk about why we're here."

Her reply is a little terse. "Fine by me."

"What's your interest in the Lorax?"

"I've been following the Lorax since his second bombing."

"Really. So what have you learned in all that time?"

"First things first," she says. "Did you kill Petrovich?"

"Christ." She doesn't waste any time. "You sure you're a journalist?"

"Why?"

"Because you sound like a cop."

"Is there a difference?"

"Yeah. A cop has to follow certain rules."

A car turns somewhere on a road above us, its headlights sweeping the tops of the trees, then roars away, tires squealing. Kids with nothing better to do — the good old days. "We might use different techniques," she says. "But we both want the truth."

"Maybe you should have started by telling me the truth —"

"Then answer the question."

"I didn't kill anybody."

"It was your knife they found his blood on."

It's frightening how much she knows, but I guess that's her business. I'm in need of an ally, even a manipulating waif with a handgun. Especially a manipulating waif with a handgun.

"My knife was stolen," I tell her. "Shortly after I got here."

"How convenient."

"Not for me. That's why I'm hiding behind dumpsters."

"Who would want to steal your knife?"

"Look, whether or not you believe me, it's obviously a set-up."

"Fine. Either way Porter, you're a fugitive. So what's the deal?"

We're making deals now. The new Telson.

"You need help," she says. "Isn't that why you called me?"

"I thought we could share some information."

"Sure. What've you got?"

"A suspect," I tell her. "What about you?"

"You've got a suspect?"

"Don't sound so excited —"

"Who is it this time?" she asks wearily.

"What do you mean — this time?"

"From what the cops are saying, you were sure it was Petrovich."

"You taking the cops to bed too? Pumping them for information?"

"I've got a scanner Porter. Hours of fun. You should get one."

"I'll put it on my Christmas list. Look — Petrovich was the set-up. I was supposed to believe he was the Lorax. I was supposed to be so sure that I'd tell the cops. That way, when he was killed with my knife, they would come after me."

"Who's your suspect?"

"A local who works for the mill."

"Again?" She groans. "I hope you dug a little deeper this time."

"Why don't you want to believe it could be a local?"

"Statistics, Porter. Locals tend to behave in their backyards. To avoid suspicion."

"Maybe this guy is getting frustrated. Or he's become opportunistic and this was just too good to pass up. He's ex-military and he knows explosives. The last bombing used C4, in case you didn't know that. He works in the industry and knows his way around the bush."

"I could find a dozen guys who fit that description."

"I'm sure you could. But there's more."

Even in this light I can see her patiently dubious expression. I don't want to tell her about the hat with the crimped visor or where I first saw it. But she just stands there, waiting, and doesn't say anything. She's using silence effectively, better than most of the pros. "You'll just have to trust me," I tell her. "This guy is involved."

"Could you be a little more vague? I'm having trouble handling this much detail."

"I saw him at the bombing scene."

"He was at the crime scene? What, was he just standing there?"

I tell her about my little hike through the woods, coming across the stranger. How he was hidden, dressed in camo and watching the cops through the scope of a rifle. How he turned on me. She stands closer and she smells familiar — too good, despite my frustration with her. When I'm finished, her sarcasm is gone. "The cops didn't pick him up?"

"They didn't believe me."

"But how do you know it's the guy who works for the mill?"

"Good solid detective work," I tell her. "He's been following me around."

"Following you? Why? Does he think you can identify him?"

"He knows who I am. He probably killed Petrovich to get me off his case."

She's nodding, making mental notes, double-spaced with chapter headings.

"What about you?" I say. "What have your years of research revealed?"

She sighs. "Not as much as I would have liked. I've made contacts all over North America in the ecotage underground. These monkey-wrenchers are a pretty connected lot, but even so, I don't think they know who's doing it. They idolize the Lorax of course — he's sort of their Edward Abbey — but they don't know who he is. Or they know and they're very good at hiding it."

"So you're pretty much in the dark."

"Pretty much," she admits. She's close enough I could reach out and grab her. I'm not sure if it would be to hold her or strangle her. Either way, it may be a losing proposition — her gun is bigger than mine. I'll just have to consider her one of the boys. "I even went to the prison where they got Kazinski," she says. "They gave me ten whole minutes with him."

"The Unabomber?"

"I'm glad to see you read the papers. He gave me some insights into the evils of technology but he says he has no idea who the Lorax is. He'd like to meet him though, shake his hand."

"I'd love to give him the opportunity."

There's a lull; we both have a lot to think about. Clouds drift in and it suddenly seems very dark. All we need are black toques and we could be on the set of *The Blair Witch Project*. As if on cue something rustles through the brush, in the direction of the river.

Telson reaches under her coat. "What the hell was that?"

A large dark shape snorts and lifts its head.

"Put your gun away. Poaching is illegal."

"What?" she says, her voice a little shaky.

"It's just a moose, making its rounds."

The gun goes away and after a few minutes so does the moose. We listen for what seems a long time to the receding crackle and slap of willows. "I hired a profiler," she says finally. "Retired FBI guy who lives down in Florida, raises crocodiles. He figures the Lorax is a loner who's using the name to identify himself with the environmental movement. He's what they call an organized criminal — highly intelligent, plans his crimes well in advance and controls the crime scene. He's not mainstream green; probably has another job. Despite his intelligence, he's got a simplistic value system. Probably white, in his twenties or early thirties, lives in the country or has a secure place to make his bombs. Like Kazinski, he feels socially alienated and prefers to work at a distance. Unlike Kazinski, he probably didn't intend to harm anyone."

I picture Nina. "The result is the same."

"I'm sorry about what happened to your friend," she says, reaching a hand toward me, then thinks better of it. "But it could have been an unlucky coincidence. The bomb was set in a machine that wasn't working, presumably so no one would get hurt. There's no way he could have known you'd be there. After your friend was killed the bombings stopped for years."

"Well, they've started again. And he doesn't seem to mind killing now."

"Yeah," she says. "That's got me worried."

"You and a lot of people."

"So what are we going to do, Porter? Can we work together?"

Sure, I tell her, we can work together. Not like I have a lot of choice. I tell her about Brotsky, ask her to look into his past. What did he do in the military? Why did he leave? Was he buddies with Petrovich? What connection might either of them have had with Hess? Where were they during the other bombings? Was there some reason the Lorax picked Curtain River Forest Products? What sort of environmental record do they have?

"Anything else?"

"Just do what you can. Look hard at this Brotsky."

"Okay," she says. "But we have an understanding right?"

She wants exclusive rights. I want revenge. It seems like a good deal.

I'm shopping at the Forest Service cache the next night. Not much selection, but good hours. For the limited selection they have, they make it up with volume. Everything comes by the crate like a wholesale grocery — all that's missing is the oversized cart. I'm in an aisle where canned prunes come by the gross; the Forest Service has to start hiring younger firefighters.

"What about batteries?" asks Carl. "You need more flashlight batteries?"

I nod and he hands me a five-pound box. I take out four batteries, put the rest back.

"You should have come to me," he says. "Never trust a reporter."

"Journalist," I correct him, as if there's a difference.

"They both buy ink by the ton," he says. "So they're always right."

He's upset I went to Telson for help. "Friends take care of friends," he says, but that's exactly why I don't want him too involved. He's done enough already — taken too many risks smuggling me back in the helicopter. He could lose his job, end up in prison. Telson on the other hand is a professional, knows what she's getting into. And she knows the Lorax as good as anyone.

"Think about it, Porter —"

Carl walks narrow alleys between high shelves stacked with fire pumps, hose, portable water tanks, axes and tents, shines his flashlight at what he thinks might interest me — Carl's fugitive emporium. I'd need the stake truck to move most of this stuff, not the backpack I'm using.

"What's her motivation?" he asks. "If they don't catch the Lorax, she can still write a bestseller."

I toss cans of beans and Spork into my backpack. "How are the cops making out?"

"They think you're dead. Either in the fire or on the river. They found parts of a canoe and your jacket caught in a sweeper below The Meat Grinder. They've got divers out there, Search & Rescue — about 20 boats searching downstream and along the banks. Looks like the Canada Day Raft Race."

"What about the Lorax?"

Carl shakes his head. "The cops seem a little distracted right now."

"How did that fire start? Was it our buddy Red Flag?"

Carl shakes his head. "Abandoned camp fire."

Creamed corn, a small campstove and a bag of rice complete the Porter Cassel survival kit. In the toiletries section I add a few rolls of posterior stationery; just because you're a fugitive doesn't mean you have to be barbaric. There's a selection of cooking gear on a top shelf. I grab hold of a crossbeam and climb up, grab for the pots. They make a noise like a two-year-old with cymbals.

Carl flinches. "We better get out of here before someone notices."

I'm just about to climb down when I see a stack of familiar cake pans.

"Since when have our cooks been baking?"

Carl shines the flashlight at me, blinds me for a few seconds. "Some of them do now that we're using base camps again," he says. "And we're getting better cooks, who know how to do more than boil pork chops."

"Did you know this is the same type of pan the arsonist is using?"

"Really?" Carl frowns. "Maybe our cooks are starting fires."

A vehicle turns into the ranger station parking lot, headlights sweeping rectangles of light across the shelves, catching me like a convict on a prison wall. Carl kills his flashlight and I scramble down. "It's the cops," Carl whispers at a window. "Someone's coming."

"Is there a back door?"

"No." He gives me a worried look. "I'll take care of it."

I watch from the corner of a dirty window as Carl leaves the cache, pretends to be locking the door. A beam of light suddenly fills the room — the cop's flashlight — and I duck away from the window. The Mountie is close enough that I hear him ask if there's a problem; Carl telling him he was just going home from the office, thought he heard something. But he did a thorough search — it must have been a squirrel or something that got inside, rattled some pots. The Mountie makes another pass with his flashlight, then shrugs. Carl walks him back to his cruiser.

I slip out of the cache as the cruiser pulls away, vanish into the shadows.

26

I SPEND THE DAY like a skunk, sleeping in the crawlspace under the burned-out old house. It leaves me smelling as appealing as a skunk, but at least it's relatively safe under there. Around noon, a group of kids come over and wake me — I hear them clomping around, the floorboards creaking; watch from between cracks in the floor as they add to the graffiti in the living room, sit around and smoke a joint. But they quickly lose interest; there's really nothing left to wreck.

By two in the afternoon it's stifling under the old house. I'm ready to give in — arrest me, just put me somewhere cool where it doesn't smell like mouse turds. I lie on bare dirt and stare at cracked boards. If this is anything like The Hole in prison, I'm doing my best to stay out of there. Night finally comes. I boil Kraft Dinner — yellow death, we used to call it — and drink a lot of apple juice. I clean up as best I can for my business meeting.

"I'm not sure this is such a good idea."

"Relax Porter. No one stops an old Volkswagen."

I'm nervous being in a car like this, on the road where the police could stop us. Telson picked me up at a pre-arranged location in a back alley. This time when I called her, I was a telemarketer wondering if she was happy with her cell phone service. She was, except for all the telemarketers. I offered her a call-screening package — the Just Say No program.

She said no; she's learning already.

Tonight she's wearing a bulky jacket, jeans and old army boots. No more shorts and halter tops — too hard to hide the big gun. I'm wearing what I've been wearing for the past several days.

Telson wrinkles her nose. "What is that smell?"

"That would be me."

"Maybe you should ride in the trunk."

Fortunately we don't drive far. A narrow trail leads to a water treatment intake along the river. The road isn't well travelled and has ruts as hard as concrete curbstops. The Bug bounces and rattles like a piñata at a birthday party — if I burst it won't be candy that comes out. We park by a cinder block building with a pocked "Town of Curtain River" sign on the door.

I look around, nervous. "Maybe we should go somewhere else."

"Relax, Porter. I doubt there's much traffic down here."

We get out of the tin can; I want to be able to look around and Telson is fanning a hand in front of her face, holding her nose. It's a beautiful, dark, starlit spring night — perfect for fugitives, teenagers and vampires. We wander toward the dim block of the intake station as though drawn to a monolith. Telson leans against the brick wall, lights up a cigarette. Another surprise.

"When did you start smoking?"

"I tend to smoke under stressful conditions."

"You weren't smoking when you met me."

"Don't flatter yourself," she says. "I was chewing Nicorette."

I glance toward the stars, wonder if Special "O" is circling somewhere up there in their Cessna Caravan, honing in on the glow of Telson's cigarette. Can they fly at night? I sense invisible eyes and ears in the darkness around us. Next — the dogs will be spying on me. Then it's a nice white room with daily doses of pharmaceuticals.

"You're not really a vegetarian are you?"

"No." She clicks shut a lighter. "Just makes it easier to infiltrate these groups."

"They like vegetarians?"

"They like anyone on their end of the spectrum with extreme beliefs."

"That what you were doing at the Mountain Guardian meeting?"

"Yeah. But they're soft core, not worth infiltrating."

I think of Reggie — he didn't strike me as soft core — and it makes me wonder what kind of people she's been hanging with that she needs to carry such a big gun. She takes a long drag, her cigarette glowing like a beacon. Enough small talk.

"So what did you find out?" I ask her.

"About your friend Alvin Brotsky? He's a bit of an enigma." A cloud of smoke drifts past my face. "Alvin was definitely in the military," she says. "That part was easy. What exactly he did is harder to ascertain."

"His tattoo said Airborne."

"Getting chummy enough to compare tattoos?"

"You know I don't have any tattoos."

"Yeah," she says. "You're pretty much a skinny white canvas. Anyway, Brotsky injured his knees somehow and they offered him a desk job, which he declined."

"Not enough action behind a desk."

Telson finishes her smoke, the glowing butt arcing across the road like tracer ammunition.

"Watch where you flick that thing," I say, annoyed. "It's pretty dry out here."

"Once a twig pig," she says. "Always a twig pig."

"Is Airborne involved in explosives operations?"

"I don't know much about the military. I'll need more time."

"So you don't really know anything about Brotsky."

"The military are notoriously protective about their records, Porter. You remember the Somalia papers? I should have bought more stocks in the paper shredding industry before the Access to Information legislation was passed."

"What else did you find out?"

"I looked into Curtain River Forest Products, into their environmental record, which, it turns out, is no worse than industry standard. It's actually a bit better. This area has such heavy recreational use that they have to be more careful than most other companies. Forget a slap on the wrist penalty, they mess up here and it's in the *National Post* the next day. Some VP has a stroke over his morning bagel."

"So they're good corporate citizens. You've been talking with Benji."

"Faust? Yeah, I talked to him. He took me out for lunch —"

"You're a cheap convert."

"He's not the only one I talked to."

"But you turned on the charm. Everyone likes to talk to a pretty girl."

A moment's pause. Telson doesn't like losing control of the conversation.

"Do you want my help or not, Porter?"

"Temper, temper. Remember the deal."

She lights up another cigarette, her face visible for a second. She's frowning.

"Anyway," I tell her, "someone didn't think they're good corporate citizens."

"That's been bothering me," she says, puffing hard for a moment, the tip of her cigarette pulsing like a warning light. "It's not consistent. Like I said, their record isn't that bad and it got me wondering if maybe there wasn't something a little less obvious. I dug some more and it turns out the company's safety record isn't as sterling as their environmental record. In the past eight years they've had 423."

"Four hundred accidents? I'd hate to see their Workers' Comp premiums."

"Most companies have a fraction of that many accidents," Telson says. She's pacing on the road now, sounds excited — the roving reporter on a scent trail. "The interesting thing is most of the accidents occurred after Whitlaw bought the company and built the new mill."

"Four hundred accidents." I still can't believe it. "Why?"

She points a finger at me. "Production baby. For its size, this mill pumps out more lumber than any other mill in the country. Benji was pretty proud of that little titbit of information but it got me wondering if there was a connection with that many accidents. So I talked to a few workers. They're stressed out, making mistakes. The machines are running so fast, they can't keep up."

I think of Leonard at Emergency, his fingers in his friend's lunch bucket.

Gonna lose our safety bonus this week —

And Linda Hess, talking about her husband.

He got frustrated sometimes. So many people got hurt —

"I did a little investigating too," I tell Telson. "Hess was concerned with safety."

"But he worked in the bush, right? Not in the mill."

"Yes — he worked in the bush, but there must be a tremendous amount of pressure on the bush operations to feed a mill that hungry. They're not unionized, are they?"

"Bingo," says Telson.

"You think Hess was talking union?"

"It wouldn't be the first time someone tried. I found some old articles from the local rag. About a year after the mill was up and running a few guys decide to do a little union rousing and get fired faster than you can spit. So they take the company to court and get their jobs back. Wanna guess how long they stayed?"

I shrug — I don't want to slow her down.

"Three weeks," she says triumphantly. "I tracked down one of the guys and he told me he just couldn't take the stress. The management and supervisors were all over him. He received threats — like what could happen to a man who fell into the de-barker. So he sold his house and got the hell out of Dodge."

Telson is close enough I can smell her perfume. And her excitement.

"They killed him," she says. "They killed Hess."

I think of Petrovich — his record of assault. "Maybe Brotsky and Petrovich were working together. They were going to warn Hess, scare him a bit, get him to shut up. But Petrovich gets carried away, and suddenly they have a body to get rid of. A bit of C4 in Hess's machine and a word spray-painted on a nearby tree, and they're in the clear. Blame it all on the Lorax."

"A plausible theory," says Telson.

A theory that clears me of Petrovich's murder but leaves me as far from catching the Lorax as the day Nina was killed. "Hess must have talked to someone about this."

"That's my next project."

I picture Petrovich with his throat cut — someone tidying up loose ends at my expense. Ronald Hess distributed over several acres of logging slash. "Maybe you'd better go to the cops with this one, let them ask the questions."

Telson shakes her head. "No way, this one is mine."

"These people are killers."

"Don't worry." She pats her jacket. "I travel with a big stick."

"I can't talk you out of this?"

"Not a chance."

We look at each other, her face faintly luminescent in the starlight. I can't think of anything more to say. "Can I drop you somewhere?" she asks, moving toward the car.

"I'm fine here."

"Probably best." She gives me a reassuring smile, but she's already miles away. "You keep out of sight, Porter. Call me in a couple of days." Then she ducks into her Bug and she's gone, tail lights dancing up the rutted road. For as long as I can, I listen to the receding sound of the engine.

It sounds like loss.

The lights are off at Carl's place by the time I drop by for my mountain bike. I should have stashed it somewhere else because as I draw near the ranger station I notice a car parked across the street. It's a Caprice Classic, a newer model, which looks harmless enough. I doubt the used clothes store it's parked in front of is open this time of night and if I looked closer I'm reasonably certain I'd find blue and red lights in the rear window, radios in the dash, a shotgun between the seats. Not that I plan on getting that close — I can't tell if anyone is home; it's parked just beyond an oblong of visible road illuminated by a weak streetlight.

I take the low road, through bramble along the creek.

Plenty of shadow. I watch and wait, perfumed by the night scent of willow. There's another scent mixed in, one I doubt would sell at the local drugstore. Odor of dead cat. Mice drag race enthusiastically at my feet, rustling under dead leaves. No other sounds — seems safe enough. Except for that Caprice. And Special "O."

We've got shit you've never dreamed of Cassel —

I'm thinking it's not worth the risk; I can borrow a bike somewhere else. Suddenly there's a flash of light near Carl's back porch and for an instant I can see everything: picnic table, lawnmower, fence. The beam swings like a lighthouse warning over my head and across a wall of dense green spruce. Then darkness comes again, much thicker, and I remain motionless while my eyes become reacquainted with the night. The cop with the flashlight is taking his time sauntering across the lawn. Then he's invisible, swallowed by shadow, a light crunch of gravel signalling his progress down the alley.

When he turns onto the road I run softly across the lawn.

The bike is where I left it and I fumble with the combination lock, feel for the raised numbers like a blind man reading Braille. The story is familiar and the lock gives. I walk the bike down the alley away from the road. In no time I'm across town.

I don't like the exposure along the highway but the bordering brush rising out of the valley is too thick to negotiate. There's nothing to do but wait for a dark stretch with no traffic then pedal like mad for the top of the hill.

I make it to the top with only one interruption — a semi-trailer forces me to drop the bike in the ditch and crouch just inside the tree line. Then it's cross-country over farm fields. In the dark I jolt and wobble over gopher burrows; there are more than 18 holes on this golf course and plenty of hazards — bovine land mines can cause a nasty skid. For navigation, I use the thin picket of fence-line trees marking the boundary of each quarter section.

Headlights ahead — the secondary road leading to Brotsky's.

The vehicle is long gone by the time I make it to the road. I heave my bike over barbed wire. At this time of night, traffic should be minimal, but I pedal hard, stash the bike in the ditch and walk the last few hundred yards.

Brotsky's place is dark, no vehicle visible. But there's a garage and I feel for my watch. It's gone — I must have lost it on the back nine. Brotsky is on early night shift and I should have plenty of time to do what I have to, but it makes me nervous to be without my watch. It has sentimental value — I got it at Mohawk with a fill and it's lasted more than a week.

I'm crossing the yard when there's a pop and I'm suddenly blinded — the yard lighting up like a prison compound. I dash into shadow beside the garage, wait for the sound of an opening door. For my heart to stop thumping. But the yard lights must be automatic, rigged for movement, because no one comes out. I sit tight; they're probably on a timer.

After about five minutes, the lights switch off. I slip into the garage.

The garage isn't empty and the occupant is familiar. Creases in the side of the old, blue Plymouth look in the shielded beam of my flashlight like the scrape of shark's teeth. In the gloom, the car's tail fins throw long shadows — like I've found the carcass of some dead marine animal. The door opens with an arthritic groan, triggering the car's interior light. I quickly close the door.

The keys are in the ignition. Not that anyone would want to steal it.

The glove box yields two treasures — a rare collector's edition of the operator's manual, still in its plastic slipcover, and a registration in the name of Alvin J. Brotsky. The manual is still good; the registration expired three months ago. I check under the seat and in the trunk but find nothing further.

The house I approach from behind, avoid triggering the yard lights. The back door is locked as are all the windows within reach. A basement window caves easily against the steel-toed tip of my boot. I wait a moment but there are no alarms, no more lights. I put on leather workgloves, pick jagged shards of glass from the bottom of the sill, lower myself through the casement.

I'm standing on something — a washing machine or dryer. Metal pops and sags. Glass crunches under my boots. I flick on my flashlight. It's a dryer; I'm in the laundry room. I jump down, inspect a shelf filled with junk and half-empty boxes of detergent. The next room is a den of sorts with a couch, TV, dartboard and pool table. The furnishings are old, the basement only half-finished, rooms roughed in. Full ashtrays everywhere and enough empty beer bottles to put a Boy Scout through college. It's a red-neck speakeasy — the posse from The Corral must relocate here after last call.

There's another room, with a locked metal door I'll return to later.

Upstairs, the house is a little more civilized; the kitchen is clean, newspapers piled in a corner. The living room coffee table is scattered with magazines, *Field & Stream, Deer Hunter, Guns & Ammo*, and survivalist magazines — chubby urbanites dressed in fatigues recommend the best all-around sniper rifle, how to build a recreational bunker. When I was a kid, bomb shelters were just going out of style. Nice to see fashion is still predictably cyclic. The bookshelf shows a wide divergence of tastes — *Nancy Drew* sits next to an old version of *Gray's Anatomy*. Brotsky must have bought the books at a garage sale to fill shelf space.

A child's room is obviously unused. Pluto and Minnie Mouse share a dusty lampshade. A baseball bat and two gloves in a corner evoke memories, guilt for breaking the window. Is the room for Brotsky's kid? Relatives? I close the bedroom door, move down the hall. Bathroom to the left, master bedroom at the end. Big bed. On the wall, a motel-quality painting of a sailing ship in stormy weather. Three dressers — nice taste in antiques; pictures on top show a family of three, Brotsky smiling. The woman is attractive, younger than him. Then more single pictures of a boy, progressively older, culminating with a high school grad picture. The storyline isn't hard to imagine — away on duty, covert manoeuvres at home. A battle, which Brotsky apparently lost.

In the closet, rifles stored without trigger guards. The Mounties wouldn't approve.

Not much to go on — you could find unsecured rifles and gun-related magazines in any house around here. I move back to the kitchen. A clock in the microwave glows green numbers. Forty minutes until Brotsky gets off work. Plenty of time. Downstairs, the locked metal door doesn't give until I find a toolbox and pry bar. Still, it takes a lot of work to get past the three deadbolts.

The room has no windows. I flick on the lights.

I'm in a military surplus store. Camo netting hangs from the ceiling, making the room resemble a large tent. Metal ammo boxes are stacked in neat rows. There's a reloading press on a workbench, enough gunpowder to keep Yosemite Sam in business. Guns in an open rack line one wall, chained together through their trigger guards. Three or four rifles are hunting models with wooden stocks. Thirty or forty of them are assault weapons. Most disturbing — a 50-calibre machine gun sits on a heavy tripod. I don't think it's a replica.

I don't think Brotsky will report this break-in.

A small bookshelf displays much less variety than its counterpart topside — reloading manuals, guerrilla warfare, tactical procedures. Next to a cluster of hand grenades I hope are duds is a photo of a younger Brotsky, black-haired and in fatigues, posing in front of a helicopter.

— they offered him a desk job, which he declined —

I rummage through metal cases, lettered on the outside with cryptic codes, looking for c4 or dynamite. A case of high explosive would make a nice parting gift for a disgruntled grunt. Or is grunt the right term for Airborne? Probably not. But there's no high explosive — the cases are filled with dried food, foot powder, spare fatigues. He's well prepared for the end of the world.

There's nothing here which directly connects Brotsky to Petrovich or Hess's death. If there is, I don't have the time to find it myself. This dig needs a full team: grids, photos, screens. But on another level, there's plenty here. Some of those guns have got to be illegal and taken in the context of recent events assume a deeper significance. Brotsky is trained in military tactics, sabotage, counter-intelligence. Explosives. He's good at his job, then he's injured and can't go out with the boys anymore. Like a football player — an injured free agent — he's suddenly all washed up. So he quits, gets another job. But he likes the toys, wants to keep up with the rest of the class. Whitlaw, his new boss, his commanding officer, tells him there's mutiny in the ranks, offers Brotsky a special mission — talk to the troublemaker, make him understand. Persuade him, for the good of the unit. Brotsky recruits Petrovich but they're a little too persuasive and there's a body to get rid of. Not to worry: Brotsky the seasoned veteran, thinks this through. The Lorax has been in the papers for years, the crimes never solved. Time for a Lorax comeback. Plop Hess in a machine and load it with high explosive. There won't be enough left of the body to prove anything.

Misdirection. No evidence. Insurance pays for the machine.

Then along comes the ex-twig pig, nosing around, looking for the Lorax. So Brotsky gives me a Lorax. He steals the starter off Old Faithful so I'll go to his buddy with the Land Rovers, who steers me in Petrovich's direction. To make sure I believe that Petrovich is the Lorax, he has Petrovich harass me, plants the incriminating resumé. Then he kills Petrovich, who has too much of a temper to remain reliable. Two birds, one stone.

And I have motive up to my eyeballs. It's such a perfect set-up, it's chilling.

Maybe I should be a good citizen, make an anonymous call, report a break-in. Rachet might find this room interesting, might begin to make a few of the same connections. There's a small locked filing cabinet I'm trying to jimmy when I hear the front door open. I lunge for the lights. Could I have been here that long or did Brotsky get off work early? Boots are kicked off, thump against the wall. Maybe he'll go upstairs and have a beer, or better yet, go to bed. I listen hard, hope to hear the floor above my head creak but there's only silence. Is he standing by the door, sensing something is not quite right, or has he padded upstairs in his stocking feet?

Is he coming down the stairs, silently, a gun in his hand?

I'm not waiting to find out, slip into the laundry room.

Shards of glass snap under my boots as I stand on the dryer. I hear the floor above me creak now — Brotsky running for the stairs — and heave myself up through the casement, scramble over the metal window well. Lights go on below, projecting a wide beam of light through the vacant window. I run sideways out of the light, to the rear of the house, away from the spotlights waiting in front. As I run, I hear the dim but unmistakable rattle of chain from Brotsky's basement. He's unchaining his guns.

My bike is several hundred yards up the road lying in the ditch and I run behind the garage, head into the scattered spruce. I'll use the dark and trees as cover to carefully work my way to the road. Barely into the trees, I hear the front door of the house slap open and stop running, crouch behind a tree. The yard lights don't go on. Has he killed them or is he coming around back?

The stars are magnificent but give only enough light to make out individual trees. The ground is black, obstacles hidden. I move slowly from tree to tree, crouching, straining to make out movement by the dark blocks of garage and house. There's a series of muted slapping sounds and spruce needles drop down the back of my neck. It takes me a few dangerously long seconds to realize he's using a silencer and those were bullets, at chest height — if I hadn't crouched, I'd be dead. But it's too dark for those shots to have been anything but a lucky guess. I make a short, crouched dash for another clump of trees and the slapping sound follows, wood chips hitting my cheek — he's shooting lower now, clearly following my progress. A pause a half beat long and I dive, lay flat behind dense branches which suddenly come alive, whispering and crackling.

Branches fall — then silence.

He's got a full automatic with infrared or some sort of starlight amplification scope and is in no hurry — he can see when I move and he's not worried about waking the neighbours. But why shoot at me? He needs me as a scapegoat.

Unless he doesn't realize it's me. Maybe he thinks it's the real Lorax.

In the quiet, my breathing sounds like Darth Vader. I could use some of the Force right now — even if I make it to my bike I couldn't outrun him; he would have no problem driving across the cow pasture that surrounds his little patch of trees. If I knew where he was, I might be able to follow an obscured path toward the road. But with a gun like that? One wrong move and I get to see Nina again — assuming I'd be travelling in the right direction.

In the distance, I hear a motor — a car turning off the highway, headed this direction. The car needs a new muffler, the roar obscenely loud. Above me, light plays across tree branches. I feel around for a rock, find one smaller than I'd hoped for. When the car is closer, I run away from the road toward the rear of the garage, use the car's noise as cover. I'm counting on Brotsky looking for me closer to the road — I don't expect him to be distracted for long. The car passes, taking with it the light. As the sound begins to recede I throw the rock toward the front of the garage, hoping to trigger the yard lights.

Either they're not that sensitive or Brotsky has turned them off.

The rock hits something metal and suddenly I see movement — Brotsky leaned up against the back corner of the garage, his rifle searching toward the road. He's little more than a suggestion, but the barrel of the gun is visible against the lighter siding of the garage. He steps quickly toward the front and I move around back, sprint across dead zone between the buildings to the back of the house, then circle to the far side and peer around a front corner.

He's a dim shape between the garage and house. I toss a handful of gravel to make him think I'm headed back into the trees and when I see his dark form head in that direction I run to the front of the house, yank open the door without entering and run for the cover of the garage.

It works. Brotsky has gone full circle around the house and is poised in front of the door, looking around, trying to decide if I really went in. If I didn't, he knows I'm not far. If I did, I could be going for his guns. He goes in. I wait a few seconds, then sprint for his truck.

The yard lights come on — the keys aren't in his Bronco. I spend what might be the last ten seconds of my life yanking open the hood, grabbing spark plug wires, flipping the clasp on his distributor cap. Brotsky must be downstairs, in his windowless gunroom. The distributor cap comes loose and I toss it as far as I can, then bolt for the garage.

I make it inside just as the door on the house slaps open.

The blue whale cranks but doesn't start. Too much noise — too little time. It catches and I gun the engine, grab the shifter. Brotsky knows what I'm up to because he's waiting outside when the big Plymouth splinters his cedar garage door. I'm ducking anyways, expecting wood to come through the windshield. I get bullets instead, throwing glass. The Bronco is a short distance in front of the garage and I use it as cover, put it between me and Brotsky, get a glimpse of a man with a rifle, pivoting like a lawn sprinkler, spraying bullets. The engine roars, the car fishtailing — I can't tell if it's gravel hitting the wheel wells or more bullets. As I leave the circle of light, I peer just over the dash and something bites my ear. The driveway curves — the road just ahead. I'm going too fast but if I hit the brakes, he'll see the lights and I don't want to give him a target. I slide nearly into the far ditch — if he's still shooting I can't hear it over the engine but the trees are in my favour now. I click on headlights to find the road, see the glint of my bike's handlebar ahead in the ditch, make a sudden decision. Maybe it's a mistake but I figure I got at least 30 or 40 seconds before Brotsky can make it to the road, maybe more with his bad knee.

I kill the lights, drag the bike out of the ditch. The back door of the Plymouth has a jagged swath of perfect round little holes, trailing across a tail fin. When the interior light goes on, the back seat looks like two cats went at it. The bike fits — couldn't do that with today's Plymouth. Something bright buzzes past like fireworks as I surge forward, spraying gravel. He's using tracer ammo. I push the accelerator flat and the big girl responds — can't do it like that with a new Plymouth either. More fireworks streak past — a celebration in my honour. In the dark, I nearly miss a curve in the road, grab for the lights. Bullet holes and cracked glass give me a high speed kaleidoscopic view of ditch and road.

I crank the wheel hard, regain the road grade.

I'm out of his line of fire.

Lights ahead — a truck passing on the highway. I pull hard into the turn, halfway into the ditch. Something in the old girl gives; the engine races too fast — victim of a bullet or a belt; she isn't going much further. I take the first secondary gravel road to the right, then another to the left. The car lurches and falters. I crank the wheel toward a meadow on one side, exit while the car is still rolling. It thumps down a ditch where I'm sure it'll stop but it lumbers on, whispering through dry grass. A hundred yards into the meadow it hits something that doesn't want to move, grinds for a moment then dies.

I remember my bike, follow the swath of bent grass.

The car is nosed into a low embankment which did surprisingly little damage to its front end. But that may be the only part undamaged — this car isn't going anywhere; it's a landscape feature now. I pull out my bike, carry it for a distance to avoid leaving a track, then saddle up and head cross-country.

At four in the morning the town looks like a scene from an old Western movie; grey and uninhabited. Soon the sun will be up, colour will return to the world and they'll be looking for me again. Time to crawl back into my coffin. But I hesitate — something is wrong. Nothing I can see but I'm developing another sense — paranoia.

I'm tired, hungry and my ear hurts like hell.

All my gear is under that house.

Those kids that stopped by yesterday — they left too quickly.

Maybe it's something. Maybe it's nothing. But I can't afford the risk.

I retreat, fade into the sunrise.

There's a plane circling over town. It could be an amateur practising his left banks but I don't think so — a Twin Otter is a bit extravagant for a student pilot. And then there's the white and blue paint job. I spend the day hunkered in the willows along a creek. I've got shade and water so it's not so bad but I'm hungry and could use a few painkillers. One of Brotsky's bullets took the bottom off my right earlobe. When it finally gets dark I pull my mountain bike out of the brush and head for a small store about 20 miles north of town. I'm not up to shopping but I remember a phone booth.

It's a long slog on an empty stomach. The hills come like waves in a storm, leaving me breathless and dizzy at each crest. But I forge on, in the second lowest gear. The store is a small wooden-sided building with an old Coke emblem over the door. A solitary light on a pole flickers like an insane asylum fluorescent during electroshock therapy. I wait a few minutes for it to die but it hangs on. There are plenty of rocks nearby but knocking out the only light might wake the owner in the house behind the store. I lean the bike against the phone booth, dig out my quarters.

I call Telson's cell phone but get no answer, then recycle the quarter. This time, after six rings, I get an answer. I change my voice. Western hillbilly. "Hello, is this the duty officer?"

"Yeah, that's me." Carl sounds like I pulled him out of a good dream.

"Sorry to call ya so late but a pile I was burnin' got away."

A deep sigh. "What's it doing now?"

"It's sparkin' up pretty good. I can see it from the house."

"Is it off your property? Or can this wait until morning?"

"We better get on this one now," I say. "Before it gets worse."

There's a pause — Carl doing a mental inventory of recent fire permits.

"What's you location?"

"You know the Mink Creek Store?"

"Uh-huh —"

"We're three miles west, two miles north, then eleven miles west again."

There's a longer pause. Carl doesn't have any fire permits in that area. The timbre of his voice changes slightly. "What sort of equipment do you have on hand?"

"Nothing," I tell him. "So you better bring lots of stuff."

"Okay. It'll take about 40 minutes. How will I know your place?"

"You'll see the fire as you get closer. Just remember to turn at the store."

My next call is long distance. Cindy answers on the second ring. She's hysterical. "Jesus Christ Porter, what's going on? The police are looking for you. You're all over the news — on TV, the radio —"

"Calm down Cindy. They can scan cell phones."

"What?" She sounds disoriented.

"They could be listening. Are you still at home?"

"No — I did like you told me."

"Good. Don't give any clues out about where you are."

"Okay." She's calmer now.

"How are the kids?"

"The kids are good."

"I need you to make a call for me. Are you near a phone?"

"I'm on the phone —"

"A land line. A regular phone."

There's a scuffling sound; Cindy moving around. "The motel has one in the room."

"Don't use that one. Is there a pay phone close by?"

Cindy's breathing is louder. "Yeah, I can see one in the parking lot."

"Good. This is how it'll work. You go to the pay phone and dial a number I'll give you. It's the cops. When they answer, you hold the cell phone to the receiver so I can talk directly with the cops. Don't say anything yourself. Can you do that?"

"Yes."

"Did you check in under your name? Use your credit card? List your licence plate?"

"Give me a little credit here, Porter —"

"Good. After the call, wake the kids and drive somewhere else."

A sigh. "Okay. Let's try to do this earlier next time."

"I'll try," I tell her. "Now go to the pay phone."

More background noise; Cindy checking on the kids, then the click of a door and faint footsteps like an old radio play. "Okay Porter —" She sounds a little breathless. "I'm ready."

I give her the number, listen to her punching keys.

"RCMP, Curtain River. How may I direct your call?"

"Sergeant Andre Rachet please."

There's a long pause, then: "Rachet here."

"Did you analyze the knife?"

A brief silence. "Porter Cassel. Back from the dead. How thoughtful of you to call."

"What did you find on the knife?"

"Where are you?" Rachet says. "We should get together, talk face-to-face."

"This is fine."

"It doesn't look good that you ran. It would look better if you came in —"

He's not just trying to talk me in, he's stalling, dragging out the conversation for a phone trace. I'm not sure how long that takes but I play along, let him talk. I want the call traced to throw them off my track. I steer the conversation back to the knife.

"We found blood," Rachet says. "Petrovich's blood. But you knew that."

"Anything else?"

"Like what?"

"Don't play games with me Rachet —"

"Okay, okay — look, don't hang up. We found something on the knife."

"What did you find?"

"Skin cells," he says after just the slightest hesitation.

"You match them with anyone?"

"You don't think they're yours?" Rachet says. "Because if you don't think they're yours you should come in, give us a sample. Pretty hard to rule you out without a sample."

"They're not mine."

"Wonderful. Then come in —"

"They're Alvin Brotsky's. Get a sample from him."

"What?" The disbelief in his voice is clear, even though Cindy isn't holding the cell close enough. Not that I blame her — I did this once for a towerman who wanted to talk to his girlfriend and had to keep moving the radio from ear to mouthpiece. Things didn't work out for him despite my best efforts — she dumped him anyway. Things aren't working out here much better — the handle on my knife is polished smooth.

"Alvin Brotsky and Zeke Petrovich killed Ronald Hess for talking union and used the Lorax as a cover to get rid of the body. Brotsky is ex-military and had access to C4. Then Brotsky set it up so I'd think Petrovich was the Lorax and killed Petrovich with my knife."

"Interesting," Rachet says. "If this is true, you're off the hook. So why not come in?"

"Pay a little visit to Brotsky. Look downstairs in his armoury. Have a look at his car."

"You can be assured we'll do that —"

"Good. When you put the pieces together, I'll call again."

"Wait a minute here, Cassel —"

"Goodbye."

There's a click; the payphone returning to its cradle, then Cindy. "How was that?"

"That was perfect, Cin. Now get the hell out of there. As soon as they complete a trace, they'll call the locals, wherever you are. They'll be looking for me but it won't take them long to figure out who you are."

"Okay." Her voice is strained. "Be careful, Porter."

I sense she wants to talk more but have to cut it short, fade into the dark. A few minutes later, an approaching vehicle flashes its lights. Not a bad response time. From the ditch I use my flashlight to return the signal and Carl pulls his Forest Service truck to the side of the road, waits in the dark. I heave my bike into the back of the truck, crawl into the cab through the rear sliding window to avoid triggering the interior door light.

Carl looks spooked. "You okay, Porter? What's going on?"

"Anyone follow you?"

He looks over his shoulder. "I doubt it."

"Just drive for now. Go east."

Carl turns on the headlights, pulls onto the road.

"What did you bring?"

He points back with his thumb. "Food, first aid kit, blankets."

I reach back through the rear slider, fumble open a box and find bread, canned meat, juice. I pull most of it in, make myself a hasty sandwich, talk between mouthfuls, tell him about my fun-filled excursion to Brotsky's house of guns. By the time I'm done, Carl is shaking his head. "He actually shot at you?"

"He turned the car into Swiss cheese."

"I'll call the cops," he says. "Anonymously of course, report the location of the car. They'll check the registration and when they visit Brotsky, they'll find the guns."

I finish my sandwich, make another. Spam never tasted so good. "It's worth a try but I'm willing to bet Brotsky will find the car first and get rid of it. The guns'll be gone too."

"Maybe." Carl crouches pensively over the steering wheel. "You're sure it's him?"

"I'm pretty sure he killed Petrovich. And Hess."

"And you think he's the Lorax?"

"I doubt it. This was just a copycat."

Carl gives me a concerned look. "What makes you think that?"

I tell him my theory about Hess being killed for talking union.

"So the Lorax was just a cover?"

The truck drifts toward the ditch. "Yeah — watch the road."

"What about Petrovich?"

A tire slips over the shoulder, spilling cans of food onto the floorboards and threatening to pull the rest of the truck into the ditch. Carl yanks it back onto hardtop, the truck swerving, leaning into its springs. I'm too tired to flinch. Dashed yellow lines scroll hypnotically past in the headlights. My stomach is full and I'm fighting to keep my eyes open. "His partner in crime," I mumble. "A loose end."

"They set you up."

I remember Star's warning. And Carl's. "I walked right into it."

Carl is gripping the steering wheel with both hands. "So what now, Porter?"

I shake my head. Despite my assurances to Cindy, I don't know.

"Where are you staying? There's cops everywhere in town."

"I'm sort of between addresses."

"I know a place. Old rail bridge over the river. I found it when I was hunting. Lots of cover and plenty of clean water. And I bet I could get the truck down the rail bed."

"That's not necessary. I can ride in."

"Not with all this stuff —"

He lights up a smoke, cracks open the window. I'm too tired to argue and not looking forward to a bumpy bike ride in the dark with a load of supplies on my back. The lighted patch of highway flows beneath like a river. The buzz of the tires is soothing —

Like the sound of rapids. I'm in a canoe —

I jolt awake. We're not moving anymore and I'm alone in the truck. Filaments of some dream linger, an impression of having been somewhere else. Through the windshield the dark structure of an old timber bridge is stark against star-speckled night sky.

The door handle is cool under my hands. I stand at the end of the bridge, the river in the valley below a ribbon of sheet metal. Behind me the truck sits on the rail bed, looking dangerously out of place.

Dawn isn't far off. How long did I sleep?

"Carl?" My voice seems too loud. "Where are you?"

"Down here." A faint voice from the valley. "Just a minute —"

There's a stirring in the bushes below — heavy willow and alder in spring leaf. A jungle. A few rocks trickle down a slope. A dark shape emerges from darker foliage, silhouetted against the river.

"How long have we been here, Carl?"

As he walks closer, Carl's expression is calm. In this light, he looks much younger.

"I didn't want to wake you," he says, smiling. "You needed the rest."

I glance back at the truck. "You sure this line is abandoned?"

"Don't worry, it goes right past town and I haven't heard a train in years." He walks onto the bridge, lifts his arms. "What a beautiful morning, Porter. Can you smell that? Willow, water and earth."

"Creosote," I add. "Oil and tar."

He drops his arms, turns around — he's still smiling. "I kind of envy you right now. I have to go back to the office, sit in a little room with buzzing radios all day. You get to stay out here, in the real world."

"I'm not terribly impressed with the real world right now, Carl."

Carl lingers on the bridge, a light morning breeze stirring his long hair. I think he's serious — envying me — and worry he's forgetting what's at stake here. I grab the supplies he's brought, set them beside the tracks, thank him for his help. As the truck thumps down the rail bed I stash my bike, lug gear into the valley, fighting dense willow. Mosquitoes hiding under the leaves ambush me as I go past. The sun is just coming up and already it's ten degrees warmer. It's going to be a long day, here in the real world.

I pick a spot under the bridge abutment, collapse and close my eyes.

The real world goes away.

27

I'M JARRED AWAKE a few hours later by an earthquake. The ground vibrates, timbers shake and groan above my head. The train takes only a few minutes to pass. My adrenaline rush takes longer. I picture a truck thumping along the rail bed, a train coming around the bend.

Carl, smiling. *Don't worry about it —*

I shake my head, creep into the bushes. The valley is steep, the willows dense. I follow a narrow game trail to a sandbar speckled with deer and elk tracks. There are bootprints here too, leading to the water's edge and back. Carl's tracks — I'm vaguely annoyed he left tracks visible to the river and sky. I'll take a drink of water then smooth over both our tracks.

The river water tastes of rocks and sediment.

I'm about to smooth over the tracks when I notice something that causes an apprehensive tingle. Carl's track is a perfect imprint in the damp sand, clearly showing a gouge in one lug, a prominent nick in another. Accidental characteristics I've seen before.

A thousand boots could leave a print like that, I tell myself, trying to shake off the notion as I climb the steep trail up the river valley. Mosquitoes hiding under leaves swarm around me. So do disturbing thoughts. The Emperador cigar box and gunpowder in Carl's basement; the cake pans in the Forest Service cache. Carl owns a two-wheel-drive Chevy pickup, which fits the suspect vehicle type from the last fire, and he depends on the overtime that fires bring. But all these things can be explained away and I'm ashamed, thinking he could be the arsonist.

He's my friend, helping me in my time of need.

Still, there's a lingering doubt; my paranoia is in full bloom. He's been keenly interested in my arson investigation and I can't help wondering if this is more than professional curiosity. His bootprint looks like a perfect match; I had a pretty good look at the print found at the last fire as Dipple demonstrated proper casting technique. I sit in the shade of the bridge abutment and worry. I'm a fugitive — looking at a long stretch in prison if I can't sort this out — and Carl could turn me in at any time. This is ridiculous — an unhealthy distraction. I've got to clear this from my conscience.

I can't afford to doubt Carl.

The Caprice Classic isn't parked on the curb anymore but the back door of the ranger station is locked. It's an old building with wooden windowsills, no security. I test the windows, discover a downstairs window can be persuaded, slide it open. It's dark inside and I wait a moment while my eyes adjust. Long table, chairs, coffee percolator — I'm in the conference room. A car passes on the road, chasing a rectangle of light across the wall. Going up the stairs I hear voices but it's only radios — the nightly soap opera as towerpeople talk to one another, bare souls and share their loneliness. A computer monitor projects green light through the doorway of the duty room like something out of an alien abduction movie. I could be on the *X-Files* but it's not those types of files

I'm looking for. The personnel files are in a cabinet behind the clerical desk.

The cabinet is locked but fortunately the keys aren't well hidden.

Carl's file is easy to find. I pull it out, lay it open. In this light, everything around me is grey, mirroring my mood. I don't much care for what I'm doing but can't stop thinking about it. The burn rate of a well-ventilated Emperador cigar leaves plenty of time to drive from the last fire to Curtain River. I compare Carl's time sheets against the dates of the arson fires. Two of them were on weekends when Carl didn't work. Three were on days Carl had off — casual illness or holidays. Another coincidence? Maybe, but I remember something Carl said.

... fire is a natural process, Porter —

Carl is into natural processes. He tans animal hides, eats wild meat; his technological concessions are limited to a refrigerator and antique phone. But I'm having a hard time picturing Carl as an arsonist. Just doesn't mesh with the Carl I know, sitting in the duty room directing fire fighting. Out on the fireline, leading crews.

When it comes right down to it, you never really know people.

"Looking for something?"

I kill my flashlight, slam shut the cabinet.

"Jesus Christ, Carl. You scared the hell out of me."

He stands in the doorway of the duty room, silhouetted in pale green light. He must have been in the duty room and I wonder how long he's been watching me.

"Carl, what are you doing here with the lights off?"

He gestures toward the duty room. "Listening to the show."

There's something in his hand — a beer bottle. How many has he had?

"The show? Right ... What's going on tonight?"

Carl takes a drink. "Old Gabe is putting the moves on that new tower girl."

"Oh, really." I try to sound casual. "Where's she at?"

"Sheep Mountain," he says. He seems steady enough when he walks. I move away from the file cabinet and there's an awkward pause as we stand in the dark. In the background, Gabe Peterson's voice is a ghost from the ether. A younger, more impressionable voice answers — Gabe is making progress. Unfortunately, he's 80 miles away and stuck in a lookout tower. Carl takes another swig of beer, looks toward the file cabinet.

"What were you looking for?"

"Tapes," I say quickly, the shock wearing off. I'm not sure I sound believable but I need an explanation to avoid the real reason I'm here. In the back of my mind, a half-formed plan begins to solidify. "I was looking for audio tapes. I thought there might be some blank tapes in the cabinet. The little ones, for the answering machine."

"There're no tapes in there," he says.

"I noticed."

"You should have asked. I could have helped you."

"I did. I went to the house but you weren't home."

There's a pause, Carl glancing out a window toward his house. "How did you get in?"

"The back door. You didn't hear me?"

He shakes his head, sits on the edge of the desk. In the oblique light coming from the duty room he's frowning, probably trying to remember if he locked the back door, which he did. "Why do you need tapes for the answering machine?" he asks finally.

"They're not for the answering machine."

"What are they for?"

"I've got one of those small recorders for taking notes —"

"Yeah?"

"I've got a plan. I'll need your help."

"Sure," he says without much enthusiasm.

"But we don't have to do it tonight — if you're not up to it."

He staggers a bit as he stands. He may already have had too much to drink.

"Let's do it," he says. "I'm tired of waiting."

After Carl leaves to make preparations, I sit in the duty room with the lights off, watch the screen saver. I'm not sure he bought my story about looking for tapes. I'm not sure we'll actually carry out this half-baked plan. I'm not really sure of anything. But I've got a phone handy and about a half-hour to kill. Maybe, if I'm really lucky, we won't have to do anything. I dial up Cindy's borrowed cell phone.

"What?" she says. "Again?"

"Again."

"Let me get the kids ready this time."

I give her a few minutes, punch up Telson's cell phone, let it ring 20 times but get no answer. Where could she be at this time of night? She's a big girl, packs a .45, but I'm still worried, frustrated I can't just go over there. I call Cindy again.

"Okay —" She's a bit breathless. "I'm ready."

I listen to her punch numbers, wait while the dispatcher puts me through to wherever Rachet spends his nights. He's a bit groggy but it doesn't take him long to wake up.

"Christ Cassel, you could call during the day —"

"I'm pretty much a night crawler lately. What did you find out about those skin cells?"

"The skin cells — right. The lab is still working on those."

"Did you get a sample from Brotsky to match against?"

Shuffling sounds — Rachet getting out of bed, no doubt frantically signalling his wife to call in for a trace. "It's not that simple Cassel. To take a DNA sample from someone you gotta have reasonable grounds — a court order. You can't just go around sampling people —"

"You don't think you have reasonable grounds?"

A faint click — I've gone public. "Hardly," he says.

"Did you check Brotsky's basement?"

"Yeah, we checked it. What exactly did you think we'd find?"

"You didn't find anything?" I'm disappointed but not surprised.

"A darkroom," says Rachet. "An enlarger. Hardly illegal."

Brotsky works fast. "And his car?"

"Claims he had it crushed a few months ago —"

"What about the union angle?"

"— which fits with his insurance, which also expired a few months ago. As far as Hess rabble-rousing for the union, no one seems to know anything about it."

"Or they're not talking —"

"Always a possibility," Rachet says. "Why are you so hung up on this guy?"

If I have to explain, they're obviously not making progress. I'm about to ask about Brotsky's fingerprints at the crime scene but realize it doesn't matter — his prints could be at Petrovich's trailer for any number of reasons. Unlike mine.

"Any luck with that resumé?"

"The resumé —" Rachet grunts. "Look Cassel, we're doing everything we can to get to the bottom of this. Best thing for you is to come in before some over-eager local yokel puts a bullet in you. Your face is all over the news. Just how far do you think you're going to get —"

"As far as I have to." At least they're buying my ruse.

"This isn't good," Rachet says. "You're not making this any easier —"

I hang up — they're not getting anywhere and I don't have time for idle chatter. Something occurred to me while I was on the phone — something that worries me more than being the prime suspect in Petrovich's murder. I don't want to but I return to the file cabinet, check farther back into Carl's work record, before the fires started. I take the file into the duty room, sit at the desk and read the yellow attendance records by the light of the computer monitor. As I flip back through the records and check dates I get a sick feeling. Almost every time the Lorax struck, Carl was off work. Except once — the bombing which killed Nina. And for that, he wouldn't have to take time off work.

This is ridiculous — Carl is my friend.

A friend with an overdeveloped environmental conscience, frustrated at having many of his penalty recommendations dismissed. What was it he said that night in The Corral? *Sometimes I think the damn Lorax accomplishes more than the Forest Service.* Maybe he called me down here out of more than friendly concern. Maybe he called me down here to keep tabs on my investigation.

Both investigations — he's asked a lot of questions.

I stare at the wall map, mentally noting the locations where the bombings and arsons occurred. I could be misinterpreting Carl's friendly concern — an option I prefer — but the bombings stopped after Nina was killed. Then the fires started. The bootprint and cigar box. Like finding the point of origin on a fire, one clue is meaningless, but many clues tend to point the way. Too many little things are starting to make sense. Once, when Carl and I were buddied up on an inspection of a geophysical program, driving new cutlines through the bush, we came across a powder mag in a clearing. Boxes of dynamite to be used as underground charges sat in the bright winter sunshine, unlocked and unguarded. Look at that, says Carl. Someone could steal a box or two and they would never know. At the time, it seemed an idle comment. Now, it doesn't seem so idle — the Lorax used seismic gel.

It can't be Carl — but I dig a little deeper, just to make sure.

I return the file to the cabinet, stand in the dim ranger station. The tower people have signed off for the night and the only sound is the faint hum of radios. In the duty room I hesitate before dialling the phone. It rings for a long time. The voice that answers is still half asleep.

"Yeah?"

"Bill, it's Porter."

A pause. I picture Bill sitting in bed, trying to wake up. Bed springs creak. "Just a minute," he whispers. "I gotta switch phones so I don't wake the old lady."

I watch the screen saver on the monitor; a high-tech lava light. A minute later there's a click, the scrape of a chair. Bill comes back on line, sounding winded like he just played the last half of a gruelling football game. "What's going on, Porter?"

"You been watching the news lately?"

"Yeah, I been watching. Why'd you run?"

"Why? Why do you think? They were watching me when I went to get the knife."

"It doesn't look good, you taking off like that —"

"Save the sermon, Bill. I know how it looks. I didn't have much choice."

I'm expecting some sort of retort but Bill is silent.

"I need another favour, Bill."

"What a surprise," he says. "What are we talking about this time?"

"Can you access the Canadian Bomb Data Centre?"

"Maybe. Why? What's up?"

"I need you to run a search on stolen seismic gel."

"You want to tell me what this is about?"

"The Lorax used seismic gel."

"I see," says Bill. "That's very interesting. But why do you need to search the database? You have a suspect again? One that's still alive?"

"Yeah, I've got a suspect."

"You're not missing any more knives are you?"

"Bill —"

A pause. "Okay. How far back do you want to search?"

Through the duty room window I watch a car cruise past. A Caprice Classic.

"Go back eight years. When can you do it?"

"I'll have to wait until morning, when the office opens."

I glance out the duty room door. Carl's kitchen light is on. "I need to know now."

"It's not that simple, Porter. I'm not a cop anymore. I gotta call people, wake them up, ask them for favours in the middle of the night. It's not very endearing, believe me."

"I thought the Mounties worked twenty-four-seven."

"Some of them," says Bill. "Not the guys I gotta call."

"You remember Carl Mackey?"

"Mackey?"

"That ranger I used to work with — the one who called me down here after the bombing."

"Oh — right."

"He's my suspect, Bill. And he's the guy who's been helping me out."

"Okay," Bill says quietly. "I'll do what I can. Give me an hour."

A half-hour later Carl has completed the few simple preparations, and dressed in a black tracksuit, he's anxious to get going. I'd prefer to wait until I've heard from Bill again but it wouldn't look good. There's a half-dozen empty beer bottles tucked in a corner of the duty room and Carl is pacing the small office like a tourist who can't find the bathroom. He may have figured out what I was after in the filing cabinet and he probably noticed when he left the ranger station that the door was still locked. Regardless of my suspicions, he's probably wondering if I trust him and may be using this as a test; I don't know what the passing grade is. And if my suspicions are correct, he'll want to know for sure who's using the Lorax as a cover.

And who knows — this just might work.

We take Carl's Chevy. He drives while I crouch on the floor mat.

"You sure she's home?" he asks.

"No, but we'll cruise past first and check it out."

I inspect the goodies Carl has put together: a small tape recorder, a big 6-volt dry cell battery, speaker wires, a digital watch, duct tape and a block of white doughy material he whipped up in his kitchen. With this, MacGyver could save the world. I'm aiming lower — save myself.

Carl glances over. "That what you wanted?"

"It'll do." The truck lurches suddenly. "You okay to drive?"

"I'm just fine."

"Be careful. I don't want the cops stopping us."

The truck slows perceptibly. I attach wires as Carl drives, put the bomb together with duct tape. Carl takes a corner too abruptly, runs over a curb. I bump my head on the underside of the dash, feel like a kid trying to sneak into an X-rated drive-in.

"We're in front of her house," he says quietly.

"Is there a Bronco in the driveway?"

"No, just her car."

"Good. Find a dark alley."

Carl's bony hand grips the gearshift. I can smell the beer on his breath. The truck lurches and I bump my head again. We're turning, the power steering pump whining. Gravel crunches under the tires and we stop. I sit up — we're in an alley. Without streetlights, it's much darker here; a sliver of moon turns backyard fences and trashcans faintly luminescent. A block away, a window is lit like a beacon. Music seeps through a wall.

"How do we go in?" Carl asks.

"I'll go in. You watch the house. Anyone comes, you lay on the horn —"

"No way, Porter. I'm going in with you."

I shake my head. "She might recognize you."

"Not with this." He pulls out a second balaclava. "And I won't say anything."

I'd hoped to do this alone, but see there's no way that'll happen. It might be good to have some help. We slip on our ski masks and move together down the alley. Carl has no trouble finding the back of the house. The gate creaks enough to make me nervous, then we're in the yard and I see the dim outlines of a garden shed, a picnic table. And a dog house. I hold up a hand.

"Don't worry," Carl whispers. "She doesn't have —"

A dark shape explodes out of the dog house, barking like a fire alarm — one of those little dogs that look like a floor mop. Its small size does nothing to inhibit its decibel level. The dog reaches the end of its chain, gives a little yelp, then catches its breath and erupts again.

"Shit," Carl whispers. "She didn't —"

I grab his arm, yank him back. We crouch in a dark space

between shed and fence. The dog is barking so hard it's hyperventilating. Maybe we'll get lucky and it'll pass out. Lights go on. Carmen's face is framed in an open window, her hair a wild blonde mess.

"Jesus Christ Chi-chi —"

The dog barks louder and Carmen vanishes from the window.

Carl moves toward the gate. "Let's get the hell out of here."

We retreat to the alley and I motion for Carl to wait. Chi-chi's barking slows to intermittent bursts as her batteries run down. A screen door creaks and we hear Carmen's murmured reassurances. I run silently across a neighbour's damp lawn to the front of the house, Carl following a few paces behind, then cautiously along an illuminated walkway to a side door. Carmen is still in the backyard, whispering sweet nothings into her dog's ear. My plan is pathetically simple. Frighten her just enough to get her to talk and catch it all on tape. Not exactly an admissible confession but I'm not expecting to use it in court. We slip into the house, carefully shut the door.

"We'll grab her when she comes in," I whisper to Carl. "Take her downstairs."

He nods — with his black ski mask he looks fairly intimidating.

"Be careful," I add. "We don't want to hurt her."

When she comes in we wait until she's locked the door, then grab her. She's surprised enough she doesn't fight for a half-second, then holding her is like hanging onto a runaway jackhammer. She screams and my hand goes over her mouth. She's kicking, using her elbows, and I'm having a hard time holding her. Then she bites my hand — hard, and I let her go. I'm holding my bleeding hand when she kicks me in the shin and I nearly go down. Carl hits her with a quick uppercut and she drops, sprawled on the stairs leading to the kitchen.

"Jesus Christ, Carl —"

"I had to do something."

She's not moving and I check her vitals. She's okay, but unconscious.

"Bring her downstairs," I tell Carl. "I'll be right there."

I use the upstairs bathroom to wash my wound — the same sink I used to wash Petrovich's blood off my hand. They say a human bite is one of the worst and I wash for a long time, the cold water taking some of the edge off the pain. I may need stitches — forget the dog; beware of owner. Carmen has a first aid kit in the medicine cabinet and I use gauze, bandage my hand as best I can. When I get downstairs, Carl has duct-taped Carmen to an old office chair. Little chance of her getting loose — he's used most of the roll. And she's still unconscious.

"What now?" he asks.

I check her vitals again. She seems okay but concussions can be tricky.

"Did you have to hit her so hard?"

"This was your idea," he says, annoyed.

I find smelling salts in the medicine cabinet upstairs, hold them under Carmen's nose. She coughs and sputters, raises her head and looks at us, confused. There's a thin trickle of blood coming from a cut on her lip. I hope Carl didn't break her jaw.

"Are you okay, Carmen?" I hold up a few fingers. "How is your vision?"

Her vision seems fine. So does her jaw. "What do you perverts want?" she asks.

"Don't flatter yourself. All I want is a little information."

She struggles against the duct tape. "Untie me and get the hell out of my house."

She's pretty brave, given the circumstances, which isn't good.

She has to be frightened for this to work. "I'm going to ask you a few questions —" I speak slowly, change my voice enough I hope she won't recognize it as belonging to Asper Hassenfloss of the Insurance Underwriters of America. "The questions are simple. If I get the answers I need, then you'll be just fine."

"And if you don't?"

I show her the bomb.

"You're bluffing," she says.

I make a production of setting the timer — fiddling with the digital watch — and carefully place it under her chair. "That bomb is C4 plastic explosive — the same stuff your boyfriend used to kill Ronald Hess. It's set to go off in ten minutes. I'm going to ask questions for about nine minutes and if I get the answers I'm looking for, I'll reset the timer for the morning, let the bomb squad diffuse it. If I don't get the answers I'm looking for, I'll just leave."

"How do I know that's a real bomb," she says.

She's sizing me up. Her face is flushed, hair plastered to her forehead.

"You don't," I tell her. "But you could find out."

There's a fairly long pause as she considers this. Blood is starting to seep through the bandages on my hand. Carl stands behind her, arms crossed.

"Who the hell are you?"

"The Ghost of Christmas Past. Why did you help Brotsky kill Ronald Hess?"

She glares at me. Behind her, Carl clicks on the mini-cassette recorder.

"You're wasting time, Carmen."

She glares at me, still more angry than scared, and I'm thinking all I've accomplished is exposing myself and Carl to needless risk when Carl walks to a basement wall and, as calm as an inner city kid with nothing better to do, lifts a spray can and starts to scrawl graffiti on the wall. But it's not just graffiti — what he writes in red tree-marking paint causes my scalp to tighten. A single, terrifying word.

LORAX

The way he does this seems so natural, like he's done it before. He pops the cap back on the can of paint, ambles to his position behind Carmen and looks at me. I can't see his face — just his eyes, and force myself to concentrate on Carmen. She's staring at the wall. This may work after all.

"We're not impressed that someone is using our name."

She swallows, looks up at me.

"To cover up their dirty laundry," I tell her. "We're very unimpressed."

She mumbles something. Carl moves the recorder closer.

"Speak up Carmen, I can't hear you. And you're nearly out of time."

"Okay ..." she whispers. Then louder, "All I know is that they were going to have a talk with this Hess guy, convince him it would be better to shut up about the union. We've had union problems before and they were just going to talk to him, convince him that it would be best for everyone if he just dropped it. But Al said something went wrong — that Zeke got carried away. Al wouldn't get carried away — he's a soldier. But Petrovich is crazy —"

Carmen trails off, a look of anguish on her face, slumped against the restraints.

"So Brotsky put Hess in the machine and blew it up, then blamed it on the Lorax?"

She nods.

"Speak up Carmen. I can't hear you."

"Yes," she whispers. "But it wasn't my idea to use your name. It wasn't my idea."

"Whose idea was it?"

She won't look at me.

Carl leans toward her, speaks harshly into her ear. "Whose idea was it?"

She flinches and I give him a cautionary glance — his voice will be on the tape and she may recognize him. But I'm wearing a balaclava and it's a little hard to communicate with facial expressions. Carl continues to press her, nearly shouting.

"Who gave the order? Who told them to go after Hess? Was it Whitlaw?"

"I don't know."

"Not good enough —"

"I don't *know*," she wails. "He never told me."

I look hard at Carl, shake my head. "Carmen, tell me about Zeke Petrovich."

"He's crazy," she says, looking at me again, her eyes wide. "Like a bad dog. He got in a fight a few years ago and nearly killed a guy. Everyone is afraid of him, everyone except Al. He thought this guy would be afraid of him too — that would be enough."

"But Ronald Hess wasn't afraid of him was he?"

"No ... I don't know. Maybe he was too new."

"When did Brotsky decide to kill Petrovich?"

She looks away, like a kid caught in a lie. "I don't know anything about that."

"Don't bullshit me, Carmen. I know you helped set it up. I know about the file."

She looks stunned. "All I did was move a few things around for Al —"

"But you knew, didn't you."

She shakes her head. "No — I didn't know. I didn't know anything about that. Al just told me this guy was going to come around, looking for Petrovich's file. When he did, I was supposed to slip in this work record, then take it out again after I called the cops. That's it. I swear to God."

"But you figured it out."

She looks miserable. "When it was over, I started to wonder."

I hope we have enough because I'm getting nervous. Time to get out of here.

"Okay, Carmen —" I reach under her chair, wrap a wire from the bomb around a chair leg. "The timer is set for six hours, plenty of time for the bomb squad to do their thing, but there's a catch so listen carefully. You gotta sit perfectly still. The bomb is wired to the chair and if you move you'll set off a mercury switch. Can you sit still that long?"

She nods carefully, as if even this might set off the playdough.

"Good girl. Sit still and you'll be fine."

I'm nearly to the stairs when I turn. "One more thing, Carmen. When the cops get here, you tell them just what you told me. You tell them about what happened to Ronny Hess and how you helped Al. You tell them that and they'll probably give you a deal. You make sure you do that because we'll be watching the papers and we'll know —"

"I can't," she says, pleading. "He'll kill me."

"We'll be watching the papers, Carmen."

Carl is a step ahead of me on the stairs, looking down. Looking at me.

"And you tell them," he says, "that the Lorax never intended to kill anyone."

Craig Whitlaw doesn't sound impressed at being woken this time of night. He's going to be even less impressed in a hurry. Carl and I are back at the ranger station. Whitlaw is on the speakerphone, routed through the answering machine, which is now recording.

"You've been a bad boy, Mr. Whitlaw."

"Who is this?"

"Spiderman, the Toxic Avenger — it doesn't really matter. What matters is safety."

"Look, I don't have time for pranks —"

"What you did to Ronald Hess was no prank."

There's a long silence — Whitlaw deciding if he should hang up. I can hear him breathing, a little faster than normal. Stumbling out of bed in the middle of the night can do that to you. So can a guilty conscience.

"I don't know what you're talking about," he says.

"Of course not." I'm looking at Carl, who has an expression close to rapture on his face. "Plausible deniability Craig — which is why you had Brotsky do the dirty work for you. But killing Hess because he was talking union was a very bad decision."

A forced chuckle. "You should read the papers. The Lorax killed Ronald Hess."

"Nice try. Did Benji dream that one up for you?"

"Look, I don't know what the hell you're talking about."

"Four hundred accidents — that's what I'm talking about. How many fingers and toes does that come out to? And running off those employees after the court told you to take them back — that's not going to look good when people find out Ronald Hess was talking union."

"That's a very creative theory," he says. "Who did you say you were?"

"I didn't. But maybe you'd like to take a guess."

He's not into guessing tonight but for an innocent man, he's remained on the line a long time. Me — I'd have hung up by now. Like a porno line, he's waiting to see if there's anything really good coming. I don't want to disappoint him and give Carl a nod. He's seated next to the answering machine — the announcement tape replaced with something a little more topical.

Carl presses a button and Carmen's tearful voice fills the room.

— all I know is that they were going to have a talk with this Hess guy, convince him it would be better to shut up about the union. We've had union problems before and they were just going to talk to him, convince him that it would be best for everyone if he just dropped it. But Al said something went wrong — that Zeke got carried away. Al wouldn't get carried away — he's a soldier. But Petrovich is crazy —

I stop the tape. There's a few seconds of Whitlaw's heavy breathing.

"That's interesting," he says. "Good acting —"

"There's more Craig. Would you like me to play it on an open phone line?"

A longer silence. Then, "What do you want? Money?"

"It's always about money, isn't it?"

"We should get together," he says, earnest now — Craig the businessman.

"That won't be necessary. We don't want money."

There's a pause. I've stumped him.

"Look, don't fuck with me —"

I hang up, wait a few minutes before calling back. He answers on the first ring.

"Temper, temper, Craig. No need for such language."

"Okay —" He's a little more subdued. "What do you want?"

"Justice Craig. Just a little fucking *justice*."

A heavy sigh from the ether — he's clearly disappointed he can't buy me off.

"This is how it's going to work. I know you gave the order to talk to Hess, to persuade him not to push the union, but I'm willing to bet you didn't mean for it to go this far. So you go to the cops and tell them about Brotsky and Petrovich. Tell them everything. Consider this your one chance to redeem yourself. You do that and I forget about the tape."

His reply is very quiet. "And if I don't?"

"Then the tape goes for you — to the cops or the newspapers, I haven't decided which first. Think about it Craig — the truth is going to come out anyway. It might look better if you came forward voluntarily, filled with remorse, and told the Mounties you never intended it should go this far. That you couldn't live with yourself anymore. Or do you think it would look better if they came after you? Think of the headlines — this is juicy stuff. Mill owner covers up murder of employee. Maybe if you're lucky, you'll get on *The Fifth Estate* —"

"Okay —" he says. "When am I supposed to do this?"

"When? Right now, of course."

"Right now?" He sounds uncertain.

"Don't screw with me, Craig."

"Give me an hour," he says quickly. "To get my affairs in order."

I look at Carl. We're grinning, can't believe this is working.

"Okay, Craig. One hour. We'll be watching."

It's a risk, but I decide to bike across town to Telson's trailer. It bothers me she hasn't been answering my calls. I've got my end of our deal to hold up. Tonight, she's going to get the scoop of her career.

I'll get my life back.

The chain on my mountain bike whirs against the gear-changer and I adjust slightly until the sound is gone. I'm in stealth mode now and peddle hard, my hand throbbing. It's cool enough there's dew on the windows of parked cars. The hotel — the only neon sign in town, is an electric red monolith. Streetlights buzz and hum like bored insects over deserted pavement — unlike a city, no one hangs around here at this hour. Even the bars are quiet, scattered pickup trucks abandoned in parking lots. I take back alleys anyway, just to be sure.

There's no traffic when I dash across the highway but a moment later a police suburban races past on mainstreet, its tires humming. It's headed out of town — a good direction; I'm headed the other way, pedalling narrow streets past trailers and older homes, no lights on. Big spruce trees cast long shadows. Closer to the river, I smell damp earth. Gravel crunches under my bike tires as I turn off pavement into the RV park. Darker here, like entering a cave. Familiar now with the winding crescents, it doesn't take long to find Telson's trailer. Her Bug is on the gravel pad and I feel a surge of anticipation like the old days — a week ago.

But she's not home.

The trailer door is unlocked. There's a half eaten pork chop and bottle of beer on the kitchen table. The beer is knocked over, a puddle on the table and floor. I've never taken her to be a slob and have a bad feeling she left in a hurry, or was taken, and I recall our last conversation, about Hess and the union. How he must have told someone.

Telson's excitement: *That's my next project.*

I look for some clue. There's nothing.

I head back to the ranger station, taking too many chances in the open, when a light swings behind me in an alley. Looking back I'm blinded, can't see who it is but when the red and blues on the bumper begin to flash it's pretty clear. I turn as casually as possible down another alley and, out of the sweep of the headlights, pedal hard toward a strip of lawn between two houses.

A garden shed, the door slightly ajar.

I wheel the bike inside, crouch beside bags of fertilizer and lawn seed.

The cruiser rolls past, silent, lights flashing.

I don't wait for him to come back. By the time I reach the

ranger station he's returned to the alley where he first spotted me, muted flashes of red and blue light bouncing off houses. The ranger station is dark but the door is unlocked. Carl emerges from the duty room, back lit by monitor light like a painting of Moses descending The Mount.

"She's gone," I tell him, breathless from the ride. "Telson. They took her —"

"I know," he says quietly.

"What?"

He leads me into the duty room, hits 'play' on the answering machine. Brotsky's angry voice fills the room. "Attention shithead. You forgot dial recall. Well, guess what. Your little girlfriend here ain't so tough. You want to keep all her parts together, you better still have those tapes. I want them and the one you're making now too. You got a half-hour to be at the old mill by the river. Don't think about copying those tapes because no matter what the fuck goes down, I'll send someone after you. And don't try to jerk me off. I don't use playdough."

There's a click, then line static.

Carl looks like he might cry. "Christ, Porter, I'm sorry —"

Whitlaw must have called Brotsky — a risk I doubted he would take. Brotsky has killed once already to cover his tracks and it must have occurred to Whitlaw that he could be next. Or he's stupid enough to think the situation can be salvaged. A bad call either way.

"I should have thought about that," Carl says. "Used an unlisted phone —"

"It's not your fault, Carl. She was always involved. She knew there were risks."

Carl smoothes back his hair, gives me an anguished look. "What now?"

I walk to the window, peer through the blinds. The street is empty but for how long? How many cops are in town? How many more will arrive when they realize I'm still here? None of them can save Telson — Brotsky has no intention of letting her live, or me for that matter. He'll have the place wired like a minefield, take out all the evidence.

"Now we go get her."

After Carl leaves to make preparations I sit in the duty room and stare at the phone. I don't want to think about what we have to do. I want to think about Carl as the Lorax even less. But I gotta know if I can trust him — not that I have much choice.

I call Bill Star one more time. He answers on the first ring.

"Christ Porter, what's going on down there?"

"What do you mean?"

"I just got the strangest call. Your buddy Rachet. Asked if I knew where you were."

"What'd you tell him?"

"Nothing, for now."

"Good. What'd you find out about the seismic gel?"

"You owe me big time," he says. "Seven reported thefts."

"Where?"

"Three in Quebec, two in BC. And two in Alberta."

I get a bad feeling. "Where were the ones in Alberta?"

"One in the prairies — Fort MacLeod. One up north, close to where you used to work."

"What's the name of the program it was stolen from?"

There's a pause — Bill switching to hands free. Papers rustle. "Catherine Creek 3D," he says, his voice tinny. "That mean something to you?"

More than I'd like — Catherine Creek was a big program, easy to remember. Lots of new lines. Lots of shot holes. A lot of dynamite. And as I recall, Carl looked after it. Which might explain his reluctance to let me go when I told him I was headed to Fort Termination to look into a few things. He was afraid I would find out. That last arson, the one that didn't fit the pattern, may just have been his last ditch attempt to divert me from heading further north.

"You there, Porter?"

"Bill — I'll have to call you later."

I set the receiver back in the cradle. The bad feeling settles in.

Outside, a cop car rolls past, its lights strobing red and blue lines through the blinds, projected on the duty room wall. They're looking for me; I'm surprised they haven't already checked the ranger station. Maybe they're just setting up, getting ready for an assault. When the back door opens I crouch, as if that'll help. It's Carl, a rifle slung over his shoulder, a backpack in his hands, black toque rolled up on his head like a Navy Seal. I wonder what's in the backpack — more Catherine Creek dynamite?

"We're ready," he says, coming into the duty room.

"You see any cops outside?"

He glances toward the window. "One, but he's gone. What's the plan?"

The plan. I look at him, wondering.

"What?" he says. "What's the matter?"

"Nothing," I tell him. "Let's get going."

28

I'VE BIKED PAST the old mill site a few times. It sits next to the river, right at the edge of town, across the street from the Legion and the bottle depot. This is where Curtain River Forest Products got its start, when it was a dinky little operation with 30 or 40 employees, probably all related. That was before Craig Whitlaw came up from Texas. Before Al Brotsky ruined his knee. Back in the days of the Old Testament. Now a new kind of religion is running the town and tonight it wants another sacrifice.

We park in an alley behind the bottle depot, walk quietly along the edge of the road. There are no streetlights and beside me Carl is a tall, dark sliver, the muzzle of his rifle jutting over his shoulder makes us look like we're grunts on night patrol. There's just enough light to make out trees on either side of the road and the high bald dome of the rusty old beehive-burner at the mill. I smell damp rock, river brush, garbage. The old mill site is fenced with chain-link topped by three strands of barbed wire. The gate — I see double posts as we approach — is padlocked. Carl and I exchange glances, then Carl gives the lock a tug.

It's not locked, just hung to look like it is.

Carl hangs the open lock on the wire, unslings his rifle. We go in.

My plan is simple. Most likely, it'll happen inside, probably in the main building. I'll face Brotsky while Carl sneaks in through the old log infeed. When the time comes, I'll key my two-way radio, press a strip of duct tape down so it'll keep transmitting, hopefully set the radio inconspicuously aside. Just before we left, Carl made a call to the Mounties, told them to listen to a certain Forest Service frequency, promised a good show. I'm not sure if the Boys in Blue can triangulate my position but that's not my point — I plan to push Brotsky as far as he'll go, piss him off enough he'll talk. It's a big risk but I'll keep my flashlight on him — he tries anything, Carl puts him down. It's not perfect, but it could work.

Providing Carl is there for me. It may be in his best interest not to be.

A breeze comes up, sighing in the trees like a ghost, making me edgy — I'm edgy enough already, wondering if Telson is okay. Wondering about too many things. I gotta stay focused. Ahead and to the right the old burner is a mountain of rusting steel. I can smell the corrosion and the faint odour of old ash damp with dew. Something else — paint? A slender conveyer runs from the top of the burner back to the mill, stark as a gallows against the promised dawn sky. The main building is a dark wall to the left. There's enough light to see to the edge of the gravelled parking lot. It's empty but Brotsky could have parked anywhere. Carl holds me back with a hand and we listen intently. I hear nothing. He points toward a corner of the big building, motions that he's going the other way. I nod and we part.

Hopefully not for the last time.

A metal door materializes against a darker backdrop and I pause, listening hard. Nothing. I want to go in but hesitate — Brotsky might have wired the door. There's no guarantee Telson is inside. Until I notice what's hanging on the door handle — a piece of cloth, coarse and lacy in my hand. Telson's panties. He wants to make sure I open that door. He gets his wish.

Hinges squeal. I cringe, expecting the worst. A frightened voice in the dark.

"Porter? Is that you, Porter?"

I can't see anything in here. The voice sounds very small and far away.

"I'm in here Porter ... Be careful."

She's trying to be brave but the timbre of fear in her voice chills me. I wait for my eyes to adjust enough that I can move around but it doesn't much help. I'll have to use my flashlight, which I don't like because it'll be a beacon for Brotsky to shoot at. I click it on, hold it as far as I can from the vulnerable parts of my body.

In the weak flashlight beam the building is cavernous. Most of the equipment is gone but long metal beds, catwalks and conveyors remain. I see only parts of this, point like a nervous lighthouse keeper. Tonight there are hazards everywhere. Telson is nowhere in sight but her voice is like the call of a distant bird.

"Farther back Porter. Be careful — he's watching."

I dart the beam of light up, search catwalks toward the rear of the building but see no one. My flashlight isn't bright enough and there are too many places to hide. I begin to work my way deeper into the building, moving between conveyors. It's like being caught in the wrong part of the subway with all the tracks at waist height — knowing the train is coming but not being able to see or hear it. I hope Carl is in position by now.

Telson calls again. She's close but on the other side of a line of equipment and I climb onto a series of conveyor belts, pan the light. She's seated on an old crate next to a large hunk of iron; an old head rig with a rusty saw blade as wide as a dinner table. Dark lines cross her chest — old rubber belts; she's been strapped to the machine.

"Porter?" She's squinting and I lower the light.

"Are you okay?"

She nods but looks pale and frightened. Behind her the hooked teeth of the rusted saw blade are frozen like a monster caught with its mouth open. I doubt the saw will ever turn again but there must be some reason Brotsky put her here. I glance around, pointing the light like a gun.

"Where is he?"

"I don't know —"

Stepping down from the conveyor I lose my footing, and my flashlight — it clatters through the iron works, but fortunately doesn't go out. When I jump down my ankle twinges painfully. I lunge for the flashlight, ready to defend myself.

Against what? Brotsky remains anonymous.

"You okay, Porter?" Telson's voice is a strained whisper.

I hobble over, examine her restraints. He's thorough; I'll have to cut them off —

"Porter, there's a bomb under this box."

I kneel, peer through a ragged hole in the side of the crate.

"He told me it's wired to a mercury switch. He told me not to move."

There's a grey, five-gallon pail under there. It could just be hydraulic fluid like it says on the lid, except it's been opened at one time, the lid pushed back on. But I don't see a timer or any wires. It doesn't much look like a bomb. "Did you see him put a bomb under there?"

She shakes her head, her eyes wide. "It was already there."

It could be a real bomb, rigged for movement, Brotsky counting on me trying to diffuse it myself. He wouldn't have to hang around, but somehow I feel he isn't one to take chances. Which means the clock is ticking.

"Hang in there," I tell Telson. "I'm getting you out of this —"

A soft slapping sound, blending into a white flash of pain. I'm hit in the thigh — the bullet pulling my legs out from under me — and drop, clutching the wound, the flashlight rolling away, bathing me in light. *The fucker —* Blood oozes through my fingers. Telson is screaming.

Move before he shoots you again. But I can't.

The radio — call Carl on the radio. I tug at my jacket, try to free the heavy radio from an inside pocket but when I let go of my leg it starts to pump blood again.

Telson sounds far away. "Porter ... oh my God ..."

I feel faint, can't get at the radio. I shout instead. "Carl!" My voice vanishing in the cavernous building. There's no response and I have a horrible thought — Carl is the one who shot me, to protect his identity. Or Brotsky has and Carl is gone. Either way, Carl is covered.

I am the Lorax. I speak for the trees ...

The cops — they're listening to the radio. I have to get to the radio.

I'm digging under my jacket, feel the radio in my hands when there's a bright flash of light — a rainbow exploding in my temple; Brotsky's kicked me in the head. On my back I look up and see him standing over me, as tall as a sky-scraper, a rifle slung over his back.

"Give me the fucking tapes," he says, his hand out.

I try to look around. There's blood in my eyes and the radio is gone. It hurts to move.

"The tapes —" Brotsky kicks me in the ribs, losing patience.

I drag a hand across my jacket, fumble for the pocket where I shoved the tapes but I'm too slow and Brotsky kicks me again, reaches down and rips the tapes out of my pocket. I miss probably my only chance to grab him — he's too fast and I'm too groggy. Telson is screaming and he backhands her, her head snapping to the side.

He pockets the tapes — pirated Captain Tractor and Sheryl Crow.

"Just couldn't keep your fucking nose out of it could you, Cassel?"

He's got my blood smeared on his hand; a hard look — the fishhook scar at the corner of his mouth pulled taught. The flashlight, my signal to Carl, is beyond reach, illuminating a heap of ripped conveyor belts. The radio — I've got to find the radio; it's there, a dozen feet away. Brotsky kicks my reaching hand. He's way ahead of me and I'm slowing down.

Telson is slumped against her restraints. She isn't moving.

"I've got to be going now," Brotsky says. "People to do, things to see."

There's something dark in his hand. Somehow, he's gotten hold of my radio.

"But don't worry, you won't feel a thing. I cooked up a little something just for you two lovebirds. C4 of course but also lots of magnesium; some powdered aluminium; a little iron oxide. A thousand fucking degrees — they won't find anything. It'll be like sitting on the sun."

It's a remote detonator. I try to rise. Brotsky places a boot on my chest, pushes me down.

"You're done, Cassel. Just lay back and relax."

Black spots hover — I'm still losing blood; sounds are becoming hollow, like I'm at the bottom of a big tin can. Brotsky leans over Telson, says something I can't quite catch. I think of her panties hanging on the door, try once more to rise. But I'm far too slow. Brotsky turns, executes a textbook spin kick, catches me in the chin. I go down.

He stands over me, pulls out a knife.

"That's what I miss," he says, grinning. "A good fight —"

An explosion — Brotsky jerks, falls forward on top of me. He's struggling; I'm not sure if it's to get the knife into me or just to get up. Either way, there's not much I can do. Then he's still, the tip of his rifle sticking out over his shoulder, inches from my nose. It dawns on me that someone shot him.

Then, Brotsky rises — Carl pulling him up.

Carl's face, too close — like a bad video ...

"Hang in there buddy."

I'm always suspicious of the wrong people, those I should trust —

He's working on Telson, cutting her loose. I hear her voice — the sound of a newborn; can't make out what she's saying. Then she's at my side, helping Carl lift me. Darkness ... swirling hallucinations ... Abruptly we're outside and it's morning, pale light. I'm weak, like a dream where you're being chased but can't run. The mill building is pale blue. The old burner has the word "LORAX" spray-painted in crude red letters.

Telson's face is close. She's beautiful. "Just hang in there, Porter ..."

"Your radio," says Carl. "Have to call the cops ..."

He stands, holds the radio close to his lips, keys the mike.

"This —"

A bright flash of light, a hard shove. Then darkness.

29

WHEN I COME TO, I'm not sure where I am. Or if I made it — I see a bright, beckoning light. Turns out it's just the fluorescents in my hospital room. I try to get up and quickly find that won't be happening — I'm hooked to a battery of tubes. My leg is bandaged but still there, so I lie back, let my thoughts float up through the lake of painkillers they must have given me.

Try to remember exactly what happened.

I remember trying to stand, Brotsky pushing me down. My radio out of reach. The rifle shot. Telson, whispering in my ear and then being outside, seeing that dreaded word painted in red on the old burner. A flash like a camera at a birthday party — something triggered the bomb. Maybe Brotsky wasn't dead. Maybe it was Carl's radio.

Then faces, distorted and leering but I think that must have been a dream —

I'm too woozy to think this hard; stare out the window. I've got a hell of a mountain view, which probably isn't covered under my basic health care benefits. The mountains look close enough to touch ...

Sweet oblivion.

I wake hours later, sensing I'm not alone.

"You're back with us," says a nurse I recognize as having bandaged my sprained ankle eons ago. She's young, with pale skin and red hair. An angel named Betty. This will be the second time Betty will be fitting me with crutches. She takes my blood pressure, her slim hand cool on my wrist as she monitors my pulse. "You've been away."

"Soma vacation," I mumble, my voice pharmaceutically calm.

"What's that?"

"*A Brave New World*," I tell her. "Savages."

She smiles — another babbling patient. "You were out for a while. You had us worried."

"How long?"

"Three days." She smiles as if I've been at Club Med. "You lost a lot of blood."

I'm hooked to a machine on an IV tower — it keeps beeping. I think that's a good sign. On a side table are several bouquets of flowers; one, I can see from the card, is from my parents; I'm not sure who sent the others.

"Good thing they brought you in so quickly," she says.

"The people who brought me in — are they okay?"

She looks puzzled. "Sure."

"Christina Telson and Carl Mackey?"

"Your friends are fine. A few bumps and bruises."

"Are they here?"

She shakes her head, pulls back the blankets and checks my leg. Removes the dressing. "We kept them overnight and released them. You on the other hand are a different story." I glance down — a bad idea. It's not that the sight of blood bothers me — just my blood. I lie back, stare at the ceiling. "You were lucky," she says. "Some damage but the bullet passed through without hitting the major artery or breaking any bones. Half an inch to the right and you'd have bled to death."

"That's me — lucky."

"Trust me," she says. "I used to work Emerg in the city. How's your pain?"

"What pain?"

She smiles again — a nice smile. "You're on morphine. Can you wiggle your toes?"

I wiggle my toes. Betty is pleased.

"Were you here when they brought me in?"

She nods, massaging my toes. I may want to marry her.

"Did they bring in anyone else? Besides my friends?"

"Like who?" she says.

Brotsky — but like Hess there probably wasn't much left of him. "Never mind."

I try a few more questions but Betty has no answers.

"I'll get you some breakfast," she says. "The doctor will be around later to see you."

Then I'm alone again with my mountain view. Down the hall, a machine sighs and grunts like someone on a stair climber. I doze. A different nurse wakes me with a tray of hospital food. I'm hungry enough that Jello and instant fried eggs look good.

Half way through the eggs I have breakfast guests — Rachet, Bergren, *et al.*

"Nice view," Rachet says. "Better than what you'll be getting used to."

"You gonna eat that muffin?" says Bergren. "I missed breakfast."

I protect my muffin. The Mounties make themselves comfortable. Rachet, being the senior, gets the only chair. Bergren and an older cop I've never seen before lean against the window, spoiling my view.

“We’ve been looking for you,” Rachet says.

“You’ve been a busy boy,” adds Bergren. “Taking out Petrovich, then Brotsky.”

I can’t believe they still don’t have this straight. But in my present state it’s hard to get worked up. When I talk it sounds like I’m narrating a *National Geographic* special on dung beetles. “I didn’t take anyone out. Talk to Mackey and Telson. Listen to the tapes.”

“What tapes?” says Rachet.

Carl didn’t give them the tapes. “It’s all on tape. Brotsky and his girlfriend. Whitlaw talking about Hess. It had nothing to do with the Lorax. Whitlaw wanted to stop Hess from talking union. He sent Brotsky and Petrovich to talk him out of it but they got carried away and killed Hess, then made it look like a Lorax bombing —”

All three cops are giving me a strange look.

“Brotsky grabbed Telson,” I say. “He wanted to trade her for the tapes.”

“You still have these tapes?” says Rachet.

“Carl has them. I left them at the ranger station.”

“I see.” Rachet is rubbing his chin. “Too bad we can’t find your friend Carl.”

“Talk to Whitlaw. Or Telson — she’s a reporter. She’ll tell you everything.”

“We’re looking for Whitlaw. As for Telson, she went back to the States.”

Suddenly, I want more painkillers. “What about Brotsky’s girlfriend — Carmen?”

“Oh, right.” Rachet is wagging a finger at me, as if making a point he’d forgotten until now. “She’s considering charges against you for kidnapping and aggravated assault. Says you tied her up in her own house and threatened to kill her. I’m willing to bet the teeth marks under those bandages on your hand match her bite imprint."

"She's in on it," I say faintly. "She switched the resumé."

Bergren chuckles. "The non-existent resumé?"

"You don't have *any* idea what happened?"

"We'll figure it out," says Rachet. "We've got you. And you're not going anywhere."

They're all staring at me, frowning, as if waiting for me to crack and confess. My head feels like rubber from the drugs but I still sense there's something wrong here. How could it be that with so many people involved, they still haven't figured it out? How could they just let Carl and Telson go like that, without getting the full story? Telson's a reporter — she wouldn't leave a story this hot if it killed her, which it nearly did. Then something Nurse Betty said clicks — her puzzlement when I asked if the people who brought me in were okay.

"You knew," I say quietly. "You knew all along."

Rachet and Bergren exchange glances.

"Not all along," Rachet says. "Far from it. But Mr. Mackey did give us the tapes. He also told us your knife was stolen a week before Petrovich was killed."

"So I'm not a fugitive anymore?"

"Not officially. But we'll want to talk with you some more later."

My relief must be obvious because Bergren laughs. "A Kodak moment."

"Why didn't you just tell me?"

"We wanted to hear the same story from you."

"And Whitlaw?"

"We picked him up yesterday."

There's a pause, filled with the beep of my morphine monitor.

I'm thinking about the old mill and the explosion right after we got out. Since we never really had a chance to use the radios, I'm wondering how the Mounties got there so quickly. "You knew about Telson," I say, looking at Rachet. "You knew Brotsky had her at the old mill."

Rachet looks uncomfortable, shifts in his chair.

"You knew and you let me go in there anyway."

It takes Rachet a lot of beeps to answer. "Yes," he says finally.

"But not until the very end. We had Whitlaw's line tapped, after you told us your theory about the union, and we picked up your phone call with that bit of tape you played. Then we picked up a call from Whitlaw to Brotsky, telling him he'd just received a call from the ranger station."

"But you didn't catch Brotsky's call to us?"

Rachet shakes his head. "We didn't have a tap on that line."

"But you knew something was going down."

"Sure. But we didn't know where or exactly what. We suspected it would be a trade of some sort but we didn't know what Brotsky had to trade. Until someone thought to check on your friend Telson. Even then, we didn't know for sure if he had her. Then we got Carl Mackey's call about monitoring the radio."

Makes sense. I wonder if it would have come out differently had the radios worked.

Yeah — I might have blown us to bits.

"How did you ever find us?"

Rachet smiles, somewhat reluctantly. "Luck. All the training and experience and sometimes you just get a lucky break. We found Mackey's truck parked behind the bottle depot. Then it just made sense that it would go down at the old mill."

I think about Brotsky shooting me in the leg. Pulling his knife.

"Why didn't you go in?"

Rachet raises his hands. "Honestly — we didn't know what we were up against. We deployed and waited, monitored the Forest Service frequency. When we had some indication of a hostage and what we were up against, we were prepared to go in."

"We could have been dead by then."

"You could have come in long ago instead of playing phone games."

Maybe that makes us even.

"But you're still alive," Rachet says, leaning forward in his chair, giving me his best scowl. "You were very lucky. Next time, maybe you won't be so lucky. Next time, maybe I won't go so easy on you. There's still about a dozen statutes under which I could charge you. Keep that in mind before you decide to investigate this Lorax any further. I suggest you stick to forest fires."

"Don't worry," I tell him. "I'm done with the Lorax."

They disconnect a few tubes and I'm somewhat mobile. I shuffle to the bathroom, towing my IV stand, frighten myself when I look in the mirror. I've got a long crescent of stitches on one temple — Brotsky's parting gift — bruises the colour of damaged fruit. I do a lap down the hall to test my leg but am apprehended at the nursing station, sent to my room. This little adventure exhausts me and I take a nap, wake to find a nurse changing the dressing on my thigh. This nurse is in her fifties, with the dehydrated complexion of someone who's spent too much time under fluorescents, but she's friendly enough.

"On a scale of one-to-ten, how's your pain?"

"Seven point three," I tell her. "If I was a machocist I'd be in heaven."

"We'll give you a little something but we're going to back you off the morphine." She points to a button on the gadget connected to my IV stand. "You know you can self-medicate. The machine is set on minimum but you can increase the frequency up to a limit."

Now they tell me. I press the button. The machine sighs. So do I.

"All done," she says, pulling the blanket over my leg. "You have a visitor."

"More cops?"

"No cops this time. A mountain man."

Carl comes in, wearing moccasins and his fringed buckskin jacket. The room fills with the odour of wood smoke and perspiration. I'm surprised they didn't decontaminate the jacket before letting him into the hospital. "How you doing buddy?" he asks. "You up for a game of soccer?"

The nurse wags a finger at me. "You stay in bed."

She leaves and Carl takes a seat, fidgets. "How's the leg?"

"Not bad. Bullet passed through without hitting bone."

"Always a bonus."

"How's that fire by the river going?"

"It's being held. It's smaller than we thought."

I nod and there's a pause. It's going to be tough getting past small talk.

"Has Christina been in to see you yet?"

I try to look unconcerned but I'd hoped she would be here when I woke up. Asleep in a chair maybe, holding my hand. "They told me they held you both overnight."

Carl nods. "That was a long night. I hate hospitals."

"I know what you mean," I tell him. "Full of sick people."

He's reading the cards that came with the flowers. "She brought you lilies."

Lilies. I wonder if there's some meaning behind that.

"If you wait a minute," Carl says, "I'll run outside and grab a handful of dandelions."

I picture Carl on the lawn, ripping out dandelions, impressing the maintenance people.

"No thanks. It's the thought that counts."

"Can't say I didn't offer."

There's a lull in conversation, Carl glancing out the window.

"What happened?" I ask finally. An open question. It takes him a while to answer.

"I got stuck in the log infeed," he says finally. "Slipped in the dark and got my leg jammed between two rollers. You should see the bruises." He's rubbing his leg, just above the knee, as if to assure me the bruises are really there. I'm not sure I want to find out if they are. Despite everything that's happened, he came through in the end. Maybe that's all you can ever expect of anyone. "I heard the shot," he says quietly. "But with the echoes in there I couldn't tell where it came from, and when I got myself unjammed it took a while to get into position."

"Well, thanks," I say. "I'm glad you were there."

He waves it off. "You'd have done the same."

We attempt small talk again but it seems cheap. Carl fidgets with the fringes on his jacket.

"I gotta go, Porter," he says. "I'll pop by later."

I'm left with my thoughts and the view. I don't want to think too hard about Carl right now. Maybe later, when there's some distance to my perspective. I need loud music and a long drive but neither is on the program. Instead, I reach for the remote control, turn on the overhead television. It's on a swing arm and has a screen the size of a cigarette pack. I doze, wake sometime the next morning. I'm rescued from a rerun of a MASH episode by Cindy and the kids.

Cindy looks beautiful. The kids, carrying model Styrofoam airplanes, commence to toss them back and forth at each other over my bed. When I was a kid, I was frightened of hospitals and would have sat in the corner, trying to be inconspicuous. Cindy's kids watch emergency room procedures on TV and seem right at home. For them, an old guy with bruises is pretty tame.

"Oh my God ..." Cindy examines my bruises. At least someone feels sorry for me.

I flinch. "Don't worry, they're worse than they look."

"Don't be a sissy. Hold still —"

A model airplane gets stuck in the IV hanger and three kids scramble after it. I grab my IV lines so they're not pulled out. Cindy orders the kids out of the room. Despite her diminutive stature, she has the voice of a general. The kids march into the hall, their enthusiasm undiminished.

"Sorry about that, Porter."

"Nice to be surrounded by family."

"I would have come sooner but I was on vacation."

"Look, I want to thank you for that —"

She waves it off; she's not good with praise. "Don't mention it."

"Really. I mean it. I couldn't have done it without you."

She looks away for a moment, self-conscious. In the hall, the kids hoop and holler.

"How far did you get?" I ask.

She smiles. "California. I'd always wanted to see it."

"Do any surfing?"

"No. They turned me back at the border. I wasn't blonde enough."

Cindy tells me about her trip. I don't tell her about Brotsky and the old mill, don't want to worry her anymore; she's done her share already. In the background, the TV mumbles, kids shout in the hall, respirators sigh and hiss. I'm content to lie still and listen.

"I'm staying at a motel here in town," says Cindy. "Until you're out."

I imagine the kids in a small motel room. "Thanks, but you don't have to."

"It's no problem," she says. "I'm on vacation, remember? And the kids haven't seen the mountains before. They don't get outside enough as it is. I'll take them for picnics, go on little hikes. It'll wear them out. They'll sleep like logs."

She's holding my hand. "Thanks," I tell her. "That'll be nice."

After she's gone, it's just me, the mountains and the television. I watch a local channel — old file images of a forest fire. There's a provincial fire ban: no open fires under any circumstances. High winds and low humidities are expected for the next few days. The Forest Service advises against backcountry camping, the announcer suggesting we stay at home, watch television. No problem on my end. I switch channels, fall asleep during an old Charles Bronson movie.

The next morning the mountains are hazy. A grey pall hangs in the air. Even inside I can smell the smoke. Nurse Betty assures me it's from forest fires up north, which explains the distinctive odour — an earthy twang, bitter like a herb. Ground fire, burning moss. I feel like I'm playing hooky. Cindy and the kids spend an hour before lunch. The kids are full of energy, can't sit still; the nurses have taken away their model airplanes. I'm restless too, the odour of smoke making me frantic, like a hunting dog that's been forgotten in the truck.

"You okay, Porter? You look angry."

"Fine Cin. I just want to get out of here. I can't handle this much relaxing."

"It's not relaxing," she says sternly. "It's recuperating."

"You sound like my nurse."

She promises to come back in the afternoon. She'll take the kids for a hike in the woods, tire them out. They'll sit better when she comes back. She slips me a chocolate bar before she leaves, which I promptly use to spoil my lunch. Reconstituted eggs have lost their appeal. I turn on the TV, hope to distract myself. The newscaster updates the fire ban. The Forest Service is advising they have a Red Flag day here on the East Slopes. Winds from the west are bringing thick smoke from fires in British Columbia — nature's smog is rolling in. Asthmatics are advised to stay indoors, close all windows. And there are fires down south in Montana and Oregon too. We're surrounded by fire and I try not to think about it, but there isn't much to do but think. And when I look outside, there it is, hanging in the air like a bad dream that won't go away. A Red Flag day. Fires in the north. Fires in the west and south. Which is where most of the water bombers and firefighters will be. It makes me wonder. Makes me worry.

What if a fire were started here today?

With the wind and dry conditions it would get ugly fast — the rate of spread would be astronomical and it wouldn't take a fire long to wipe out most of the timber between here and the mountains. Forget camping for a decade or two. Forget logging for a century. Then it occurs to me who does the logging around here and how pissed the Lorax must be that someone used his name for their own purposes — that a sawmill used his name in vain, and I get really worried.

For a few minutes I lie in my hospital bed, staring at the grey air outside, the odour of smoke in my nostrils, and wonder what to do. Should I call Carl and question him about my suspicions?

Ask him not to start any more fires? Or should I call the cops? The Forest Service?

Could Carl really be the Lorax? Could he be Red Flag?

What about the bootprint? The seismic gel? The timing? The cigar?

There's a phone on the nightstand, which a sticker proclaims is just for local calls. Good enough for my purposes. I'll call Carl, just to see if he's in the office today, chained to the duty desk. The receptionist at the ranger station tells me Carl is not at work today. He had a family emergency. His mother is ill. I thank her, hang up, try to call directory assistance but am intercepted by the hospital switchboard. No long distance calls permitted. I tell her it's an emergency and she points out that I'm already in a hospital, tells me to call the nursing station, press the little red button by my bed. I lose her when I try to explain that it's a different kind of emergency. I'll call Cindy — she can find the phone number to Carl's parents — but when I ring her motel room there's no answer.

Then I remember she's taking the kids for a hike. In the woods.

I call the ranger station again, hear radios and voices in the background. The receptionist sounds busy, isn't thrilled when I ask her to dig up the number for Carl's parents. Nothing on file and he didn't leave her the number. She hangs up halfway through saying goodbye.

I pull out my IV line. There isn't much I can do in here.

There are crutches in the closet, clothes on a shelf above. I use the local phone to call a cab and wait in my room until I see it pull into the lot. Betty at the nursing station isn't happy to see me dressed and out of my room.

"Where are you going?"

"I'm checking out," I say as I swivel past.

She chases after me. "You can't do that. The doctor has to authorize it."

The automatic doors part in front of me. "Sorry, I can't wait."

"Don't make me call security." She's getting tough but I've seen security — a guy so old he should use a walker. A fight between the two of us would be pretty pathetic. I'd have to cane him with my crutch.

"This is a hospital," I tell her. "You can't keep me here."

"Mr. Cassel ..." She's hovering around me, clearly distressed.

"Keep my bed warm, I might be back."

We're outside now in the parking lot. The cabbie gives me a strange look as I fumble with the door handle, a nurse at my side wringing her hands. He reaches over, pushes open the passenger door, and I see why he didn't bother getting up. The suspension must have extra heavy springs on his side. He can steer with his belly.

"Mr. Cassel, I really must protest —"

"You can come along if you want."

She looks uncertainly back at the hospital. "I'm not allowed to leave the grounds."

"Thanks for everything, Betty. Here, help me get this crutch inside."

Betty hesitates, then sighs and hands me the crutch. "Bring them back," she says.

"Ranger's honour," I tell her. "Ranger station," I tell the cabbie.

When we arrive at the ranger station five blocks later, he assesses the minimal $2 charge but I only have 75 cents left in my jeans from my fugitive phone account. The cabbie can't believe it, tries to grab my crutches as collateral. I wrestle them free, get out of the car. He sits inside and glares at me but decides the effort of getting out of the car isn't worth $1.25. He'll probably bill it to the Forest Service anyway, which suits me fine.

Inside the ranger station, I stagger up the stairs — thank God for handrails — and lean against the counter, catch my breath. Already, I miss nurse Betty — I could use a hit of morphine right now. The receptionist is the only one in sight, hunched over her desk, on the phone. She's a shipping-lane-sized lady with curly hair. She sees me, smiles and waves. I grimace, wave back, motion her over. She takes a minute to finish her call, then faces me across the counter.

"Well if it isn't Porter Cassel. The Fugitive."

"Not any more," I say, panting. "So Carl didn't leave a phone number?"

"That was you on the phone?"

"That was me. Look, I really need to get a hold of Carl."

"Well, he didn't leave a number."

"Could I use a phone to call directory assistance?"

"Sure." She shrugs. "You don't look so good. Kinda pale."

With all the bruises, I'm surprised she can tell.

"I'll live. Just show me where I can sit down."

She lets me into the inner sanctum, points me to Carl's office. I sit at Carl's desk and call directory assistance, looking for his parents. They live in some small prairie town in southern Alberta, something that starts with a "B." I play verbal charades with the operator until she comes up with an L. Mackey in Brooks. A man answers.

"Hello. Mr. Mackey?"

"Yeah?"

"Is this the Mackey whose son is a forest ranger?"

"Yeah."

"Is Carl home?"

"He doesn't live here anymore. We don't have a lot of trees in Brooks."

"I can appreciate that. Mr. Mackey, is your wife okay?"

A stony silence. "What?"

"Your wife — is she ill?"

"My wife died three years ago. Who the hell is this?"

"No one," I mumble. "Sorry for disturbing you."

After I hang up, I sit still for a few minutes, look around Carl's office. Desk, file cabinets, pictures of forest fires, of Carl holding up a big fish. This could be any ranger's office. This could be my office. I shake my head, gather my crutches, make my way into the duty room. Chief Ranger Gary Hanlon is manning the desk. He's on the phone and is faxing something at the same time. He looks at the end of his rope, eyes twitchy, ball cap crooked, polyester shirt hanging half out of his pants. I stand by the door until he notices me.

"I'm on hold," he says, punching numbers on the fax machine.

"Chief, do you know where Carl is?"

"Gone," he says. "Hell of a time too."

"His mother passed away years ago —"

"You look like shit," he says, as if noticing for the first time. "You ready to work?"

I'm on crutches and he wants to know if I'm ready to work.

"We got a serious cross-over," he says. "Wind out of the west at 40, gusting to 70. One active fire on the verge of going UC again. And to top it all off, half my standby resources just got commandeered to go to a fire near Slave Lake. Red Flag day is a fucking understatement. I need bodies. Can you fly a patrol?"

"Keep your resources here," I tell him. "It's going to get worse."

"What?" he yells into the phone. "I don't give a shit. Order more yourself." And he hangs up. "I want to stick you in a fixed wing," he says. "Fly the slopes." He's moving past me while he talks, crouching over the duty desk and staring at the screen, reaching for the radio at the same time. Like fighting a lynch mob, he's taking shots in all directions.

"Listen to me Chief. You've got bigger problems."

He stares at me, still crouched over the desk, the radio mike in his hand. A phone rings but he doesn't answer, just looks at me. His brain is playing catch-up but it's finally sinking in that I'm trying to tell him something.

"What?"

"You know that arsonist I've been investigating?"

He gives me a blank look, then nods.

"Well, I'm pretty sure he's here and he's planning something big."

"If this is a joke," he says, reaching for the phone, "you've got a sick sense of humor."

"This is the only part of the province he hasn't hit," I tell him. Hanlon has the phone to his ear and I'm not sure he's listening but I keep going anyway. "You got a Red Flag day and no resources to speak of. This guy knows fire weather and is probably monitoring the resource allocation. If I wanted to start a devastating fire, I'd do it now. Light up the East Slopes."

He sets the phone back in its cradle. "You're sure about this?"

"Think about it. It's a perfect set-up."

He doesn't want to think about it but like a good dispatcher is weighing the options.

"Nothing we can do about it," he says.

"What?"

"We don't know if he's here. And the fires up north are real."

Tough call. "Look, I know he's here. I can virtually guarantee it."

"You can guarantee it?" He's understandably sceptical but I don't want to tell him about Carl. I'm thinking maybe no one ever has to know. If I could just talk to Carl —

"And if you're wrong?" he says.

"I want to be wrong. I just don't think I am."

Hanlon takes a minute, which, for a busy dispatcher, is a long time.

"Jesus Christ Cassel — this I do not fucking need. A fire under these conditions —" He shakes his head, stares at the wall map. "There are people out there camping — half the fucking city. What do we do about them?"

"My sister and her kids are out there too. Evacuate."

He stares at me. "Evacuate the fucking *West Country*? Do you know what that'll take? Two million acres. Every damn helicopter in the province is on a fire or sitting in the bush waiting for one. We don't have the resources."

Would Carl endanger that many people?

"Well, you've gotta do something Gary. Warn them. Put it on the radio."

Hanlon paces the confines of the small room then suddenly sits behind the duty desk, his ball cap in his hands like he's praying. For a few minutes he doesn't move, just stares blankly at the floor. I'm not sure if he's thinking or is just frozen. Stress can do funny things. Personalities change. Tempers get short. People don't think straight. It's a sort of a psychosis and it hits everyone differently.

"Gary, I need a helicopter. I think I can find him."

Another minute of lethargy before he looks up at me. "What?"

"If you let me use the fire growth model on the dispatch computer I think I can figure out where he'll hit. I'm pretty sure this guy has been using something like that to plan his fires."

A look of hope dawns on Hanlon's face. "You think we can stop him?"

"It's worth a try."

Hanlon stares at me but doesn't move.

"I'll need to sit there, Gary."

"Oh, sorry." He gets up. "I'll call headquarters, plead for more helicopters."

I take a seat behind the dispatch desk. There's a computer and battery of phones, radios and microphones in front of me. This is the first time in three years I've been in the hot seat but it doesn't take long to slip back into the role. Stress is like falling off a bike — it hurts but you get used to it. I start up the fire growth model, find it's a different version from the one I used to work with. Abacus to calculus different. The tool I used was simple, monochrome and two-dimensional. This one is interactive, spatial, like a video game. I look around for Hanlon but he's nowhere in sight — probably in his office trying to panic the regional and provincial dispatchers. I look for an option to replay the last simulation, hoping Carl didn't erase it, but find nothing.

Okay, think this through.

Bring up the vegetation inventory, themed by FBP Fuel Type. Punch in present and predicted weather. The growth model is almost as easy to use as a video game. Factor in slope and aspect ...

With the parameters set, it's obvious the entire area is at extreme hazard. I need to find the areas which would result in the most dramatic fire growth because that's where Carl will set his devices. Wind is predominately from the west so I click on an icon of a little flame, initiate a few spot fires in gullies along the toe of the mountains, watch them grow eastward across the screen. Even considering the condensed time frame of the simulation, the rate the pixels on the screen turn black is frightening.

"Holy shit." Hanlon is breathing down my neck. "That's fast."

"See these areas here ..." I smudge the screen with my fingertips. "These areas show the most rapid fire growth. If I was the arsonist, this is where I'd start my burn."

Hanlon is nodding. "What makes you think he knows that?"

"He knows what he's doing. Think about his other fires."

"Yeah, real burners," he says. "I was on that Vermilion fire." Hanlon is leaning on the desk. I turn the screen so he can see better but he's too intent to back off. "By the looks of this," he says, "that Vermilion fire was a picnic compared to what this could be."

I run a few more simulations. They're all frightening.

"If you think you can stop him," Hanlon says. "You better try."

"You manage to get any more helicopters?"

He shakes his head. "They said they weren't prepared to reallocate resources based on a hunch. They've got too much real fire going up north, even had the nerve to ask if I really need the two machines I got left."

I think of Cindy and the kids, tripping through the woods. "You call the cops?"

"Yeah —" He hesitates.

"What?"

"They didn't seem too concerned when they heard your name."

I grab the phone, call the local detachment, suffer through an overly polite, bilingual, politically correct receptionist. "Is Andre Rachet there?"

"No sir, Mr. Rachet has departed."

"What's his mobile number?"

"I'm not at liberty —"

"Put me through. It's an emergency."

A stiff silence, then: "I'll put you through to the duty officer."

A click, then a casual voice. "Bergren here. What's the nature of your emergency?"

"This is the duty officer at the Forest Service. I have reason to believe a serial arsonist is in the area and intends to start a significant fire in the next few hours."

"What is your name sir?"

I hesitate. "Porter Cassel."

"Cassel —" His tone changes. "Aren't you supposed to be in the hospital?"

"Never mind that. I'm a fast healer. We've got a situation here —"

"You're not *calling* from the hospital are you?"

I grind my teeth. "No, I'm not calling from the hospital —"

"Because this better not be a prank. We still got plenty —"

"Listen Bergren, you may not think much of my contribution to your investigation but I know fire and I can tell you this. The bush out here is drier and more dangerous than it's been in a century, which is about the frequency of large fires in this area. Most of our suppression resources have been moved out of the area to fight fires up north. The guy who's been lighting the fires knows this and if he starts a fire today that fire is going to be at your doorstep by nightfall. There are a lot of people camped out in the bush and if the shit hits the fan they'll be trying to get out at the same time. You ever been in the city during rush hour? Well if you think a few thousand office workers trying to get home is a big problem, imagine them driving motorhomes. Then imagine a one-lane dirt road and a wall of flame two hundred feet high, chasing them. You getting the picture?"

There's a brief silence. "Yeah, I can picture that. What do you want us to do?"

"Evacuate the campgrounds, do crowd control, make sure everyone is safe."

There's a longer pause. "Okay, we can handle that. What are you guys doing?"

"The only thing we can. We're getting ready for the fire."

After I hang up, Hanlon looks paler. "You really think it'll hap-

pen?"

"I hope to God I'm wrong."

"If you're wrong, they'll crucify you."

I don't answer. If I'm right and can't stop Carl, there'll be no way to stop the fire.

For a few minutes, Hanlon and I sit together listening to the radios squelch and crackle, overwhelmed by the task ahead. My leg is throbbing.

"I need a helicopter, Gary. Right away."

Hanlon stands, goes to the window of the duty room. It's windy outside, plastic bags and trashcans rolling past like tumble weeds. It gets much windier it'll be difficult to fly. He watches the street for a few more minutes.

"There's a machine based at the tower," he says. "Call him in."

Looking down through the bubble, pine trees ripple in the wind like wheat in a field. Ready for harvest. Ready for consumption. Nature, begging for a fire. But I'm more interested in the view west, where the fire will start. The wind has thinned the smoke but there's still enough to give the mountains a distant, tombstone sort of look.

"So what are we doing?" asks the pilot. He's an older fellow, soft spoken, with grey hair and wrinkled hands. I've flown with him maybe a dozen times over the years. He's worked for the Forest Service long enough to know something unusual is up if he's been pulled from man-up in these hazard conditions, with only one passenger.

"Just a patrol," I say. "Keep heading west."

We pass the small fire by the river, far to our left. Sections of dozerline are visible and smoke blows in a steady stream just above the canopy. Bright spots of orange flicker on the ground. The helicopter bucks and weaves in the strong wind. I look ahead, concentrate on the forest at the base of the mountains, looking for new smoke. The pilot glances at the map, spread out over my lap.

"You got anything specific in mind?"

"When we get to the Rocks we'll start here," I tell him, point to a series of circles I've scribbled on the map. "Work our way north. Fly at about 2,000 feet. Keep the Trunk Road on my side."

"You looking for anything in particular?"

"Smoke," I say, then hesitate. "And a light blue Chev half-ton."

The pilot nods and we fly in silence. Usually, pilots are fairly talkative, interested in what you're doing. Flying all day can be boring. But he's quiet, a concerned look on his face. The helicopter shudders, maxed-out against the head wind; we're doing half the normal speed. Hanlon's nervous voice blares in my headset.

"YHH, this is dispatch. You see anything yet?"

I fumble for the volume control, turn it down. "Negative dispatch."

"Keep me posted."

"Copy. The cops started the evacuation yet?"

"Roger. They've got it on the radio."

We pass over a road, see a small herd of motorhomes kicking up dust, headed out of the forest. Cindy wouldn't have taken the kids too far into the bush, but I still worry. You don't appreciate the power and speed of a fire under these circumstances until you've seen one. Close to the first circle on my map the pilot turns against the wind, the helicopter slewing, and we drop to 2,000 feet. I'm interested in a draw of dense spruce in line with a gap in the mountains. It's next to the road, offering easy access, and a steady wind would push a fire into the crowns of the trees, accelerate it up the slopes.

"This good?"

I nod to the pilot, motion for him to circle the area, stare down through Plexiglass.

Dense green forest. Nothing else. "Follow the road north."

The Forestry Trunk Road winds along the transition between foothills and the Front Range. Rugged country here, sheathed with dense pine. From above, sporadic cutblocks look like missing pieces of a jigsaw puzzle. There are few cutblocks this far west as of yet, not many roads; the Trunk Road is the only artery. It's here that log trucks and campers mix it up during summer, friction running both ways. The Trunk Road is also the only way the arsonist could get here by vehicle and I don't think Carl has a horse.

Nothing but forest at the second and third spots. We pass several campers tucked in the trees just off the road. I'm tempted to stop and warn them but don't want to waste precious time finding a landing spot and hiking down the road. They'd be at the tail of the fire anyway and with this wind would be fairly safe. We pass the fourth then fifth circle on my map without seeing anything suspicious.

"Now what?" The pilot has been reading my map. Nothing else is circled.

"Go back. We'll do it again, heading south."

The helicopter makes a wide turn. Buffeted by the wind, we fly sideways, the machine jerking. Suddenly we drop, zoom toward treetops, the pilot pointing to something. "You see that?"

I look but his vision is sharper, more experienced. Then a flash off metal or glass. We turn hard, auguring against the wind, G-force pushing bile up my throat. The horizon tilts unreasonably, then levels and I see something among the trees along a trail so narrow as to be nearly invisible from the air. A light blue Chevy half-ton. Carl's truck.

"Look for a landing spot."

We circle once more. Not far from the truck there's a strip of dense spruce along what must be a creek. This is where he'll be, looking for a spot with a lot of fine fuels and dense low branches. I lose sight of the creek and truck as the helicopter levels, then tilts downward.

"I can set you on the road, about a quarter-mile down."

"Do it, then take off and land farther away. Monitor the radio."

I don't want Carl spooked by shutting down the helicopter so close. I'd rather he think it was just a routine patrol, curious but passing over. As we circle into the wind and settle toward the road, I'm not sure what I'll do when I come face to face with him. Are we still friends? Will he have his shotgun with him? His rifle?

Will he give me the chance to face him?

The skids settle on the road and we're engulfed in a coffee-coloured dust storm. I grab my belt radio and step out, eyes squinted against the swirling grit, and crouch on the road. The roar and dust recede and suddenly I'm earthbound, surrounded by trees, smelling a faint odour of smoke. I start down the road, jogging, the radio slapping against my thigh.

I don't jog far. A half-dozen steps and my injured leg blazes with pain. The dressing wasn't intended to take this much movement and spots of blood blossom in the fabric of my jeans. I'm weak, dizzy. We should have landed closer. Should have brought the crutches. I stumble into the trees where it's a bit cooler, where I'm out of sight and there's something to hold onto. The bruises from Brotsky's boots come to life and my ankle refuses to take much weight. The forest is dense enough that the lower boles of the pines are branchless and I see the truck soon enough. I approach quickly, in too much pain to be cautious.

It's Carl's truck all right: plastic jerry cans full of gas and diesel in the back. The truck is unlocked, a map on the seat similar to the one I left in the helicopter. But there are a lot more circles on this map and I get a really bad feeling — he isn't just lighting one spot, he's lighting them all.

Hopefully this is his first stop, not his last.

I take the keys from the ignition, toss them as far as I can, lock the truck and start toward the creek I saw from the air but I'm too faint to go far and decide to wait by the truck, sit on a carpet of pine needles and lean against a tire. A squirrel chatters. Treetops sway against the smoky sky. Trees rub and groan. The forest seems nervous, waiting. I check my radio. It's fine. I try to think of what to say to Carl. I can't. I hear footsteps crunching on dry ground, muted whistling. He's having fun, enjoying his little project. I push myself to my feet, ignoring a swell of nausea, see Carl from across the hood of his truck. He doesn't notice me right away. He's carrying a backpack, looks relaxed, like he's just come back from a fishing trip.

"Hey buddy, what are you up to?"

Carl freezes, his smile vanishing. When he sees it's me the smile creeps back — a different smile now, wistful rather than relaxed. "Porter, what are you doing here?"

"I'm here to stop you. To take you home."

We're faced off, on opposite sides of the truck.

"Stop what?" Puzzled, like he doesn't know what I'm talking about.

"It's just me, Carl. Let's not play games."

"What are you talking about?"

I'm dizzy, like I'm still on heavy painkillers, and it makes everything a little unreal, as if this wasn't unreal enough. I notice I'm not the only one with a Forest Service radio. I swallow hard, force myself to concentrate.

"Look, Carl ... I know what's going on."

"What's going on?" he says. "Tell me what's going on, then we'll both know."

"The fires. The bombings. I know you're the Lorax."

"Me?" He looks shocked. "You think *I'm* the Lorax?"

He can lie better than that. "Your mother passed away years ago."

He doesn't answer — he's been caught and knows it. He frowns, looks away and then walks to the truck and drops his pack in the back. I move along the side of the truck, keeping it between us, face him across the open box. "I want you to diffuse that thing you just set."

He leans against the truck, stares down like an unresponsive child.

"How long until it goes off?"

He doesn't respond, just stands there gripping the edge of the truck box.

"How long, Carl?"

Nothing. I unholster my radio — I've got to call dispatch, get an initial attack crew out here, mobilize suppression resources. If they can get here fast enough, maybe they can catch it small. But my radio doesn't work and it takes me a few seconds to realize why. Carl has already keyed his mike, walking over my signal so I can't transmit. By the time I realize that all I have to do is shout and his radio will pick it up, he's come around the back of the truck and knocked the radio out of my hand. He backs up, holding both radios.

"Sorry about that, Porter."

For a few seconds I'm speechless, staring at this stranger.

"Carl, this is crazy. Let's talk about this."

He's staring at me, puzzled. "Jesus, Porter, look at your leg —"

My wound has opened, blood blotted into the cloth of my jeans.

"Just give me a radio, Carl."

He shakes his head. "You shouldn't have come."

"I had to, Carl. You have to stop this."

"That's not why you came."

Now I'm the one who's puzzled. "What?"

"You came because you hate me. Ever since Nina was killed."

"Carl —"

"That's why you want to stop me." The anguish in his features is painful to watch. "But that was a mistake. I never should have pissed around with dynamite. It was just so convenient. Grab a case, toss a few sticks into a machine. But I never intended to hurt anyone." His voice cracks. "I never could have hurt her —"

"Carl... I don't hate you. I just want this to be over —"

"I should have started with fire." His expression changes — he's determined now. "It's natural and much more effective. Blowing up a few feller-bunchers was never going to change anything. Insurance pays for them and they're back in business the next day. I was going about it all wrong. Fire — now that's a different story. Fire belongs here."

I catch a whiff of smoke. New smoke, not the stuff blowing in from BC.

"Put it out, Carl, before it grows."

"It's all about balance. You of all people should understand."

I take a step toward him. It's painful and I'm way too slow.

"The whole system is way out of balance. That's what the Forest Service is supposed to do, maintain the balance — that's why I became a ranger. But it's out of control. So I'm fixing it, Porter. I'm re-establishing the natural balance. You should be able to appreciate that."

"This isn't the way to do it."

"You think there's another way?" He laughs. "Don't be naïve."

"You've got to stop."

"I couldn't stop it if I wanted to."

I have to get that radio but I'm dizzy, my vision blurry.

"This isn't the only one, Porter. There's about 20 more, all with fuses set to go off at the same time. I've found something much better than cigars. It'll be like running a drip torch along the Trunk Road."

"Jesus, Carl."

I hear a gush of flame. A few hundred yards away a clump of spruce trees candle like a blazing yellow torch in the wind. The flames turn orange, leap energetically into the air, fanned into the crowns of neighbouring pine. Already, it's out of control. We need a helicopter with a bucket. In a few minutes, even that won't be enough. And if there's 20 more of these —

"Look at that, Porter. See how natural that is?"

Carl looks hypnotized — maybe I can take a radio from him, call dispatch. But in my condition, I doubt it. Turns out I don't have to. The helicopter is approaching. The pilot has seen the fire or a tower called it in.

"YHH calling Cassel. You want me to put on the bucket?"

Carl lifts a radio. "Negative YHH," he replies. "Pick me up at the road."

"Send the bombers!" I holler. Too late — Carl's no longer transmitting.

Reluctantly, he turns away from the fire. "Time to go, Porter."

He moves past me, tries to open the truck door. "Okay, give me the keys."

"They're gone," I say quietly, watching the flames.

Carl grabs my arm. "Stop kidding around, Porter —"

He rummages through my pockets, looking for keys. I lean on the truck, watch the sway of the fire, flames leaping high above the treetops. Even at this distance, I can feel the heat. If the wind were blowing the other way, we'd already be dead. Carl swears — I barely hear him over the howl of the fire. Mixed with the roar of burning trees is the thump of a circling helicopter — two sounds which in my mind always exist together. Then I can't stand anymore and begin to fall. Carl's arm is around my waist, holding me up. I stumble beside him through the trees, nearly pulling us both down. Ahead on the road the helicopter waits, powered up, its rotors buzzing like an immense angry insect. I'm deafened by the scream of the turbo engine as Carl helps me inside then climbs in next to me.

The ground tilts and drops away. Below us, the inferno is already several acres and running in the treetops, soon to be beyond our suppression capability, creating its own weather, turning day into night. As we go higher, I see more fires — a line of similar spots growing together, driving east. Carl has his blazing conflagration. But he's not watching his creation. He's staring at his hands, smeared with blood from when he helped me into the helicopter.

He gives me an anguished look. "Jesus Christ, Porter —"

I notice too late that he isn't wearing his seatbelt and when he opens the door the most I can do is a frantic, grasping fumble. The helicopter rocks suddenly and he's gone, the door rattling in the wind. "What the hell was that?" yells the pilot, looking back over his shoulder. For a few seconds I'm too stunned to do anything but watch the chattering door.

Finally, I manage to pull on my headset.

"He fell," I say slowly. "He didn't have his belt on."

30

I WANT TO GO to the ranger station but they take me straight to the hospital. Nurse Betty has been expecting me and I receive a stern reprimand — I've opened the wound again and risked infection, not to mention bleeding to death. The doctor is equally unimpressed, seeing his handiwork undone. I'm patched up, given another shot of painkillers and shown to my room. Rachet is waiting for me. He stands as they wheel me in, watches them tuck me into bed, hook up the machines.

"Christ, Cassel," he says as the nurse leaves. "You just can't stay away from this stuff."

"You told me to stick to forest fires."

"Yeah." He nods. "Well you sure got one going now."

"How big is it?"

"Big," he says expressively. "And getting bigger."

"You get everyone out of the way?"

"I think so. You made a good call."

"What about my sister and her kids?"

"They never left town. One of the kids wasn't feeling well."

I lie back, let out a sigh of relief.

"About Mr. Mackey," Rachet says. "What exactly happened?"

"He was the one starting the fires," I admit. "I didn't figure it out until the end."

"That's usually how it goes. I'm sorry it had to be your friend."

I picture Carl in his buckskin jacket. Sitting in The Corral. At the duty desk. "So am I."

"Why did he do it?"

"Overtime," I lie. "He needed the overtime."

"Hell of a way to get a few extra hours."

We're both silent for a minute. The painkillers have reached their full potential; I think they gave me a double this time, to keep me in bed. I blink hard, try to remain conscious. Rachet drums his fingers on the side of my hospital bed. "Tell me about Mr. Mackey's fall."

I'm tempted to tell him that I think it started years ago, and that I should have noticed. "He didn't put his seatbelt on," I say. "He was peering down at the fire as we lifted off, trying to get a good look. I think he was leaning against the door and it popped open as we banked to that side. He just lost his balance."

"He lost his balance?"

"I think so, but I can't be sure. I was a little distracted."

"I heard an interesting theory," Rachet says slowly. "One of my colleagues, a Mr. Kirby — I believe you know him. Apparently, he had this notion that whoever was lighting the fires could also be the Lorax. Said there was a possible connection as far as motive might be concerned. Went so far as to suggest it might be worth looking into."

"That was my suggestion," I say, looking directly at Rachet. "A misguided notion."

"You're sure?" He's trying hard to read me.

"I didn't push my friend out of the helicopter."

He looks at me hard a few more seconds, then smiles ruefully. "Of course not."

I think that was the question he was waiting to ask because he leaves soon after, unconvinced. For Rachet, nothing is ever over until the evidence has been logged and the case makes it through court. He's going to be disappointed this time.

I wake the next morning to a familiar face. She's wearing a dress.

"How long have you been here?" I ask groggily, lifting my head.

She smiles, comes to the edge of the bed and offers me her hand. "Let's start again," she says. "From the beginning. My name is Christina Telson, and I'm a journalist, but this isn't an interview. I'm not a vegetarian and I didn't grow up on a farm. In fact, hamburgers are my favourite food and I have only a vague inkling where they come from."

"Cows," I say. "Beef."

"I had my suspicions," she says.

Her hand is still hanging in space, wavering just slightly. I shake it.

"Porter Cassel," I tell her. "Unemployed firefighter. Romantically helpless."

"Wonderful," she says. "I love a challenge."

ACKNOWLEDGEMENTS

I WOULD LIKE to thank the following members of the Royal Canadian Mounted Police for their patience in the face of my ceaseless questions; their input greatly enhanced the technical accuracy of the story: Cpl. Vaughn Chistensen, Didsbury Detachment; Sgt. Larry Moore, Explosives Disposal Unit, "K" Division; Joe Deak, Chemist, Crime Lab, "K" Division; Sgt. Larry McLeod, NCO, Athabasca Detachment; Cpl. Gordon Petracek, Forensic Identification Specialist, Red Deer Detachment. I would also like to extend my gratitude to Paul Steensland, USFS Special Agent, for reviewing the manuscript, and Randel Yopek of Explosives Limited for advice on dynamite configurations and legalities. Thanks also to Dave Garbutt of Hub Cigar & Newstand for information on the Emperador cigar, and to Marc Côté of Cormorant Books for his interest and encouragement.